C000295615

Something Blue

A Dystopian Romance

KNicolle x

By Kristy Nicolle

First published by Kristy Nicolle, United Kingdom, April 2017

FIRST EDITION (1ˢᵗ EDITION)
Published April 2017 by Kristy Nicolle
Copyright © 2017 Kristy Nicolle
Edited By- Jaimie Cordall

Adult Dystopian Romance

The right of Kristy Nicolle to be identified as author of this Work has been asserted by her in accordance with sections 77 and 78 of the Copyright, Designs and Patents Act 1988.
All rights reserved. No part of this publication may be reproduced, stored in retrieval system, copied in any form or by any means, electronic, mechanical, photocopying, recording or otherwise transmitted without written permission from the publisher. You must not circulate this book in any format.

Disclaimer:
This ebook is written in U.K English by personal preference of the author. This is a work of fiction. Names, characters, businesses, places, events and incidents are either the products of the author's imagination or used in a fictitious manner. Any resemblance to actual persons, living or dead, or actual events is purely coincidental.

ISBN: 978-1-911395-06-5

www.kristynicolle.com

For the nefarious Doctor Moo,

Who despite her best efforts couldn't stop this book's journey to completion.

I know you're pissed that you aren't the Something Blue but we've talked about this.

P.s. Mark is still mine.

"According to Greek mythology, humans were originally created with four arms, four legs and a head with two faces. Fearing their power, Zeus split them into two separate parts, condemning them to spend their lives in search of their other halves."
— **Plato**, **The Symposium**

Glossary of Terms

Holo-dash: A touchable interface, kind of like a computer, but with more stringent usages.

Hard-Light: Light interfaces that can be touched.

Soft-Light: Used for non-touch broadcasts such as television shows and commercials.

Upcycler: A modern device that can take away rubbish and produce objects selected from the hard-light Catalogue.

Tubemail: Mail direct from Bliss Inc. headquarters, such as upcycler notices, holo-dash update instructions and engagement rings/ wedding invitations.

Synths: Robots controlled by the human workforce in the labour districts. Synths can fly and are responsible for keeping Monopolis clean, fed and served.

Hard-Light Holograms: Bliss Inc. latest technology, whereby labourers in the labour district can take hard-light form in Monopolis. They take the form of hard-light bodies that can move and think, and are monitored closely by Bliss Inc.

Prologue

A beginner's guide to the Jigsaw project.

———————●◗●———————

Hello, and welcome to your comprehensive and simple guide to Pippa Hart's life changing formula and corresponding programme: The Jigsaw Project. Please read this information carefully, as full understanding of this programme is vital to your success. You matter to us here at Bliss Inc., so to prepare you for this life changing process, we have provided you with a quick and complete guide to the matching process, a brief overview of the history of the programme, and a clear and concise explanation of why your future happiness is so important to us.

What is the Jigsaw Project?

The Jigsaw project is the process by which matchmates are made using the formula for true love. This formula was first developed by Dr Pippa Hart after she watched Humanity become self-destructive due to excessive overpopulation. The Formula is necessary because during the 21st Century, the Internet blossomed, leaving humans with too much choice for reproductive partners. As non-nuclear families, a.k.a. divorced families, became more prevalent, as well as mother's producing infants from multiple male genetic donors, humans began to exhibit increased negative traits, such as violence, loneliness, laziness, unfaithfulness, loose sexual morals and an inability to see their behaviours as self- destructive. These traits led to a continuation of irresponsible behaviour, and therefore a steady incline of children being born to poor, uneducated families. This, in short, led to the population of the western world spiralling out of control. As humanity faced mass famine and poverty due to over-population, the west launched a programme of mass sterilisation across the developing world. After this the western world realised they had made a mistake as the system of people who had upheld their lavish lifestyle began to collapse from lack of bodies. The numbers of people in the west began to far outweigh those who were providing for them in the third world, leading to wars over resources.

Living on a war torn and ravaged planet, Pippa Hart realised that science was humanity's last hope. She conducted research secretly on her own family, over a course of fifty years, developing a formula which resulted in a ninety-nine percent success rate in producing lasting marriages and therefore, happy, contented children. These children then grow to become happy and contented adults, allowing humanity to progress. The implementation of blind arranged marriages has in fact been so successful, that our society no longer needs prisons, police or safeguarding.

What does the Jigsaw Project have to do with me?

If you are reading this document, it means you are about to take one of two kinds of match test. Whether you be fifteen and taking the primary match test to determine suitability for the Jigsaw Project, or this be your monthly readiness test, you will always be asked to sign at the bottom of this document, giving us your consent to continue participating. If you have been selected for the Jigsaw Project, congratulations! Selection occurs at fifteen, and means that you have been deemed as having a mate with whom you can achieve perfect happiness, making you eligible for the privilege of reproduction. Once the matching has occurred, you will attend your tattooing ceremony on your 16th birthday, where you will be marked in anticipation of your move to Monopolis. Once you are situated in the city, you will continue to take a physical and psychological test once monthly to determine your readiness for married life. When both partners test positive and are deemed ready, you will be notified and planning your wedding can begin.

What are the benefits?

Benefits of the project are limitless. The matching tattoos on the inside or back of your wrist, which are assigned at acceptance in the programme when your match is made, unlock endless possibilities when scanned post-nuptials. You will be given the best society can offer you, because we know your gift, that of a child created as the scientific product of true love, has greater value than any single material thing that Bliss Inc. can offer.

How long does the Jigsaw Project Last?

The Jigsaw Project can last a lifetime, but your happiness is paramount to us, and so for 100 days, you will receive once weekly sexology and psychology counselling as a couple. If our experts deem you and your matchmate happy, which 99% of our participants are, you will be moved onto Fantasia Pastures, the conception and pregnancy settlement to begin your happily ever after once the 100 days conclude.

Why is the Jigsaw Programme Important?

The Jigsaw programme is the result of Pippa Hart's formula for marital bliss (aka true love.) The formula remains top secret, even today, but has saved mankind from self-destruction, as well as allowing each individual paramount levels of pleasure throughout their lives.

One

I sign my name confidently on the paper, watching the holo-ink glide over the translucent sheet as I glimpse at my tattoo, calling out for its other half, glowing neon blue on my pale skin. I sigh, taking in the intricate crenulations which match only one other, a nervous knot balling in my stomach at the thought of this not being the last readiness test I ever take.

The white-walled, clinically sterile corridor rises around me, pure, clean, and safe. The seat I'm sitting in senses my anxiety, softening beneath me as the smart foam of its clutch relaxes, lowering my blood pressure and heart rate simultaneously. I gaze to the other women sat in the office; each one is beautifully nervous in complexion and twitching, feet bobbing up and down, fingers twisting around each other. Their bodies are clad in the single-status suit, or a variation of it, and they are all wondering the same question:

Will this be it? Will I finally be ready?

I sigh again as the door at the end of the corridor opens and a woman walks out, her face relaxed and shoulders set back into the single-standard white and pale pink suit. The edges of her jacket are creased too sharply and her brown eyes shine out into

1

the bright light of the space, full of hope and thoughts of her wedding day. How do I know this? Because I've taken exactly sixty-one of these tests and with each month that passes, I wait, on the edge of my seat, for it to be my turn. All of my friends who had entered the Jigsaw project with me are long gone by now, some even on their second or third child, so I have to wonder if there's something wrong with me.

I feel ready to meet him now, ready for marriage and yet each month I sit, incessantly checking my tubemail, only to have nothing arrive but the odd council notice about throwing non-compatible items down the upcycler in my apartment wall.

The doorway fills with the shadow of a woman with violet hair, her pale skin and brown eyes similar to my own as her voice fills the air around me and I feel my heartbeat accelerate.

"Valentine Morland?" she calls out into the barren, minimalistic space.

"Yes!" I snap, overly excitable and yet impatient. Every time I've come for the test this year I've felt more and more pressure piling on my shoulders. So much so that I'm scared I'll never be ready. Then again, I've never heard of that happening. The formula has determined I am a match for whoever has the other half of the tattoo, the person I spend my life searching for, despite the fact I know I will never find him here. Especially when I haven't laid eyes on someone of the opposite sex since I was fifteen other than at my sisters' weddings, and that was also the last time I saw my father.

Getting to my feet, I take step after nervous step, hurrying into the stark office of the woman who had called my name.

"Hello, Valentine. Nice to see you again." She smiles, pity in her wide hazel eyes. She knows me well, mainly because I'm one of her longest attending singles and despite this fact I refuse to learn her name. I mean, getting friendly with the technicians really is the nail in the coffin of the pathetic-ness I call my life and so I refuse, referring to her only as the technician and staying reserved.

As I take a seat in yet another white, smart foam chair, which heats slightly as I feel a chill run up my spine from the open window opposite the door, I hand her my clipboard and form, hoping to God that it's the last one I ever fill out. We're required to read the information each and every time we test, so I know it back to front and left to right by now. Yet the prospect of what it details never fails to cause my heart to flutter in my chest, excited at finally discovering the true love which I've been dreaming of since I knew what dreams were.

"Right, the physical examination first," the technician decrees, pulling out a scanning wand from the white desk at which she perches herself. "Can you stand?" she asks me, not meeting my gaze as she reads through the transparent form with my signature in neon blue at the bottom. She nods, satisfied, before letting the wall take it from her and sending it off to the filing clerks in the basement. "Arms out," she demands, as I move and proceed to watch as she waves the wand over me, first examining the external skin of my body through my clothes.

The computer monitor behind her reflects my pale and sweaty complexion back at me. My honey blonde hair falls in thick waves down my back and over my left shoulder as my almond shaped hazel eyes widen, surrounded by thick black

3

lashes, and I take myself in. I watch her examining the freckle above my lip and the beauty spot by my left eye, probably checking for cancer, though nobody gets that anymore. Well, I suppose some people in the labour districts do, but no one from the Jigsaw Project, no one chosen.

I lower my arms as I begin to feel uncomfortable and she finishes the surface examination before moving on to examine my internal organs. "Do you have any questions for me?" she queries, not even looking at me as she scans over my heart, which pulsates, grotesque and too real before my eyes on the screen. I feel myself become distracted as I watch its beat race, the curves of it tremoring and empty, alone.

"Well, why is it taking so long?" I ask her, knowing her answer will be the same. I have asked the same question every time I have been in this office for the past year, feeling myself wasting away and my body becoming older, creeping towards menopause and causing me to panic. I'm only twenty-five, but that's still four years older than the average recipient of a positive readiness test, so with each month that passes, I panic a little more.

"At Bliss Inc., your happiness is important to us, Valentine. We won't let you commit to a total stranger until you're both ready, even with a ninety-nine percent success rate of our formula producing true love, these things still take time," her reply comes as an irritating repetition of the answer I get every time I ask her this question, almost as though she's reading it from an invisible script.

I sigh as she scans down to the floor, going over my thick and short legs. I'm a curvy girl, mainly because I always make sure to

4

eat ten percent more calories than I'm supposed to, I've been doing this ever since I saw on the Childcare Channel that a little extra weight can help you conceive and carry a baby to term successfully. I had always been slim until that day, but as the years had gone by with no positive readiness result, I have gained weight, wondering if this is the reason I'm not deemed ready to meet my matchmate.

"Okay, everything seems good here." She places the wand back into the desk drawer, which opens at a mere swipe of her finger over the edge of its flawless white surface. I sit down, bored of the monotony of this already. She turns back to me, her eyes glimmering as her purple hair shakes. "Are you ready to take the psychological exam?" she asks me, her face plastered with a kind and gentle smile.

Her teeth are extremely white, her skin is flawless, and neither falter in their perfection as something terrible occurs to me.

"So, I do have another question," I tell her, biting down on the soft flesh of my lip as my heart begins to race again and the seat softens automatically beneath me. This time though, its reaction does nothing as I feel stress weigh on me without reprieve.

"What is it?" she asks, making a few selections on the neon blue, hard-light of the holo-dash, where the next part of the test is conducted, and not looking at me even still.

"What happens if you're never ready?" I suddenly blurt, feeling my curiosity and fear push me into an action that isn't natural to me. I'm scared. I had never heard or seen on any soft-light broadcast channel any mention of someone not being ready until it was too late, but what if I'm the first? What if I'm an odd

5

one out, or they've made a mistake? What if I'm not chosen at all? I feel myself panicking as she frowns.

"Trust in the process, Valentine. You will be ready. Trust me, I've worked here forever and I've never seen someone fail all their readiness tests," she comforts me, placing a stiff hand on my shoulder and giving a deliberate and unnaturally strong squeeze.

"Okay. Sorry, I'm just nervous. This is my sixty-first test," I admonish and she frowns.

"My, that is a lot. But I've known individuals who have as many as eighty, sometimes ninety. Worry not. You will be ready, and so will your matchmate. Remember, it's not always you. Sometimes it's them." She straightens, breaking the contact between us and I relax. She is right. It might not be me at all, it might be him. Besides, if she knows individuals who have as many as eighty or ninety tests, then I suppose my record isn't so bad.

"Are you ready to begin?" the technician asks me as I inhale and she pushes the hard-light holo-dash toward me. It swings on an invisible axis to lie before me like a desk.

"Yes," I reply, speaking to the dash now instead of her. "Valentine Morland, psychological readiness exam, take sixty-one."

Outside the test centre, which is only one department of the Bliss Inc. Headquarters, I stand in the sunlight and feel myself relax. The test is over for another month, and now all I have to do is wait for the result, or lack thereof.

The day is new, as my tests are always scheduled frightfully early, and I watch as the high-speed monorail glides overhead, moving along its transparent glass and steel tracks with a seemingly fluid abandon of physical laws. I gaze around me at the headquarter district, the pristine gardens with that special genetically modified grass which stops growing once it reaches its perfect height, the trees with leaves spread differently, depending on the time day, to maximise their oxygen production, and the countless women who walk around me, all dressed in white and pink, waiting to be promoted to the status of 'Bride.'

As I stare back to the gargantuan skyscraper from which I've just come, I wonder if the man I've been waiting for is close. The Headquarter district is like a buffer between our two worlds as it's the only destination that the male, female and newlywed monorails frequent. As I look to my left, I see the border between the female and male districts, invisible and lethal to anyone who tries to bypass it when they shouldn't. I examine the lone security synth as it hovers, watching us from above like we're ants.

I know I shouldn't linger, I should be on my way, but every single time I stand here, I wonder if I can catch a glimpse of him. Of course, I can see nothing past the border. In fact, I'm pretty sure it's a hologram made to look transparent, when really it's only a screen.

After all, I can't imagine that the male testing centre is as barren as it seems. I watch the synths as they buzz, to and fro, before pivoting on my heel and deciding to board the monorail back to the centre of the female district, from which I'll walk back to my unit.

My journey back into the heart of the female district of Monopolis passes swiftly, and I decide to walk leisurely home, knowing that I have no readiness classes for the rest of the day because my test day is always kept clear. I have a fair amount of possibilities for activities, but eventually change my mind, deciding that rather than practicing on a hard-light piano or going to the local hover-rink, that I'll go and visit Egypt instead.

I look down at the hard-light watch on my wrist. It had taken me a whole year's worth of readiness study credits to obtain, but it was totally worth it, even if it did have limited capability in the singles section of Monopolis. I mean, everyone thought I was mad spending my cred on this kind of tech, which is usually reserved for matchmade couples.

My friends might have judged, especially Egypt, but they didn't understand. I think the majority of my friends, who I'd met at my acceptance into Monopolis party at 16, had been gone by the time I was 22, having been single for maybe only a year after their readiness tests began. I, on the other hand, am finding myself having to make friends with much younger women now, and Egypt doesn't even take the readiness exam yet, because she's only 18.

I walk through the crowded, yet pristine white paved streets. A pop up soft light screen blocks my path and I walk through it, disrupting an advert for some kind of new hard-light technology. I've seen the advert a hundred times, but I can't really remember what the new technology is for. I brush away the thought, almost running into a synth that is polishing the blank, slick pavement tiles. It always amazes me how sufficient the cleaning synths are around here, because everything is always just a little too bright. I mean, compared to Pearl Falls where I had grown up, this is a single girl's paradise, but honestly it has never felt truly like home.

I tap on the hard-light screen of my watch, keying in Egypt's dash number and waiting the obligatory two rings before seeing her face pop up on screen. Her hair is dishevelled and she's still in her district-standard pyjamas amongst the simple white duvet and pink pillows of her single bed.

"Hey! How did it go?" she asks me with a yawn, her raven locks fuzzy around the edges of her face from sleep.

"Same old, same old," I shrug, not wanting to discuss the test. I feel like every single month I get bombarded with the same questions now, like if the test had felt different or if I'd answered the questions any differently. Being honest, my answer is always no, because I fear being told I'm ready when I'm not, through dishonest answers. As hard as being alone is, the technicians are always quick to remind you that failing the 100-day evaluation with your spouse is irreversible and holds even worse consequences, though other than a few rumours which have always circulated, no-one ever says what happens to the couples who don't make it. I guess they must segregate them somewhere, because there's no way I'd want to live in a society where ninety-nine percent of people achieve true love, having to live with the embarrassment that I couldn't make it work like everyone else.

"Do you want to come around and binge watch the wedding channel?" she asks me, moving to lie on her stomach in front of the camera and placing her chin in her palms, which are propped on her elbows, digging into the smart foam of her mattress.

"Yeah, I don't have readiness classes today. I thought I'd use some of my cred to get us a pizza or something later," I suggest this and her eyes light up immediately. Being eighteen her income sucks, and because I've been here so long mine has been collecting in my account for far longer than usual, so I like spoiling her.

"Oh my bliss! Valentine you're the best!" she squeals from inside the watch face and I smile back at her, quickly brushing a loose strand of my hair behind my ear.

"Okay, I'll see you in a minute," I promise as she kisses the screen. I give a tiny wave with my free hand before ending the holo-call and laughing at her insanely bubbly personality. She's certainly a lot younger than me in spirit, that's for sure.

As I walk down the main high street of the Female District, I take a moment to calm myself, watching women walking past in their white variation clothing, so wrapped up in their daily buzz that I wonder momentarily what lives would be like if everyone had jobs. I mean, I know I'm lucky. Being selected as eligible for the Jigsaw project means I am work exempt, because my job is to get ready for being a wife and mother. However, I'd never heard enough about the labour district to know what people with jobs lived like. Or how they survived. Neither of my parents had worked either, so I can't help but find myself curious. I know that some of the people in the city are from the outside, but I can never find the courage to ask them, one way or another, what their experience entails.

I stare into cafés, wistful as I pass their wide glass windows that sheen, looking in upon the holo-dash menus as people place their orders. I watch a couple of girls sitting together, one of them examining the other's ring. I sigh.

When is that going to be me, dammit? Where the hell is he? I cuss silently, feeling my heart rate skyrocket as I bite down on the soft flesh of my lip, trying to bridle my impatience.

I turn from the window, realising I've stopped, and continue in my leisurely stroll down the pristine white sidewalks.

Looking up to the light blue sky I appreciate its endless beauty, and I'm grateful to be a part of a city that survives on totally sustainable energy in order to preserve it. I'm even more grateful that I was born now and not back in the 21st Century, where pollution had been rife and everyone had been having sex with everyone else. I feel proud of the fact I'm still untouched, and as I reach the end of the high street and turn a left, I come to the city's inner limit and exhale.

I'm on the edge of the water, where an enormous lake sprawls forth from the urban jungle home only to females. I feel myself dwarfed by the natural beauty of the manmade lake, but even more than that, I find myself wishful, I find myself curious.

As I gaze across the water to what lies on the opposite side, walking beneath the enormous towering rail of the high-speed monorail once more, I see it. The male district of the city. The place where I have never, nor will ever, visit. I wonder where he is right now. Whether he's as tired as I am of waiting. Whether he's standing on the opposite side, gazing back at me.

I feel my chest constrict, the loneliness that I have been craving to release me tightening its hold. It does this every night, when I falter in sleep, reaching out, seeking him and watching the lonely blue glow of my solitary tattoo, incomplete as my hands sprawl into the cotton sheets, wanton.

I look down at it, the jigsaw puzzle piece without a companion, just like me. I find myself getting emotional, so pull my feelings back, knowing I need to remain strong a little longer. I've never been in love, and I've been almost completely out of contact with men for the last 9 years. I miss contact, real contact, like an embrace, a kiss. Even the kind a parent can give would be better than this wasteland of flesh, where everything is formal. Everything is contained.

I long for him as I stand at the edge of the water, like I do every single time I take this test, looking upon the city of men and willing him to find me.

Trust the process. The technician's words call out through my memory, the whisper of comfort they provide as fleeting as my last human contact. I twist my mouth, running my hand back through my honey blonde hair and sighing. This isn't the end. It's the beginning. I just have to wait and be patient. As I have always been.

<hr />

"Hey! I'm here!" I call out into the camera at Egypt's apartment. I hear her excited babble saying something too quick for me to catch before a loud, high pitched tone sounds and the door before me slides aside. I step into the entryway, scanning the tattoo on the inside of my left wrist over the turnstile as I pass through. The elevator descends, sensing my proximity and opening in a swish rush of silent sleek motion. I stride into it, scanning my tattoo once more over the sensor labelled with the floor I wish to ascend to, and glad for the company of people like Egypt.

Taking the test always makes me emotional, but today it's worse for some reason. The loneliness and unrequited love for a stranger is slowly becoming overwhelming and terrifying with every month that passes, and I wonder how much longer I can really carry on like this.

As the elevator moves upward soundlessly, I hum, feeling the emptiness of the inside of the space making grabs for me and threatening to fill me with dread. Too slowly I reach the floor where Egypt's apartment unit sits and so walk out quickly, feeling tears prickling my eyes and threatening to spill over.

The door opens before I even reach it to knock, and I fly forward crashing into an unsuspecting Egypt and hugging her, happy for the contact, even if she does stand stone still, obviously confused.

"Whoa! What's wrong?" she asks as I burst into tears, my voice failing me as I sob, standing in the doorway of her apartment unit. She pulls me through the door and walks me across the small studio space, taking hurried paces alongside me and sitting me down on her white couch, which sits next to the standard single bed.

"I'm sorry," I sigh, feeling the tears falling down my cheeks like an antidote to my pain, the desolation within me spilling outward.

13

"Don't be sorry. What happened?" she asks, looking concerned and pushing her messy dark hair behind one ear. Her eyes are hazel just like mine, and I see my blotchy, tear stained complexion reflected back at me in her genteel features.

"Nothing! That's the problem. This is my sixty-first test Egypt. I'm twenty-five and I'm alone!" I cry, feeling the weight of the years I have lived here, training, waiting, dreaming, weighing down on me like they've all been for nothing.

"Whoa, I thought you said you were happy it was taking longer, because you'll be ready!" she reminds me, stroking my hair with her long fingers.

"Of course I said that. I don't want you to see me like this. I'm so tired of waiting, Egypt. My friends, they all have their second child, even third child by now," I express my distress as we sit on her couch and I cry, letting my emotion out as Egypt wraps her arms around me.

"Shhh. It's not so bad, Monopolis can be fun. You've got loads of hobbies, ice skating, painting, pottery, and you know you kick my ass at ballet." She tries to make me feel better but I sputter, laughing at her naivety.

"Yes, but that's only because most of the people my age are long gone by now. I've had so much time by myself, Egypt. It's driving me crazy," I confess the reason I have put so much time and energy into my studies and recreation, not only building my cred considerably in the process, but also because I can't stand to stay in my unit alone anymore. I can't stand the feeling that nobody cares about me, that I'm not on anyone's mind.

"Well, you're not alone now. I'm here. If you don't want to go home tonight, I understand. You can always stay here, you know that. I only have a single bed, but we can squeeze." She is so kind, so sweet and I'm immediately grateful for her and glad that I decided to walk the five blocks to see her. I need company. Even if it was only of the female friend variety.

Getting up from the couch she pads across the breadth of her single unit on bare feet, reaching the wall upcycler and asking clearly for what she requires as she says, "tissues," before scanning her tattoo. I watch her, remembering how I'd struggled using an upcycler for the first time when I'd moved here. My parents had been the only people with access to the ones in my childhood home, and so upon moving here, I had wasted no time in spending my first week's cred vocally flicking through the options for single status individuals and ordering the most ridiculous things in the catalogue I could find, like a carrot sharpener. The food cycler had been just as bad, and I can't help but laugh internally as I remember sitting, surrounded by vegetables that I'd ordered just for the sake of it, sharpening carrots and trying to get over how stupid I'd been to go on such a spending spree on my first night.

As Egypt waits patiently, the upcycler beeps before spitting out a small package at her, which she throws at me as she launches herself onto the bed next to the sofa. I look to her and ask the simple question with a weak smile.

"Do I look tragic?" She frowns, not answering with a cheeky glint in her eye. "Hey! You're supposed to say no," I complain, taking a tissue and throwing the rest of the packet at her. She puts her hands over her head and deflects the projectile, laughing.

"I'm not going to lie to you!" she smirks as I wipe my eyes, feeling utterly pathetic.

"Well that makes me feel just great." I roll my eyes, letting them finally drop into my lap where I scrunch up the tissue in my palm.

"Well, I know what always makes me feel better when I think I look like crap," Egypt replies with a crooked smile and I smile back, knowing full well to what it is she's referring.

"You wanna get the holo-boards and I'll get the markers?" I ask her and she nods, smiling.

"Let's rate some ugly-ass dresses," she winks, and with that, we set to work.

Two

The door's holo-dash buzzes, grabbing my attention away from the high definition soft-light of the catwalk. The wedding channel is definitely my favourite thing to watch, and even better is when new designers showcase their latest collections, especially when they're horrible.

"Pizza time! YES!" Egypt does a fist pump and leaps from the bed on which we're sprawled, landing with feline elegance on the balls of her feet and making a dash for the door, before she scans her tattoo on the door's holo-dash, causing it to slide open.

Outside in the hall, the delivery synth hovers at head height, square and plain white, holding a clear plastic pizza box in its mail compartment. I'm momentarily distracted by the soft-light channel, which switches from the wedding dress showcase we've been watching to a Bliss Inc. advertisement. I turn my attention to the screen almost automatically, my eyes resting upon the pixelated outline of Pippa Hart the Eighth's perfect face.

"Here at Bliss Inc., we believe in true love. Why? Well, because we have the formula which makes it possible!" her high pitched girly tones echo off the walls of the apartment as I hear Egypt taking the food and the synth saying "Thank you for your

17

custom," before she walks back across the room toward me and the door slides shut silently, leaving us once again alone. I turn towards her, tuning out the background noise as Pippa Hart begins the open house tour of the Bliss Inc. headquarters.

Egypt places the box on the bed and opens the top of it, the smell of processed cheese and meat fills the air around me and I sigh, relaxing at the comforting smell of my childhood. My dad had always made the most amazing pizza when I was a kid, and it is still my go to for when I feel crappy.

Passing me a slice, Egypt sits on the bed and looks at me, beginning to chew on her own slice thoughtfully.

"You know, I never asked you, what do you think he'll be like? You know, your guy?" She asks me the question straight up and I ponder this a moment, chewing considerably before answering.

"Blonde hair, dark eyes, strong, tall." I list off the characteristics that I imagine every single time I picture walking down the aisle.

"Oh my bliss, he sounds hot! What about his personality?" she questions me, taking another bite of her pizza and getting cheese on her chin. I frown. I'd never thought about his personality as much as his face, always figuring that I'd automatically love everything about him. After all, what was the point in matchmaking couples via a scientific formula if their personalities didn't match as well?

"Someone who's kind and sweet to me. Someone who loves me," I reply to her and she looks kind of odd as her expression twists into a curious one.

"Is that it? What about him? What about what he is on his own, without you? Like sense of humour? Family man?" I feel like

I'm being interrogated, but instead of being irritated, I feel my eyes widen. I realise that perhaps I had been lazy in my assumptions. I had thought the formula would give me exactly what I wanted, but I wonder how it can do that when even I don't know what exactly it is I want.

"What about you?" I ask her, deflecting the question and cocking my head. I lean back against the wall her bed is against, next to the windowsill of the unit, and watch as her face turns animated.

"Someone who knows how to cook and who's funny! Oh, and someone who wants to travel, like maybe take me to one of those holiday resorts like the honeymoon complex. I'd like someone physically fit. Someone who likes to cuddle." Her answer is short, but it's better than my complete lack of one, and so I smile at her as her eyes sparkle, so clearly picturing the imaginary face she's given her matchmate.

"That sounds nice," I reply and she shrugs.

"Yeah, I guess. It's what I put on the match test when I took it anyway," she replies, grinning as she helps herself to another slice of pizza.

"So what about the dress? I think I know what you don't like by now, but I'm curious to hear what you do want! What's the flavour of the week? Have you thought about it recently?" she asks me a question she's asked me several times before, but every time I change my answer, so I can see why she's asking me again.

"Something princessy I think. I want that big sweeping skirt. I think they're breath-taking. Maybe not even white, like blush?" I speak, licking my lips and looking up, imagining myself standing in the Marriage Complex, ready to get married. I see myself carrying my large skirts down the steps of Bliss Hall, feeling my heartbeat accelerate as I take step after measured step, heels making sure that my movement is deliberate and careful, even if my pulse isn't.

"I think I want a red dress, you know. I'm not really traditional," she expresses, closing her eyes as she takes a third slice of pizza, eating so quick I'm sure she thinks I've just purchased the last pizza on the planet.

"I think you'll look beautiful in red! White flowers?" I enquire, finishing my slice of pizza and chewing through the fluffy crust firmly as I speak.

"How did you know?" she giggles, reaching out and squeezing my knee.

"Well, you've had the same wedding layout since I met you at sixteen, if I don't know by now I'd say I've been deaf or an extremely bad friend for the last two years." I remind her and she smiles, suddenly looking sad.

"I'm going to miss you, you know, when you go," she sighs, and I frown. I haven't thought about leaving her behind. It has always feels like I'm going to be stuck here until long after she's gone.

"I'll miss you too, but hopefully we'll be close by when we get to Fantasia Pastures." I remind her that it's not the end. I may get married before her, but after completing the 100-day newlywed period, I'll be moving onto Fantasia Pastures until my first child reaches the age of one. It is quite possible we will be neighbours, and even if that doesn't work out, Pearl Falls houses thousands of families for extended periods of time, because you can't move on to Jasmine Grove to prepare for retirement in Rose Gardens until all your children have passed the age of fifteen.

"Do you think our children will grow up together, Val?" she looks like she might cry and so I nod, hoping more than anything we can be neighbours in the future.

"Of course! You'll be chasing me around Rose Gardens on a walker-synth for sure!" I smile, hoping to Bliss that I'm right.

———————————•●•———————————

"You sure you're okay to go home?" Egypt asks me and I force my lips to turn up at the corners, dreading returning to my apartment, but hoping the walk back to my unit will be enough to clear my head and tire me out for some dreamless and easy sleep.

"Yeah, thanks for the offer, but I have readiness classes early tomorrow, and you know how brutal the alarm can be if you're not fully rested when it goes off," I reply and she nods, still wearing the pyjamas that she'd slept in the night before.

"Yeah, I know exactly what you mean. You saw my hair this morning when I answered your call, right?" she chuckles, touching the back of her head, self-conscious, and I roll my eyes.

"Yeah well, you think that's bad... remember that chick we saw who thought high fashion hair would be suitable for her wedding?" I ask her and she guffaws, snorting slightly at the memory.

"Yeah, that's right! They back combed it and her groom's fingers got all caught in it. Then, after the ceremony, she fell through a window trying to remove her veil, I think?" she reminds me of the *real wedding disasters* episode and I giggle.

21

"Yep. That's the one!" I pull her into me for a hug, enjoying the contact before she releases me gently and I step through her open doorway.

"Come again soon, okay?" she requests and I nod, glad for the return invite. She's my closest friend, if not one of the most genuine people I've ever met.

"You bet." I wink at her and walk from the apartment, waving as she sees me off. I step across the pristine lobby, housing six other apartment units, and into the elevator, watching Egypt's beautiful, caring gaze disappear as the doors slide shut.

I scan my wrist across the ground floor section of the holo-dash and feel my stomach lurch slightly as the elevator begins its too quick descent. Stepping out into the lobby as the doors slide open quickly, I exit the building and walk out into the cold night air of the city streets.

⎯⎯⎯⎯⎯•◉•⎯⎯⎯⎯⎯

As I walk the five blocks to my apartment unit, I find myself curious. Egypt had asked me what I wanted in a man, and it's made me realise that other than his aesthetic, I have no idea. I don't even know any men, other than my dad, because I'd grown up with two sisters and no brothers. I always assume the formula will take care of my happiness, of love, but how do I know what I'll love in someone when I don't even know what love is? I wonder if love is like how I feel about my mom and dad, but then I remember the look in people's eyes when I see them in Bliss Inc. adverts. There's something special there, something I'd never seen anywhere else. Like they both know some great secret and

22

are keeping it between themselves, savouring the fact that nobody else knows.

I sigh, running my fingers through my hair and stepping off the curb, walking across the street as I catch the high-speed monorail gliding overhead in the distance, a silent, glistening glass bullet that cuts through the dark night sky like it's nothing. I wonder where it's headed. If it's taking new brides and grooms to the airport for their honeymoon. Whether it's headed to the Marriage Complex, or whether it's bringing couples back to their new homes after their three-week honeymoon. I am never usually this curious, and I wonder if my emotions are skyrocketing out of control because of the test, though you'd think I'd be used to taking them by now.

You're just being impatient. I scold myself, knowing I need to wait for him. I need to trust in the process.

As I reach the corner on which my apartment block sits, I turn, suddenly coming parallel once more to the giant lake which separates me from my other half, from the newlyweds who have the happiness I so desire.

I vow now to think more on what I want *in* a man, rather than what I want him to look like. After all, he might look the total opposite to what I've always fantasised, and I worry that when, If I ever do, finally walk down the aisle I'll look like I've been slapped with disappointment. I hate that thought, knowing that if my groom looked like that at me, I'd most certainly burst into tears.

Scanning my wrist on the holo-dash, I enter my building, which is exactly identical to Egypt's except reversed in floor plan. The architecture bores me; plain white, clinical, clean, barren. It's

23

almost as though the buildings for singles are designed to make you feel alone, because on the adverts I've seen, apartments on the Newlywed Island Complex are absolutely nothing like any architecture I've ever found here.

As I walk through the turnstile, scanning my wrist and stepping into the elevator, I ponder the apartments I have seen. The fact they have wooden floors, something that is kept only for married couples, because wood isn't a finite resource. I've also seen that they have colour. So, where the bland white and pale pinks of the Female District creates a macrocosm of space, the colours in the Newlywed Complex created a kind of cosiness in the units, like they are a home, rather than somewhere you just sleep and eat.

The elevator swooshes up, taking me to my desired floor, which I promptly walk across, not even trying to be quiet as the surrounding units are sound-proofed. I scan my wrist once more, gaining access in a careless fashion that's become only too routine the last 9 years. I fall through the doorway as my door slides open and the lights turn on, feeling dread as the space is revealed.

It's pretty standard, but with a few more decadent white and pink furnishings, my apartment is a large square studio too. I have a three-quarter sized bed, something else I'd saved for, even though I have no one to share it with, as well as a simple kitchen with an extortionately expensive coffee maker and a juicer. My small studio, however, is decorated, unlike Egypt's, which has only been lived in for two years.

My back wall is covered in e-magazine print-outs, the only images of men I can easily get my hands on, plastered into collages of what I might want my wedding to look like, what my groom might look like. I am a very visual person, I guess, so maybe that's why I haven't thought about his personality.

As I stand in the stark fluorescent light of the room, I suddenly feel exhausted at the collection of images that fill my field of vision. The collages are of my dreams, of the gown I will wear, of the ring he will pick for me, of the flowers I will hold... but right now I feel so far from any of that, it's draining to take it all in.

I close my eyes, letting myself give into the urge to take a break from the brightness of it all, quickly deciding I need to sleep.

I strip my clothes off, after scanning my unit's holo-dash active and saying 'fog' so that my windows crystallise, shielding my curvy nakedness from view. Turning on my heel once, I shove my clothes into the upcycler's in-device trash chute, quickly saying 'pyjamas' and longing for the machine to hurry up as it selects the single standard garments from the hard-light catalogue and spits out the folded, white cotton top and pants. I slip them on, walking across the room and sitting on my bed, before I look into the hard-light of the holo-dash which takes up the large wall on the end of my bed. The size, another upgrade I have paid for, allows me to see that I have absolutely no messages. It's not really a surprise, considering that messaging others via holo-dash, just like via my hard-light watch, costs you quite a bit of cred, and everyone in the Single Districts only has what readiness courses allow. I suppose though it doesn't matter, it isn't like I could message a man, or even my sisters in Pearl Falls, because communications are restricted to same-sex, same-class only. Still, at the thought of noone reaching out, my heart fractures and the loneliness I had felt before, the despair that my sixty-first test had brought, returns.

I flop back onto the smart foam mattress which heats, hugging me like the body of another. This only makes me more depressed as I call out, "sleep" and watch as the lights flicker into nothingness and my curtains draw, shrouding me in the dark.

I lie in the black, eyes closed, imagining that the arms of my groom are holding me, imagining that I'm not alone, that I'm not cut off. I imagine that he's here and that he's perfect. As I envision this, I fall slowly into desperate dreams of closeness, heat and most heart-breaking of all, true love.

———————●●●————————

I wake, groggy, to silence. This isn't normal. Usually, I'm given a miniature heart attack by the buzz of my alarm from the holo-dash.

I stir, wondering why I'm awake early, but then as I open my eyes I realise that the light streaming in through the window is brighter than normal.

Did I oversleep? What happened to my alarm? I wonder, sitting up straight and scowling, hoping I haven't missed too many classes due to this unusual and irritating technical difficulty.

I move forward, pushing myself onto my knees as my legs curl beneath me and allowing my body to fall forward into the mattress. I sweep my wrist over the scanner next to the far end of the bed and activate my holo-dash, pulling it up and watching as my forehead crumples when the time comes up on the home screen. It's 12:30pm.

What in the name of Bliss is going on? I wonder, looking up next into the left-hand corner of the dash. My mailbox is bleeping, crowded with ten messages.

I blink, bringing my hands up to wipe my eyes, making sure I'm not seeing things or still caught in a dream. I kneel up, bringing my finger to the mailbox icon on the dash. I click on it, before I suddenly notice something flashing out of the corner of my eye.

My tubemail, which is attached to the wall behind my coffee maker and out of easy reach due to lack of use, is blinking neon blue. I turn toward it at a slow and measured pace, eyes widening.

Could it be?

No. I refuse to get my hopes up. It's probably another notice about the upcycler, or a new holo-dash update notice. My heart rate falters, giving my unwanted excitement away as my blood pounds in my veins, becoming audible in my ears.

I put my warm feet down onto the radiant cold of the unit floor, cooling my soles. I push up from the mattress, standing straight and walking across the room, around the lonely kitchen island and over to the tubemail compartment, where the blinking neon blue light continues to ebb as I push my coffee maker out of the way.

Inside the transparent plastic tube, I'm surprised that I'm not greeted by the sight of the usual roll of transparent acetate Instead, there's a square package wrapped in white paper. Not something you typically ever see outside of the wedding district.

At this thought, the realisation that my life may well be about to change, my heart bursts into an all-out sprint and I feel my body begin to tremble. This isn't how I'd pictured this moment. I only took the test yesterday, and yet here I am, standing in my pyjamas with my face unmade and my hair looking like I've been dragged backwards through a genetically modified topiary.

I stop, remembering that this might not be it. It might be something else. After all, today has been unusual; my alarm hadn't gone off for readiness classes. A small voice inside me whispers, *maybe it's because you're ready,* as I swallow hard and my hand lurches forward before I can even think to do anything else.

I wrap my fingers around the parcel as I push open the transparent seal around the tube, feeling the thickness and uncharacteristic matte of the paper as I pull it from where it has sat, waiting for me.

I turn away from the wall, holding it in my hand, and notice that the paper is wrapped around the parcel with a bright blue ribbon, tied in a neat flower design on the top, as I walk toward my bed. I sit down upon the smart foam mattress, my heart racing and my breath coming in short shallow wisps.

Once I'm sitting, I don't look to my holo-dash, still transfixed by the parcel as I pull on the ribbon, watching it unravel like I hope my life is about to, coming apart with such ease that it's as though the silk has been waiting for my nervous touch. As the paper around the tiny square package falls flat, I see it, the words. The words I've been waiting for.

SAVE THE DATE.

I scream. I can't help myself as a bubble of pure, unbridled excitement moves up from my stomach, past my heart and into my windpipe, bringing a smile to my face as I close my eyes, throwing my head back and clutching the box inside the invitation to my chest.

Oh my bliss. It's happening. I'm getting married!

I can't take my eyes off the invitation as I pick it up in my left hand, fingers clutching the soft ring box in my right. I scan down the page, a smile on my face I can't get rid of.

You are Cordially Invited to Attend the Wedding of

Valentine Morland and Matchmate
On the 10th of October

Location: Bliss Hall - Suite Thirteen

Time: 12 noon

Family and friends are invited to join Valentine and her new Husband in the suite after the ceremony for drinks, cake, silver service and well-wishes.

Please arrive at 1 o'clock proper in formal best.

See RSVP card on reverse for food and drink choices.

———————————— ●●● ————————————

I cannot help but find myself teary at the announcement of my wedding. *My wedding.* I'm going to meet him. Finally. After all this time.

I look at my hard-light watch, which sits on my nightstand where the noise of my alarm usually resounds. Today is the 3rd of October. I have a week. I will be married in a week. I feel my heart falter, not only in excitement, but also in fear. I have seven days to prepare, to make sure I look my best, to get ready to make my first impression.

I let my hand with the invite in fall to the bed, slack, as my mind begins to race. I have to find a dress... and lingerie... and flowers.

Oh bliss, OH BLISS.

Suddenly, I'm freaking out, but as my breathing quickens even more, my eyes fall to the box of soft material in my hand. I've never seen this type of material before, but I kind of want to stroke it as I put my left hand on the lid, readying myself to pull it open. I inhale, suddenly nervous.

The ring is a big deal; I have always known this, especially because it's the only part of the wedding, other than his suit, that the groom gets to choose. I've heard rumours that they have a whole street just for rings in the male district of Monopolis, and you have to book an appointment to go and buy it and everything, just like wedding dress shops here in the female district. There's no limit on how much a groom can spend on the ring, because the state of Monopolis pays, a part of the perks of the Jigsaw project. Besides, real diamonds hadn't been found in years, so almost every single ring out there is now synthetically made, and merely sentimental.

As the lid pulls back, it reveals a ring unlike anything I could have imagined. I certainly never would have picked anything like it for myself. A note card falls out of the box and my heart flutters again, remembering how many of my friends had received first contact via an anonymous letter from their grooms. I turn the card over as I stare between it and the ring. Disappointed. It merely says.

Platinum Band with 1ct Blue Diamond solitaire, Princess cut.

I exhale, turning it over and checking the back for something, anything from my groom. There's nothing, so as I continue to stare at the blue diamond engagement ring. Pulling it out of the box to slip on my finger, I can't help but deflate.

I stare at the band, fitted by the jewellers, who are some of the most highly ranked people in Monopolis as they have the right to request information on the matchmate of the men they serve. The jewel sparkles in the light, blue and cold. I wonder why on earth anyone would want a blue diamond. I mean, I've seen coloured stones before, but never blue. After all, most of the women I knew owned nothing blue, because all the clothes in the female district are white and pale pink.

Maybe he wants you to stand out. I think, a reluctant smile gracing my lips at the thought. Feeling better, I turn around to my holo-dash, knowing now why my mailbox is so full. Hopefully it'll be family and my wedding planning instructions.

31

The light streams through the window, which has automatically cleared at the bright hue of the day, causing my privacy to dissolve along with it. I sigh, letting it bathe me and realise that I'll only be stuck in my tiny shoebox apartment for the next seven days. Then I'll be free. Whisked away to a life of luxury, sun and perfect love as I finally grasp the happily ever after I've longed for, for nine years.

I open my eyes, ready to begin as I tap on the first message in my mailbox with my index finger. As the window opens on the interface, I see it's from my mom. Apparently, according to the timestamp, she had known about my engagement before I did, having received her invitation at 9:00 am this morning.

Dear Valentine,

Congratulations on *finally* receiving your wedding date. I'll be in town tomorrow for wedding dress shopping and planning. I only hope we can find a dress for someone as curvy as you. After all, we weren't all blessed with my perfect figure.

All the best.
Your Mother x

I roll my eyes, feeling the scrutiny of my mother's gaze resonating through the screen. I love my mom, don't get me wrong, but she has high standards. I remember when my sister Portia had called me crying because mother had told her she hadn't gotten back into her pre-baby body fast enough.

I shake my head, knowing that wedding dress shopping is going to be a nightmare, and hoping that I can convince Egypt to

32

come along for emotional support. After all, my sisters would do anything to avoid the scorch of Cynthia Morland's stare, especially throwing the scrutiny on me. I've heard that they provide champagne at the fittings, which I've never had, and can only pray that it has the same calming effect that all the e-mags claim.

Thinking about this I open the next message down, knowing exactly what's coming.

Valentine,

Congratulations on your wedding announcement! My baby sister is finally getting married! You better not look better than I did! Kidding! Seriously though.

I hope you know mom is also going to be a complete nightmare during shopping, and that she's decided that we're all coming to see you tomorrow. Don't worry, I'll bring you some invisible earplugs. Just, for the love of bliss, don't let her in charge of the registry scanner, you should see the amount of hideous crap I ended up with because I got drunk at the bridal boutique and gave her free reign over my registry list.

Anyway, see you tomorrow!

Portia

P.S Don't give me a shocked look when you see how incredibly fat I've gotten. I have two kids and a third on the way and I want to see how you look when....

I laugh as the message cuts off, as the word count has been exceeded. Portia hates my mother, and as the middle child, she and I definitely share the opinion that we are merely less successful attempts at recreating my eldest sister, Eve. Realising that I've probably gotten a message from her too, I scroll down the list, letting my eyes search for telling words or phrases. Finally, the last message I find tips me off and I open it, rolling my eyes at the title: **I hope you know this puts a major imposition on *my* marriage.**

> **Valentine,**
> **Of course, your wedding would be on the day I'm next ovulating. I have no idea how you do it, but as if dragging out your single life over nine years so I have to listen to Portia whine about never seeing you and missing you isn't enough, now I'm probably going to have to miss my predicted conception date. As if managing three children isn't hard enough, Desmond and I are now trying for a fourth, mainly because I'm pretty sure Portia is trying to win favour over me with our mother by giving her more grandchildren. Anyway, congratulations, blah blah blah. See you tomorrow.**
> **Eve**

Oh my bliss, that's so Eve. I think to myself, wondering how she became so self-centred and competitive. I mean, when I think about it, I probably got the worst of our mother, and I'm not like that at all.

I had been left alone in Pearl Falls with my mother once Eve and Portia had been accepted into the Jigsaw Project, and those two years living at home with her had been the worst of my life. I'm a talented girl, I know that, but in a large way I wish I wasn't, because that would mean my mother wasn't the pushiest woman on the planet. Head of the home-pride committee at the Falls,

Cynthia Morland's children were expected to fully exude the values of Bliss Inc., giving her a reputation of being the perfect mother and wife. These claims were not merely gossip either, as she had a full trophy case to prove them. She had given me the best childhood I could have asked for, home schooling me, taking me to ballet lessons, piano lessons, ice skating lessons, art classes. I even speak three languages.

However, it isn't because she loves me. It is because she wants others to love her. To want to be her. She has, in a way, made me desirable, talented and skilled, but she has also tried to make me so for her own benefit. My mother is the head of the schooling programme, the head of the activities and holiday committees too, and I can't help but wonder why she is like this. Why she is so determined to work a hundred-hour week bettering the community when none of the other wives had to, nor desired to. It is nothing short of strange.

I also know I'm lucky I've been accepted into the project at all, because there's no way in hell my mother would have accepted any other result from me.

I open the next message in my inbox, rolling my eyes and shaking my head at my mother's insanely condescending tone which is echoing through my mind, before I stare down at myself, at my curves, loving them all-the-more because she disapproves.

Scanning down the list of messages, I open an official looking-one next.

Dear Miss Morland,

Find enclosed a list of numbers for floral shops, salons, bridal dress stores, decoration suppliers, as well a list of shops

you should be registering with in order to select wedding gifts in anticipation of your first home as a couple. You will need to be prompt in making appointments as times are given away on a first come, first served basis, and at the discretion of the shop owners. Food and Drinks are provided by Bliss Hall for your reception.

We congratulate you on your wedding and wish you a lifetime of Bliss with us.

Pippa Hart VIII
Bliss Inc. President.

I find the list of numbers at the bottom of the page, instantly wondering how I'm going to be able to pay for all the calls that I'll have to make. I mean, I'm not hard up, but my sisters had both been on hold with their bridal consultants for at least three hours, and that wasn't going to come cheap. Then I remember something; something that makes me smile as I lean back, moving to grab my watch off the bedside table and checking my account balance with a simple swipe of one finger. I let my eyes linger on the screen as I see that my old account is gone. Instead, I see a new account, with no cred balance, but simply two words that make me smile.

STATUS: **BRIDE**

Three

As I lean against the singular kitchen island, which marks the end of my kitchen and the beginning of the living area that holds my three-quarter bed, sofa, and holo-dash, I take a moment to breathe. Holding the warm cup of coffee in my hands, which I have successfully managed to make after three failed attempts due to shaking fingers, I close my eyes.

This can't be real. I must be dreaming.

I don't want to believe that this is all really happening. After all, I only took the test yesterday. How has everything managed to change so dramatically so fast? Is it a mistake? Is it so fast because it had taken me and my matchmate so long to both finally be ready?

I open my eyes as I exhale heavily, taking another sip of the bitter, warm liquid in my cup. My ring catches in the light, shimmering blue and cold back at me. I stare at it a few moments, still transfixed by this heavy and unusual addition to my hand. It's beautiful, but it's certainly not my dream ring. Or something I would have chosen if it'd been me in the store. I wonder if this means my groom will be nothing like I expect also.

37

Scrunching up my forehead, I look to the back wall of the unit, at the images and collages of my dreams.

In a moment of aloof detachment, I twist, placing my coffee cup down on the flawless white of the kitchen island, before taking three long strides across the room and reaching up high to where the layering of images ends. I slide my fingers under the loose parts of the acetate which has been stuck to the wall with gum stick. Pulling, I rip the images down from the surface one by one and let them scatter on the floor like the leaves of trees, genetically designed to turn red and fall to the ground in one synchronised plight.

After I've cleared the wall of fantasies, of that which will never be reality, I gather the pictures up from the floor, stacking them in a disarrayed pile before throwing them haphazardly into the upcycler trash chute with a determined vow that I won't make this difficult for myself. My expectations are based off nothing more than what I've seen in e-mags. What if my matchmate isn't attractive? Or he eats with his mouth wide open? Or he snores... The possibilities begin to stack up and I feel myself start to panic.

Before I get a chance to completely freak myself out, I take a few quick and unbalanced steps across the and slump onto my bed, scanning my wrist to activate the interface and saying, "call Egypt," in a loud and measured tone, the one which I reserve for speaking with technology.

The interface buzzes exactly once before Egypt accepts the call, and her over-excitable babble fills the room, echoing around me in surround sound.

"Oh my bliss, I've been waiting for you to call! I got my invitation this morning! Congratulations!" She's almost too excitable, though I can see that her eyes are red, almost like she's been crying. Of course she got her invitation already, though I can't deny it's kind of unsettling how Bliss Inc. keeps tabs on whom you're spending time with.

"Egypt, I'm freaking out!" I groan, falling back just as quickly as I've propped myself up among my unmade sheets.

"What? What happened? Is the ring hideous?" she asks me, her eyes wide. "Speaking of the ring, can I see it?" My mouth twists into a grimace as she blinks a few times, curious and impatient as she brushes her dark hair behind one ear. "Okay, that's it. I'm coming over there. Who in the name of Bliss doesn't want to show off their engagement ring? This is an emergency! I'll be ten minutes!" I open my mouth to protest, but she ends the call and the interface goes blank. I blink a few times, realising that I'm still in my plain white cotton pyjamas, but unable to summon the energy to care. I'm an emotional wreck, stuck somewhere between mind numbing fear and ecstasy.

What the hell is wrong with me? I should be celebrating.

I sigh out, climbing off the bed and swiping my holo-dash closed as I go, not wanting to deal with the world, even if that means booking an appointment with a bridal boutique, which you'd think I'd be freaking over the moon about. Instead, I just lean back against the kitchen island, sipping my lone cup of coffee and enjoying my last few single moments before my life turns upside down.

I hear the holo-dash at my door buzz, alerting me to the fact Egypt is outside. I walk over to the door, the last dregs of my coffee all but gone as I swipe my wrist tattoo and command the dash to allow her entry.

I wait a few moments, nervous as the elevator moves at what I am sure is a pace far slower than normal, hopping from foot to foot and continuously looking down to my ring and then back to my tattoo as the thoughts of how drastically everything is about to change whirl around in my head.

Finally, I see the shadows of feet appear under the door and hit the holo-dash to open it. As it slides to the left, Egypt is revealed behind the door, a worried expression plastered on her face.

"Hey! Valentine, what's going on? Are you okay?" She strides across the threshold, looking me full in the face as she passes before her eyes drop automatically to my hand.

"Yeah, sorry. I'm just panicking," I mumble, walking back across the compact unit and watching as the door slides shut behind her. I place my empty cup in the kitchen upcycler, which takes it away to be cleaned.

"I'd say! What's going on?" She sits down on the sofa, crossing her elegantly long legs and brushing her hair behind one ear, intent on listening.

"I just, everything is happening in this giant blur. I'm scared," I admit, biting my lower lip as she rolls her eyes at me.

"You, are a complete moron, Val." Egypt laughs and I can't help but laugh too. "You're the only person I know who is crying about being alone one day, and then crying about getting engaged not twenty-four hours later! Now come on, be honest, is it the ring?" She cocks an eyebrow at me as her eyes dart down to my hand again.

"Well, the ring... it's just." I hold up my hand to her as I take a step forward. Her long fingers grasp my palm, pulling me toward her as I sit down on the sofa beside her and her dark eyes widen.

"Val, it's beautiful! A little unusual perhaps, but what's the problem?" she asks me the question and I breathe, relieved. She thought my ring was beautiful. So maybe I'm just being neurotic.

"I just, it isn't what I always pictured..." I begin and she laughs, exasperated.

"Valentine, as long as I've known you, you have never had a single idea about how you want this to happen. You have a million ideas, but they change every other day. How can you expect a stranger to possibly know what you want, when you don't know?" she speaks reason, despite the fact she's younger than me, and I feel like crying all over again. She's right. What was I expecting? Did I think this stranger could read my mind? I mean, I suppose we've been matched as one another's true love, but that doesn't make him psychic.

I let my gaze linger on the cold blue of the diamond, which throws light back on my face as I admire it. I guess it is kind of unique.

"Okay, you're right. I'm being crazy. Sorry." I apologise and she grins at me, placing a hand in mine.

"Hey, it's okay. You only took the test yesterday. That *is* fast. Even I thought so. Still, you have a week until the wedding. I've taken the time off already from classes. Though you might have to help me out with some cred. Seeing as I'm missing classes and all." She winks at me and I smile, wiping my eyes, which have become teary too quickly at her kindness.

"You didn't have to do that," I remind her, worrying that she'll suffer without her income.

"Of course I didn't, but did you think I was going to miss out on a trip to the wedding district? Though first, you'll have to announce me as your official maid of honour," she reminds me of the million and one formalities I must take care of. The maid of honour is important, and I am glad she's suggested herself, because I can't bear to think about having to choose between my sisters.

It would be my maid of honours job to help me get ready on the day, as well as helping me get my unit ready for departure. While the ceremony is private, reserved only for the bride, groom and registrar, the maid of honour would be there right before I walk in, and right after I come out. I need Egypt there with me, just like I needed her this morning, so I smile back at her.

"Okay, of course I'll register you as my maid of honour on the license. I wouldn't ask anyone else." I say, thinking aloud.

"Have you not started registering yet?" she demands, looking impatient and excitable as I shake my head.

"Not exactly. I've just sort of been... sitting." I say, breathing out heavily and finally managing a genuine smile. Egypt being here makes everything seem so much simpler.

"Well, and cleaning." She gestures to the wall behind me and I give her a sheepish look.

"I told you I was freaking out," I explain and she nods, rolling her eyes.

"You are a disaster, but don't worry, I'm here. We'll sort everything out together. But first, we need to get you registered for a marriage license." She gets to her feet and begins to flurry about my apartment, re-making my bed as I watch her.

I know that the marriage license is the most important thing, and I probably should have got to that by now. It is the only way in which people will be granted access to the wedding suite after the ceremony, because everyone knows invitations are only formality, and that the guest list is purely down to the choices of the bride and groom when they filed their individual claims. I also remember, now, that it grants people from the settlements visitation into Monopolis in the week leading up to the wedding, so leaving it this late is probably stupid of me. My mother and sisters will need to have that visitation so they can come and see me tomorrow.

"Have you done anything so far except sit and freak out?" Egypt berates me, as I walk over to the scanner and present my tattoo, bringing up the hard-light interface for her to look at.

"No. I haven't done anything. I've still got to book a bridal shop appointment, file for a license, pick flowers, and decorations. Oh, and my mother is coming up tomorrow." I sigh, feeling utterly useless.

"The *infamous* Cynthia Morland?" She looks surprised as she cocks an eyebrow and licks her lips.

"Yes, unfortunately." I roll my eyes.

"Well, then, in that case, I'm definitely glad I'm going to be your maid of honour." She smiles at me, eyes sparkling and I laugh. She really has no idea what she is getting into with my mother, but unlike me, I bet she can't wait to find out.

Everything is happening too quickly and, in the blink of an eye, I'm standing outside a five-star breakfast restaurant, wide eyed and alert, waiting for my mother with Egypt by my side.

"This is insane!" Egypt squeals, looking around at the decadence of the district. Building fronts are decorated with silver and gold filigree designs, and the streets smell like the inside of a flower shop, mixed with the scent of thick cake batter and icing. I inhale, letting the aroma calm me as I feel my palms becoming sweaty. My mother is coming to Monopolis, and I'm beginning to wonder if I may get away with running in the other direction. I'm wearing the traditional white pantsuit, but now I am also sporting a blue sash around my waist like a belt, an outward symbol that I'm carrying the status of bride.

"I know. I'm crapping..." I begin, but before I can finish I'm cut off by a high pitched and demanding voice.

"Valentine Ophelia Morland! Language!" As the voice of my childhood echoes in my ears and I cringe, I pivot on the spot, beginning to wish that I'd made a run for it earlier.

"Mom." I acknowledge her as I look into the full force of her gaze.

My mother is a tall, willowy creature of six foot one. Her hair is dirty blonde and kept too straight until it stops in an abrupt acuteness just below her shoulders. She's wearing a black suit with a red and pink ombré blouse beneath it, and she looks like a too beautiful poker, stood straight and proper in the middle of the street. Behind her, my two sisters are stood, giggling at me beneath purposefully placed hands.

"Yes. That's me." She smiles, her lips tense and her expression strained. The odd thing about my mother, which strikes me only now that I've not seen her in maybe three years, is how she ceases to age. I must remember to ask her what kind of face cream she uses, because for all I know she could be immortal.

We hang in the silence a few moments before Egypt saves me and my mother's gaze shifts, changing instantly in classic Cynthia Morland fashion from disapproving to adoring.

"I'm Egypt," Egypt says into the awkward silence, side stepping me and presenting herself. "Valentine's maid of honour," she explains as my mother's well-hidden but undoubtedly vacant expression proves she has no idea I was bringing someone. She holds out a thin wrist and long fingers, taking Egypt's hand and shaking it vigorously.

"Well, this is a surprise. I had no idea Valentine had already chosen a maid of honour, but I suppose it's for the best. You're a beautiful girl, and both my other daughters are in-between pregnancies or expecting right now. You're perfect, very photogenic." She reaches up and twists Egypt's head from left to right in her palms, completely intrusive as she examines my friend's strong features and jawline in the middle of the street.

I cough, interrupting them as Portia smiles at me and I examine her for a moment, noting that she's not that much bigger than me in size as I recall her email, wondering exactly how much pressure my mother is piling on her.

"Shall we go in?" I ask and my mother tuts loudly before looking to Egypt.

"Well of course, I think we have a lot to discuss." She sounds exasperated, making me feel like a complete and utter idiot. "You didn't plan our appointments too close together did you, Valentine? You know that you don't want to arrive at these types of things flustered. You're a bride now. Composure and Complexion, the two C's, are everything." I see my sisters shoot borderline hysterical glances at each other. I had heard these speeches twice before already, as had they, but I notice they have no problem getting along when it comes to my discomfort.

"Of course. We have two hours until the bridal gown appointment," I reply, turning and entering the restaurant as its glass door slides open, blasting warm air down onto me and making a nice change from the chill of the inner-city streets, which are becoming more and more like a wind tunnel with each passing day.

"Good, we have much to discuss," my mother repeats abruptly, more like she's a dictator than a caring parent, but I don't know what else I expected. This is Cynthia Morland all over.

●●●

Taking our seats in the restaurant, we sit by the window at my mother's request, no doubt because she wants to watch the new brides walking past, mentally rating them on scales of obesity and ugliness to assure herself that she's just as beautiful as any of the new and upcoming brides. I smile; trying to enjoy the experience because it's a luxury for me to even be in a place with service, as every restaurant in the Female District is self-service.

As I sit and my mother orders a salad for me and my sisters from the service synth, taking away the joy of novelty, Egypt frowns to herself before ordering the same. I can tell she's heart broken, especially because there's bacon and eggs on the menu,

46

which you can only get in the wedding district before marriage. The holographic menus flicker out of existence on the table, leaving us with nowhere to hide and no distractions.

"So, let's see it!" my mother demands.

"See what?" I ask her, looking away from the window, which I've been using to distract me from her scrutiny.

"The ring of course, Valentine! Goodness, if I didn't know any better, I'd say you were in a carbohydrate induced coma!" she snaps and I hold my hand out, the ring glimmering under the fluorescent lights of the café. It's a stark contrast to the woman I had passed in the restaurant the morning of my test. She'd been overjoyed to show off her ring, but my mother is judge, jury and executioner when it comes to marital fashion, so instead I merely feel dread, worrying she'll make me feel worse about a ring I'm already unsure if I like.

"Is that a blue diamond?" she asks me, looking from my hand to my face and back again.

"Yes, platinum too," I reply with caution.

"Well, I'd say we have a fashion-conscious groom on our hands. Coloured diamonds are coming into fashion in a big way." She smiles at me, approving and I exhale. Eve grabs my hand next, slapping away Portia who sits back into her chair, pouting. The blue reflects in the deeply chocolate eyes of my eldest sister and she nods her head in approval, blonde hair immovable in a stylish beehive.

"Well, it's not as nice as my ring... but it's pretty different." I think that's as close as I'm going to get to a compliment from her, so I smile.

"Thanks," I reply, moving my hand to Portia so she can check out my ring too. Her eyes glimmer, envious. I know that she had hated her ring. It was a teardrop shaped diamond, and she had gone on for her entire wedding week about it being a sign that she was going to spend her married life crying.

"You're lucky." She scowls at me and I laugh, having missed her sense of humour, more than I've missed the other two members of my family combined.

"So, you're thinking blue for the colour scheme of the wedding I assume?" My mother asks me as five service synths swarm in the air around us, setting bowls full of lush green salad on the table.

"Why would you think that? It's my wedding, right?" I ask her, stabbing at my salad with my fork and looking up at her, nervous.

"Well, Valentine, yes. But I'd be remiss in my motherly duties if I let you go out there, in front of your future husband, looking like you've walked out of one of the working settlement jumble sales. You need to match. You're one package. I'd say blue needs to be a major theme. I mean, you can't wear pink, it'll clash terribly with a ring that colour!" She looks at me like I'm insane.

Portia smirks now beside my mother, knowing that my ring isn't such a blessing after all. At least with her clear diamond she had free reign over her colour scheme, and I start to feel a little less sympathetic about her registry list disaster. Egypt perks up beside me.

"What kind of blue exactly were you thinking Mrs Morland?" she asks, trying to be polite and gracious, but I can't help but want to kick her under the table.

"Well, perhaps, periwinkle or baby blue, with greys and the bridal gown in a pure white?" she suggests, glaring at me as I pop a ripe tomato in my mouth and juice and pips burst out between my lips. "Oh for heaven's sake, Valentine, you're about to be somebody's *wife!* Can you at least act like you weren't raised in a barn?" She condemns me and I feel my temper raging inside my chest as I bring a napkin to my lips. I didn't even want her here, and if it weren't for the fact she'd already been invited by the stupid people at Bliss Inc., I wonder if I'd have invited her at all.

As the people at the table sit and begin planning my wedding for me, I listen to plans of grandeur about greys and periwinkle blues which I don't want, wondering if I'll have the energy to fight for the thing which matters to me. The dress.

After the meal is over, my mother, Egypt and Eve walk out of the restaurant as Portia and I make a quick dash for the bathroom. I don't even need to go, but I do need a moment to collect myself, especially if I'm going to spend the rest of the day in the company of my mother.

"You okay?" Portia asks me as I sit up on the hand decontamination unit.

"Do I look okay?" I ask her, cocking an eyebrow as she walks into one of the cubicles and shuts the door, continuing the conversation.

"No, you look like you want to commit matricide. Or throw up, or possibly both."

"You know me so well," I quip and I hear her snort. "I don't want a blue wedding.," I express, feeling my heart hammering at the thought of losing all control.

"Well, try telling that to our mother. No really, do it, I could use a good laugh," she replies, tittering, and I sigh, knowing she's right.

"It's just not what I pictured," I express and she laughs.

"Things rarely are, Valentine. I mean, you're engaged now, so I can be honest with you, right?" she asks me and I nod, though she can't see me. She coughs after a few moments of silence and I vocalise my thoughts.

"Yes, of course."

"Well then, I'll be honest. The wedding isn't the thing you should be worried about. It's the marriage part. Men are, well, they're people too you know." She sounds kind of put out at the sentiment and I feel my lips quirk.

"You're just saying that to scare me. The formula takes care of the rest, you know that." I speak the company line aloud and she snorts.

"Uh, yeah, the formula can match you, but you have to learn about each other. You're marrying a stranger, Val. That's scary and hard, whether you're matchmates or not," she expresses this as she exits the cubicle and I swing my feet, feeling my stomach drop.

"I guess. I hadn't really thought about it that way," I confess as she moves forward, placing her tattoo under the hand decontamination unit and waiting as her hands are washed and dried.

"I know. Neither did I," she admits and her eyes cloud over, her blonde hair falling over her shoulder as she turns towards me.

"Look, my advice, as much as it's worth, is to go into this with an open heart. Try not to get offended by every little thing. Don't worry about the wedding. Your relationship and passing your one-hundred-day assessment is what's important. Okay?" She looks deeply into my eyes, like she's giving me some earth-shattering advice that will save my life. I know she's being dramatic, but I can't help but feel my heart falter at the stare she gives me, her brown eyes boring into mine.

"Okay. I promise I'll try to keep an open heart," I express, feeling my breathing slow as I concentrate on relaxing. This should be the most exciting time of my life, and yet my family is stressing me out to the point where I just want to run away. Portia gives me a pity-filled smile as we exit the bathroom, and I ready myself internally to head back to the bridal party, knowing that it's time to go in search of 'the one.'

———————●●●———————

After a hurried walk down the main street of the wedding district, I finally take a left, looking down to my hard-light watch for direction as it beeps, alerting me that my appointment time is only 5 minutes away.

"Having short legs isn't an excuse for lateness, Valentine, do hurry up!" My mother is ten strides ahead of me already, her colossally long legs dwarfing my steps by an alarming differential. Egypt walks beside me, grabbing my hand and pulling me forward. I'm by far the shortest here, and so feel myself flushing as I lag behind even Portia, who is three months pregnant.

"Your mother is certainly... high strung," Egypt whispers to me as I practically jog down the street, rolling my eyes and feeling my cheeks flush with colour as the wind whips my hair back from my face.

"You noticed that, huh?" I ask her and she laughs under her breath. Finally, we reach the bridal store, where my mother is already scanning her tattoo over the holo-dash and speaking into the interface. I scowl.

Shouldn't I be doing that?

"Yes, party of five for Valentine Morland," she announces promptly, brushing her hair back behind one shoulder and looking to me as I watch on, unable to stop hurricane Cynthia from taking over everything in her path. Unfortunately for me, the thing in her path is me and my wedding.

The intercom buzzes and the clear glass doors of the bridal store glide open. I barge past my sisters, pulling Egypt with me, determined to be the first one in after my mother. I won't have them ruin this for me.

"Hi, I'm Valentine." I glide past my mother's long strides, scurrying with my short height and moving right into the centre of the glorious pastel space. I'm so flabbergasted by the decadence of my surroundings, that I hardly notice who it was my mother is moving to greet. Two women stand before me, or, they look like women. They're entirely made of coloured light, and if I didn't know any better, I'd say they're ghosts. Their dark hair is pulled back into tight topknots and flawless expressions of serene calm are plastered onto their faces.

"I'm An," says the first woman, grasping my hand with a slim wrist adorned with a million bangles. Her face is stunningly Asian, and her eyes shine out from her face, dark and divine in their chocolate hue. I gasp as the hard-light comes into cold contact with my skin, alarmed at the difference between inanimate and sentient hard-light projections.

"Taylor," the second woman admonishes, her kind, wide eyes glimmering dark under the soft yellow light, which bathes the bridal suite in an eerie and non-fluorescent aura.

"What are you?" I hear Egypt blurt from behind me, a little unorthodox, but I'm pretty sure it's what we're all thinking. When I'd been to Portia and Eve's bridal fitting they'd been seen to by synths.

"We are hard-light holograms, Miss. You must have seen us advertised," they reply in unison, it's sort of freaky actually. Then I realise that they must be what I've seen advertised all over the place. Hard-light holograms. Labourers, but made of hard-light and projected here.

"I'm Valentine. The Bride." I say my name again, adding my title with determination, knowing that I need to own it, become it. Otherwise my mother and sisters will have their way with my big day.

"Welcome to Starlight Bridal store. Congratulations on your wedding!" they say in unison, pulling me into a group hug with them both. I scowl slightly because this kind of physical contact with strangers isn't usual. I mean, I barely hug my mother like this and it's especially weird because they don't really exist, but can still touch and feel. I step back from them quickly and my mom takes over the conversation.

"My daughter needs something that will make her look slimmer and take her up by about a foot," she demands, looking back to me as the bridal consultants nod in agreement.

"We're thinking something princess style? What do you think, Valentine?" An asks me, moving out from the side of my mother's shadow and staring with directness upon me.

"Well, I was thinking a really full skirt. Something classic," I respond, ignoring my mother as she glares at the two women that are both staring at me.

"Right, well you come this way. I'll take you through some options," Taylor says, moving past my mom and gripping my hand in hers.

"You ladies can have a seat right over there. Champagne? Fresh fruit?" An asks the remainder of the bridal party and they all nod, taking a seat on a soft apple green chaise longue.

As I'm taken back from the front of the store, which holds only seating and no dresses that I can see, I find myself exhaling when we move into a back room, which expands for at least a quarter of a mile. Racks of dresses spread out across the lush expanse of baby blue carpet, as cream and silver walls rise on either side. It's huge, and I know I made the right call when I'd chosen this store. They had bragged the best choice in Monopolis, and now I know why.

"So your mother, she's pushy." Taylor exclaims as I stand, gaping at the room full of gossamer, silk, diamantes and dazzle.

"Yeah, sorry about her." I apologise, sighing and running my hands through my hair.

"Don't apologise. I see it all the time, that's why we started storing the dresses in the back. This should be your choice. Not hers." Taylor smiles kindly at me and I laugh, shaking my head.

"Yeah, I don't get the impression that she thinks of this as my wedding. It's more like her wedding take four." I sigh and Taylor smiles.

"Can I see your ring?" she asks me, eyes darting to my hand as I raise it up under the gentle caress of the yellowing light.

"Wow, a blue diamond! I haven't ever seen one that colour! You must be thrilled!" She practically screams with the level of excitement she exudes, making me smile as the light around her ebbs. She'd *never* seen a ring like mine? Wow.

"Hey, I have a question. I originally hated this idea, but do you have any dresses in blue? Like, are they popular?" I ask her and her eyes narrow as her lips form into a pucker of delight.

"Blue? No, they're not that common, but I think we stock them in the back. Let me just..." She is cut off by the angry and rushed tone of An, who comes steam rolling into the back like her head is on fire.

"Tay, please, for the love of bliss. Go and deal with that *woman*. I'm going to slap her," she demands and Taylor laughs.

"I always had more tact than you anyway." She rolls her eyes and I snort, unable to help myself.

"Sorry about my mother. Though, trust me, it's harder being related to her." I apologise again and An shakes her head.

"You are a hero in my eyes, Valentine. How have you not... you know?" She runs a hand underneath her chin and across her throat.

"I have no idea," I say, shrugging as she takes a step forward.

"You definitely deserve a beautiful gown... so, what are you thinking?" She asks me. I hold up my ring, showing her the blue of the stone.

"Well, I hated the idea when my mom originally suggested it, but maybe blue? I mean, that's not common, right?" I question her as we stand among the fields of white dresses, interspersed occasionally by the odd coloured rack, as they expand out, creating an odd fabric macrocosm.

"A blue wedding dress?" She looks excited at the challenge.

"Yeah, I know it's not normal, but maybe standing out could be nice," I say, thinking back to my sister's weddings. They'd both been in white, and they'd both been in slim fitting gowns. They'd had the traditional roses. It'd been done. So maybe something different and unique would be cool.

"I think it's a great idea. You're a daring bride and that's great. White is boring anyway." An shrugs it off, flicking her long manicured nails like she's brushing away the idea of white wedding gowns all together. "This way."

She leads me down the narrow corridors created by the rows of dress racks, being made even narrower as we pass dresses with overly full skirts. After walking for around three minutes, she halts, bringing me to a place that's close to the back of the room. Right in the corner is an entire line of dresses in a multitude of blues.

"I don't want anything over the top bright," I muse, glad in this moment that my family is waiting outside. I've been dreaming about this moment for a long time and the last thing I want is the shrill tones of Cynthia Morland shattering my bridal fantasy.

"Okay, here, take those gloves." An gestures to a box of transparent film gloves, and so I pick up the box, wondering how far her abilities as a hard-light hologram extends. I slip the gloves on as she moves across the rack, placing her hand on her hip and narrowing her eyes in concentration.

"So I guess you're not married," I assume, thinking about to the commercial I'd seen about hard-light holograms. They were a way for people to work in the city while never leaving the labour districts if I remember correctly.

"That would be correct," she replies too quickly, like she's sick of being asked the same thing over and over.

"Ah, I'm sorry," I admonish and she frowns slightly.

"Don't be sorry. I never wanted children. I wanted to make something of myself. So now I make beautiful things for others." Her tone turns harsh and I worry I've offended her.

"I'm sorry, I didn't mean to..." I begin, but she silences me.

"It's okay, you don't know any better," she replies and it's my turn to be taken back. *Don't know any better?* What the hell is that supposed to mean?

Cautiously I take a step forward and start looking through the gowns, fingering the delicate fabrics through the film of my gloves and allowing my pupils to dilate fully, taking in the beauty of each gown. They truly are wearable art.

"What about this one?" she asks, pulling a dress down from the rack. She's not wearing any gloves, but I guess that's because she's made of light, which doesn't leave stains behind. I examine her against my better judgement, noticing her tattoo is red and stark against her pale skin, different from mine. I blink, realising I'm staring, and adjust my focus so it's on the dress she's

57

suggesting. It's a deep midnight blue, with a corseted bodice, sweetheart neckline and a full princess skirt. It's covered in diamond looking crystals, dripping in them in fact, and looks not unlike something one would wear to a coronation, back in the old days.

"No, it's too much. I don't want something so obvious." I'm blunt with my assessment, no longer caring what An thinks of me. She's clearly got some kind of issue with not being allowed to get married.

"I know what you're thinking," she accuses me, placing the dress back on the rack.

"What's that?" I reply, cocking an eyebrow as I pull out another dress, examining it closely and purposefully keeping my gaze averted from hers.

"You're thinking I must be jealous, right?" she demands, and I shrug, not committing to any response, my eyes widening with alarm. This girl is intense. "Well, I'm not. I've just seen what happens when marriages go wrong. You young girls, you come in here with your happily ever after fantasies, which you've been fed by the whackos up there at Bliss Inc. You have no idea what's actually going on." I let the dress in my hand drop as my heart starts to hammer. What the hell is she talking about? Marriages going wrong?

"Marriages don't go *wrong*. The formula has a ninety-nine percent success rate. You know that," I protest, narrowing my eyes and scrutinising her expression as it turns serious.

"Look, I'm sure you and your prince charming are going to be very happy together. Just, don't you ever ask yourself... what happens to the one percent that aren't happy? No one around here ever questions a damn thing that comes out of the mouth of Bliss Inc., but of course, that's none of my business." She sighs at me, raising an eyebrow. I blink at her, wondering what she's getting at. "Just think about it." She smiles at me, somewhat apologetic and suddenly I hear Taylor's voice calling out into the room, bouncing off the walls and making me startle.

"Did you find anything yet?" she calls, and I watch as her brunette topknot comes into view above the rows of dresses.

"Not yet!" I call back, feeling my heart racing in my chest. I can't shake the impression that there's something very wrong with An. Is she so jealous about marriage that she's scaring young brides? Who the hell does that?

As I scrunch up my nose in distaste at this woman putting stupid ideas into my head, when I'm already worried enough, my eyes latch onto something. It's a pale, baby blue gown with a white lace overlay. I reach out to it, gripping it through the film of my gloves as I cock my head to the left and pull it out of the rack.

"Can I try this on?" I ask An, keeping my gaze firm as she nods, her expression now appearing pity-filled, which just goes to annoy me further.

"Of course, you go back to the dressing room and I'll follow in a few minutes," she expresses, moving to pick the dress I've selected off the rack.

I stride, at a brisk pace, down the makeshift corridors of gowns, meeting up with Taylor as she's now on her way to find me.

"I found one," I say quickly, wondering if she can sense my alarm.

"That's great! Hey, you okay?" she asks me, reaching up with her hand to touch my face. I slap her away.

"You really need to be careful how you speak to brides you know. You can't just go around putting doubts in people's heads a week before their wedding!" I bite out, irritated.

"Huh? Wait! What happened?" She grabs my elbow and I notice she doesn't have a tattoo like mine, instead of having a jigsaw puzzle piece, she has a luminous red circle made up of two curving arrows, etched into her wrist just like An's. It's one of the tattoos given to those who work in the labour districts, though which one it belongs to, I'm not sure.

"An, she basically said that my marriage is doomed because the formula is only ninety nine percent effective. Who the hell says that?" I exclaim, feeling my rage bubbling at an uncontrollable level. She looks shocked as her eyes widen, before they settle into her face again and she becomes reserved.

"Valentine, I'm so sorry. An, she's having a tough time. Don't listen to her. You and I both know she's probably just jealous. It can be hard working around brides and never being one yourself. Especially now this new technology allows us to have face to face interaction with our customers." Taylor's eyes implore me to calm down, so I do, taking a large breath and removing my arm from her grip.

"I know, it's just not very kind is all. I mean, I'm nervous as it is," I explain and she nods.

"I'll talk to her. You go back and get undressed. I'll get your dress and be in to fit you into it in a few minutes." She winks at me, making me feel slightly more relaxed as I spin on my heel and stride out of the labyrinth of decadence.

Back in the shop front, I sit on one of the large lilac poufs while my mother, Eve and Egypt sip on champagne, and Portia looks like she might slap them all as she shoves grape after grape into her mouth.

"What's taking so long?" My mother gets to her feet, tutting as her heels click melodically on the floor, and that's when we hear it.

"An! You can't just say that to her!" Taylor's voice is only just audible from deep in the depths of the storeroom.

"She deserves to know! They all do!" I hear An's voice resonating again, followed only by inaudible mumbling as I strain to hear more.

A few moments of silence pass, before Taylor suddenly comes storming in from the back room, her face flushed a deep and angry red.

My mother glares at her, completely disgusted by her attire and the service, apparently. Though I have to admit, this has been far from my dream experience. Then again, maybe trying on the dress will be when I'll finally start to feel like a bride.

"Alright, Valentine. Let's get you fitted into this gown." Taylor smiles at me, brushing her hair to one side as she lifts her arm higher over her head, making sure that the now opaque dress bag doesn't drag on the floor.

I look to Egypt, who is watching me like a hawk while sipping entirely too fast on her champagne. I wave to her, smiling nervously as she grins back with noticeable envy in her eyes.

At the back of the shop floor, a single dressing room is fitted seamlessly into the wall and I step inside as Taylor opens the door.

"Sorry about that, Valentine, truly." She apologises again after she's closed the door behind me.

"It's alright. My mother makes people crazy. It was probably just her pushing An over the edge or something." I shrug away the issue, keen to forget about the nastiness and doubt I have been feeling, so I can move on to something I've been looking forward to.

"Okay, so this is only the first dress, don't worry if it's not right. You have the shop for the next few hours. The first one you try on is often more of an indication of what you don't like, than what you do." I smile at her, knowing that's probably true. The further I get into planning this wedding, the more I realise I have no idea what it is I truly want.

●●●

As I step out from the dressing room, I feel myself humming, vibrating with excitement. The gown is perfect, in a palest duck-egg blue with a white lace overlay, the bodice has a plunging neckline. The skirt billows out from me as I lift it, understanding the problem my mother has with my height only now I'm practically tripping over my skirt. I walk across the shop floor, feeling like a princess in bare feet. An is back, sitting and talking with Egypt as they both halt in mid-sentence, turning to look at me.

I step up onto a cream circular platform in front of a semi-circular mirror, which has been set up so I can assess myself.

I stare at my reflection. The dress makes me look slimmer than I am, and as the platforms lifts me above the floor, the skirt hangs at its proper length, only just tracing the floor at the front, with my train billowing out and pooling in a fabric puddle behind me. I breathe in, feeling my mother's eyes baring into the back of my skull as I turn, facing her and letting the skirt swish around me in a billowing wave of lace and gossamer silk.

"Oh, Valentine," she gasps, placing her hands to her lips. "You look so…. Slim and tall." She continues, diminishing her initial reaction with some semblance of a compliment as I roll my eyes. Her opinion isn't the one I care about though, as I stare at Egypt, who is getting teary eyed.

"That's perfect, with the blue. It's so unusual," she exclaims, beaming at me. I feel my heart flutter, knowing that all the compliments in the world cannot match the cold, dead envy which is seeping from both my sisters as they continue to sip champagne and stuff their faces with fruit. I look down at the crystals in the lace, shimmering, and hold my engagement ring up to the light. It glistens a shade darker, but undeniably matching, in blue.

"It's perfect," I say, looking down upon their faces. I make the decision in an instant, knowing immediately that I'll never find anything I love more than this gown. I can only hope that my reaction to the groom is as certain.

Four

The week has flown past me in a flurry of calla lily bouquets and the taste of blue velvet cake with cream frosting, which still makes my mouth flood with saliva. The remainder of my pre-wedding shopping trip had been stressful to say the least, and without Egypt, I surely wouldn't have made it out alive.

"So, I'm thinking that you should take my juicer and my coffee maker. You know, and anything else not tied down," I announce to her as we sit together on my bed. It's my final night in my apartment unit, and she's been helping me clean and organise stuff all day. If I'm honest, I hardly own anything. Everything in my apartment, other than the few luxuries I'd splurged on, is standard single issue and readily taken away and replenished by my upcycler in exchange for cred. Still, I want to give Egypt the few things I do have, she's earned it.

"You serious?" she replies, cocking an eyebrow as I nod, feeling my fingers touch the hard-light of my watch gingerly and knowing that I'll wait to give it to her until tomorrow.

"Yeah, of course. I mean, you've helped so much this week. Plus, I worked hard for this stuff and I can't take it with me.

Someone should benefit." I reason with her, knowing that a sentimental reason as simple as 'because you're my best friend' was going to leave her guilt faced.

"Thanks, Val. Really." She leans over and gives me a hug as we sit here in the apartment unit that I've inhabited for nine years.

I remember the very first day I'd stepped inside this place, how my mom warned me not to get fat and to keep up with ballet and ice-skating for my health. This place is my home, even though it's not big enough to hold more than about three people. I've lived here, been happy here and dreamed of what my life is going to be here and I can't deny, no matter how silly it may sound, that I'm going to miss it.

"You okay?" Egypt asks me, grasping my hand in hers. My ring twinkles, making this all the more real.

"Yeah, I'm just sad I guess. I've lived here a long time," I express, looking around at the bare walls and floors that encase us.

"Come on now, don't be sad. Everyone knows single apartments suck. Your next place will be so much nicer. Plus, think about all the food you're going to be enjoying, and all of it will be free!" She looks dreamily upward as she licks her lips.

"Yeah, I guess. I'm going to miss my crappy coffee maker though." I sigh and she laughs.

"You are funny, Val." She shakes her head and I feel myself getting emotional. I'm being ridiculous, but I can't help myself. I guess being here for longer than anyone else makes me feel all the more attached to everything about being single.

"I know. It's stupid, but I've been here so long," I say, getting to my feet and walking across the room. I stretch up to the white kitchen units and pick out two of the identical white mugs.

"Coffee?" I ask Egypt as she moves to the sofa, watching me with interest as she goes.

"Mhmm." She nods in reply and I put the two mugs down on the counter with a clang. It is a familiar sound, one that shouldn't irk me, yet it does. I can't help but wonder if my next place will have a coffee maker, though I suppose I'll oversee the décor and the furniture with unlimited funds. If I want one I can just order it.

It makes me wonder about the man who I'll be meeting in what is now merely hours. What will my new husband be like? Will he like coffee? Will he like tea? I wonder if he'll take milk and sugar. Or maybe he likes it black? These are only a few of the million and one questions I have, despite being small, which matter.

As I put on my coffee maker and the familiar smell of bitter richness fills the room, I turn, waiting as I watch Egypt staring at me.

"What?" I ask her and she laughs.

"You're asking me that. Shouldn't I be asking you? I can't even imagine what you're thinking about." She puts her chin on top of her knee, which is pulled up on the couch, and I cock my head.

"Actually, I was just wondering if this man I'm meeting tomorrow will like coffee," I admit, biting down on my bottom lip with nervous butterflies fluttering around my stomach.

"Of course he will! Who doesn't like coffee?" she asks me and I giggle.

"I don't know, but I wonder, you know? I have no idea what he'll be like. What if I don't like him..." I speak the fear aloud and am taken back to how I'd felt standing with An in the bridal store.

"Of course you're going to like him, Valentine. I'd even go as far as to say you'll probably love him. He's your matchmate. This isn't like before when people believed in soulmates or something stupid like that. It's science." She is trying to comfort me and before I can help myself I'm blurting my true fears into the open air.

"The formula is only ninety-nine per cent effective, though, right? So, that must mean that one percent of people do not live happily ever after, right?" I ask her and her face suddenly looks funny. She stills for a moment, blinking as though the thought had never occurred to her, before brushing it away and responding in her usual optimistic tone.

"Yeah, but it's like bleach, right? I mean bleach kills like everything, but they have to put ninety-nine percent on the bottle for legal reasons," she explains and I feel my heart lift. Maybe she's right.

"You're right. I'm probably just freaking out again. Thanks for being here. I know I'm a nightmare right now." I apologise for being so up and down as I hear the coffee maker beep and turn, moving to pour the sensuously, dark liquid into the mugs.

"It's okay. Bliss knows I'll be freaking out like this, if not worse, before my big day. You will come back for me, right Val? You know I'm an only child. So, I'm counting on you to help me deal with my mom," she pleads at me with her stare as I turn back, looking at her over my shoulder. I grab both the cups, and move across the small space between the back unit and the island, placing them both down and pushing hers across the space toward her. She rises from the sofa and skips across the floor, closing the distance between us.

"Of course I will. You know that," I say, bringing the cup to my lips and blowing on the coffee, inhaling deeply and closing my eyes.

"You know, we probably shouldn't be having coffee this late," Egypt comments and I open my eyes.

"I don't think that'll mean much to me. I mean, I doubt I'll be getting anything even resembling sleep." I groan, knowing that my mind is far too busy to be shutting down anytime soon. I'm getting married *tomorrow*. That's only one sleep away. Then I'll be whisked away with a stranger on my honeymoon. Tomorrow night I'll be in a totally new bed, with a totally new husband.

At the thought of this my stomach drops and I stop mid-inhale as I go to blow on my coffee again.

"What is it?" Egypt asks me, her eyebrows raising and pinching together in fluid and quick motion.

"I just realised, I'll be sleeping with a man tomorrow night," I whisper, feeling a shiver run up my spine, though from excitement or fear I can't tell.

"Yeah, I was wondering when you were going to start panicking about that. I'm surprised it's taken you this long. I thought that would be the first thing you'd be freaking out about." Egypt chuckles to herself and I let the breath I've been holding go, releasing with it a hysterical giggle.

"I mean, surely he wouldn't expect..." I begin, but she cuts me off.

"Oh, *they expect*." She laughs my naivety off, waving a hand.

"How do you know?" I ask her and she snorts.

"There's a reason they separate us you know. I mean, if you look back at history, it's pretty obvious that women aren't the ones that needed to be controlled in that area," Egypt blurts and suddenly what she says startles me.

"History?" I ask her, my eyebrow rising in surprise.

"Yeah, when I was a kid, my dad was a collector of all these old books and stuff. I used to flip through them. He even gave me one once, to explain why I'm called Egypt. It was the name of this beautiful country, with golden sands and these statues..." She starts going off on a tangent and my eyes widen. History? Like, *old* history? I have never heard anything other than how bad life had been before the formula from my home schooling and readiness courses, but what Egypt is describing doesn't sound bad at all.

"But I thought the world was all like, bad and stuff? Like wars all the time and crime? It wasn't safe," I stutter, feeling like the rug has been pulled from under me. Egypt is younger than me by seven years, so I was usually the one explaining things to her, not the other way around.

"Well yeah, but there were times of peace. People used to be free to travel at will as well! I mean, obviously marrying whoever they liked didn't work out so well, but can you imagine being able to see the world bit by bit?" She sounds super excited and I cock my head, giving her a nervous look as I bite my lip.

"Egypt, how many people know about your dad's books?" I ask her and she shrugs.

"Not many I guess. Maybe just family, and now you, why?" She looks curious, and her facial expression appears to mirror her age as I stare at her, unable to conceive what it is I've just heard. I have never heard of history books before. I thought everything like that was lost during the wars that had ravaged the planet.

"No reason. I just wondered." I shrug, putting the information back where it belongs, in the past.

Suddenly, Egypt's stomach rumbles. I check my watch, realising that I've been stood here for longer than I thought.

"I suppose I'd better feed you." I roll my eyes, giving her a cheeky grin.

"Yes, and order two pizzas!" She scowls at me.

"One each? I've got to fit into a wedding gown tomorrow!" I exclaim and she rolls her eyes.

"Valentine, I have no intention of letting you eat any of this pizza. I simply want one for tonight and one to take home before the ceremony tomorrow. After all, this will be my last opportunity to steal food from you. So why not make the most of it? You will be eating the single standard ramen. After all, you never know, you might miss the taste of cardboard noodles, seeing as how you're almost crying over a crappy cupboard sized apartment," she jokes, fidgeting as she takes a sip of the now lukewarm coffee in front of her.

"Now, *that* is something I won't miss."

<hr />

I wake, groggy and with an immediate ball of nerves weighing heavy like lead in my stomach. I groan, knowing now that staying up all night and watching back *Monopolis' worst wedding fumbles* was a *terrible* and I mean *terrible* idea. My eyes open and

I'm lying, still fully dressed from last night in white cotton sweat pants and a pink cotton camisole.

I sit bolt upright, realising that Egypt isn't here as I turn, looking to my kitchen, where my coffee maker, juicer and the spare pizza from last night are gone. She must have taken them.

I crawl forward, unable to muster the strength to move any other way, and sweep my wrist across the scanner that has activated my holo-dash for the last 9 years. The dash wakes up in one single cyan flash of light and I shield my eyes, finding myself blinded. I take a moment, blinking, then as I turn away, I realise that the light is still dim as it falls upon my face.

I breathe out, calming myself, as the fear that I'd overslept fades and I check the time on the dash. 6:30am. *Phew.*

I see a flashing note on the interface and swipe it open. Egypt had left a message before she left.

Val,

Left early to take stuff home, I'll be back before you know it. Get some beauty sleep!

E x

I exhale, breathing slowly and allowing my palm to rest over the cool skin that covers my heart. It's fluttering, gentle and yet incessant in its rhythm.

"Calm down," I whisper to myself, willing my body to stop humming. Today's the day, the day I meet him, and as I get to my feet, I feel myself getting lightheaded. I inhale and exhale a few times.

71

Trust in the formula. Trust in the science, is all I keep telling myself over and over.

I walk over to my kitchen island where I lean, my skin covered in goosebumps at the chill of the early morning air. I could really do with some coffee, but Egypt has already taken my machine. I feel my heart palpitating, the walls of the apartment closing in on me.

I decide on an impulse to go and get some fresh air, quickly requesting some clothes as well as a hairbrush and toothpaste pills. I get dressed, chewing on the pills and letting the taste of mint neutralise away the feeling of nausea climbing up my throat.

Finally dressed, I run the brush through my hair a few times before slapping the hard-light watch on my wrist and scanning my tattoo before I exit my apartment.

Tapping my foot nervously I wait for the elevator to descend, not even thinking to have grabbed a jacket as I'm sweating with goosebumps running down my arms.

What is it? Why am I feeling like this?

I've been dreaming of this day for nine years, and yet here I am, running hot and cold like a broken heater and so nervous I might vomit. The elevator doors sweep sideways and I practically fall into the lobby of my apartment building, quickly scanning my wrist through the turnstile and rushing through the glass doors into the cold October morning of the city outside. Wind whips my hair from my face as I feel my heartbeat climb again. I should be happy, but instead, I feel like I might pass out with the overwhelming urge to run away.

I let the impulse grab me, beginning in a jog down the street as I let my feet pound against the matte white of the sidewalk. There's nobody around except for the service synths and so I let myself run, my hair streaming out behind me in ribbons of honey blonde as my face flushes red and my chest heaves, sucking in the cold air like it's a drug.

I make it to the water's edge, seeing the Newlywed Complex in the middle of the lake. Behind it, the Male District of Monopolis stands, and somewhere among the men that inhabit it, my husband is waking up, or maybe sleeping. I'll be meeting him in under six hours, and suddenly my heart falters in my chest.

I'm scared. I'll admit it. I've been reminded of the only unconditional love I've ever known from my mother this last week, and I'll be honest, I don't like it. I don't want to be legally bound to someone who will criticise and not listen to me. I don't want to become my mother to my future daughter. I don't want that. I want someone who loves me for who I am, whatever that means, and helps me discover who I am for myself without continuously pushing me for more than I can give.

I let tears stream down my face as I gasp, breath caught in my throat as I struggle to feed my muscles what they need. I'm only a small way from my apartment, having found the cold grabbing at my insides despite the heat running through my veins.

Suddenly, I hear my name.

"Valentine?" It's Egypt, no doubt returning from her apartment. She spots me from across the street, walking at a hurried pace toward me as I suddenly feel the need to hurl.

I'm going to be sick. I'm going to be sick.

Then, suddenly, I am sick, horrendously, and with gut wrenching accuracy over the guardrail of the lake.

Oh bliss, what the hell is wrong with me? I feel myself shaking as an arm grabs around my shoulder and Egypt pulls me into a bone-crushing hug. My face buries into her raven locks as she pulls me into her, hushing me like I'm a child.

"It'll be okay. Valentine, look at me!" she says, pushing me back from her. She looks at me with unbridled intensity. "Repeat after me," she demands and I nod in return, wiping my mouth on my arm and feeling a calming emptiness settle over me. "I am getting married todays" she states, firm, and I laugh, unable to believe those words.

"I am getting married today," I say, hiccupping in between my vocal affirmation as tears continue to stream down my cheeks.

"It is perfectly normal to be nervous," she says and I repeat after her again.

"It is perfectly normal to be nervous... even if I have just thrown up and am getting hot and cold running chills," I sputter, shaking my head.

"Do you want to do this?" she asks me and I look at her, my eyes still brimming.

"I don't have a choice," I reply, feeling the truth of my own words slap me, like an ice wall, in the face. I am right; I don't have a choice. Bliss Inc. says I'm getting married. So, I'm *getting* married. Maybe that's why I'm so incredibly afraid, because I don't like not being in control. Could it be I'm more like my mother than I'd realised? "I'm so scared, Egypt," I whisper and she hugs me again, smiling and wiping tears from underneath my eyes.

"You'd be insane if you weren't, Valentine," she whispers back to me as the wind whips her hair back from her face.

"You really think?" I ask her, my eyes wide as they stare up at her through tears. I need the truth.

"Yes. I really do." She frowns and looks thoughtful. "You're binding yourself to a stranger. Whether or not he's the right stranger, is beyond the point. You're allowed to have doubts, but you've seen couples that have already been through this. Think about them." She reminds me of the couples I know. About my mother and father, and how despite their differences they always became a team when they needed to. How my father looks into my mother's eyes every year on valentine's day, the anniversary of when I had been conceived, and routinely adorns her neck with diamonds and pearls. My sisters, and how they have both fallen so deeply in love with their husbands that they have transformed into something much more than the shallow creatures they had once been.

I straighten in Egypt's arms.

"I'm ready," I declare, my tears ceasing as my breathing rate regulates in my chest.

"Okay. Let's go," Egypt whispers to me, putting her hand in mine and pulling me along the sidewalk. I let myself take each step at a time, knowing that she's right. I do have a right to be nervous. My sisters had both been nervous before their weddings, though their nervousness had manifested as excitement and a rabid urge to tell everyone that everything they were doing was wrong. I should be excited, but maybe I can't be because I'm scared that I'm not enough. What if this person I'm meeting today doesn't love me, or think I'm beautiful? What if he thinks I'm too curvy, or finds my sense of humour irritating?

You're overthinking things. I remind myself, exhaling as I blink a few times. *I need to give this a chance.* I vow, realising that if I write off my husband before I've even met him, that I might miss out on the best day of my life, through being too worried to relax and enjoy things. After all, 99% of the couples matched went on to a life of bliss, so really, the odds are in my favour. As we reach my apartment building and climb up the stairs to pass the time until we'll board the high-speed monorail to the Marriage Complex, I wonder why I've been so scared.

After all, everyone else seems happily married, so I guess I really do have nothing to fear.

I'm nervous as we approach the station, realising that I've never been to where we're going before. What if I get lost? Or worse, what if I miss my ride? The settlements of the city are placed in four opposing locations around the lake which lies central to it all, with the Newlywed complex being placed on an island right in the middle. The Marriage Complex is the smallest by far, reserved only for the colossal halls in which the unions of the Jigsaw Project take place, and I've only ever seen it in Bliss Magazine or on the wedding channel.

As I delicately climb the glass steps that rise toward the platform, Egypt in tow, I feel surprisingly light. I don't have any baggage. Only myself and my friend, because all our wedding clothes and accessories have already been sent over to the bridal suite which attaches to wedding suite thirteen, where I'll be getting married. The monorail track connects to the district at opposite sides, depending on where it is coming from. When it is arriving from the female district it arrives from the west, and when from the male district it arrives from the east, meaning that Brides and Grooms, who are delivered into a station which runs right through the complex housing the halls, will never run into each other before the ceremony.

"Is it this way?" I ask Egypt, feeling confused as I look down at my hard-light watch. The message is confusing.

You will be picked up at 8:30am from your corresponding platform.

That's all it says. I frown at it as I reach the top of the stairs, and Egypt inhales sharply.

"Look, over there! It's one station but the different carriages all have separate platforms. Platform thirteen! That's you, I think," she explains and I nod, finally understanding. Corresponding platform means that it corresponds to the number of your suite inside the Marriage Complex, though why they haven't made that clear I don't understand. I sigh, looking down to my watch again and seeing that the time is 8:25am, but considering we got lost on the way here and had no idea which way we were going, it could be worse.

"We have five minutes. So, I think I'd better give you this before we board." I unhook the watch from around my wrist, deleting my account from the interface by scanning my tattoo across the back three consecutive times in practiced motion. As I do this, I glimpse my ring; glimmering in the light, reminding me that everything in my life is about to change.

I pass the watch to Egypt, who has wide eyes and a surprised expression.

"Val, you can't give me that. It's like… too much." She looks concerned and I roll my eyes at her.

"Come on, it's not like I can't just get another one for free once I'm married." I snort, throwing the watch and observing as she scrambles to catch it. I don't know why but she jumps, reaching out and grabbing it so quickly she nearly falls forward and off the platform as we reach the edge. I laugh at her over-the-top care; I mean everyone knows hard-light can't exactly smash.

"Thank you," she breathes, placing it around her wrist and sighing. "I'm the luckiest girl ever. Even if I am losing my best friend." She smiles sadly and her dark eyes sparkle. I exhale, miserable that today might be the last time I see her.

"I hope we'll be together soon. I mean, it's only 2 and a half years until you start taking your readiness tests. Who knows how soon after you'll get married. You'll be joining me before you know it!" I exclaim, full of optimism, though I know it's entirely possible that by the time she's taking readiness tests, I'll have my first or maybe even second child.

As she examines the watch and the time on the face glows 8:30am, I hear the hushed whirring of wheels on a single, slick, glass track, and watch as the other women waiting in the same station, but separate platforms, turn to the monorail as it glides into the space. The oblong transparent bubble halts smoothly and the door glides open as I swipe my tattoo on the upright scanner, revealing the innards of the individual carriage assigned to this platform. I step across the air-filled gap and into the monorail with wide eyes, taking in every detail as Egypt scans her tattoo after me and skips inside before sliding in front of me, taking in the carriage too.

The seating is plush, red, and made from the same material my ring box had been smothered in. It's soft to touch as I run my hand across it and the buttons that upholster it gleam golden.

The light is equally golden, exuding from a small hanging fixture adorned with many yellowing crystals, which shakes slightly as the carriage door closes behind us. I have never been in a bridal carriage before, mainly because when I went to both my sister's weddings I had been in a passenger carriage with the other guests, which was nowhere near this nice.

On the far side, a small shelf is stocked with crystal bottles, presumably filled with some sort of alcohol, and fine stemmed glasses. It doesn't surprise me, after all, a lot of brides turn up to their weddings a little tipsy; they say it helps with the nerves.

"Do you want some champagne?" Egypt asks me, immediately spotting the glasses and bottles and looking to me with a mischievous grin. I shake my head.

"No, I already threw up today. Let's not add alcohol." I admonish and she winks, clicking her teeth.

"Good plan, chief." As I hear a tone sound throughout the carriage, I take a seat, feeling odd and out of place as the monorail lurches into motion. It pulls out of the station like a bullet from the barrel of a gun, like the ones they used to show on those really bad TV shows about the past. I think back to when I was a child, about how I had become slowly more and more enamoured with the concept of meeting my matchmate and getting married. I had been seven years old when I had first played 'wedding' with my sisters, only being allowed to be the officiate while Portia got stuck being the groom and Eve was always the bride.

As we rise high into the sky, I get a rare view of the sparse buds of new trees growing out in the wilderness. The land, which sprawls out in endless distance that I cannot even begin to comprehend, is a work in progress, being made clean and new again by those plants which were deemed perfect in terms of genetic modification. As I look into what Bliss Inc. has planned for our world, I seek a smidgeon of comfort.

How can a company making our world beautiful once more, be bad?

At the asking of this question, my heart begins to race in my chest.

I had never thought I would be this nervous, and as the carriage takes me away from the Female District of Monopolis and I leave my old life behind me, I look at Egypt and find myself hopeful. My excitement grows as I look out the window, watching the frothing waters of the lake flash past as we travel beyond the limits of the place where I have spent the last nine years. I look back on the skyline for a moment before turning away, staring only toward where I'm going, and forgetting where I've been.

Five

The monorail slows to a halt, smooth upon the tracks as it devours the miles like they're nothing. The journey has gone too quickly and as we still in the station, a tone sounds once more through the carriage.

I depart, taking Egypt by the hand and stepping out into the bright morning light of the Marriage Complex station.

My feet find the floor, clad in flawless white stone, marble perhaps, which spreads out before me like someone has spilt milk.

"Whoa." Egypt's expression is simple, but falls from her lips, mirroring my awe-struck face and affirming my own reaction. The Complex towers as a gigantic, glass, bubble-like structure, and as the other brides depart from the monorail, I look around, finding that each segment of the enormous glass complex is home to a differently named marital hall. I'm getting married in the main one, Bliss Hall, but there are others, such as Joy Pavilion, Ecstasy Hall and Elation Pavilion, which are easily identifiable from the spot in which I'm stood, taking it all in and realising that this is really happening.

"Come on! Let's get inside!" Egypt takes a few steps forward, pulling me with her as I continue to gape, watching as the monorail departs to where it had come from.

I wonder how many people get married here, especially seeing as how the high-speed luxury monorail was reserved only for brides and their maids of honour. Guests would arrive on the outskirts of the complex, not central to it as we are.

I step across the slick surface of the station, making sure not to hurry so I don't slip. I also want to take in as much of my surroundings as I can. The halls are encased in beautiful topiaries, with butterflies that flutter from leaf to leaf, as though they've gathered in this place, celebrating everything that it stands for.

As we near the wide front steps, rising into Bliss Hall, which stands only ten metres from where the monorail has just dropped us off, I notice men in white uniforms standing by the door. They're wearing edgy, pressed cotton suits with short hair that's slicked back and dark glasses that hide their eyes. I stare at them as I begin to climb the stairs, Egypt pulling me all the way. I haven't seen a man for so long, except for those on the wedding channel, or in magazines, that I double take at the sight of them. They take a step forward in unison, pulling the white double doors open as the first bride reaches them.

The rest of us pick up pace as the innards of Bliss Hall are revealed. It's so beautiful, that as I pass the threshold, the first thing I can think to do is look up, my eyes settling on the ceiling mural, showing brides and grooms, embracing one another and happy.

The hall, on first appearance, seems to be just that; a long hallway, with many doors on either side, broken up by columns with vases and flowers on top. I look at them as I pass, finding each door numbered and with the word *bride* or *groom* beneath in swirly font. I feel my heart palpitate. The rooms where we will get ready, where we will prepare for the ceremony where we will first meet, are but a wall apart. He may be only metres away as I get ready.

As I step through the hall, watching the numbers on the doors slowly ascend, I wonder if he's as nervous as I am.

Oh Bliss, I hope he's not awful.

"Here we are, number thirteen!" Egypt squeals, moving to the door with *Bride* written on the front and the number thirteen above. I scan my tattoo on the panel next to the thick wood doorframe and Egypt turns the handle before she pulls me in behind her, where we're greeted by magnificence in every direction. This room truly is a woman's paradise. There's a full buffet and a bar stocked with a variety of alcohol. The walls are lined with mirrors on two sides, reflecting me back at myself from a multitude of angles. I guess I am going to be on camera for this, so I need to be able to see myself as they will, to look perfect from every possible angle.

The suite is lit in a stark and fluorescent way, highlighting the flaws in my appearance, and is scattered with white sofas, vanity counters, dress rails and baskets which are filled with the flowers that have been dropped off for the ceremony.

I stand in the doorway as Egypt darts forward, rushing from one side of the room to the other as she begins to examine everything. My dress hangs on the rail, freshly cleaned and altered, ready for the cameras. Next to it, Egypt's dress hangs, even though she won't be involved in the ceremony.

I feel my heart begin to pound again at the sight of my bridal gown and close the door behind me, hearing the gasps of other brides as they reach their own suites. I step forward and, under the scrutiny of the fluorescent light, find myself feeling oddly lonely. My reflections bounce from the mirrors as Egypt moves into the colossal sized bathroom, which lies to my right. All I can see is myself, surrounded by replicas and nobody else. I turn full circle, looking at my lone figure, made multiple by the glass of the mirrors.

"Valentine, you have to see the size of this bathroom!" Egypt comes back to the doorway of the washroom, widening the crack in the door and causing the mirror on the opposite wall to create a macrocosm of yellow light, which seeps outward. I walk, as though in a dream, across the thick silver carpet and toward her, stepping past her and looking into the expanse of the bathroom. There's an enormous shower beside a Jacuzzi bathtub and everything is clinical white, as I had expected. The carpet is plush, spongey even, as I step onto it. The whole room smells like synthetic lavender, which relaxes me despite my better judgement, and I turn to Egypt, only to find that she's gone. "Hey, Val! There are instructions here!" she calls back to me, and I follow her, unable to keep up with her excitable pace as I trail behind like a stray dog.

"Really?" I call, moving back out into the main bridal suite.

"Yeah, check this out, a remote thingy!" She shoves the hard-light remote to me, which she's taken off a vanity where the jewellery I have chosen for today lies. Beside it, there's a transparent sheet of acetate with holo-ink upon its surface. It reads:

To the bride,

Please find here a remote that can be used to call our service synths to you, should you need anything. Beauty synths are also at your disposal, and will attend to you once you have selected hair and make-up options from the in-suite holo-dash. Should you need anything, anything at all, please do not hesitate to press the 'call' button, and someone will attend you.

We wish you a fantastic wedding day, and hope you are ready for a lifetime of bliss!

Bliss Inc.

I scan the page twice, noticing the advert at the bottom, which reads:

Coming soon- hard-light, holograms! Bringing the human touch to your big day!

Before handing the sheet to Egypt who promptly reads it and then smiles.

"I was wondering what we were going to do about your hair and make-up" She expresses and I push my lips together so hard they're almost white.

"Yeah, me too, I've never had a synth do my make-up before. I guess that must be why brides always look flawless," I shrug and

Egypt puts down the note before she moves over to the buffet table, picking up a pastry and shoving it into her mouth.

"I think I might take a shower." I suggest and Egypt nods.

"You do that, I'm good here." She turns back to the food as I place the remote on the vanity and make my way into the bathroom, shutting and locking the door behind me before sinking down against it and onto the floor. I exhale hard, letting myself catch my breath as my toes bury into the carpet. I close my eyes, allowing a feeling of sudden exhaustion to fall over me. I'm bone tired from all the emotion that has led me to this moment, and as I take a second, a gentle smile forms on my lips despite my weary heart. This day is finally here, and I can only hope that he's everything I've dreamed of.

After a few more moments of slow, even, breaths and the sanctuary of the darkness my closed eyelids provide, I get to my feet, climbing up off the floor and walking over to the shower.

I strip, letting my white pantsuit fall to the floor, shedding it like it holds all my fears and attachments to single life. I step into the shower cubicle, something completely unlike anything I've had access to in Monopolis. The shower in my old apartment unit had a scanner, which once I pressed my tattoo to it would allow a hot water stream to fall over my body in a slow, low-pressure torrent. The shower was also on a timer, so after ten minutes the water would cease, leaving me cold and shivering. I had made the rookie mistake of taking too long when I had first moved to Monopolis, finding myself with soap all over my body and still in my hair after the hot water had long since run dry. The result had been a hideous sponge wash in my sink afterward and a large amount of cursing.

This shower, however, is nothing like that, and as I step into the white tiled cubicle and the glass door slides closed behind me, the advanced piece of technology wakes up, dimming the lights of the space.

"*I can sense you're tense, Miss. Relaxation mode?*" the shower asks, making me smile and reminding me of my childhood. My shower at home in Pearl Falls had been just like this, and I had missed it.

"Yes." I speak aloud, as the scent of jasmine is blasted from the aromatherapy ducts in the walls to my left and right. With that, the hot water comes on, spouting from six shower jets on either side of my body and three overhead. The hot steam mingles with the scent of the flowers as the high-pressure flow of the water hits my skin, turning it red and flush at the intense power of the water. I let my arms rise from my sides, pushing the hot trickles of water down my skull and allowing my hair to become slick against my head.

All the tension in my body seems to lift as my skin prickles, sensitive. I wonder whether his touch will do this to me, how it'll feel to be in a man's arms, to be naked under the scrutiny of his gaze.

I sigh out, looking down at myself. I'm not slim, but curvaceous as my hips bulge outward, creating the base to the figure eight of my hourglass shape. My breasts aren't small either, hanging heavy now under the heat of the water. I wonder if he'll see the million and one flaws that I do when I look down at myself. My too big thighs, the small layer of fat over the top of my stomach, how entirely too short my legs are.

"*Adding soap,*" I hear the shower announce and close my eyes, letting the scent of lavender now mingle in with the jasmine as suds fall down over my body from all angles, made thin and bubbly by the jets that allow water to mix with the soap before it hits my skin, creating a frothy lather.

I sigh, *this is just what I need,* and as I enjoy the rest of the sequence the shower has in store, I let myself drift away on thoughts of white and baby blue calla lily bouquets and the finest pearl jewellery.

After I'm out of the shower and wrapped in a giant, white, towelling robe, I pad through to the bridal suite, where Egypt is examining her bridesmaid's dress on the rail next to my gown.

"Yay, you're done! You were ages!" she complains, dropping the white silk of her dress so the garment hangs straight again. She bounds over to me, grasping my hands in hers with an excited glint in her eye.

"Yeah, remember those really fancy showers they have back in Pearl Falls?" I ask her and she shakes her head. I find myself puzzled, creasing my brow. I thought all the people in Pearl Falls had the same housing.

"Nah, but I was an only child. Everyone knows that the more kids you have, the better housing you get." She shrugs and I continue to frown. I didn't know that.

"Oh, well, they have these programmes you can choose from, like *relaxation mode*, or *wake me up mode*, or *quick mode.* It's all different types of aromatherapy and water pressure. Like the relaxation one is all lavender and jasmine, but the *wake me up*

88

setting is citrusy and leaves you feeling rejuvenated. You should have a shower!" I suggest and she laughs.

"Wow! Fancy! I'll have to try that!" she replies, moving to sniff me. "You smell like a flower shop," she notes, grinning and I nod, my wet hair still trailing down the back of my robe.

"Yeah, I'm hoping my groom likes it," I whisper, feeling embarrassed about referring to him so frankly. I have always talked to Egypt about my future husband, but I have never been so close to meeting him, and I feel like anything I might say now may jinx me or something. I know it's probably silly to be superstitious, but he could be only metres away.

"Do you know if the groom is here yet?" I ask her and she shrugs, lowering her gaze and brushing her dark hair behind one ear.

"I don't know, I went to look and there was some guy posted outside the door. You know, one of the ones in the white suits." She frowns, her expression troubled at this, and so I shrug.

"I guess they're strict about us seeing each other, even if it is only just before." I reason and she smiles, accepting my logic.

"Why don't you go and check out the hair and make-up options while I take a shower?" she suggests and I nod, half-eyeing the buffet behind me as I turn to move toward the vanity, where the remote for the special holo-dash lies.

I contemplate grabbing a pastry as I pick up the remote, but then decide against it, remembering how I'd thrown up earlier. "Don't pick anything without me!" Egypt adds, as she closes the bathroom door behind her and locks it.

I move over to the place in the wall where the holo-dash is. I've never operated a holo-dash with a remote before, and I

89

wonder if it has something to do with how they're wired to service and beauty synths. Regardless of the reason for needing one, I push the 'ON' button on the remote, finding it refreshing not to have to scan my tattoo.

As the soft-light of the special holo-dash pops up from the wall, immediately displaying another advert for hard-light holograms, I realise the need for the remote. This holo-dash will allow me to trial make-up and hair styles on my face virtually before I actually call the beauty synths into the room, making my decision-making process a lot easier. They'll also automatically know what option I've chosen, meaning I won't have to explain anything.

Just as I'm thinking how easy this will make things, I press the hair button and the library of styles opens. My mouth drops open as the screen reveals that there are over a million styles to choose from.

Oh my bliss.

This could take a while.

Egypt has joined me on the floor of the suite as we sit, bickering about what style is going to make me the most unforgettable.

"Look, I still think style #11147." She pouts and I shake my head.

"No, Egypt! It makes me look like a poodle!" I protest and she smirks.

"Poodles are cute!" She argues back and I roll my eyes.

"Well, I think something on the side with the flowers will look nice. Like this one..." I show her style #33351 and she rolls her eyes.

"I'm telling you, you're going to look like a crane! Too much neck." She runs her hand across her own neck in a slicing motion and shakes her head.

"Fine, what about something simple, like this one?" I point out style #475896 and she puckers her lips, cocking her head to the left and letting her hair tumble down over one shoulder.

"I like it... but on the other side... and with a little more volume on the front." She snatches the remote from me for the hundredth time this hour, scrolling left in the style line-up a few times before she finds one she's happy with. I'm surprised at the one she lands on, mainly because I actually like it.

"Okay, that one. Just pick that one!" I exclaim, so ready to be done with the choices. There is such a thing, I think I have decided, as too many options.

"Okay! What about makeup?" she asks me as she selects style #476898 and then presses a few buttons to move to the make-up selection library. After the hair selection has been made, the door of the room is opened by a man in a white suit.

"Beauty synth!" he calls out as I move to the vanity, watching Egypt in the mirror.

The synth swarms into the room, its body pink as opposed to white, distinguishing it as different to the normal service synths you see everywhere. The bot zooms toward me, halting and scanning across my face in a blur of blue crossing lasers.

"Please sit," it asks and I pull out the chair by the vanity, moving it behind Egypt so I can make sure she doesn't hijack my make-up choice.

"Okay, so let's look at *natural* looks, Egypt. I don't want to look over the top or anything like *that*," I instruct her, pointing to the clown-like make-up choice she's pondering. I take my seat in the chair and the synth extends fluidly moving metallic arms, each equipped with various combs, scissors, blow dryers and styling wands.

I lean back into the smart foam of the chair, letting it heat around my muscles which have begun to clench again, aware that the hours are slipping away too readily and that my wedding is drawing closer, second by second.

"What about this?" Egypt asks me, scrolling through the 'natural look' section of the make-up catalogue. The image of my face, which has been made up with her selection looks too gaunt, with contouring that's too hard on my light skin tone.

"No, I want my beauty marks uncovered and my cheekbones less prominent," I instruct, finding myself becoming more confident with asking for what I want. I'm not a single any longer, and that means that the world is opening to me, presenting the pearl of its wealth and experiences. I just need to be brave enough and confident enough to take them in palm and make the most of the opportunity.

"Okay, like this?" she asks, showing me another look. It's different, with eyeliner that curves up slightly in a creamy, light blue at the corners of my eyes. My cheeks are a pale pink, not contoured, but highlighted with blusher. My lashes are a thick black and my lips pale, exaggerating the beauty spot by my left eye and the freckle above my lip. I think she's got it.

"Yes! That one!" I burst, almost rising in excitement at my virtual beauty, but quickly calming down as I feel the synth tugging at my head as I move.

"Ow!" I exclaim, rolling my eyes and crossing my arms across my chest. I should really have better sense than to try and get up when a synth is attached to my head with hot irons, but I guess I'm just too dazed by everything that's happening.

Another knock at the door interrupts my internal condemnation of my own stupidity.

"Beauty synth!" the doorman calls again, letting another pink synth zoom into the air of the room. It faces me, scanning my complexion and beginning to extend out its arms, though this time they're attached to eyelash curlers, blusher brushes and foundation palettes. Egypt giggles as I cough when the synth begins to dab my chest with lightly sparkling powder.

"Hey, don't laugh! You're next!" I remind her and she stops giggling. I smirk and she looks down to the remote.

"I better get choosing, I guess. I've got to get you into lingerie and your dress, after all," she exclaims and I nod, knowing that I probably should have let her go first, but also knowing there is nothing I can do about it now. I look at the time on the dash and as she re-enters the hairstyle selection library I inhale, bringing more sparkling powder particles, which still linger in the air, into my lungs, causing me to cough once more.

"Please sit still, Miss," the synth requests as it begins applying foundation to my face while my hair is pulled up and twisted around a blistering hot curling iron. I look at the dash again, trying to make sure I am not mistaken. Nope, it's 10:30am already. Only an hour and a half to go.

"Is this right?" I ask Egypt as I examine the lingerie I'm stood in. It's unlike anything I've ever worn, and as she looks at me, she laughs.

"I'm pretty sure that's a garter belt. It goes around your hips, not your waist, come here." She beckons for me to come closer and I blush, embarrassed that it's so obvious I have absolutely no idea what I'm doing.

As I approach her, I see that she's fully dressed in the gorgeous, Grecian-style, white gown I'd chosen for her. The fabric bunches at her left hip, before draping across her torso and pulling up over her right shoulder in an asymmetric design. It contrasts with her dark hair and I'm glad that I decided it should be she who wears white and not I. It suits her far better.

"You look beautiful," I compliment as she pulls the garter belt down around the stiff white silk corset of my lingerie. She attaches it to my stockings and then looks up to me, her brown eyes sparkling.

"Are you scared?" she asks me and I sigh out, moving up to run my fingers through my hair, but realising that doing so will mess up the style.

"Terrified," I admit, breathing out in a deep exhalation and trying to dispel some of my fear.

"It's okay. You look stunning. He won't be able to resist you, Valentine. He's a lucky guy." She pulls me into a hug and I hug her back.

"Thanks for being here with me." I say, knowing that I can't get too emotional, because I don't want my makeup to get smudged.

"You're more than welcome. Shall we get you into your dress?" Egypt asks me and I nod, looking back to the time again. It's now 11:30am, I only have thirty minutes.

"Yeah, let's do that. Does this look okay?" I ask her and she nods, shaking her head. I hadn't had a say in the lingerie. My sister Eve had picked it out, seeing as how I couldn't bear to have my mother accompany me into the store. Egypt had no experience with men either and so doesn't know any more about what they like than I do.

"Valentine, I'm not sure it's really appropriate right now, but you look hot." She laughs and I giggle too. She walks over to the rail where my dress hangs. "Oh my bliss, there's like a million buttons back here, you better sit down. This could take a few minutes," she expresses, beginning to unbutton the back of the gown. I walk over to the vanity, where my jewellery still lies, glimmering.

I pick up the pearl choker and place it around my neck, clipping it together magnetically just beneath my hairline and then putting in the pearl stud earrings my mother had insisted I buy. As I begin to wrap a pearl bracelet around my wrist I catch my reflection in the mirror of the vanity. I look different. My hair is swept back up into rose like formations on the right side of my head, pinned with a comb of icy blue pearls, and a loose curl falls before my left ear. My hair is swept back smoothly from the front, and looks sleek, as though it's been set in some sort of spray.

I examine my face too, finding my makeup is soft, with metallic blue eyeliner and nude lipstick offsetting my natural beauty. I catch my beauty spot as I turn, and smile, glad that this small individual mark hasn't been erased by the mass-produced styling of brides.

"You done yet?" I ask her and she shakes her head.

"Nope, still like ten more. Two secs." She undoes the final buttons on the back of the dress, before slipping it off the hanger and holding it up.

"Step in," she instructs, and so I do. I put my arms through the pastel blue sleeves, which end atop my shoulder and are embellished with the white lace overlay that covers the entire gown. I stand, watching the dress becoming increasingly fitted to my form as Egypt does up the many buttons which fit the gown tightly to my spine. When she's done, she moves over to the corner of the room, where a white shoebox sits next to the basket in which my bouquet lays.

"Okay, sit down. I'll put these on for you," she says as I take a seat, careful that no makeup has been spilled on the flawless white of its smart foam cushions before I do so.

Egypt pops the shoebox lid off and places it on the floor, bending at the knee and pulling out one of the two high heeled blue pumps which are encrusted with glitter. They tie onto my foot with pale blue silk ribbon, which she undoes before slipping my foot into one.

"Got it?" I ask her, as I feel my heel slip in seamlessly.

"Yes, Cinderella, you shall go to the ball!" she exclaims and I smile. I love the story of Cinderella. It had been my favourite as a child. I wonder now if that's maybe why I'm partial to the big dress.

Finally, Egypt puts on the other shoe and then ties the ribbon around my foot. She helps me stand, giving me a hand as I pull myself upright and smooth my skirts around myself, feeling the weight of the dress, as well as what's happening, colliding in a single moment and making my heart pound. "Okay! Bouquet!" Egypt takes no time before she bounds over to the basket that holds my flowers, bringing the bunch back with her and handing it to me as the synthetic scent of calla lilies fills my nostrils. My flowers are beautiful, being white and fading to blue in their centres they create a macrocosm of ombré throughout the circular arrangement. I lift them to my nose, breathing in heavily and allowing the aroma to wash over me.

"Mmm." I hum, lowering them and holding them in front of me, like a real bride.

"You look so..." Egypt begins, but then starts to get teary eyed.

"Don't cry, Egypt. Or I'll start," I warn her, smiling and putting my arm around her shoulder.

"I know, I'm sorry... you just look like a real bride is all." She expresses.

"Thanks. I suppose that's better than looking like a fake bride." I make the joke, trying to break the tension that is forming in my gut.

I look at the time. It's 11:55am. How had getting into my dress, putting on some shoes and picking up some flowers taken twenty-five minutes? Surely, there's a mistake!

"Can Miss Valentine Morland step toward the door at the end of the suite? It is time to prepare for your entrance." The voice comes from nowhere, just like the voice from the shower had, and it makes me startle.

Egypt grips my hand and walks me toward the door at the end of the room where the holo-dash had come out of the wall.

I haven't noticed it before, mainly because it doesn't look like a door. It looks like a design in the wall. As I step toward it, it slides open, revealing nothing on the other side but shadow.

Egypt looks up to me, her eyes watering and her face resolved that she won't break down. I know her too well, and it's meaning I can read her face when I wish I couldn't.

"Egypt, I'm scared!" I burst, suddenly startled. I don't want to walk through the door. I can't.

What if he's awful? What if he's all wrong?

Egypt puts her hands on my shoulders and looks deeply into my eyes now, trying to steady us both.

"Valentine, you're a beautiful bride. Good luck." She says the words to me, my last form of comfort disappearing as she turns and runs from the room.

I'm left, startled by her abrupt departure, holding my bouquet along with the left side of my sweeping skirt.

I turn, reaffirming that the door leads to a place with no light.

I step through it, not knowing what is going to happen once I do.

"Valentine, the doors in front of you will open shortly. Don't be alarmed. There will be flashes, but it's just the media synths. Don't forget to smile!" The automated voice rings out around me as I stand in the dark and the door from which I've come slides closed. The only source of light in the room is that which is seeping from the crack of the doors a few paces in front of me. I take a step forward so I'm directly behind them.

I breathe in, and then out, clutching my bouquet with fumbling fingers. This is it. I'm going to meet him. I'm not going to cry. He's going to be perfect and I'll know it as soon as I see him.

I look down to my imperfect, blue diamond, engagement ring as I think these things, heart hammering.

Suddenly, as my heartbeat becomes so loud it's thudding in my ears, the doors open.

Six

As the doors swing forward, I find myself blinded by the sudden and unbridled flashes from the bulbs of a million media synths. They swarm in the air around me as I stand, revealed to the hall in which I'll take my vows.

I blink once, twice, before realising that it's now my turn to move, to step forward. I smile, remembering the words of the automated message in my last moments alone.

I take a step forward, careful and measured in my pace. The synths follow me, tracking my every motion and relaying my image back to the wedding channel, where thousands, if not tens of thousands, of single girls will look upon my face, scrutinising me and judging my choice of attire.

I focus, realising that this isn't about them; it's about me and him. I find my vision now unobscured as the flashes of bulbs recede and the synths back away from me, getting a wide shot of my dress.

I see him and inhale, waiting for me at the end of the colossally long aisle. It is longer than it appears on soft-light. In comparison to its vast length, my steps are tiny, and I find myself, perhaps for the first time ever, wishing I'd been able to live up to my mother's expectations and been tall and leggy, just like she is.

I blush as I stumble slightly, my shoe catching on the front of my dress. I try not to let the error shake my confidence, but as I near the end of the aisle, I finally manage to get a proper view of him. My groom. The man who has scientifically been matched to me.

He's nothing like I imagined and his face sends my stomach plummeting as a wave of disappointment hits me. He's not blonde, he's not got brown eyes, his face isn't warm. His face is instead hard, angular and utterly cold in its distinction as he stands, jaw clenched and dark black hair glistening under the too bright light.

I watch as he turns to me, as though he's a machine, and his eyes rest on me. His expression doesn't turn to one of excitement, or one of joy, or even interest. He is merely unfeeling and cold in his gaze as it falls upon me like ice water.

As I finally near the end of the aisle, I move up the three shallow steps toward the platform where the officiate stands behind my groom, looking at me with kind and sympathetic eyes.

Maybe he knows something I don't about the groom. Maybe he is awful. Oh bliss... I start to panic as I distract myself with passing off my bouquet to a synth, which swarms close to me, nudging my bare arm and causing shivers to run rampant up my spine. Once my bouquet is handed over, I'm left with no other choice but to turn, taking the strangers hands in mine, which are glacially cold, and gazing up, finally, to look him in the eye.

He's tall, taller than I would have thought at maybe six foot four or five. His hair is thick and black and falls in lustrous waves across his head, where it tapers off in a million dreamily layered segments. He looks like he could be a model, or maybe an actor like those they pick for the bridal magazines. The thing that's most remarkable about this man though, isn't his hair, or his height, or the coldness in his expression. It's his eyes.

I have never seen anyone with blue eyes before. I know that most men have their eyes augmented for magazines when other colours are required for editorial shoots, but this man, his eyes are so intensely deep blue that I almost gasp, their sapphire depths, though cold, taking my breath unwillingly away.

"Clark Cavanaugh, it is my deepest pleasure to introduce your bride, Valentine Morland." The officiate announces his name. Clark Cavanaugh. The two words echo through my mind, which is turning slightly numb at the events unfolding before my eyes, like a bad dream I can't wake from.

"Hello," I whisper, my eyes searching his deeply for any sign of compassion or mercy he might be feeling. I know he can tell I'm nervous, I mean, I'm basically shaking like a leaf in late autumn, and yet he merely coughs, clearing his throat and announcing a single syllable.

"Hi."

He doesn't do anything to alleviate my nerves. He doesn't smile. He just speaks, his voice reminding me of a razor cutting stone with the clipped, glacial nature of his tone. The officiate shifts on the balls of his feet, clearly uncomfortable as I flush, looking away from Clark and toward him. I guess keeping my eyes away from him and on the officiate, who looks like he has the utmost sympathy for me as his gaze wanders between us, is probably the safest way to ensure I don't make a bolt for the door.

I look back down the long aisle for a moment, wishing Egypt was here or even my mother, anyone to distract from the awkward and cruel tension which is clutching at my heart and twisting like a vice. At the end of the white marble aisle, two men stand in white suits, guarding the door. Their sunglasses remain on and their expressions are plain as I turn back to Clark. The atmosphere is so tense you could hear a pin drop, and so I look to the officiate, begging him with my gaze to continue speaking, so neither of us have to make an attempt at conversation.

"We have brought you two together today, to sanctify the connection which you were scientifically pre-destined to create. It is an irrefutable connection, a connection based on that which can be quantified, and on the fact that the moment your eyes connected, you felt an immediate rush of emotion you cannot describe in any other way than by naming it *true love*." A small and hysterical giggle escapes my lips at this line and I slam my hand over my mouth, dropping Clark's cold skin and finding my eyes widening with shock at my own lack of decorum.

I take a few breaths, coughing as though something was caught in my throat and then nodding for the officiate to continue. He scowls, clearly not pleased with the interruption. As he rolls his eyes, Clark's stare deadens and I peek up at him through my lashes, heart hammering, terrified.

"As I was saying, you are here today because you have been deemed worthy of the privilege of love in this life. We here at Bliss Inc. are proud to have brought you together, and know that you will go on to make exemplary citizens, and furthermore exemplary parents. You are not only here in service to the love that will grow between you, but in service to humanity. We thank you for this service. If you have vows, I would ask that you now exchange them." He looks between us and I curse internally. I know what I want to say. What I want to promise the man I will be spending the rest of my days with, but standing here, right now, considering the cold masculinity and rough stubble of my matchmate's face, I'm speechless.

The silence echoes out into the hall, poisonous and awkward before the officiate clears his throat once more.

"Of course, some love, some emotion, no matter how we scientifically conceive it, is beyond words, beyond expression. So, I will now substitute in the pre-approved vows." He looks to Clark, summoning forth a synth with the customary pillow holding our rings. He passes me the man's band, and then my more delicate ring to Clark as he looks between us, his expression bored.

"Do you, Clark Cavanaugh, take Valentine Morland to be your wife?" He asks Clark, who swallows, his gaze never wavering from the cold scrutiny under which I'm practically cowering.

"I do." He says the words, gulping down air, as the only noticeable change in his demeanour is the escalated rising and falling of his chest within the broad width of his suit. He slides the blue, diamond encrusted, wedding ring onto my finger in slow and gentle motion, not shaking, or visibly nervous. He's simply unfeeling and cold toward me, making the cool blue of my dress only too adequate for the entire affair.

"Do you, Valentine Morland, take Clark Cavanaugh to be your husband?" He asks me the question and my mind starts to race.

This entire ceremony has been awful. I've been stood here, sweating and practically hyperventilating, wondering why on earth I bothered to get so dressed up over a man who was just as cold as the blue diamond he has chosen for me. I might as well have turned up in a paper bag for all he would have noticed.

"I do." I say the words automatically, as though I've seen the wedding ceremonies so many times it is no longer me accepting the vows, but rather walking through a commercial, as though it isn't my life, or my choice, it's just what you say. I slip the ring on his finger, pushing it down the length of his knuckle with a shove as my temper flares.

"You may kiss." The officiate nods to us, his brows pinching together as he takes a step back. Clark inhales as the media synths swarm and his body visibly tenses. He inhales, like he's getting ready to eat a meal he detests.

His hand pushes its way around my waist, pulling me into him forcefully and crushing his lips to mine in a fevered and angry embrace.

I stand, kissing him back, so shocked by the sudden forwardness of this act that when he breaks the kiss he leaves me both breathless and exposed. He turns away from me, facing the aisle from where I've come as he bends his arm at the elbow and looks to me, his gaze darting quickly downward as though I don't deserve actual words. I take the hint, looping my arm through the crook of his elbow, which is clad in a black tux which I only just take in now.

I have been so enraptured in his face, in its unexpected cruelty and hardness, that I've barely taken in the hall, or what he's wearing. So, as he pulls me forcefully down the shallow steps and the double doors at the end of the hall open, unleashing a torrent of guests into the room who have been watching the ceremony from outside on a soft-light monitor, I scrutinise him. He's wearing a slim fit black tux with icy blue accents, no doubt because he's been informed of the colour scheme by his tailor after I'd picked out my flowers and dress.

"Hi, I'm Valentine. I know you're probably nervous. I am too. I've been terrified, but it is nice to finally meet you," I admit, as he turns to me, surprised. His eyes soften slightly as I feel my own start to prickle with tears, a torrent of emotion rushing through me.

"Likewise," is his only reply as he bows his head curtly, his lips pulling at the corners into a grimace-like smile. I pucker my own lips sideways, frustrated. I have been hoping that we'd laugh about the absurd way we're meeting, or find mutual ground in our discomfort, but he's acting reserved.

I don't want to push, so instead I turn only to see Egypt dashing toward me.

As the guests pile in, service synths begin to transform the hall for our reception. They take the vast space, which is pure white with only a blue runner down the middle that leads to the altar at the end of the room where I'm stood, and transform it before my eyes, setting up and laying tables in only moments. The guests pour in, watching as they make up the room, hanging large periwinkle blue banners from the walls and ceiling and fastening them at intervals so they bulge, making the ceiling lower and creating a more intimate atmosphere.

"Oh my God, Val! I thought you were going to pass out or something! You okay?" Egypt comes hurtling toward me, wrapping her arms around my neck as I move from Clark, who stands like a statue, to embrace her back.

"Hey, I'm okay," I whisper, finding comfort in her familiar warmth and bubbly personality. She is the kind of person who can make any awkward situation easier, so I turn to Clark.

"This is Egypt, my maid of honour and best friend." I explain as Egypt turns to him, her expression becoming serious as she holds out a hand. He takes it, shaking it once firmly and nodding to her.

"Thank you for coming," is all he says, his expression remaining blank. She looks at him, alarmed at his lack of effort to continue with the conversation.

"Well, you're a lucky man. Valentine is a wonderful girl," she continues and he smiles at her, the expression not reaching his eyes.

"Thank you. I'm sure she'd say the same about you," he replies, his tone odd. The entire conversation becomes stilted and so I take to watching the arrangement of the tables by the synths rather than my new husband. Egypt shoots me a worried glance as she moves back into the crowd of mine, or more rightfully, my mother's guests. With this thought, something else occurs to me as I look around the people who begin mulling around the space and seats are set around the tables in automated time. I find it odd that there's hardly anyone I don't recognise. Where are his family?

"Don't you have any family here?" I ask him, suddenly curious and unable to stop myself. His eyes widen sharply, as though I've taken him completely off guard. I don't think it's an unreasonable question, so why should he? Don't I have a right to be curious about the family I've just married into?

"Just my brother," is his only reply, short and clipped.

"Oh, you have a brother? Where is he?" I ask him and he frowns.

"I don't know," is his answer. Evasive, frustrating and infuriating, I begin to feel anger coursing through me as embarrassment flushes my face red. I don't mind so much that he's not being forthcoming, after all, we only just met and we're suddenly man and wife. However, he could at least pretend to act semi-interested for the sake of not making me look like I've just married the equivalent of a robot with good hair.

As I stand in the middle of the room, within which the lighting begins to dim to a cold blue, setting the mood for the afternoon reception and late night dancing, I spot a change in Clark. His face suddenly transforms, going from bored to intense, as a man who I've never seen before moves from the crowd and makes his way toward us.

This must be his brother. I deduce, though I know the only reason I assume this is because he's the only person here I don't recognise. He looks nothing like Clark, who has cold and acutely angled features making him reek of masculine power. Instead, his brother has soft blonde hair and dark eyes, which are wide as they rest on my form. I feel my heart flutter in my chest at the sight of him as some kind of recognition sparks. It's like I've seen him before, but that's impossible.

"Clark!" he exclaims, widening his arms and bringing them around his brother's wide gait. He winks to me as he pulls back, offering me a hand.

"You must be Valentine." He grins, his crooked smile making me feel slightly better. I take his hand and shake it, grinning back at him.

"I must be," I reply, flushing. Clark rolls his eyes next to me.

"Hey, she's my bride, remember?" he snaps, possessive, and the man immediately turns to look at his brother.

"You could have fooled me. You looked like the equivalent of a constipated statue during the ceremony. The poor thing probably thinks there's something wrong with you."

"Jason, for the love of all that is sacred, shut up." Clark glares and I watch him, immediately wishing it had been Jason at the end of the aisle instead as he looks between us and sighs.

"Well, it was lovely to meet you, Valentine. Should I have been so lucky as to qualify for the Jigsaw project, I can only hope my bride would have been half as beautiful as you." He raises my hand to his lips and plants a quick kiss. The room silences around us as the public display of affection causes the people around me to stop and stare.

This isn't regular behaviour and is highly unorthodox and so I flush, looking to Clark and feeling my embarrassment heighten at his brother's over amorous behaviour. He doesn't look angry, or surprised, but merely uninterested as his expression becomes once more masked with cold reserve.

"Would it be alright if I were to steal my brother for just a moment?" Jason asks me as I begin to panic at the eyes on me. I nod hastily, glad of the opportunity to lose myself in the sea of other guests, drawing attention away from the fact I'd received a nicer greeting from Jason than my groom.

The two men stride away, both clad in the same colour and style of suit as they move to the back of the hall, stepping back through the door from which Clark presumably entered. I stand in the middle of the space as the conversation of the guests begins to pick up again. Shortly after the groom's disappearance, guests begin to converge on me, the first of whom is my mother.

"Valentine! Oh, he's so handsome!" She doesn't compliment me, but instead the ice sculpture I have married. I smile, accepting the compliment as graciously as I know how.

"Thank you. Did you see his brother?" I begin and she flicks her wrist as her expression turns stern. She's wearing spotless white, and as my father catches up to her, being only five and a half feet, she begins her critique of me.

"Yes, why would you let him kiss you like that? Especially when you're married to that... well, hunk," she asks me, her eyes so intense they practically melt the skin off my face.

"I didn't know he was going to do that. It was completely inappropriate!" I protest and she nods, satisfied with my response.

"Good! Now say hello to your father. He hasn't seen you since Portia's big day! I mean, you can't deny you did take your time getting married!" She condemns me again, so I waste no time shifting my gaze.

I turn to my father, looking into his deep brown eyes and feeling my heart inflate. Where Cynthia Morland is a storm, he has always been the calm that follows. I have missed him so much and so I immediately rush forward and wrap my arms around him, feeling the familiar smell of wood and musk fill my nostrils, comforting me when I need it most.

"Dad," I whisper and he looks to me, eyes tear-filled.

"I missed you, poppet," he whispers back, stroking my hair and looking up to me.

"I missed you too." I break the embrace, only to find my own eyes watering with tears. It's the most wanted I've felt all day, and I can't believe it's my father and not the groom who is causing me to feel this way.

"Valentine!" I see my sister Eve raising a hand and pushing through the crowd of people so I step between my mother and father. As I do so, my foot catches the inside of my skirt and I go flying, splaying out across the slick marble. The room collectively gasps as all eyes turn to me and my bracelet snaps, sending pearls skittering everywhere.

Silence falls afterwards, well, except for one voice, which rings out loud and clear as I lay, splatted on the cool floor like a humiliated blue pancake.

"Jason, I don't care what you say. I am NOT falling in love with her!" The voice is cold, cruel and makes me wish the ground would swallow me whole. Clark's deep voice rings out in the cool vastness of the space, and as Eve and Egypt rush forward to help me to my feet, while the final pearl finishes its course across the floor, I find myself scarily close to tears of panic and despair.

As my mother scurries over to condemn me, the door at the end of the hall loudly opens and the crowd turns away from my teary eyes and toward the altar. Clark and Jason move out into the hall, none the wiser that anyone had been privy to their conversation.

"Valentine, are you alright?" Eve asks me, looking into my eyes with a pity-filled stare. There's no glee in her gaze at my

111

misfortune, merely concern, making me want to cry all the more. This must be bad if my eldest sister isn't using it to point score.

"Yes, I'm fine," I mumble, brushing my skirt down and gathering myself. I watch as Clark and Jason walk over to the crowd, curious as to what the commotion is about. People part as my husband moves toward me, his expression having softened somewhat.

"What happened? Are you alright?" He looks to me and then the pearls scattered around me on the floor.

"She's fine, she's just clumsy is all! She fell over. Classic Valentine!" My mother laughs it off, embarrassing me further and Clark rounds on her.

"Excuse me? Who the hell do you think you are?" he accuses her and my eyes widen as her mouth pops open.

"I, *young man,* am your new mother in law." My mother narrows her eyes as well and Clark squares himself up to her.

"No. You're a bully. I don't give a damn if you're her mother. In fact, that makes what you just did *worse.* Apologise. This is her day. Not yours." His words echo around us and my sisters inhale sharply beside me.

I stand, stone still, watching my mother, unable to so much as blink. She's surrounded by her friends, by the people who think so much of her, and so I wonder what exactly it is she'll do now.

"Well... I suppose that was a little bit harsh. I'm sorry, Valentine." She apologises and I scrunch up my forehead. What the hell is going on here? My mother getting put down? Me getting defended? Maybe being married isn't so bad after all.

"It's fine. I just banged my elbow, that's all," I announce, trying to defuse the tension as the synths break the silence by clanking their metal arms against the delicately stalked glasses, signalling that we should move to be seated. Clark moves over to me, staring downward and examining the floor, which is still scattered with pearls.

"I'm sorry about your bracelet, and her…" He gestures to my mother, who now scurries over to her set seat as my father stands, transfixed and watching Clark with a half impressed-half dazed smile.

"It's alright. I'm used to it." I express and he frowns.

"You shouldn't have to be." He grunts back in response, taking my hand firmly in his and walking me over to the beautiful top table, which is finally set up.

I watch him curiously. Why would someone so cold stand up for me and defend me so fiercely. Is this normal?

He pulls out a seat for me, which I sit in, looking out over the hall where the rest of the guests are taking their places too. The centrepieces glow blue and consist of tall glass vases filled with some kind of neon liquid. The eerie light casts shadows on Clark's face as he takes a seat next to me and watches his brother, who stares at him and makes a face which I find unreadable.

"So, what did you choose from the menu?" he asks me, picking up the card in front of him with his name on and examining it, not looking at me even still. I place my hands in my lap and cross my ankles, unsure of what to say. He's really asking me something so simple? Doesn't he want to know more about me?

"I think I picked the chicken. You?" I ask him and he laughs.

"I picked the steak. All we can get in the male district as standard is chicken, I'm so sick of it," he announces, revealing something I hadn't known.

"Really, that's funny. All we can get in the female district as standard is steak." I laugh and he shakes his head.

"That figures." His reply is simple as his blue eyes finally catch mine, but he looks away again quickly and I'm left not knowing how to reply. I want to ask him a million and one questions, but I feel awkward.

As I open my mouth to say something witty about the food choices, the service synths begin to buzz around the room, each one holding six steaming plates. I realise instantly that I'm starving, so, as the first synth brings over our plates and puts them down silently on the table, I dig in, trying to look elegant in eating but undoubtedly failing as I realise how hungry I really am.

The meal passes in silence as we both keep our eyes trained on the guests, who watch us like hawks.

Seven

The first dance is about to begin, and I'm stuffed from the food. Clark hasn't said anything to me, just sat and watched as the speeches took place. I wonder what his deal is, why he's not happy. Am I not what he expected? Did I choose the wrong dress? Am I a disappointment? I'm afraid that all these things might be true, and to top it all off, I can't help but replay his voice in my head saying *I am NOT falling in love with her.* Am I that grotesque? That repugnant that he knows from merely a few words spoken that I'm all wrong for him? Are we the one per cent? Are we the couple the formula got wrong?

The glasses are clinked again as a stereo somewhere begins to play the song I had chosen. It's one of my favourites, because my dad used to play it to me when I was a child, and like all music now it's ancient.

My funny valentine seeps out into the room. Clark and I stand and he takes my hand, before holding it out from him like I'm infectious, as he storms through the maze of tables.

When we reach the dance floor, which remains clear in the centre of the room surrounded by tables holding dirty plates and full guests, he wraps his arm around my waist, tight in his clutch on me. He pulls my body into his and I find his lips by my ear.

"Smile, Valentine." He whispers, sending a shiver down my spine. His tone is deadly, like if I don't do as he asks there'll be dark consequences.

He places my hand over his heart, grasping my fingers in his like I might run away. I look up to him, my eyes beginning to sparkle as I feel terror clutch at me. My husband looks down too, his gaze unreadable. In an unexpected and sudden motion, he rests his forehead against mine, his expression becoming pained like it physically hurts him to be close to me.

We sway, his eyes closing as he pushes me out from him, rejecting my proximity and swirling me in a calculated and emotionless pirouette. The skirt of my dress billows outward, before he pulls me back into his body, yanking me so hard that I feel like he's pulling my arm from my shoulder socket.

"Did I do something wrong?" I whisper to him, and he exhales, laughing.

"No, Valentine. You did not. Now, dance with me." This is his only request as he spins me, bending me back over as I feel my stomach flutter. His cold reserve is making me nervous, but for some reason I'm excited while dancing with him, whether it's me being stupid or not though, it's too soon to tell, but I let him possess me as we dance.

He is in complete control as we move around the floor, so much so that I have to do little but look into his eyes, marvelling even still at the deep sapphire blue of his irises. Every few minutes he grimaces, placing his forehead on mine and I wonder if it's just for show, if he's forcing this act of affection. He looks physically pained by my closeness and I count down the beats until the song is over.

The song ends and I feel myself exhale as he spins me one final time. The blue light reflects off his black hair as he bows to me and I curtsey, blushing as his expression flashes between scorching hot and icy cold, like he can't quite decide whether to bother acting like he's interested in me or not.

As the song changes to something else, my sisters come forward together, Eve with her husband this time, as Clark walks off toward his brother who beckons him. I watch as he bends down and his brother whispers something into his ear. Clark laughs and I scowl, turning to my sisters and exhaling.

"That, was hot," Portia leans in and whispers to me.

"Was it?" I ask her, dazed by her reaction as I start to feel the emotional weight of the day catching up with me.

"Oh my God, did you not notice his whole, 'I'm wanting to rip this girl's clothes off but I must restrain myself' vibe?" She asks me and I frown.

"What the hell are you talking about? He can't stand me. I think that's pretty obvious," I snap and Eve raises her eyebrows.

"Don't be so sure, men are funny creatures. Isn't that right, honey?" she asks her husband, Desmond, and he suddenly checks back into the conversation.

"Oh, uh yes. Of course," he replies and I laugh. He so totally wasn't listening.

"See, Desmond and I agree with Portia. He's into you." Eve announces this and I shake my head.

"You guys are crazy." I say, placing both my hands on my waist.

"I think you're forgetting that he also took on mom, and like totally won. I mean, if you don't want him, I'm sure Desmond won't mind sharing me," Eve cocks an eyebrow as she nudges Desmond, whose eyes have wandered to Egypt, who is now trying to get people up onto the dance floor and moving.

"Oh yes, of course, darling." Desmond replies and she slaps him on the arm.

"Can you listen to me for like two seconds." She rolls her eyes and Portia and I look to one another with a smirk.

"Well, I guess we only just met. I don't know, he just... seems cold to me. And where is his family? Like, his brother is here... and you heard what he said about me." I start babbling and Eve's eyes widen.

"Yeah, that's true. I mean, what the hell is that all about? Where's his family? You know fine architecture like that doesn't just spring up out of the ground." She looks to Clark and I roll my eyes. Can we all just ignore the fact he's not completely ugly for one second. The man is practically a robot.

"I guess... I suppose time will tell," I reply and Eve and Portia both nod. I had never thought those words would fall from my lips on my wedding day. I have always held the belief that as soon as I laid eyes on my matchmate I'd know, but the fact is, he's a stranger.

"It's true, once Stephen and I went on honeymoon, that's where we really connected for the first time. The wedding is all formality," Portia relinquishes this information and I frown. Hadn't she always been preaching about how as soon as she saw Stephen she knew he was right for her?

"Yeah, I still have no idea where we're going." I shrug and she smiles.

"Yeah they tell you on the high-speed monorail on your way to the airport. Have you thought about where you want to get assigned?" she asks me and I think back on the three options. Clark and I will be going wherever we're sent, as you don't get a choice where you honeymoon, but I have always wanted to go to the island resort Jungala. It is way more appealing to me than somewhere cold or rainy.

"Jungala," I say and she grins.

"It's great there, you'll have a fabulous time." She winks at me and I know she's secretly happy I want to go where she honeymooned, just one more thing for me to be jealous of. Knowing me, I'll probably end up getting sent to Twin Peaks, the ski-resort surrounded by snow. Maybe it would be fitting, especially seeing as how my husband has about as much personality as a snowman.

"You should probably go and sit with your husband, Valentine. You know it doesn't look good with you two avoiding each other," Eve prompts me and I twist my mouth. I don't want to go and push myself on him.

"Okay," I sigh, turning from them and walking swiftly across the dance floor.

As I approach the table at which he and his brother are sitting, I take a seat. He looks at me with a scowl, as though I'm not wanted.

Instead of feeling offended though, I decide to try to get to know him. Even if I have to interrogate his brother to do it.

"So, what can you tell me about Clark?" I ask Jason and his brown eyes sparkle as he takes in my face. I smile at him, hoping that his instant kindness will mean he will shed some light on my husband.

"Why don't you ask him yourself?" he suggests, getting up and moving over to Egypt, who has begun to walk toward me. He diverts her and I catch Clark mumbling, "You are such an asshole," as he passes. I catch his sentiment and feel my heart finally giving out. I've had enough of him and his standoffish games. I get to my feet, moving to leave the table again and wondering why I even bothered.

"Wait, Valentine... Wait!" he calls out, but suddenly, the lights brighten and a voice comes over the speakers.

"We would like to thank you all for attending the wedding of Mr and Mrs Cavanaugh. Their high-speed shuttle to the airport will depart in only 20 minutes. Please say your goodbyes and make sure you take all personal belongings with you when you leave. We here at Bliss Inc. would like to wish Valentine and Clark a future full of bliss. Congratulations!"

The message that routinely ends the reception rings in my ears, and as Clark grabs onto my wrist to stop me walking away, I yank it from his grasp, storming across the dance floor towards Egypt and launching myself at her.

"Egypt, I can't go with him! He's awful!" I whisper into her ear in a rush. Her fingers dig into my back as she holds me.

"Be brave, Valentine," she whispers back, "Give him a chance. You have to, for me. I'm going to need you in Pearl Falls, okay!?" She's desperate now, her voice becoming high pitched.

120

"You'll call me when I get back, right?" I make her promise, knowing that there's no communication with the outside world within the honeymoon complex.

"Yes, as soon as you're back. Be strong okay. Don't let him ignore you. Just be patient, but don't give up trying." She makes me vow and so I nod my head, feeling like I'm going to cry. I let her go and back into Clark who has followed me.

"What?" I turn and snap, wondering why he's hanging around me like a bad smell when he clearly wants nothing to do with me.

"I just thought we should get going? We don't want to miss the shuttle," he mumbles, now changing in his demeanour so he looks like a lost schoolboy.

"I need to say my goodbyes," I say and he blinks, standing aside without a word.

As I move to go and say farewell to my family, I realise that soon I'll be alone with him for three weeks. I remember my readiness courses, what they had taught me and sigh, knowing now that no amount of training could have ever prepared me for the mystery that is Clark Cavanaugh.

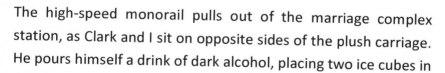

The high-speed monorail pulls out of the marriage complex station, as Clark and I sit on opposite sides of the plush carriage. He pours himself a drink of dark alcohol, placing two ice cubes in the glass, which clink together, reminding me of us.

I'm exhausted. Too tired to want to make any effort with him, too tired to want to make small talk, or be angry. Instead, I sit in silence, looking out the window.

As he stands, taking a sip of his drink, he moves toward the envelope that sits on the counter next to the ice bucket and glasses. He slips his fingers under the seal and opens it, scanning the page twice before looking to me and announcing, "We're going to Jungala." I don't look up at him, just turn back to the window and put my feet up on the plush hold of the crimson padded bench that lines the space.

I should be happy, we're going to the honeymoon destination I wanted, and my husband isn't ugly, well, at least not on the outside. Instead I'm ambivalent. Not caring.

It doesn't matter if we're off to some island paradise, for me, because I'm in bad company. Yes, Clark stood up to my mother, he defended me, but it's hours into our marriage and I still know nothing about him other than the fact he has a brother, can dance and has decided that he will one hundred percent not fall in love with me. I'm sick and tired of getting whiplash from him, and it's only been an afternoon.

The sun is setting outside the window, and as I worry about what sharing a bed with this man might entail, I listen to the continued sound of his lips taking in alcohol and ice cubes clicking against glass. My blue dress billows out around me on the seat, taking up enough space so that I can make sure he's nowhere near me.

As we race to the airport the carriage fills with everything that isn't being said. This entire day has been nothing like I expected, and as my heart settles into the cold clutches of disappointment, a tear leaks from the corner of my eye. I brush it away, knowing that for all the credit in the world, I will not let Clark see me cry.

As we sit in the airport departure lounge for Jungala, I glance around. Everything is a slick grey, merging from the black and traditional whites of the brides and grooms who file in slowly from their shuttles. Brides have taken their heels off, walking barefoot across the silver carpet with their pricey shoes slung over one shoulder, or their veils crumpled up in their groom's hand. Clark is at a coffee shop nearby, getting us some coffee.

So, I know he likes coffee, I just wish he was open to the same feelings about me. I wonder if it's not so much his attitude, it's the fact I haven't been given the chance to even know him, or him me, before I've been written off as something he detests, which bothers me so much.

I stare around the lounge; Brides and grooms are sitting, still dressed in their wedding attire and talking to one another. They all look so enraptured, so caught up in one another's eyes and voices, that I know time is moving at a different speed for them. When you have someone new to learn about, there is never enough time, but when, like me, your husband makes you want to irrationally hit things, every second drags on for an eternity.

Clark returns, staring at a couple that are kissing amorously behind me and flushing. I wonder if he thinks I'm expecting this from him, which makes my stomach turn.

"I hope I got your order right... I don't know what you take or anything..." He says, looking me in the eye and coughing as the woman sitting next to me hitches up her skirt and proceeds to climb on her new husband's lap.

"You know, you could have asked." I bite his head off, irritated that he didn't even think to communicate with me. I'm supposed to be his wife for goodness' sake.

"Sorry." He wavers beneath my scorn, clearly too tired for an argument, or not bothered enough to ask me what I prefer even though it is too late. I wonder how the man in front of me can be the same man who took on my mother and won not a few hours ago. Right now, he looks like the equivalent of a kicked puppy.

I sit back in the smart-foam of my seat, taking the coffee from him and sipping it immediately. I wince, burning my tongue but not wanting to let him know I'm in pain. I don't want his sympathy.

"That's hot," he says simply, watching me as I pull a face against my better judgement.

"No shit. Wow. You must be a detective." I scowl up at him, my tone dripping with disdain.

"Would you like me better as a detective?" he asks me, totally not understanding why I'm so clearly agitated. What, is he trying to be cute with me right now?

"I'd like you better if you'd give me some space. I'm tired," I admit, blowing on my coffee and watching as he walks over to the other side of the rack of chairs, which are all connected by a metallic looking bar. He takes the seat behind me, so our heads are practically touching and I exhale. This guy is riding on my last nerve.

"You realise you're technically closer to me right now than you just were?" I say, not bothering to turn to look at him.

"How about you draw a line, princess? Would that make you happy?" he growls. I roll my eyes. I'm married to a jackass. Great.

124

"How about you shut the hell up," I say, returning to ignoring him as he sniggers, laughing like a child behind me.

Instead of letting him get to me, I pick my weary ass up off the seat and take a stroll, moving to look in the windows of some of the shops.

In the display windows, there are pictures of happy couples jetting off to their honeymoons. I look at the images, then down to myself and over to Clark, who is sitting, watching the soft-light holo-dash which shows our boarding time.

This really is *nothing* like I imagined.

It's not like the wedding channel has made it out to be, or the magazines which I've obsessively scanned since I was old enough to read. Clark isn't just a groom in a tux with a perfect smile. He is a person; a complicated, infuriating person but still an individual none the less. I can't help but feel short changed, and as I look around the departure lounge, we seem to be the only couple that isn't caught up in one another.

I sigh, hearing the double tone signalling our flight is boarding. I've never been on a plane, so as it is I don't know what to expect. One thing I do know, however, is that the thought of being alone for however many hours and in a confined space with my new husband is making me overcome with dread. I don't want to deal with his smart mouth, or his cold expression. I just want to sleep.

After the plane has taken off soundlessly into the air, Clark falls asleep next to me. His eyelids close and his expression softens as he falls into dreams, which I'm utterly sure don't include me. I watch him as the light in the wide cabin dims, unable to believe

I'm really flying as I look about. His angular face is attractive, but perhaps my expectations have sold him short.

He has long black eyelashes, of which I'm completely jealous. His lips are sculpted perfectly, not too thick or thin. His hair is black and glossy, and he has stubble on his chin, jaw and cheeks, which is just starting to break through his flawless pallor. His face is missing the stark sapphire of his gaze, and yet I like looking at him when he's like this. He seems less intimidating by far.

I look away, restraining myself as I fear he may wake, but, as I find there's nothing else to look at except the soft-light holo-map of our projected flight path and a few other couples who are kissing, I cannot help but return to staring at his face.

As I step off the plane, the air is humid and sticky on my skin. Clark helps me onto the tarmac of the runway, where a monorail awaits to take us directly to our hotel.

Jungala has three main resorts *The Palm*, *The Oasis* and *The Dune*. We're stationed in *The Oasis,* and I feel my spirits lift a little as I get a whiff of the salty air. We're close to the sea, something I've only seen in adverts for this place.

"This is amazing!" I gush, letting Clark pull me forward with vigour as I stop to take in the starry filled night sky. It's beautiful.

"Come on!" He pulls me forward hard and I try to inhale as I find myself out of breath in the heat, not letting my temper get the better of me, and not wanting to let him ruin this experience for me.

As we climb the glass steps to the station, Clark scans the arrivals board, checking for the next shuttle to *The Oasis*. It's in five minutes, so we hurry across the slick glass floor, my feet aching in my wedding shoes and my heart hammering as Clark removes his jacket, revealing a bulging torso clad in white cotton beneath. He takes his cravat off too, loosening his collar with his free hand and exposing a spattering of chest hair.

"Hot?" I ask him and he doesn't reply, making a sharp right at the platform and scanning his tattoo, which I now notice is on the back of his wrist, not the inside. He drags me into another plush carriage; pulling me so hard I nearly trip on the edge of the platform and fall forward. I catch myself, yanking my wrist from his grasp and taking in the transport as I fall onto the padding of a bench. This time the seating is mint green and the glass of the monorail is faceted with the designs of palm trees.

"What the hell is your problem!?" I demand of him, wondering why he had rushed so frantically.

"I didn't want to miss the monorail. It's been a long day. Did you want to have to wait another hour?" he asks me with a cocked eyebrow. There are bags under his eyes. He'd slept most of the plane journey, where as I hadn't been able to switch off, and so I wonder why he's not more rested.

"Did you have to pull me so hard!?" I bark, scowling and rubbing my wrist where he'd grabbed me. His expression becomes pained, reaching out gingerly as the carriage begins to move. I let him take my wrist in his fingers, and what he does next surprises me. He lifts it to his lips and kisses me, causing a shudder to run rampant up the length of my arm.

127

"I'm sorry," he whispers, looking all of a sudden like he's going to cry.

"It's fine. Sorry I shouted. I'm tired too," I admit, biting my bottom lip and watching as he takes my hand in his, placing it on his knee and looking out the window as we speed through the night.

I turn away from him, alarmed as my hand remains entwined with his. It becomes hot and sweaty after a while as the carriage races through the humid stickiness of the air, so I shrug him away, hoping he doesn't take offence.

After only ten minutes, the carriage slows to a halt. I rise to my feet, feeling my shoes pinching as I exit without looking to Clark. As I step out onto the carpet, which is patterned with more geometric palm trees, I stop, not looking behind me for my husband as I do, and hitch up my skirt, undoing the blue silk ribbons before taking off my pumps.

"Feet hurting?" Clark asks me, and I nod. We walk toward the desk which is blatantly labelled 'reception' and I limp slightly, as I realise that the shoes I've been wearing have been biting into my heels so hard I have blisters.

Clark moves quickly, sensing that I'm hurting, and checks us in. I watch as he scans his tattoo again and the pristine looking hard-light hologram behind the desk nods, saying something I can't hear over the roaring of a nearby fountain. I catch up to Clark, as he turns to me.

"We're on the top floor," Clark observes and I look to him. Shoes in hand. I'm exhausted and his eyes fill with pity. "Come on." He moves around me, bringing his arm beneath me and scooping me up in both his arms. I feel him holding me as my skirts flutter, and the man behind the counter gets a sweet smile as I rest my head on Clark's chest, hearing his heart racing beneath.

Well, at least I know he's not a robot. I think to myself as I yawn.

As my new husband carries me into the elevator, I scan my tattoo, working together with him as the doors close and sweep us upward. I'm too tired to take in any of the resort, seeing only tall palm trees and many levels full of hotel rooms through the glass of the pod, which carries us to the top floor.

"You look exhausted," Clark observes, looking down to me as the doors of the elevator ping open and a robotic voice says *'level one hundred'*.

"That's what happens when you're a bride. It's tiring looking this fabulous," I admit, knowing that if Egypt were here she'd appreciate the joke.

Instead Clark just puts a small, sweet smile onto his face and begins looking at door numbers. When we reach the entrance to our room, which seems to take forever as the corridor seems unending, he puts me down on the balls of my aching feet.

I'm a little disappointed, I mean, I wanted him to carry me over the threshold, but I suppose that's asking a little too much from a man whose regular demeanour makes him more like an ice sculpture and less like an actual person.

We scan our tattoos together this time, a first, and as we do I manage to take in the design of his. It fits into mine exactly. I know immediately because I've spent nine years memorising my own tattoo, but I'm still startled at how exactly it fits. Every crenulation, every gap, filled by his. The door opens wide and I go to step through.

"You don't want me to…" He begins but then stops himself.

"What?" I ask him, curious.

"Nah it's stupid." He retorts.

"Clark, what?" I demand, feeling my exhaustion making me impatient.

"Carry you in?" He cringes at his own words and I smile.

"Um… okay," I say, hopping into his arms and allowing him to carry me across the threshold. I knock my head slightly on the frame and giggle. "Ow! Careful! I don't have that many brain cells that I can afford to lose a bunch!" I exclaim and he chuckles too, setting me down in the centre of the suite, a smile making his face beautiful for the very first time.

I look around; a giant bed is covered in white silk sheets. The walls are a muted shade of aubergine and the floor is a luxurious cream. I drop my shoes against the bed, feeling his eyes on me, as I turn to him, somewhat expectant.

Suddenly, everything is awkward again. I look around the space, noticing that this is only the first room and that a door in the left wall of the suite leads to a paler and more spacious living area and kitchen. Clark turns, following my gaze, before he looks backs to me, his face turning from relaxed to glacial in a few seconds.

"Goodnight," he announces in a clipped tone, walking from the room and slamming the door of the living room shut.

I stand, unsure of what's just happened.

Did I do something wrong?

The bed beckons me, but first I know I need to get out of this dress. I turn, realising I can't get out of it myself.

Sighing, and wishing I'd picked something with a zipper, I turn on my throbbing soles and walk toward the door that Clark has just slammed. I move to put my hand on the doorknob, which gleams gold, but instead I stop, hearing his voice coming in muted sound from the next room.

Who's he talking to? I wonder as his tone becomes angry. I know that there's no communication to anyone outside the island for the next three weeks, so maybe he's talking to himself?

My heart flutters in my chest. I'm afraid to know what he's saying. I thought him carrying me, caring for me, was a sign I'd been doing something right, that we were becoming closer to speaking the same language, but as I stand here in a blue wedding dress that I can't escape, I realise that I'm deluding myself.

I run from the door, wanting to evade his voice, terrified of hearing something which will make everything worse.

I crawl onto the bed, my skirt spreading out like a flower around me. I'm too tired to even care anymore, so as I suddenly and unexpectedly find the energy to burst into slow falling tears, I cry myself to sleep alone.

Eight

I stir from sleep, the heat of the sun pouring in through the glass double doors, which act as windows, warming my skin and causing my eyes to flutter open. I look up, staring at the ceiling as I realise that this isn't my apartment. It's the hotel suite that I'll be staying in for the duration of my honeymoon…. *Honeymoon.*

Oh… crap.

I sit bolt upright, hearing the rustling of organza as I realise that I'm still wearing my wedding dress. My eyes are sore from all the crying I've done, having never felt so emotionally perplexed or alone in my life.

As I sit here, trying to work out how exactly my dream of the perfect husband had so spectacularly gone to pieces, the door to the living room opens. Clark steps through the doorframe, a tray in his arms. His eyes are wide and bright in the early morning, showing he's clearly slept better than I have. He looks to me and then his eyebrows rise in surprise.

"Why are you still wearing that?" he asks me, his lips quirking up in a half-amused smile. I scowl, looking at him from top to bottom. He'd had no problem stripping out of his suit and

132

replacing it with a pair of fine cotton pyjama bottoms and a white t-shirt.

"I couldn't get out of it by myself," I mumble, not having the energy to act as mad as I really feel.

"Oh. I'm sorry, Valentine. Why didn't you come get me?" he asks me, as though the thought hadn't even occurred to me.

"Well, you did sort of slam the door in my face, Clark. Not exactly a sign that you'd be willing to help me." I scowl and he sighs, placing the tray he's carrying down on the table near the far wall of the room, beside the double doors that lead out onto a sizeable balcony.

"I'm sorry about that. About yesterday in general. I want to talk, but first I think you need a shower, and breakfast." He gestures to the tray he's just set down and my eyebrows twitch, not sure I'm ready to forgive him for being such an asshole just yet.

"You made me breakfast?" I ask him in a surprised tone and he sighs.

"Yes. I wanted to make it up to you, for yesterday," he admits, as he moves over to the bed, crawling over the sheets. "Let's get you out of this dress," he says, indicating I should move. I do, twisting and perching on the edge of the bed.

His hand sweeps across the back of my neck, moving away tresses, which have fallen from my up-do during sleep. I shudder as his touch leaves a lingering heat and close my eyes.

A few moments later he taps me on the shoulder.

"All done. You should be able to get out of it now," he whispers, too close to my ear.

I hold the top of the gown to me, and look around the room for the bathroom. He smiles, gesturing behind me.

I turn, spotting a dark mahogany door in the wall on the right side of the bed. Stepping forward, I pull the blue skirts of the dress up around my calves with my free hand, and walk into the bathroom, feeling relief as the cool black tiles touch my still sore feet. Closing the door behind me, I hear Clark call, "I'll be on the balcony!" but I don't reply, too tired and cloudy from sleep to keep up with the extent of his early morning personality transplant.

I spin once I've let the dress fall to the floor and kick it to one side, treating it now as I am the dreams that my husband would be my perfect match; a load of ceremonial, artificial rubbish.

Staring into the wall-long mirror, I'm taken back. My eyes are shockingly mascara stained, my lipstick is smeared and my eyeliner has been smudged so the fine lines it had formed are beyond recognition. I look down at myself, stood in lingerie, and almost laugh. Did I really think I'd lose my virginity on the first night? No. I suppose I hoped otherwise, but I have heard men can be demanding. Instead, I ended up alone and with a door slammed in my face.

I let out a sigh, wondering if perhaps Clark's frosty reception of me had been nerves, or just because everything is changing so fast it's hard to keep up. I mean, I suppose I'd been less than ladylike to him in some ways, but he'd also treated me less than perfectly.

Turning and stepping into the shower, I vow to shed the doubts and quarrels of yesterday and try again today, as I wash away the makeup and glitz. After all, today is where the real work begins. Because compared to putting on a priceless gown and simply walking down an aisle, marriage with this man now seems an uncertain and terrifying feat.

Once I'm showered, I request some loungewear from the upcycler in the wall and I'm surprised to find I have hundreds of options on the hard-light holo-dash catalogue. When I'd been single, everything had been white, but now I'm a married woman, I've unlocked endless options for clothing. I select lilac as the colour for the pants and teal for the shirt from the catalogue on screen, wait as the upcycler rumbles, before the window opens and my clothes are revealed, perfectly pressed and warm. Dressing quickly, I slip the shirt over my head, shoving my lingerie down the shoot quickly afterward as I collect it from the floor, not wanting Clark to think I'm a total slob or to know that I had half expected to climb into bed with him.

I mean, I looked like some sort of monster this morning, with my tear stained face, so God knows what he thinks of me. I look to the wedding dress, but I can't quite bring myself to throw it away. So instead, with the hair dripping down the back of my t-shirt making me shudder, I pick it up and stroll back into the bedroom. There's a wardrobe against the wall next to the door that leads to the living area, which surprises me. I stood right beside it last night, but I'd barely taken in anything about my surroundings, being both too tired and too angry to care much for the decor.

I don't bother hanging the gown, but merely shove it inside and push the doors shut again. As I hear them click closed, I feel

135

my stomach rumble. I've not eaten since the reception, and I'm starving.

Clark should be on the balcony, so I pad across the room in bare feet, waiting as the balcony door slides open automatically, and shield my eyes from the glare of the extraordinarily bright sun. There's a hot tub on the balcony, though I've never been in one before. In fact, I only know what it is I'm looking at because of the amount of magazines about honeymoons I've read.

There's a table with boxy, square seating, on which a plate with a silver cloche is sitting, with cutlery beside it, gleaming. In a small vase, next to a glass full of orange juice, is a white and blue ombré calla lily, presumably the one Clark has saved from his suit jacket. I smile. It's a small gesture. But it is, nonetheless, a start.

"Morning." I say, finally letting my eyes rest on Clark, who is stood, leaning over the balcony and looking out into the sun that dangles lazily above the horizon.

"You look much better," he compliments, turning and taking a seat at the table.

"Aren't you hungry?" I ask him, but he shakes his head.

"Nah, I'm not a breakfast person." He replies and I smile as I take my seat.

"So you made this just for me?" I look between him and the silver lid as I lift it. Beneath lies bacon and eggs with a side of pancakes. I haven't had this kind of breakfast since I was a child and I can't help but get butterflies at the thought of eating it again.

"Yes," he replies, not giving anything away, but watching me with reserved interest.

I pick up the glass of orange juice, something else I haven't had in an age, and take a sip. My eyelashes flutter as the tangy zest awakens my senses, driving them from the depths of sleepiness.

"So, you said you want to talk?" I ask him and he nods, coughing slightly as he covers his mouth. His eyes become intense.

"I did. I feel like it's important we establish... boundaries before this goes any further, Valentine." He looks deeply into my eyes, his expression beyond serious. I swallow hard, the acidity of the orange juice still coating my tongue. Looking down at the plate before me, I'm suddenly not so sure I'm hungry.

"Boundaries?" I ask him, cocking one eyebrow and he nods.

"I'm going to be very honest with you. Are you alright with that?" he asks me and narrows his eyes, scrutinising my response as I lean back in my seat. I nod my head, my heart hammering in my chest.

"Okay." I don't know how else to reply. It feels like I'm about to hear some kind of dark confession.

"So, here's the thing. I have no interest in having a relationship with you. Not in the traditional sense. We're married, it's true, but as you know, entry into the Jigsaw Project isn't exactly optional." He takes a deep breath.

"What do you mean?" I ask him and he laughs.

"Well, have you ever heard of anyone who's turned down Bliss Inc.?" He asks me and I ponder this a moment. After a few minutes, I realise he's right. I have never heard of anyone being accepted into the Jigsaw project and rejecting the opportunity.

"No. I haven't," I reply. He nods.

"I thought as much. Well, my point is, I didn't choose you. You didn't choose me either. I don't believe that should mean we're forced into a life of unhappiness. Do you?" he asks me and I cock my head, wondering what on earth it is he's insinuating.

"So, you're saying you want to leave me?" I ask him, my breaths coming in small and shallow wisps.

"I can't do that, Valentine. I need this marriage to work. I'm getting older..." he begins, but I cut him off.

"How old are you?" I ask him, feeling my mind race. This isn't the conversation I had been expecting.

"Twenty-eight almost twenty-nine," he replies, his eyebrows pinching together, clearly finding my question absurd.

That's why I've been waiting all this time.

It wasn't about me at all. It was about him.

"So, what are you saying? You don't want to be married to me, but you need to be married to me? Why?" I feel myself getting both confused and stressed as panic begins to set in.

"Do you know what happens to people who don't pass the one-hundred-day assessment?" He asks me and I frown again.

"No," I reply, sitting back into my seat and watching his serious expression remain unchanged.

"Don't you ever wonder where they go? The couples that don't work out?" he asks me and I shrug.

"They get reassigned to one of the labour settlements, or that's what my friend Egypt's friend Cloe said," I reply and he laughs.

"Not exactly. Regardless though, I need this marriage to work. I'm willing to treat you well, Valentine. I'll care for you. I hope in time we'll become great friends. But that's where it ends. It has

138

to. I'm not the kind of man you want to be close to." He finishes the sentence and I blink, pinching the skin on my arm to make sure I'm not in some hideous nightmare.

"Why?" I ask him, staring at the flower in the vase between us. How can a man who had worked so tirelessly over this meal, claim he doesn't have feelings for me? It's only breakfast, but it's the nicest thing anyone has ever done for me.

"I'm not saying this to hurt you, Valentine. I think you're beautiful. Sweet. From what I know of you, anyway. I just hope I'm not too much of a disappointment." He reaches out to try and touch my hand, which rests, stone still, on the edge of the table. I notice that he's not wearing his wedding ring.

"What about children?" I ask him abruptly, my mind immediately jumping to Egypt. We have always hoped our children would grow up together.

"I think it's a bit soon to be discussing that, but perhaps in time… perhaps…" He stutters.

"What? You'll do me a solid and inseminate me? Wow. How kind of you!" I get up from the table to storm away, but he grabs my wrist, his palm too firm on my tender skin.

"Valentine, stop," is all he says, standing. "I'm trying to protect you." I turn back to him at these words.

"From what? What exactly do I need to be protected from?" I yell at him and he comes close to me, his eyes so intense, I wonder if he might hit something.

"Look. I'm trying to be honest with you here. I know myself, and I know that I'm not capable of being in a romantic relationship, alright? I'm offering you an alternative, where we'll both be happy. Isn't that good enough? What would you rather have me do? Leave? Do you really want to find out what happens when a marriage fails?" he asks me, practically growling.

I slump in his grasp, suddenly terrified.

It's true. I don't know what happens if you fail the marriage evaluation. I don't know what my future will be like if he isn't in it. I certainly can't picture me being in Pearl Falls, Fantasia Pastures or any of the other family settlements without a husband. I look up at him, angry and helpless all at once.

"I guess I don't have a choice then. Do I?" I ask him and he shakes his head.

"No. You don't. That's the problem with this. All this. You didn't choose me, and you deserve better. I'm going to try to do my best by you, Valentine. I promise. Even if I can't give you love. I think I can give you friendship. After all, we're going to be spending a lot of time together." He sighs, pulling me into his body. It's the first time I feel he's intentionally made contact.

It's only us on the balcony, and as the breeze stirs around us gently, his arms wrap around me. I rest my head against the hard muscle of his chest but as soon as I feel tears begin to sting my eyes, I clench them shut, not wanting to show him how utterly rejected I feel.

"Clark?" I whisper and he replies instantly.

"Yes?"

"Maybe, if we get to know each other first, maybe... love could come later?" I ask him and he steps back, putting a large distance between us.

"I hope for your sake that's not the case," he replies, his eyes stone cold. He walks swiftly from the balcony, leaving me alone with the sound of my own breathing and the glare of the too bright sun.

— ●●● —

I sit, my plate cleared, as I contemplate the predicament I'm in. The sun beats down on the back of my neck as I gaze through the glass half-wall of the balcony. Beyond the limits of the space, palm trees sway in the light breeze and too-bright blue waters shimmer in the distance. The waves kiss flawless expanses of white sand, which from here looks like the talcum powder they show new parents applying to babies' bottoms on the latest Bliss Inc. commercials.

I sigh, finding the too edenic surroundings nothing short of irritating as my supposed happy ending has come crashing down around my ears before shattering into a hundred jagged and cutting edges.

Looking down at my wedding ring, I wonder about Clark. I wonder why he's so afraid to even give romance a real chance. Maybe it's something serious, or maybe it's just fear getting the better of him, but either way, I suppose I'm stuck with him now. I could be a child and cry about it, but instead I wonder if a positive attitude might be a better approach. He had been right when he said we would be spending a lot of time together, so perhaps friendship isn't such a terrible idea. Maybe it could be like what me Egypt and I have.

I sit here and think back now to the boys I'd known as a child. I'd always been afraid to get too close, because I knew I was leaving and would likely never see them again, but maybe now it is time I open the door to that kind of relationship with my husband. Perhaps love is made to seem glamorous and desirable, just like the commercials make everything else about the Jigsaw Project seem. Could it be that love is in fact just as disappointing as everything else when compared to the ideal picture I've been painted? Will friendship be better in the long term? He says he wants to care for me, to give me the life I deserve, so he isn't a bad person. Maybe getting to know him better will shed some light on his problem with romance and how to fix it.

I ask myself all these questions and twist the band on my finger, knowing that I'm done crying. I can't cry over something that never was, because technically I haven't lost anything. Clark is never going to be the perfect man. I am never going to have a happy ending and maybe I'm not what he was expecting either. I realise, as I look down on a world that seems like paradise, that this disappointment is just a result of the story I've been fed since I was fifteen. It's been coming a long time, I have just been too naïve and blinded by the façade to see it. In fact, I'm beginning to wonder whether any man could live up to my expectations.

I stand from my chair, deciding to be pro-active and ask Clark if he'd like to go and take a walk, maybe talk some more. I hope he says yes, because this silence isn't solving anything.

Nine

Clark agrees to the walk, and as we step into the elevator and scan our wrist tattoos before selecting the lobby as our destination, I feel the air turn uncomfortable between us.

"Look, I don't want this to be awkward, Clark," I say, and he growls slightly under his breath, not replying. I feel myself becoming annoyed, so instead focus on the view I'd missed out on last night, when I'd been far too tired to take in much of anything.

As we descend, I look out over the cyclical hollow of *The Oasis* resort. The centre of the resort is filled with fountains, the middle of which holds multiple palm trees. The reception desk is circular, filling most the space, and I watch on as hard-light holograms go about their daily business. I wonder what life here must be like for them, watching newly wed and happy couples when they themselves cannot achieve the same. Now that I think about it, it must be awful.

As I stare around the outer rim of the lobby, I notice that it seems to hold several restaurants as well as what appears to be the entrance to a spa. I cannot help but wonder whether Clark and I will still visit these places, even if we're not attempting a romantic connection.

The doors swish open and we step out into the muggy air of the lobby, looking up I see natural light filtering in from the ceiling which is made entirely of transparent glass. The cylindrical hollow of the hotel's architecture is sliced vertically every ten or so feet, separating its one hundred floors. I take in the overwhelming size of the surroundings as a monorail enters the hotel from a tunnel in its left side, the carriages leading straight out into the lobby where we'd departed last night.

Clark grabs my hand and pulls me forward, I'm dawdling I know, but the man has no right to complain. After all, I could be making a scene, marching up to the front desk and demanding a separate room, if they'd even allow such a thing.

I rush my steps as I sense his impatience growing, the flat sneakers on my feet are comfortable beyond anything I'd owned this last past nine years and I'm grateful after yesterday's wedding shoes.

As we pass through large glass doors, which slide apart effortlessly, the early afternoon heat hits in waves of muggy humidity. The entire island spreads before us, as the hotel is close to the sea and the doors lead us in the opposite direction of the beach. Ahead, thick jungle, the mingled crowing of tropical birds and low hanging, potentially fake, fruit beckons. Once we're out in the open and a reasonable way from the hotel, Clark visibly relaxes and I frown slightly.

"What?" he asks, twisting to look me straight in the face as he notices me staring at him.

"You're odd," I reply, and his lips quirk.

"Thanks."

"What? It's my observation. It's like you ignore me one moment, and then as soon as we're outside you're totally different..." I say and he narrows his eyes.

"You're pretty observant for a woman," he admits, smiling. The expression reaches his eyes this time and I relax as we begin our walk down the perfectly paved path, which twists through the jungle just ahead.

"For a woman?" I query his expression.

"Well yes... I thought you'd be more... I don't know, emotional," he replies.

"Well you're pretty presumptuous for a man," I counter as he brings his hand up to his hair and runs his fingers through it.

"Fair enough. I suppose I should get rid of my expectations, as should you." He lays down his words as though they're law, so I bite back without hesitation.

"Already done. Now, are you going to tell me why you're acting like two totally separate people?" His eyes narrow again as he stares at me, probably contemplating whether to lie.

"Alright."

"That was easy," I say and he laughs.

"I'm not some great mystery, Valentine. I'm really very simple." We continue to walk, our steps falling into relaxed, synchronised time.

"You going to elaborate on that?" I push him for answers.

"I don't like them listening in on our conversations," he admits, eyes scanning the air, and I scowl.

"Who? Strangers?" What an utterly odd thing to be worried about.

"No, Valentine. Bliss Inc." He enlightens me and my eyes widen.

"Oh. You really think they care about what you have to say, huh?" I ask him and he laughs.

"You're naïve if you think otherwise. Why do you think I'm not wearing my wedding band?" He brings up something I'd noticed earlier. I'd thought he wasn't wearing it to try and make it obvious to me that he isn't interested. Apparently, I was wrong.

"I thought it was to hurt me," I admonish, looking into his eyes, which turn surprised. I have to admit, knowing he's not interested in a romantic relationship has taken the pressure off me. I no longer care what he thinks. If he doesn't like me then that's his problem, especially seeing as how he's been so clear about being true to who he is.

"Valentine, I'll never intentionally hurt you. I'm not a bad man. Just because I'm not in love with you doesn't mean I hate you, or even dislike you. I really do think you're sweet." He looks nervous at his own words and I flush in response.

"Well then, why won't you give this a chance?" I can't help myself as the words fall from me, desperately hopeful to the point I feel myself cringe internally.

"Look, I've seen passion, I've seen it and I watched it die. Don't you want something long lasting, something solid? Especially because we're stuck with one another. Love and volatility go hand in hand. I don't want to risk that. It's not worth it." His words send a shock through me.

Is he in love with another woman? I want to ask him but I'm suddenly afraid. If I ask and he says yes, then I'll never be able to even attempt a relationship with him.

"Sorry. You've been clear with what you said and honest. I've just been waiting for nine years for love... it's taking me a little time to adjust my expectations. I'm scared," I admit, taking a steadying breath as we turn the corner and pass the first line of trees in the jungle. The smells of simulated greenery and the sounds of long since extinct birds envelop me, causing me to perspire.

"Don't be scared. I'm your husband. I just don't want to get emotionally caught up with love or sex. I want a friendship... that's all I can handle," he explains, but I frown.

"You say this like it's all something you can control, Clark. I'm not sure that's how it works..." I express and he laughs.

"Bliss Inc. has been creating and controlling our emotional connections via a scientific formula for years... If they can do it, why can't I?" he asks me and I sigh. The conversation is exhausting me; mainly because it's making me question things I've known as fact my entire life.

"I guess... Though if you're not interested in a connection at all, why waste your time with friendship?" I ask him, tired of arguing.

"Please don't think this means I'm not interested in you. I am. I want to be friends more than you know. I want to know you. You seem lovely, wonderful even. I just don't want things to get messy, especially when we're stuck together." Suddenly, I find myself understanding what he means. I know my parents' marriage seems great, but I've heard the muffled angry voices behind closed doors after my sisters both left for Monopolis. I know, somewhere in the back of my mind, behind all of my dreams and fantasies, that marriage is binding, sometimes suffocating. Maybe going slowly and being friends isn't such a bad idea. I mean, it's not like we don't have the rest of our lives for something more. Perhaps, if whatever we're supposed to have, according to the formula, grows from a friendship, we'll be more likely to avoid fighting and emotional hurt in the future. I suppose caution never hurt anybody.

"Okay. I think I understand where you're coming from. What you're suggesting, however unorthodox, is sensible. I get the sense that you've given this a lot of thought and you know yourself better than I do. I guess I'll just have to trust you." In this response, I let go of all expectation, focusing instead on what is, rather than what could have been. There's no use me trying to fit Clark into a mould, it wouldn't be fair to either of us.

"Great! I'm so glad." He turns to me, his face becoming so animated he's almost unrecognisable from the statue I'd first laid eyes on at the end of the aisle.

"Okay. So, can we talk? There are so many questions I want to ask you," I say, feeling excited all of a sudden.

I remind myself quickly not to get too carried away, because if this is going to work, I need to make sure I don't end up falling for someone who can never love me back.

"Ask away," he replies, seeming more at ease than I've seen him so far. He places his hands in his pockets and relaxes into his stance, staring down at me with a small smile.

"Well, what do you like doing in your free time?" I ask him, deciding to start with something simple.

"Sports. I used to run a lot back in Monopolis, I don't like being cooped up, or being in any setting which requires me to dress or act formally. I don't like the fake interaction. If you couldn't tell yesterday." His answer is detailed, he clearly knows himself well, obviously better than I can claim to know myself.

"You did look sort of like you wanted to run away, or hit things... it was kind of hard to tell which." I giggle at him and his expression turns sly.

"Well, at least I didn't fall over." I flush at his response and he laughs, carrying on the conversation as he says, "So what about you? What hobbies do you have?"

"Ice skating, ballet, piano... I enjoy a variety of things really. My childhood was pretty productive." I elaborate and he cocks his head.

"Wow. You sound talented. You'll have to play for me sometime." I blush, immediately feeling my fingers twitch at the thought of tickling ivories again. The jungle hums around us and the genetically modified flowers bloom in perfect synchronisation as we walk past, expelling the latest fragrance from Bliss Inc. called *Ecstasy*.

"Maybe I can teach you," I suggest and he laughs again, the definitive structure of his facial features softening.

"I don't really think I have the soul for music," he admits and I frown,

"Why would you say that? You seem pretty tortured to me." It's supposed to come off funny, but instead his expression drops. My heart falters in its beat, knowing I've said the wrong thing. "I'm sorry... I didn't mean to offend you." I whisper quickly, shrinking back into myself. At seeing my apologetic expression, his becomes confused.

"Do I scare you or something? Every time I pull a face you pull away. It's almost like you're flinching." He asks me, stopping in his step now. I'm surprised at his reaction, wondering if I've done something wrong again.

"I'm sorry I..." I begin but he raises a hand.

"Valentine, you have nothing to be sorry for. Stop apologising. I'm not a monster. I'm not going to hurt you. We only just met, odds are it's going to take some time before we know one another well enough to avoid saying the wrong thing. Please, don't flinch away, it hurts me to see you scared." His gaze is so intense, if I didn't know any better, I'd mistake it for lust mingled with fear. Instead though, because I know he can't stand romance or passion, I guess it just means he cares.

"You just seem so angry," I admit and he sighs, shuffling his feet as his gaze drops to the pretty pebbling of the floor.

"I am. I am angry. But not at you. I'm angry because we've been stuck together and it's not our choice. I'm angry that there are people out there in the labour districts who are in love, deeply and unequivocally, but aren't allowed to lay a finger on one another because they're deemed undesirable by a company and their stupid policies. I don't mean to be harsh, or seem cold, but honestly the entire wedding has just brought up these feelings and I'm having a hard time pushing them back down where they came from." I'm amazed at his openness, at his honesty with me. We barely know one another, and yet he seems to have become a completely open book.

"Why are you telling me all this?" I ask him and he sighs again, taking a step closer and looking into my face.

"Because you're going to be my life from now on, Valentine. How can I keep things from you? Don't you think that will make both of us miserable for a very long time?"

"I suppose," I reply.

"You have a right to know how I feel about the Jigsaw Project, especially because I don't want you to mistake my disdain, for this process, as hatred for you. Yesterday, at the wedding, you were the embodiment of the entire Project walking toward me down that aisle, and I acted wrongly. I was harsh, cold, awful toward you. I realised last night that it's not you I have a problem with. It's this entire system. Okay?" He finishes the rant and I relax. He's exhausting, paranoid and most of all fighting against a system that I don't think he can possibly overcome. He's just one person, and though it's true that the system must seem awful if you're a labourer, we aren't, so what's his problem?

He begins walking again, this time ahead of me, and so I think about everything I know of him so far. Suddenly, it comes to me.

"Your brother... is he in love with someone? In the labour districts?" I ask him and his head turns so swiftly it's a wonder his neck doesn't break.

"How did you know that?" he demands of me, and my forehead creases.

"He mentioned yesterday about not being in the project, so I just wondered... you seem very passionate about the rights of labourers for someone who isn't one." I rationalise my thought process and he looks kind of impressed.

"Yes. He's been in love with the same woman for ten years, a woman who he speaks to via the holo-dash interface where he works. He's in the telecommunications sector you see. Responsible for the soft-light broadcasting and such..." He admonishes, looking around. He really is paranoid.

"If they're listening, why aren't you worried they'll hear you now?" I ask him, wondering if pointing out a flaw in his behaviour will show him how crazy he's acting.

"These trees, they interfere with the monitoring technology. The sound of the leaves makes it hard to pick up noise on the ground. Jason told me, he knows everything about surveillance because the woman he talks to, the one who he loves, works in that department. They're in communication because sometimes the broadcasts he works on use clips from the surveillance cameras." He explains and I nod. He doesn't seem to be lying, so I glance around, wondering if, perhaps, we're being watched right now. At this thought, the hairs on the back of my neck rise. I exhale, vowing to myself that I won't let his paranoid logic get to me.

"Okay. I see. So, where did you learn to cook?" I ask him, changing the subject now. I don't want his theories to take away from me getting to know him.

"Readiness courses. Did you have cooking on your schedule?" He asks me and I shake my head.

"No, I had a lot more physical activities on mine. So, I guess that figures now that I know how much you like to jog," I reply. We turn a corner and Clark slows down again, shortening his steps until I'm by his side once more.

"I'm assuming you like food then?" he asks me and I roll my eyes.

"Well, I think most people like food, Clark, but yes, I am certainly glad that you can cook. I can make ramen, and that's about it. I mean, most of my food came out of the upcycler. I never ordered ingredients to make my own meals. Seemed like too much cred to pay for me to go burning stuff," I reply. He laughs.

"There was this one time, I smoked out my entire apartment trying to roast a chicken for class. I got in so much trouble." His eyes sheen as he recalls the memory and I feel my heart inflate. He looks so much younger right now, more carefree in his rebellion.

"Yeah, I'm not that brave. I've been living off ramen and take-out where I could afford it since I left Pearl Falls," I admit, placing one foot in front of the other slowly and glad now we're taking getting to know one another at the same pace.

"Was your mom a good cook?" He asks me and I snort.

"Not likely. She was too busy being wonder-wife to mess around with that. My dad did all the cooking," I recall and he nods.

"So, if you lived off take-out, you must have had quite a bit of credit. How did you manage that? I was barely scraping by," He admonishes and I wonder why. He had been in the project longer than me, so how come he hadn't been able to save like I had?

"I just did a lot of modules on the readiness syllabus. I was there long after my friends all left, so I didn't really have anyone to go out spending with," I reply and he nods again, taking in my answer before launching into his next statement.

"Your mom, she seems like a... difficult person to get along with." He looks nervous, like I might be mad at the accuracy of his assessment.

"You think?" I cock an eyebrow with a smirk and he snorts.

"Yeah. It just seems like nothing you do is ever good enough for her, am I right?" he queries.

"Exactly. That's why I got so good at so many things when I was younger. I always wanted her approval. It's sort of why I've been dying to get married. I wanted someone to love me for me. Not some ideal version of myself I can never live up to," I admit, realising something that makes me feel a little sick as I continue. "Actually, now I think about it, she's probably part of the reason I had unrealistic expectations about you. I thought I'd lay eyes on you and be instantly happy forever. I guess that's sort of silly..." I admit and he looks kindly at me now, as if he's swept up in what I'm saying.

"Valentine, you've been fed lies about what marriage is truly like for years. Most women have. It's not as bad for men, I mean, we have more channels than just *The wedding channel* to tune into. Jason says they allow us to watch the labourers fighting in boxing matches to help curb aggression. It's brutal, but at least it's not something completely fabricated. At least it's real." He explains this and I nod.

"My expectations have left me feeling disappointed. Not in you. Just in the fact they painted me a faux paradise, instead of showing me something that's real. I mean, is true love at first sight even possible? Even if you have a formula, how do they measure it?"

"I don't know. It's top secret isn't it? Must be pretty damn complicated, and even then, they say it's only ninety-nine percent effective," he replies. I blink up at him, feeling hopeless now that he's shattered the illusion I have been living under for so long.

"I wish it were true. I feel so lonely, Clark. I thought it was because I was waiting for you, but now I'm not so sure," I admit, feeling vulnerable as I utter these words. I don't want him to think I'm asking for love, or desperate. I'm not. I just want to feel like someone else on this planet other than Egypt looks at me and sees *me,* not some stupid standard they think I need to live up to.

Clark looks at me with empathy. At first I mistake the stare for pity, but then I realise there's understanding for what I've been through mixed in with it too.

"I can't give you love, Valentine, but companionship I can give. I don't want you to feel lonely anymore." He smiles at me and I return it, knowing that we have more in common than I first thought. He might hate Bliss Inc., he might hate that we're married, but I'm certain we have at least one thing on which we agree. We are two people who have fallen victim to a beautiful lie.

Ten

After walking and talking for what seems like only an hour at most, we return to our honeymoon suite, finally exiting the muggy heat of the jungle only to find that the sun is beginning to set. Scanning our tattoos together, he catches my eye as I glimpse him examining my face.

"What? Is it that obvious I'm sweating like a pig?" I say, patting the damp slickness of my skin.

"No, you look fine. I'm sweating too. It's so hot here!" is his only reply, as the door slides sideways. We walk across the threshold and into the bedroom before I continue through to the living room for the first time since we arrived. The space is open and beige, with tall glass windows without blinds or curtains. They give an uninterrupted view of the water and the sunset, which, by all standards, is glorious. I move past the arrangement of long, lilac, smart-foam sofas and over to the window, where I place my hand on the flawless cool of the glass before staring out over the bay below.

"It's quite something, right? You'd never see something like that in the city. Even if it did wake me up at 6am." Clark complains and I turn to him.

"You know, you didn't have to sleep in here," I remind him and his eyes narrow, their sapphire blues coming alive in the fiery light of the sunset behind me.

"Oh, but I did. Don't want you getting any ideas." He comes across as cocky now as he purses his lips, and I can tell he's really starting to relax.

"You mean because you're oh-so-attractive? Give me a break. I was more likely to give it up to my friend Egypt than I am to you, and we shared a bed all the time," I explain and his eyes widen. He places his fingers to his lips and walks across the room, grabbing my elbow.

"Be careful with whom you share that little bit of information, Valentine," he whispers, a glossy black strand of his hair falling across his eyes.

"All I'm trying to say is that you can share the bed with me if you want. I don't have a problem with that. We'll both be clothed." I shrug and he looks into my face, his mouth slack with surprise.

"That's uh, very generous of you, but I think I'll stick to the sofa," he replies. I turn back to the sunset, no longer content with looking at him in his intensity.

"Suit yourself."

"I always do," He informs me with a slight chuckle. It's true, he's not exactly the most selfless individual I've ever met, or from what I know of him so far, anyway. For all I know he's just placating me so I don't go running to Bliss Inc.

"So what about dinner? What do you want to do? I can cook..." He begins to offer, but instead I interrupt him, deciding to do something for myself. Something that I want.

"I actually want to go out. We're not here that long and I'd like to make the most of it. The food at these places is supposed to be amazing. Plus, there's dancing and stuff too..." He looks surprised at my forwardness, though I don't know why he should. He's the one who told me not to hold back, or to be scared to say what's on my mind.

"You want me to take you dancing?" he asks me and I nod.

"Yeah, I enjoyed our dance at the wedding," I admit and he laughs.

"You didn't act like it. You acted like my suit was on fire with the distance you tried to put between us." Placing his hands in his pockets, he stands, stiff in posture, gauging my reaction.

"Well, so maybe then you owe me another, when you're not being a complete ass," I jest and he gets a slightly scared look.

"You want to dance, as friends?" he asks me, making sure the lines of propriety are correctly and unmistakably drawn.

"Of course, Clark. What else would we be? It's not like we're married or anything... Oh wait." I smirk and he rolls his eyes as a look of reluctance overtakes his face.

"Fine. Dinner and dancing it is."

I dress in the bedroom while Clark changes in the bathroom, the door separating us as we become vulnerable, shedding our clothes. I pull a black dress over my head, admiring the dark sparkling beadwork. It's a V-neck and has a billowing skirt. It's the most decadent thing I've ever worn except my wedding dress, and as it falls past the lace of my black bra and panties, I feel relief flood me.

As I tie the ribbon that runs around my waist at the back, I step into a pair of black heels. I don't know why I'm going to so much effort, but it's probably because I don't want to appear slobbish in front of the other guests. It's one thing that I don't care what Clark thinks, but I do care that we look as if we're any other couple. The door opens as I step into my second shoe and Clark is revealed. I'm surprised. He's made a real effort too. His black hair is slicked back against his head and his stubble has been clean shaved. He also smells like cologne, which fills my nostrils as my eyes widen.

"Well, look at you all fancy," I exclaim as his eyes lay on me and his lips curve unwillingly into a smile.

"I could say the same. You've gone to a lot of effort." He accuses me and I snort, looking him up and down and taking in his black shirt, which is tucked into dark coloured jeans.

"Don't flatter yourself. You have too." I flutter my lashes, which I have just lacquered with mascara.

"It's a show, Valentine, just like it will be when we have our first sexology and couples therapy sessions this coming weekend." He reminds me of the assessments. Of the things we have to overcome, of the people we will have to lie to in order to get this to work. The bigger question is, do I want to lie? What If I tell them the truth and they pair me with someone else? What if they're totally understanding and I'm happier out of this? Or

159

what if they don't and I end up working in an industrial sweatshop?

Oh bliss.

"You're right. We have to be believable." I nod, wondering why it is I'm agreeing to go along with this, but knowing my only real choice is to secretly hope everything will work out for the best.

As I stand here, my legs elongated in black stilettos, I wonder why I think this after everything I have always thought to be true has spectacularly fallen to pieces.

Or maybe it hasn't. Could it be that the formula just didn't work on Clark and me?

I step past Clark and into the bathroom, moving to spray on some of the perfume that sits in a glass bottle on the counter top.

"Don't..." Clark says before he can stop himself.

"Excuse me?" I say to him and he looks guilty, or angry, or maybe both.

"Uh... I just don't think you need it. You smell nice anyway," he admits and I scowl as he moves to turn away from me in a hurry.

"You've been smelling me? How friend-ish is that, Clark?" I ask him, incredulous.

"Sorry." The word falls from him as he walks from the doorway and I look down at the bottle in my hand. After a moment, I put it back against my better judgement and sigh, feeling my heart flutter a smidgeon.

I walk out of the bathroom and Clark's eyes sweep over my body as I meet him and take his hand in mine. His ring has been placed on his finger once more and I feel it, cold against the skin of my palm. He looks down at my grip on him, and I can swear he goes to complain before sighing and smiling instead.

"Come on then, let's go."

Down in the lobby, we walk across the geometric palm trees of the downtrodden carpet. Moving past the reflective mirror surface of the spa front, I catch my reflection, hand in hand with his. I could swear we actually look like a couple, but then I remember that I know better.

"So, what first, dinner or dancing?" he asks me, looking eager to get into one of the in-resort facilities. He always looks so uncomfortable in this lobby, and I wonder if his paranoia finds disdain in the watching eyes of the many hard-light receptionists. I don't suppose I can exactly blame him for this though; they truly are extremely unnerving.

"Dancing! I don't want to dance on a full stomach, and I plan on eating... A LOT," I explain and he smiles, his eyes reflecting a reluctant fondness.

"Good idea." He looks around, choosing a venue promptly called *Stars in your eyes.*

We scan our tattoos, and as we walk in through the double glass doors, which open silently, I'm hit by a sudden and gorgeous sound, as unpredictable as it is moving.

"Jazz," Clark announces, watching my reaction as a smile breaks out across my lips.

"I've never heard music like this before," I reveal and he shakes his head.

"You wouldn't have. It's considered too promiscuous for Monopolis. I haven't heard it since I was a child." He spills this piece of information and I find myself suddenly curious about his childhood. I am about to open my mouth to ask him something about his mother or father, but then another song starts, and I find my voice lost against the jibber jabber of various instruments.

We walk into the main space of the venue after travelling the length of the entrance hall and Clark's face transforms so he is beaming too. The pallor of the skin surrounding his lips, which has been shaved bare of stubble, makes his smile appear even larger than usual.

"Wow." I exhale as I take in the scene before me.

Couples move around the holographic dance floor as a hard-light band plays up on the stage. They too consist of hard-light which is projected from the floor beneath, but they once again look scarily indistinguishable from real people, making me double take when I glimpse them from the corner of my eye for the first time. They hold instruments made of light, which I don't recognise, and the music is so loud I can feel the beat of the song in the balls of my feet, which I suppose I should be grateful for as it might help me dance better.

"You ready?" I ask him and he looks to me as though I'm challenging him.

"After you." He gestures for me to go ahead and so I skip forward on the balls of my feet, brushing past two dancing couples, whilst gazing down at the floor beneath me, entranced if not slightly disoriented.

Where the holographic dance floor hadn't appeared to look like anything other than blue light from the edge, now that I stand upon it, it looks completely different. Stars and galaxies swirl beneath my feet, glimmering in a mind-blowing macrocosm of space.

"Whoa, this floor is trippy," I hear Clark say as he reaches me, placing his arms around my waist. He pulls my body close to him and I inhale the heady scent of his cologne, still looking down and unable to believe the way in which the pattern can make me feel like I'm walking atop a whole universe.

"This is amazing," I whisper to him as I pull him into me. It's weird, his hands are on my waist and yet I don't mind. His proximity doesn't bother me... in fact it makes me feel wanted. Is this what friendship with him could be like? This kind of closeness? Or was this just an act to keep me happy and everyone else convinced that he's in this marriage for love?

The music flows on, and he twirls me out from him. I catch his gaze as I spin, he's watching me like a hawk, so I let go of his hand and twist my hips, going solo on some dance moves as one of the instruments follows in a solo of its own.

I raise my hands above me, throwing my head back and letting the long tresses of my blonde hair fall down my spine. The music washes over me and for the first time since the wedding, I let go, smiling and enjoying myself. Clark watches me with a tiny smile; his eyes flickering back the light of a thousand stars upon me. This part of the honeymoon, at least, can meet my expectations, so I let it.

We've been dancing for so long I've lost track of the minutes, maybe even hours. I let myself move in his arms, getting close to his body and allowing the melody to set me free from the anxieties of the last few days. The songs slow as the night draws on, and I end up with my head on Clark's shoulder as we sway.

I feel myself slipping into something dangerous with this man. Not love, but fondness, and most certainly a place where the boundaries he'd set so easily this morning are beginning to look blurred. I know I don't want to leave this place, but I need to, or I'm going to end up hurt.

"I'm hungry," I announce, raising my voice over the music and looking up to him as I take a step back. He looks bereft as I leave his arms, but shakes it off, quickly straightening and nodding. He offers me a stiff arm which I take, more sure than ever that this is an act.

I've never met someone so capable of flicking a switch and altering his demeanour without thought. It's almost like his emotions aren't real, or if they are, they don't go deep enough to make a difference to who he really is.

He's so confusing, but as we walk from the dance floor and back out into the lobby, I remember that I've only known him a day. Even if it feels like much longer. I can see now why the honeymoon is so important. Everything is condensed here. Where living a normal life whilst getting to know one another would allow you to break things up, here we're trapped in a suite, on an island, with no distractions.

Clark coughs as we walk up to a restaurant front with *Fusion Fix* hanging in neon hard-light over the door.

"How about here?" Clark asks me and I nod. I don't even know what any of the restaurants serve, let alone what *Fusion* is.

"Sure."

We scan our tattoos once more and the door slides open before we walk inside, where immediately a hard-light hologram escorts us to a table in the corner of the restaurant. The entire place is coated in neon peach light, which gives the space a warm feel, and I bask in it as I smooth down my skirts and sit.

The menu is on the hard-light holo-dash as usual, but I see here that we order via the menu and not via a service synth. Now that I think about it, I haven't seen a single synth since we arrived here.

"I'd just like to say, you look beautiful," Clark compliments me as he examines the restaurant's selection, which I can see is vast. I'm taken aback at the statement, even if he said it without making eye contact.

"You know, that's not very friend-ish either," I express and he rolls his eyes.

"It's an observation, Valentine. A blind man could see it. I don't have to be in love with you to tell you what's true." I roll my eyes at this. He's far too slick with his words.

"Right..." I reply with a sly glance at him. He doesn't look up at me, merely continues to consider his menu. "Hey, I have a question for you..." I begin, remembering how curious I'd been about his family earlier.

"What?" He asks me, this time raising his eyes to mine.

"Well, I wanted to ask you about your family. I know you have a brother, but what about your parents? What are they like?" I ask him, leaning forward on my elbows.

His expression turns immediately sullen and reserved.

"I don't want to talk about my family right now. Not here," he expresses and I frown.

"What do you mean? Is there something wrong?" I ask him, looking around for any cameras or surveillance that could be bothering him, and he scowls, the features of his face becoming more acute as his discomfort grows.

"I just... I don't want to talk about it," he says, sighing heavily. I shuffle in my seat, crossing my ankles and feeling a panic growing in my chest. I press him for an answer.

"Why not?" I ask.

"Dammit, Valentine, just drop it!" he bursts, yelling at me as he slams down his fist on the table and rises to his feet with a jerk. The hard-light of the holo-dash flickers and his eyes flash dangerously cold.

I flinch back and he scrunches up his expression, as though he's in pain. I wonder if he hurt his hand. "I'm not hungry. You eat. I'll see you later," he growls, storming out of the restaurant before I can even turn to say something that might stop him.

I sit back, my plate cleared. It seems to be becoming a pattern. Clark and I have an argument, and then I end up eating my feelings. Oh well, at least the food is excellent.

"All done, Mrs Cavanaugh?" the hard-light hologram asks me, it's ghostly eyes looking right through me as he speaks.

"Yes, thank you," I reply, getting to my feet and watching as my plate is cleared away. My new title makes me feel uneasy and

166

restless, so I decide to venture outdoors, as the heat of the restaurant becomes stifling.

As I emerge back through the sliding glass doors of *Fusion Fix*, I walk past the crowds of couples, who are now heading back to their rooms. It's getting late, and they no doubt want to be alone.

It makes me almost laugh, the last thing I feel like I want is to be alone with my husband, and so I envy them as I quicken my step, feeling the need to flee this place.

I exit the resort at the opposite end than I had earlier, when I'd been with Clark, and let myself be swept up in the scent of salt air as it hits my skin.

The Oasis leads out, on this side, to the beach and so I take off my shoes, breaking into an almost jog along more pretty, pebbled pathway and hurry through the dark shadows of the night.

When I reach the beach, I see that several couples remain along its sandy expanse, holding hands and walking leisurely, too busy being lost in one another's eyes to notice me.

I've never been on a beach before, and so find myself feeling like I'm in a layout of Bliss Magazine, as I let the sand cling to my feet. I hear the rush of salt water and look out over the sea. I've seen it from the distance, but now I'm close, the water beckons. I look back over my shoulder, to the resort, as my eyes glide up to the top floor. Somewhere up there, Clark is taking advantage of being alone, so why shouldn't I?

Feeling suddenly angry, I whip my dress over my head, leaving it in the sand. I take off my underwear; sure that this is completely not allowed but not giving a crap. Bliss Inc. has robbed me of my happiness by using some stupid formula to pair me with the most infuriating man on the planet. So, I don't really care much for their rules right now.

Nude, I let the warm air of the night caress my skin, like the fingertips I had so longed to feel from my new husband, it runs across my flesh, leaving me with goosebumps. I'm so damn frustrated and as I run into the sea's crashing waves, the water the temperature of a lukewarm bath, I feel myself simmering.

I didn't ask for Clark. I didn't ask for any of this, and so far, it seems like I would have been better off staying single with Egypt for company. At least she didn't make me crazy, at least she didn't snap like a bear trap with no warning.

I swim out into the sea, recalling my readiness course on swimming, and let the unpredictable currents beat against me as my rage builds. I slash my arms against the water, enjoying the bite of the surface tension. I still, coming up for air before finding myself transfixed by the moon above. It's huge and kisses the horizon, and suddenly under its muted exposure I feel myself crashing like a wave as my emotion mounts and tears begin trickling down my cheeks.

"Why me?" I whisper, wondering why I've been stuck with this man. I should have known something was wrong, when it took so long for us to pass our readiness tests. I just wanted to be loved. I've paid my dues. I lived in a wasteland of loneliness for so long, and now Clark says he can't give me anything I want.

I thought I was okay with Clark's proposition, but how can we be friends, when he's so closed off? How can we make one another happy when I don't know who I am? How can he possibly make me happy when he has no desire to share who he is?

I feel my heart breaking right here under the full moon.

As the night wears on, I return to the shore, dripping wet, cold and sober.

———————●●●●———————

I let myself into our suite, dripping onto the carpet and sure I'm going to catch my death under the strong air-cooling of the corridor. I walk across the threshold only to find Clark sitting on the bed. His eyes are watching me expectantly as I enter the room; clearly, he's been waiting for me.

"Valentine... I... Wait, why are you all wet?" he asks me as I slip my shoes off and walk straight past him.

"I went for a swim," I reply, curt and irritated in my tone.

"Without me?" His forehead creases and his eyes look sad.

"Well yes, Clark. What did you expect me to do? Sit in a restaurant and cry over you?" I snap, whipping my dress over my head. After my swim, I'm numb, and I don't give a crap if he sees me naked or not.

"No I..." His eyes glide over my body, which is clad in the black lace bra and panties. "Do you have to strip in the middle of a conversation?" he accuses me and I roll my eyes as I turn away from him.

"Clark, I get it. You don't want to be in a relationship, but you're stuck. Still, I'm not going to get changed in the bathroom for the next sixty years because you're a prude, so get used to it." I practically snarl and his expression turns surprised.

"Fine," he barks, whipping his t-shirt off over his head and standing in one fluid motion. "If we're going there. Let's fucking go there." He stands in the middle of the room, his chest bare, gazing into my eyes with intensity as they widen. He's absolutely stacked with muscle.

Lucky me. I think. *Only I could get paired with someone who I actually find hot as hell, but is a complete asshole. What is this? A sick joke?*

I inhale deeply before exhaling again and running my fingers through my wet and knotty hair.

"I'm taking a shower," I bite, before spinning on my heel. As I turn, I swear I can hear Clark sniggering under his breath. "What?" I bark at him, turning back to look over one shoulder as I feel my temper flare.

"Oh, nothing, Valentine." He turns, walking across the suite and leaving his t-shirt behind on the bed.

He glances back over one shoulder a few moments later, mimicking my motions and looking me up and down as I catch the cocky swagger in his stride and the wicked gleam in his eye.

Eleven

Standing in the shower, I find myself slick and foamy with the scent of citrus. I can't bear the thought of relaxing right now. Not when Clark is making me want to hit something, preferably him, extremely hard.

I think now of his chest, of the thick muscles that bind his heart beneath the spattering of dark hair, on the tight and taut masculine edge of his structure.

Ugh.

Why can't he be ugly? Wouldn't this be so much easier that way? Then I could pretend I wasn't even slightly interested. Unfortunately for me, I suck at lying, so I can only hope my acting skills are sufficient and that they prevent him from ever noticing I actually think he's gorgeous. I know, I'd been horrified when I'd first laid eyes on him, but just like when I'd first opened the ring box, it seems I have no idea what I want.

I step out into the bathroom and dry myself in a heated towel from the upcycler. I'm vigorous with the towelling, getting out some of my frustration as I dry my skin so hard it flushes bright red. I let out a sigh, picking up my underwear off the floor and flinging it into the upcycler, before requesting some pyjamas from the catalogue and standing impatiently as they arrive.

Once they do, I put on the black silk shorts and a button up shirt. I'm enjoying wearing all this black I must admit, especially since for the last nine years I've been stuck in white. Black fits my mood, the despair and the rage I'm feeling. White, which all pre-nuptial women wore, now reeks of dreams that will soon shatter into a million pieces along with their virginity. I think about that now. It's only my second night with Clark, but I wonder how long I'll be a virgin.

Years?

Probably.

I shake my head, exiting the bathroom and climbing into bed alone. As I do, Clark enters from the living room, once again fully clothed, and looks at me with a soft expression.

"What do you want?" I demand, wondering if he's decided to take me up on my offer to share a bed. I hope not. I don't want to be sleeping next to someone who clearly wants nothing to do with me. It just seems... wrong.

"I just, I wanted to apologise about dinner," he explains and I cock an eyebrow.

"You're apologising an awful lot considering we've only been married like a day. Have you thought about just not being an asshole?" I ask him, deadly serious. He looks suddenly ashamed of himself as he moves over to sit on the edge of the bed.

"You're right. But let me explain. My family, they're a touchy subject for me. I don't like talking about them, and certainly not in public." He explains himself with what he clearly considers a satisfying response, whereas I merely find it cause for further confusion.

"That's not an explanation, Clark. I got that part already from the screaming and storming off." I reply, not letting up.

"Okay, well I'll keep things to the point then. My parents died when I was a child, Valentine. I don't like talking about them. My brother and I worked hard to let go of the past, and bringing it up just isn't good for me." He relinquishes the truth and suddenly I feel awful. He looks like a lost little boy, and I want to hold him, tell him it'll be alright. I reach out a hand and place it atop his.

"I... I'm sorry," is all I can say. He shrugs me away.

"You don't need to be. You didn't know. I shouldn't have stormed off though. You're curious about me and you have every right to be. Just don't ask me about my childhood, please." He's so rational now, it's almost like he's devoid of emotion about the entire subject.

"Can I ask you something?" I request and he smiles.

"Of course you can," he says this like the last twenty-four hours haven't happened. It's obvious that he doesn't understand how scared I feel about pissing him off.

"Well, you're so logical. You just... you brush these emotions away like they're nothing. Why? Why do you do that?" I ask him this and he cocks his head.

"I'll be honest, emotion is just messy, Valentine. It's why I don't want to get involved with you, in spite of myself." He says these last four words and I feel my heart rate quicken.

"What do you mean?" I ask him, leaning back into the smart foam pillows. He cringes.

"Nothing, I just. I like you. It's hard... to always be... clear cut."
He looks like he might throw up, as though feelings are a disease
and it's catching.

"Could have fooled me." I shake my head and he shrugs.

"I'm trying my best, but I am sorry about the restaurant. I had
a nice night with you. Dancing was... well, I enjoyed it." He rises
from the bed and I go to say something, but I can't quite bring
myself to spill the words. Instead I exhale.

"Clark..." I speak, watching as he turns, his expression
hopeful. I smile, realising it is his reaction I want to see, not a
question I need answering at all.

"Yes?" He asks me, taking a step forward without thought, as
though my stare is having a gravity-like effect.

"Goodnight." I yawn, snuggling down into the cream silk of
the sheets.

"Goodnight, Valentine. Sweet dreams," he whispers back
and, with that, he separates us with a wall.

I wake to the smell of food.

Sitting upright, I get out of bed, my stomach rumbling and
overtaking my foggy, sleep-saturated mental state. I tread across
the carpet and over to the door, which separates my half of the
suite from Clark's, knocking on the wood three times before I
hear him call through.

"Come in."

With this, I turn the golden handle of the door and enter the living space, which envelopes me with the smell of frying meat and batter.

"You're cooking me breakfast again?" I ask him, as he looks to me from the stove.

"Yes, I saw how you enjoyed yesterday's. I thought we could go out and have some fun today, so you'll need your energy." He gives me a mischievous grin and serves up the food he's cooking onto a plate. I take a seat, moving past the lilac sofas and toward a pristine white and gold kitchen island. It reminds me of the one in my old apartment and suddenly I'm nostalgic.

"This looks great. Thank you." I pull the plate toward me, losing no time in skewering a rasher of bacon and placing it in my mouth as the salty juices run rampant across my taste buds.

"So, what do you want to do today?" I ask him as he relaxes against the edge of the kitchen surface next to the hob. He's visibly far more relaxed than yesterday for sure.

"Well, I thought we could go to that amusement park." He suggests this and immediately I'm excited.

"Oh my bliss, you mean Enamoury Park?" His mouth twists into a smile at my excitement and he nods his head.

"Yeah, that's the one. I'm quite the adrenaline junkie, so I thought it could be fun." He reveals this small piece of information and I realise that getting to know each other doesn't have to be an interrogation with bright lights from which neither of us can hide, it could be, as he suggests, fun.

"Yeah, I'd like that. I think fun is exactly what we need. Things have been so..." I begin, but he finishes my sentence.

"Intense?" he asks, crossing his arms, and I nod.

"Exactly," I reply, chewing more bacon and beginning on a pancake. This morning they are blueberry. "I'm sorry too. About yesterday... I did push you. It's just hard to forget we barely know each other. We've been through so much change in such a short time. I'm kind of panicking about everything. Plus, we're in this suite and can't escape each other. It's like... there's so much pressure," I admit, realising that I was perhaps the one being pushy yesterday. It hasn't occurred to me that Clark could have issues surrounding him that are sensitive, because it wasn't until two days ago that he had popped out of my fantasy bubble and turned into a real person.

"It's alright. I appreciate your apology, but there's really no need. I just think we both need a little breathing space, some relaxed time with one another. We've barely been out of the resort since we arrived," he reminds me and I nod. I'd enjoyed last night, but it wasn't friend-like at all. It had felt like a date and the pressure to avoid feeling something was most definitely there. Maybe that's why I'd felt the sting of his rejection so strongly. Am I confusing his friendliness for attraction, and it's screwing with my head because we're surrounded by so many other people who are utterly infatuated?

After I've finished my breakfast, Clark clears my plate away. I get down from the stool on which I'm sat, turning to him.

"Okay, so I'll get changed and then we'll go?" I ask him and he acknowledges me with an eager nod. Suddenly, I notice he's in the same clothes he was wearing yesterday. "Clark, why are you still wearing that?" I ask him. He looks down at himself and shrugs.

"I, uh, didn't want to disturb you." He looks shy, an unusual expression for him.

"But you changed before... from your tux..." I remind him and he looks embarrassed.

"I crawled across the bedroom floor that morning to the bathroom, not that there was any need. You were comatose," he explains this and I giggle. What am I going to do with him? He's hopeless.

"Oh my bliss, that's crazy. Don't worry about waking me up, like, you must have a bladder of steel if that's the only bathroom. You've barely used it at all!" I exclaim in surprise and he nods.

"Yeah, I haven't had a proper drink since we got here. Soon you'll come in here and find me as a raisin," he jokes and this time I do laugh, almost crying at the image in my head.

"For future reference, please use the bathroom whenever you like." I curtsey slightly, as though giving my official blessing.

"Why thank you, wifey. How kind," he snorts and I laugh.

"Come on, you must need a shower. You slept in those clothes," I remind him and he pushes his lips together so hard they go white.

"Alright, you talked me into it. But I don't want to hear complaints about me leaving the seat up." He passes me in the doorway and I exhale, feeling as if overnight he has once more transformed from opaque to transparent.

After I've pivoted in the doorway, I walk across the bedroom and into the bathroom, ordering some clothes from the upcycler catalogue quickly. Clark enters behind me, shutting the door and turning on the shower. As I turn, I catch him beginning to take his trousers off.

"Clark!" I exclaim, squeezing my eyes shut.

"What? Weren't you the one complaining about not being prudish, and then saying I can use the bathroom this morning?" he protests, his laugh throaty as it reverberates against the tiles on the walls.

"Yes, but I don't want to see your... thingy. I've never even seen one!" I explain and he chuckles again.

"Valentine, I'm wearing underwear," he explains and I feel his arms on my elbows as my eyes open.

"Oh," I exhale, half relieved, half disappointed. I look him up and down as he's standing right in front of me. He's wearing black, tight fitting shorts and once again there's his well-muscled chest and body. I sigh.

"What?" he asks me, his eyes sparkling down on me in shimmer sapphire.

"I just... I don't know. You're not exactly hideous, are you? I'm not like... ahhh it burns my eyes." I don't know what I'm doing, but as the upcycler beeps to signal my clothing is ready, I'm glad of the distraction.

"Well you did close them at the thought of my... what did you call it, oh yes, *thingy*." He mocks me and I flush bright red.

"You think you're so damn funny, Clark Cavanaugh, but with all this *thingy* talk a girl could mistake you for having feelings. You need to be careful. Because I'm not talking about friend-ish feelings either," I snipe, grumpy. I'm like a dehydrated man looking at an Oasis, only to realise it's a mirage and not for the taking.

"Oh, don't worry, Valentine. I'm very aware of how this looks. I just... I can't help myself with you." Now it's his turn to flush. My heart rate picks up and I start to get excited. Then, I realise what's happening only too soon.

I have to shut this down.

"Well, try. Please. I can't be having this getting all confusing," I announce, turning and taking my clothes out of the upcycler.

"Alright. My apologies. I'll just uh, wait until you're done to get in the shower." He looks down at his naked feet and then leans against the shower door, which begins to fog as the hot water starts to evaporate, making the room as muggy as it is outside. I brush through my hair and move to put on perfume, but then stop, placing the bottle back again. I order a toothpaste pill from the upcycler, and begin chewing it as I exit the clammy clutch of the space. I close the door behind me, shutting the steamy atmosphere, Clark, and his *thingy* inside.

Enamoury Park is only a short walk from the resort, so Clark and I make the journey in casual time, taking lazy steps and letting other couples pass us by on the walkalator.

"Hey, can I ask you something?" I suddenly feel the urge to query him as I catch the cold blue of my engagement ring, flashing in the sunlight.

"Yeah, what's up?" he asks me, now in a dark blue t-shirt and eye-wateringly bright shorts.

"Well, my engagement ring, it's so unusual. What made you decide to choose a blue diamond?" I ask him, and he smiles, knowing the answer immediately.

"When I was a child, my mother used to tell me that my eyes were my most precious asset, because they're so unusual. A recessive allele she said. So, I guess I had her in mind when I was looking at all the precious stones." His explanation is sweet, short and personal. He'd told me not to ask any questions about his family, but he's bringing it up now, like he's a totally different person once again.

"Oh. That's really nice, Clark," I relinquish, proud to be wearing the ring on my finger now.

"Thanks. Besides, I didn't want you to have some boring ring like everyone else's," he admits.

"I'm surprised you put so much thought into it. I mean, you hate the project." I remind him and he smiles with an awkward laugh.

"Yes. I know. But I didn't want you get short changed. It's bad enough you got stuck with me for a husband." He shrugs, his eyes glittering with a pained sheen in the mid-morning glare of the sun.

"You're not so bad," I admit, feeling worried he'll see right through me. See that I'm beginning to like him more than I should.

"I'll admit, because I'm trying to be honest here, that maybe I jumped the gun about this whole marriage thing." My head snaps sideways and my eyes widen. What's he saying?

"What does that mean?" I ask, desperation so evident in his stare.

"Nothing really..." he begins and I scowl. Why is so withholding? And why is it that he gives information freely with one hand and then becomes secretive with the other. I'm so confused, and once again, I'm left feeling like I've got whiplash. I straighten my spine, not wanting him to flip out like he had at dinner, but knowing that I need to know what it is that he's talking about. If I don't, the curiosity might just kill me.

"Clark, please tell me what you mean. I feel so... up and down about all this. It's confusing the heck out of me," I explain and he sighs, yielding to my request with a reluctant but small smile.

"Nothing, I mean, I guess part of my objection to us having a romantic relationship is wanting to stick it to Bliss Inc. Show them that they can't really control my feelings. I control my own, you know?" He says this to me and I blink. Does this mean he's having feelings in spite of himself? That even though he's trying his hardest to keep things platonic that he's failing. My heart flutters and my hopes rise.

He catches it on my face and speaks quickly. "That's not the only reason I don't want us getting involved though, Valentine. So, don't think that this changes anything." My hopes are dashed before I've had a chance to process them. So I drop my gaze, heart sinking. Why do I care so much? I barely know this man. Why do I all of a sudden feel like I want to cry?

"Come on, we better get moving. If we get there too late, the lines will be long." I change the subject, deciding that the best way to get through the emotional minefield of my marriage will be to deny any and all emotional attachment to Clark. After all, he doesn't want to get hurt, and neither do I. So then, I wonder, why does it seem so fake to act like I don't care?

As I'm pondering this, the outline of Enamoury Park comes over the horizon and I inhale, excitement flooding me again. I look at the roller coasters, realising that if I'd been scared of them before, that now, by comparison to my marriage, they're really nothing to fear.

———————●❍●————————

The walkalator carries us all the way from the resort to the front of Enamoury Park, the entrance of which is signposted with giant, neon lime, hard-light lettering, hovering in a graceful arc overhead. Clark is leaning against the railing of the long stretch of moving conveyer belt, carrying us toward the park.

"So, what do you want to go on first?" he asks me, trying to catalyse a conversation. It's been kind of awkward since he admitted he's treating me like some sort of problem just to rebel against a company, but I guess that's to be expected.

"I'm not sure, I heard they have one of those VR coasters though, so that could be fun?" I suggest and he smiles with a slightly awkward expression, looking up to the skyline, which is made up of twisting hard-light vines and dancing neon lights. I can hear screams beginning to penetrate the muggy air as a ride car moves seamlessly over the light of the tracks, twirling and whirling in a physical assault on the fragile human bodies inside.

"Yeah, I heard one of them makes you feel like you're flying through space." His eyes light up slightly, making him look young, and I sigh. Why is he so damn attractive? Why can't I just stop engaging with him in this dance of to and fro?

I watch him as he examines me, before I realise he's waiting for me to continue to conversation.

"Valentine, are you alright?" he asks me as we begin to creep closer to the walkalator's termination point.

"Yeah, I'm fine," I reply, not wanting to give him any reason to get mad. He straightens, readying to step off the moving white rubber of the conveyer beneath our feet. We depart, stepping down onto flawless white ceramic looking tiles. As my foot makes contact with the surface, light ripples out from my footprint, causing a firework type effect.

"Huh. That's cool," I hear Clark note as we walk forward toward the arch of the letters marking up the entrance. Turnstiles separate us from the inside of the park, and so I swipe my tattoo over the metal panel of the machine before the glass barriers slide away, letting me loose on the technological paradise.

Clark is granted access after me and he taps me on the shoulder as I gaze up at the colossal tangle of track and décor that makes up the park.

"Where to first?" he asks me and I shrug, suddenly not so much in the mood for this place. It's too blatant, too obviously full of happiness, that I'm afraid to give into the pleasure I should be experiencing. I don't want to let myself enjoy it, in case Clark sets off another emotional landmine.

"Let's go to the virtual reality coaster first," I decide, watching as a ride car swoops around a corkscrew, leaving nothing but a trail of screams behind in the heat of the morning. "Is there a map?" I ask him and suddenly the paving stone I'm standing on comes to life, projecting a soft light map from its surface in front of me like a pop-up table.

"Well, that's convenient." Clark replies, standing close to me and leaning over my shoulder to stare at the map. His breath tickles my neck and his proximity makes me inhale as the heat radiating from his pectorals coats the back of my spine. I shudder a little.

"So, the coaster is here." I point and he nods, exhaling heavily. If I was one for assuming, I'd say he's in a large amount of discomfort being this close to me, but who am I to say what he's thinking. He's a complete mystery.

"Okay, let's head there. Come on." He ushers me forward, grabbing my hand in his without a care for the feel of his skin on mine or what it does to me. Electric tendrils begin to creep, clutching my synapses in their curves and causing me to shudder again.

"You okay?" Clark asks, pulling me through the crowds and past the rising smell of processed sugar and batter, which make my stomach grumble. I look to the stands wistfully.

"Yeah, I'm fine, just cold and hungry," I admit. He looks to me with an amused expression.

"Cold? It's like a hundred degrees out! And hungry? I cooked you breakfast like an hour ago!" he exclaims and I cross my arms, scowling at his judgemental tone.

"Do you want to see what happens when a short, curvy woman gets hungry, Clark? Because I can guarantee you it's scarier than any ride in this place." He rolls his eyes at this, stopping in his forward motion, which is causing the floor to illuminate brightly from his brisk pace.

"Fine, what do you want? Whipped sugar?" He looks to me and I nod, licking my bottom lip without thought. He shakes his head, clearly finding me hilarious as his lips quirk up at the edges. In this glance, he's so damn good looking I almost want to stomp my feet and get irrationally angry, but as a guest, who is too busy ogling the surrounding rides, barges into me, I feel my frustration dissipate.

"Hey, watch it!" Clark snarls back at the man. He backs off immediately, putting his hands up in a show of apology.

"Clark it's fine, he only bumped me by accident," I explain as Clark's eyes blaze furious and then sad as they lock with mine.

"This crowd is mad, I don't want you getting trampled. Come on." He pulls me out of the mash of people and places me next to a stall with holo-fencing. I stand, looking at him with a scowl.

"But I wanted..." He laughs.

"I know! You'll get your food! What do you want? A pink one?" he asks me and I nod.

"Yeah, large!" I explain and he darts back into the crowd. I find myself smiling against my better judgement. He's treating me like I'm precious to him, which both scares me and makes me furious. Why is this so confusing?

I watch two people behind me fight in the holo-fencing booth, the hard-light of the neon blue swords clanging and clattering as they dart in and out of each other's personal space.

"Valentine..." My name is like a breathless whisper on his lips as I pivot and find Clark has returned. He's watching me intensely and as I look down to what he's holding, I see that he's had my whipped sugar manipulated into the shape of a rose. His eyes blaze with fondness and I want to hit him. What the hell is he doing?

"Urrm... thanks," I express my gratitude with surprise, taking the white stalk of the sugar rose from him and quickly taking a large, and intentionally ungraceful, bite.

"You have…" He leans in, placing a thumb on my cheek and wiping away a dusting of fine pink sugar. I flush, and it makes me mad.

"Can you just stop?" I ask him, scowling again as he straightens.

"Yes. I'm sorry." He licks his thumb and takes my hand again, leading me through the avenue of macrocosmic light trails that illuminate with every step we take. I wrap the thick tangle of whipped pink sugar around my tongue, closing my eyes and letting the sweet crackle of it dissolving overcome me.

I continue to eat as we walk past a hard-light horror house, simulators and a booth where you can have your photo taken dressed as one of the old-fashioned rock-stars from before Monopolis had even existed. It had been called something else back then, but what I can't tell you.

Finally, we reach the entrance to the VR coaster I've been watching all the way here. It's called *Meteoric Rise*. I look up at the glow of the dark, hard-light from the ground, suddenly feeling anxiety pool in my stomach.

"You sure you want to do this?" Clark asks me, sensing my reservations as I pull on his hand. I finish off the whipped sugar quickly, perhaps too quickly, and nod, not wanting to spoil his fun.

"Yeah, sure! Let's go!"

One hour of waiting in the interactive queue later and we're being strapped into a ride car unlike anything I've ever seen. The restraints come down across my chest as the smart foam of the seat senses my utter terror and turns to putty beneath me. The VR headset falls down over my eyes and uses my height to determine position before it comes in closer to my face, suctioning on around my brows and cheekbones.

"You alright?" Clark asks me and I nod, pursing my lips together. "Valentine?" Clark calls out again as I realise that he can't see me because of his headset.

"I'm good," I bite out, feeling my stomach turn slightly.

The car jolts forward and suddenly the VR headset flickers to life. First, a short Bliss Inc. commercial plays, an advert for Jungala, alerting us to all the awesome things we can do during our stay together, including the perks of the new hologram staff. I look forward, having no choice but to watch the advert as we begin to climb. The car on the track is silent, but the speakers in the VR headset begin to emit a clunking sound, like a chain is being pulled through a metal loop. I feel my body tilt as the VR headset flickers to a new scene.

I inhale slightly as I turn my head in the headset. I'm surrounded on all sides by a galaxy of infinite majesty. The stars twinkle, glowing out into the abyssal dark in a bejewelling of colour.

As we reach the height of the coaster, I feel my stomach fall as I begin to plummet toward the surface of a shimmering diamond planet. We twist, surfing the curve of the planet's gaseous rings, gliding effortlessly through the gravity-less void. I'm blinded by diamond sparkle as we soar around a bend toward a lilac sun. The sun burns bright, sparking indigo, violet and lavender when we curve, corkscrewing upside down and over again as we lurch forward to slingshot around a moon, moving at a million miles an hour while the feel of cold air rips my hair back from my head.

My eyes widen and I put my arms above my head, which I realise were clenching onto the restraint so hard my fingers are numb. I let myself scream as we loop over a shooting star, the cool of its icy trail tickling my skin as the mask emits a small puff of cold air. The floor seems to fall from beneath us again as we go down another enormous drop, before zig-zagging left and right through a meteor storm of terrifying proportions.

I know it's all fake, but it's easy to forget when the coaster gives you the sensation you're actually moving. I lower my arms again as the coaster begins to slow and suddenly feel Clark's hand clasping mine as the ride comes to an end.

As the car glides back into the docking station, the VR headset retracts and I see him. He's beaming, his hair is all ruffled and his eyes are glistening with the intensity of the diamond planet we've just surfed. It's too much and when the restraints release us both, I stumble out onto the exit platform, feeling sick. What's worse is I don't even think it's the coaster.

I run down the steps, which lead back into the theme park, leaving Clark chasing behind as I cover my mouth with one hand.

It's too much. Whirling around space with this gorgeous man who as it turns out is really just as glacial as a shooting star.

I find a genetically modified bush, which has been programmed to grow in the shape of a moon, and throw up in a gut wrenchingly spectacular pink supernova of half-digested sugar.

"Valentine!" I hear Clark's exclamation as he yanks my hair back from my face. I continue to be sick, ferociously, until I'm empty of all substance.

I slump sideways onto a holo-bench next to the topiary. I don't speak, just pant, catching my breath and letting my heart hammer against my ribs. Clark looks down on me with pity in his stare. "Are you alright?" he asks me and I shake my head.

"I'll be fine. That coaster just... ugh. Too much motion is bad." I speak without really knowing what I'm saying, making up the lie on the spot. I know I can't admit to him that it isn't the coaster that made me feel sick at all.

It was the realisation that I could really fall in love with a man who will never love me back. In that single look, I know that Clark is someone I can't help but become attached to in the worst possible way.

<hr />

Clark is the perfect gentleman. He doesn't push me to go on any more of the attractions, but instead we walk, taking in the stalls and small vendor booths, picking only things we can do together.

"Nice shot!" he exclaims after I hit one of the targets in a shooting booth. I surprise myself, placing the hard-light gun back in its holster as I cock my hip.

"Why thank you, Sir." I wink like a saloon girl from one of the latest Bliss Inc. soft-light shows. The vendor hands me a giant stuffed heart. I thank him and Clark looks to me, brushing his hair back from his forehead with one swooping motion of his hand.

"You look better, are you feeling alright?" he inquires as we turn from the stall after he places his gun back in the holster.

189

"Yes. I feel much better. I'm sorry we haven't been on any more of the rides. Do you want to go on something? I can sit and wait?" I offer, but he shakes his head.

"Nah. I didn't come here as a single man. I think we should do stuff together," he expresses and I smile. If you'd have told me yesterday he could be this sweet, I would have strongly disagreed, but it's like something is slowly shifting within him. I just hope it lasts.

As the sun begins to lower in the sky, we walk hand in hand and I hold my giant heart underneath one arm. I'm glad I wore sneakers today, because my feet are starting to ebb.

"What about if we go in there?" I suggest, seeing the hard-light horror house as we turn a corner. It's got soft-light ghosts, which pop out of the windows to scare bypassing guests, and I feel my stomach muscles tighten. I don't know how well I'll hold up being scared, but I want to do something fun for Clark, he's been so patient.

"You sure you're up for that? I don't want you throwing up again." He looks down at me, his beautiful gaze tainted with concern.

"Sure. I mean, it looks like a walk through from here," I say, gripping onto the fuzzy curves of the heart beneath my arm.

"Okay. Let's do it!" He claps his hands together as he quickens his pace. I lag behind him, unable to keep step with the long length of his stride.

We reach the front of the hard-light horror house and I stare up at it, with purple walls on the outside, a giant tentacled man is breaking through the roof with bulging biceps.

"Look at that," I say to Clark, nudging him as the holographic man moves and cocks an eyebrow, cackling down on bypassing walkers.

"Yeah. Scary... Not. I mean come on, a guy with tentacles? That's just... well, crazy!" He stutters in his expression, small bursts of laughter catching in his throat as he chuckles to himself. Once we walk in through tinted, dark, glass doors which slide away, I tighten my grip on his palm, cuddling the heart to me and feeling my senses prickle as the darkness falls over us like a thick blanket.

"Okay... so what is going to happen do you think?" I ask him, trying to make conversation to shrug the feeling that something is going to jump out at me.

"I don't..." he begins, but suddenly, a large demon looking creature emerges from the shadows, baring its teeth in a snarl. I jump, continuing to walk as quickly as I can past it. Inside I recite the mantra.

It isn't real, it isn't real.

As my feet pick up into what is almost a jog, I feel a finger tap me on the shoulder, and so turn, expecting to see Clark. Instead, I see the face of a hideous clown. I cry out, screaming and losing my hold on what's real and what isn't. It's hard-light, so I should have known things would be touching me, but it sends a torrent of terror through me, chilling me to the core and making my heart break out into a sprint as my palms become clammy. As I'm stood on the spot, staring into the face of the most hideous thing I've ever seen with too long pointed teeth and insane bloody hair, I feel something stir at my back.

"Clark?" I yell out, spinning on the spot and staring into the shadow, scrutinising the black to see if he's found me yet. I pray silently in my head, the dark walls that produce the holograms rising high around me and closing in as I feel a breeze run through the maze. "Clark!" I yell out again, but he's nowhere to be found.

I turn back, and suddenly something is swooping down from above with fangs and glowing yellow eyes. Having had enough, and with my heart in my throat, I take off, not looking which way I'm going but seeking light and a way out, knowing I can't take much more of this so called 'fun.'

Finally, after about five blood curdling minutes, I break out into the dim light of the lowering sun. I walk, searching for Clark, but he's nowhere to be found, he's still inside.

Oh bliss. That was terrifying. I admit internally, putting my hands around my ribcage and feeling my blood pulsating around my body like a high-speed monorail. I've got a stitch and my lungs are burning as I bend over in the middle of the walkway, catching my breath and close to sobbing as tears leak from my eyes. Then I realise that I've dropped my giant cuddly toy somewhere, and I cuss. I haven't had a cuddly toy since I was a child, and it might have made the nights sleeping alone feel less lonely. I sigh, knowing that I should have been more careful, but also knowing that I'm not going back in there. Not for all the cuddly toys in Jungala.

"Valentine!" I hear my name called, and so turn, as my hair is blown back from my face in a sudden gust of warm wind. Clark is running towards me, my cuddly toy heart clutched in one of his hands. "Hey, are you okay?" He can see I've been crying, more out of shock hitting my system than anything else, and comes in close. Too close.

"I'm..." He doesn't let me finish, but instead pulls me into his chest, crushing me. I go stone still, like a statue, not letting myself collapse into the heat of his body.

"Clark..." I begin, stepping back as he looks down to me.

"I'm sorry," he apologises, holding out the heart for me to take.

"Thanks," I reply, looking deeply in to his eyes and wondering what exactly we're caught up in together.

"You should be more careful with that..." He gestures to the heart I'm holding and I wonder if he's really talking about the stuffed toy or not.

"Uh, I will. Thanks," I reply, cuddling the heart to me as the heat of the tropics chases away the chill that had clutched at my insides.

"I think we should get you back to the room. I'll cook you dinner," he offers and I smile.

"That would be nice." I grin at him, suddenly starving because I haven't had anything to eat all afternoon for fear I'll be sick again.

Hand in hand, we walk from the park, optic fireworks bursting in our wake.

We're sitting on the balcony, the sun has just set over the horizon and the sky is a deep aubergine. Clark and I have just finished the meal he'd cooked and I'm now sipping wine. I've never had it before, but it tastes good and I'm feeling way more relaxed than I have in a while.

"Did you have a nice day?" he asks me, leaning back with his left ankle propped on his right knee.

"Apart from the almost passing out from fear and throwing up in a moon bush it was perfect," I chuckle and he sighs.

"Yeah, I say we try some low octane fun tomorrow. Any ideas about what that could be?" he asks me and I think. There are a few things I'd like to do, but right now I feel so exhausted that I wonder if I'll have enough energy to enjoy them.

"Well, how about if tomorrow we go and explore the island a bit? Maybe stop somewhere to eat?" I suggest. He nods.

"Okay." The conversation falls to a standstill, so I take another sip of wine, watching the stars twinkle above. It reminds me of throwing up earlier, so I try not to think so much on the fact that I'm stood on a revolving mass of rock in an endless sea of hundreds more.

"Clark?" I say aloud, suddenly feeling bold.

"Yes, Valentine?" he replies, sensing that I'm changing the tone of our casual small talk.

"Can I ask you something?" I request this of him, tracing the tip of my index finger around the rim of my wine glass.

"Of course." he encourages my curiosity, inhaling.

"Do you find me... you know, attractive? I know you said you have your reasons for not wanting to get involved, but it's not just because I'm hideous, is it? I mean, I'm not a disappointment?" I ask him, hearing the waver in my tone as I find myself vulnerable. Is it the wine talking? Or the fact that when I had been running from the monsters in the horror house, the only person I'd wanted was him?

"Valentine..." he begins, taking his own wine glass and tipping it upward, emptying the contents in one single glug, which causes his Adam's apple to bob. "You are the furthest thing from a disappointment. I swear to you. How can you possibly think you're hideous?" he asks me, raising one eyebrow and cocking his head with an incredulous stare.

"I don't know... I just, I keep hearing you talking to someone else. I wondered if you've found a way to contact someone off the island. Are you in love with someone else? Or was it you talking to Bliss Inc. for a replacement, is that it?" I ask him and he laughs.

"No. My brother works in the telecommunication sector, and well, he used to show new recruits around this museum. It had loads of old technology in and taught them about how we need to treat it with respect and stuff... he gave me this thing. It's called a cell phone. It works anywhere. I've been calling him." He explains this and I let go of a breath I didn't even know I was holding. "Also, you know that you can't request a replacement matchmate, right? Even if I hated you, I couldn't do anything about it. We're stuck."

"Oh," I exhale. He laughs.

"You're awfully suspicious for someone who's just a friend. Are you sure you're not... you know, feeling things?" he grills me with his stare and I scowl.

"Are you?" I counter, deciding not to answer.

"I asked you first." he retorts with a deadpan expression.

"No. Of course I don't have any feelings." I bite out, taking another gulp of wine and letting the fuzziness overcome me.

"Well, I don't either. You don't have to worry about that with me... and before you say anything it's nothing to do with how you look, or other women. I just know I can restrain myself," he retorts and I latch onto his sentiment like a predator.

"So you're having to restrain yourself? That means you *have* feelings Clark!" I burst and he crosses his arms.

"I don't." he bites, stern once more.

"Then what is it exactly that you're restraining yourself from?" I ask him, teasing, and he gets to his feet, laughing.

"Go to bed, Valentine," he orders me, though his stern resolve seems to be fading as quickly as it came.

"How about you admit what we both know is true?!" I call out. He walks back through the glass doors, taking our plates with him and I can almost swear that I see him grinning to himself, as he calls back,

"I have absolutely no idea what you're talking about."

Twelve

I awaken, opening my eyes to a rather unusual sight compared to my normal Friday morning view back in Monopolis. Clark emerges from the bathroom and is dripping, with a towel around his waist, body rippling in the early morning light.

I peek out over the silk sheets, which are wrapped around me like a cocoon, with one eye, trying to get a glimpse of what I know is completely forbidden. I've never seen one, and with his frosty reserve I probably never will. I just can't help but be curious in spite of myself I suppose.

"Valentine, stop staring at me please," I hear him say as he stops, turning to face the window and taking a sip from a glass of cold water on the table next to the sliding glass doors that lead out to the balcony. I cringe, knowing I'm being far too obvious, so squeeze my eyes shut tight, pretending that I've been asleep this whole time. "Valentine, bacon or sausages for breakfast?" he inquires and before I can stop myself I'm sitting upright.

"Bacon of course! How is that even a question?" I snap, realising that I've walked right into his trap.

"You know, you suck at acting," he quips, walking back into the bathroom to get dressed with a smirk. Then I suddenly realise, he's come out here undressed for no reason. He needs a drink of water that badly he can't wait to get clothed first?

"Yeah you too!" I call back, jumping out of bed and moving through to the living area, still clad in black silk pyjamas.

I take in the new sun of the day, which hovers delicately over the glistening waters. I think back to the last two days, how Clark and I have developed a kind of routine with one another, tip toeing around the edge of anything remotely emotional. We're kind of like friends now I guess. We've spent the days going on long walks, stuffing ourselves and getting fuzzy on alcohol while making fun of the non-stop soft-light romance movies that seem to dominate every single channel. Every time we see a couple swooning we laugh, or make stupid faces, or mimic them in the worst way, and I wonder if it's really because we're becoming friends, or if we're just both too afraid to admit it could be something else. I lay back into the smart foam hold of the lilac sofa, and the smell of him envelops me. This must be where he's sleeping, because his cologne seems to have seeped into the too soft material, causing the fog of my early morning bed head to clear.

"Right, breakfast," I hear Clark say, before the sound of him clapping his hands together and then rubbing them against one another reaches me. He walks over to the Kitchen upcycler, requesting the ingredients, the same ones he uses every morning to make me breakfast just the way I like it, and waits as they pop into the compartment.

"What are we doing today?" I ask him and he glows.

"I have a surprise for you." he reveals, his eyes spilling a mischievousness glint from their blue depths.

"A surprise?" I ask, suddenly nervous. I hate surprises. My whole future has been one terrible surprise, so I'm pretty much over them for now. I want things nice and predictable thanks.

"Yes. I planned a day out for you. I thought we could both use some alone time. Then I've got something planned for us together, tonight," he explains as he begins to chop oranges to put into the juicer. His hands are dextrous as they slice through the peel and the zing of the juice seeps out into the room.

"A day out for me?" I enquire, curious, as he begins to squeeze the oranges, extracting juice before handing me a glass. I take a sip, enjoying the feel of it in my arid mouth.

"Yes," he replies, looking between me and the bacon he's now separating to cook.

"What is it? Where am I going?" I ask him and he laughs.

"You really don't get the whole surprise thing, do you?" He cocks his head and I giggle.

"I've had enough surprises with you to last me the rest of my days, Clark. I'm done with surprises." He looks surprised at my answer and then a little sad.

"I suppose I am quite the shock compared to those cookie cutter grooms. But at least I'm not boring!" He smirks.

"Oh, you mean the boring ones with feelings and the ability to fall in love? Oh yeah, they must suck." I roll my eyes and his face saddens.

"Does it really mean that much to you? Romance and love?" he asks me and I nod, unable to help myself.

"Of course. Everyone deserves to be loved," I reply, not wanting to keep eye contact but finding myself unable to look away. He replies, turning away from me in that familiar way he does when he's trying to avoid talking about anything that matters.

"Not everyone deserves love, Valentine, trust me."

● ● ●

As I zoom downwards in the elevator towards the lobby, alone, I keep hold of the transparent acetate paper with my appointment time and number on it. Clark had told me not to open the envelope with it inside until I left the room, and when I had, I was pleasantly surprised to find he's booked me in for a full day at a spa, including an appointment for a new hair-cut.

I look down at my split ends, wondering what I should ask the stylist to do with my hair. I've had it long my whole life, mainly because I didn't want to be limited on my wedding day to what style I could choose. Now I'm married, maybe it's time for a change.

I step out of the elevator when it hits the lobby floor and make my way past the enormous circular desk and over to a spa called *Cloud Nine*.

As I step in through the glass double doors, a rush of fresh air hits me, it smells like peppermint and fruit of some kind, but I can't place it. In the entrance, a large and immaculate white desk sits in front of a hard-light hologram, sitting with her legs crossed, filing her nails.

"Name?" she asks me, not looking up from her air. She's also chewing, which I find odd because hard-light holograms can't eat, or drink. I mean they're just programming and light.

"Valentine Mor... uh... Cavanaugh." I correct myself; slightly hating the fact that now his name is mine. She looks me up and down.

"Just you today?" she asks again and I frown, why is she asking me that? Is she expecting me to say yes and then confess my husband is invisible?

"Yes. That's right. Just me." I huff and she nods, using the database that makes up her brain to check my details.

"You have a salon appointment at three o' clock. Correct?" she asks me, her eyes flickering with ones and zeros as she stares right through me.

"That's right, for my hair," I reply and she nods.

"And nails. That's all part of the package. They've been told to do your face as well," she says this so fast I almost miss her words.

"My face? What's wrong with it?" I ask her and she looks at me blankly.

"That's for the make-up artists to decide. Not me." She sounds annoyed so I shrug.

"Okay. Do I go through here?" I ask her and she goes back to filing her nails.

"Great, you do that. Head on through to the Salon at three. Until then, enjoy the facilities." She points toward the glass turnstiles as I take a few steps toward them and scan my wrist, watching as the barriers give me access to the space.

I walk on into the spa, looking around and taking it all in. There are couples everywhere. In bathing suits, shorts, or clad in robes. Walking hand in hand, kissing in the Jacuzzi or practically having sex on a lounger from what I can tell. I creep through the place, which is supposed to make me feel relaxed, but instead I feel my anxiety getting worse. I want to look away, but everywhere I turn, there are another two bodies intertwined and kissing passionately.

I realise quickly that I'm jealous. This should be my honeymoon. Wrapped up in Clark, kissing him, touching him and learning everything there is to know about him. Instead, I'm here, alone, in the spa. He didn't even want to come with me, says we need alone time. What the hell is that about? I know I should be grateful that he's set all this up, but I can't help but wonder if it's a brush off.

As I find the changing rooms, which are lit upwards from the heated flooring in day-glow orange, the frosted glass door slides sideways, allowing me to move into the space which is full of benches and lockers. I scan my tattoo across the front of one, which promptly opens, revealing a white bathing suit, towels and robes. I undress quickly, feeling oddly vulnerable as men and women get naked around me. I try not to stare at the men, but it's difficult in spite of my inclination to ogle. I realise all too soon though, that Clark has a better body than all of them put together.

For the love of bliss. I cuss, wishing once more that he was hideous, that he was undesirable. That's the problem though. He isn't. He's desirable as hell.

I want him. I admit internally. *Dammit.*

I slip on the white bathing suit, which shrinks so it fits me perfectly as soon as it touches my skin. It's quite cute, with a hole cut out of the material on my left side and a halter neck tie. I grab a robe and stuff my clothes into the metal locker, before scanning my tattoo, noting the number on the outside and hearing the distinct click of a locking mechanism.

I slip my robe over my shoulders before spinning on one heel and walking back through the frosted glass doors and out of the warm orange glow of the changing area. Once I'm outside. I spot an upcycler, in the wall next to the doors on my left, and so take a few steps over to it. Above the unit, the word 'Information' is displayed in a glowing mint green. I click the catalogue interface at the top of the machine, scrolling through the options before requesting a treatment guide.

As I wait patiently for the acetate to print out, I keep my eyes trained on the wall, careful not to become transfixed by the couples lost in one another. This is less of a spa and more of a sex club if you ask me.

I cross my arms, impatient, as the sheet finally prints and I grab it, and groans travel through the air intrusively. Averting my eyes from my surroundings, I walk over to where the shallow pools and Jacuzzis froth and bubble uncontrollably. I read the list of treatments and one catches my eye immediately; in an ocean of seaweed wraps and hot stone massages, is the desersion tank. According to the description underneath, it allows you to immerse yourself in a lucid dream-like state and reveals your innermost desires. I shrug, I guess that's as good of a way to pass the time as any, and far better than watching other couples getting it on without apology.

I shake my head, disapproving and seething with jealousy as I find the room number where the tanks are kept.

It doesn't take me long to find the room as I follow more hard-light signage which is plastered on most of the pristine white walls. I step in through the door, only to be greeted by the same hard-light hologram woman I had seen at the front desk. She appears to be babysitting a bunch of silver egg-shaped pods while continuing to file her nails behind yet another desk.

"Hey, it's you again," I observe, surprised, and she rolls her eyes.

"Yes. I do everything around here you know." She puffs out, moving to hand me a pair of sticky, transparent, gummy circles with a haphazard motion of one hand.

"What are these?" I ask her and she sighs again.

"Temple plugs. They tap into your desires or whatever. You put them on your temples. Hence why they're called temple plugs, if you haven't already guessed. Just get in one of the pods. Number two is free." She gestures to one of the eggs behind her and I shrug. She's possibly the rudest hard-light hologram I've ever met. You'd think that they would fix her programming for being like that, because it's certainly not helping me relax.

"Thanks," I snap as I brush past her, moving over to the pod labelled *Two*. There's a handle on the side, which I pull on promptly, using my frustration as fuel to shift the weight. It comes away from the curved edge of the egg until a sharp click, followed by a short hiss of air, emits and the lid rises of its own accord. Inside the human shaped egg, I find the entire bottom half is full of water, that looks lukewarm and almost surreal as it doesn't move at all. I look back to the hard-light hologram, who I see now is perched on a white stool behind the desk of the room. She doesn't turn to face me, but instead acts as though I don't exist. As though I'm the ghost and not she.

I stare down into the egg-shaped bath and let my robe fall to the floor, not bothering to hang it on the provided hooks. Lifting one leg carefully, I let my toe test the water as it rounds the curved edge of the path. The water is exactly my temperature, or so it seems. It's strange, because though I get into the bath and immerse myself in the water fully, it's as though it isn't there at all.

Once I'm comfortable sitting, I quickly stick the temple plugs onto the sides of my forehead and let myself lean backward so I'm lying on my back, floating and weightless. As I do this, the egg suddenly closes of its own accord once more, sealing me inside and taking the last of the light from the surrounding room with it. I lie in the dark, wondering what I'm waiting for as my body becomes irrelevant to me. The dark, coupled with the water, takes me away from myself for the first time in days, so I willingly close my eyes. Once I do, I realise I'm no longer inside the egg, I'm no longer even in the spa. I'm a hundred floors up, standing on the balcony with Clark. It's so real, the way the wind is blowing my hair around me, the way his cologne fills my nostrils. The way the stars light up the sky above, reminding me how I am so very small. I instantly forget where I am.

"Valentine..." My name is a whisper on the breeze as he steps close to me, his hand coming up and caressing my face. His eyes aren't his own. These are different, the way they look at me entirely devoted and overcome in but one closing and opening of his alabaster eyelids. His lips come down on mine, erasing the last kiss we'd had, the kiss of our wedding day and causing my heart to break out into a sprint. His fingers curl into my hair and he lifts me off my feet.

Continuing to kiss me, he strides with brisk certainty through the sliding glass doors and into the warm aubergine of our honeymoon suite. His eyes capture the flames of a hundred flickering candles and I can feel his heartbeat against my chest as he collapses atop me on the white silk sheets.

I'm suddenly nervous as he begins to move down my body, lips lingering on my stomach as he pushes up my shirt and places soft kisses. Goosebumps run rampant across my flesh, which is hot to touch, and so I wonder if I'm not coming down with a fever. I've seen videos in the sexual education readiness modules, but they were nothing like this. Why didn't they warn me about the fact my heart is hammering so hard in my ribcage that I feel like it might explode, or the fact that the place between my thighs is starting to develop a sweet ache? Why didn't they tell me how terrified I'd feel at the thought of touching him back, and yet that I'd be unable to stop myself as I sit up and pull his shirt over his head.

I place a trail of kisses across his heart, before he pulls my face up to his and kisses me so intensely that a small and feral sounding moan emits from my throat. I have never felt like this, and I wonder why it feels like my body is waking up from some sort of deep sleep. He pulls my head back as his hands bury in my hair again and I break the kiss, crawling up the bed backwards and looking at the fine specimen before me. His eyes are passion-filled, intense and hungry for me as I bite down on my bottom lip and willingly undo the top button of my shirt. I undo another and he growls, going to unbutton his fly as he crawls forward like a predator, caging me in with his arms. His fingers come forward to my blouse, which he quickly tears open, moving down low to kiss my cleavage, a place I had never known could be so sensitive. He looks to me with a wanton glance before reaching down to unbutton the skirt I'm wearing with one hand and caress my inner thigh with the other. As I'm just about ready to combust with a feeling I have no idea how to describe, I watch him, excitement coursing through me. That's when he does it. He reaches down into his jeans and....

"Desersion simulation terminated..." The voice shocks me and my eyes break open as I jolt back to myself. I'm not in Clark's arms, I'm not even in the hotel room, I'm in the desersion pod... alone.

"What the bliss?" I shout, frustrated as the hood of the egg-shaped pod emits a hiss and opens. As I sit up, I feel the ebbing between my thighs dissipate too slowly and realise that my skin is flushed and covered in goosebumps.

Oh my bliss... What was that about? I think to myself, rubbing my arms and breathing outward, trying to steady myself enough to get out of the tank.

"Why did it stop?" I ask as the hard-light hologram swivels on her stool and I exit the pod, shaking.

"There's a two-hour time limit you know. Desersion tanks are addictive." She smirks as my brow furrows, disappointed.

"Oh." I reply, completely disoriented and she laughs.

"That good? What were you a Queen or something?" she asks me and I shake my head, picking up the robe off the floor and placing it around my shoulders.

"Something like that..." I reply and she smirks again.

"Don't you have a hair appointment in a little while?" she reminds me and I nod, not bothering to reply. I rush, flushed, out of the desersion tank suite, trying desperately to forget the last two hours have ever happened.

•●•●•

I walk out of the Salon after two and a half hours of pampering. My hair has been cut and curled so it comes just below my jawline, my nails lacquered in black and my eyebrows waxed and shaped. I feel cute and sexy wrapped up into one, which is exactly how I wanted to look because I've decided I want to make things for Clark as hard as possible.

If my fantasy in the desersion tank had been anything like how real sex could be, then I'm missing out. Then again, my impression of sexual desire could be completely off kilter. I mean, how do I know it's not like in those sex education videos? How do I know it won't be technical and awkward? What about if with Clark it's just not that good? What about if my mind is making things into ideals just like it had done with my wedding day?

I ponder this as I walk across the lobby, now fully dressed in my clothes from this morning. The sunlight of the day is dimming, and the light flowing into the space through the numerous glass panes of the structure is peachy as it falls across me like a slightly warm blanket. I step into the elevator, taking in the gorgeousness of the resort in the late afternoon, and scan my wrist tattoo which causes the doors to automatically close, before whisking me up to the top floor.

I walk down the hallway, nervous all of a sudden. My skin becomes flush at the thought of seeing Clark again after the day's events. It's stupid, me getting so worked up over something that isn't real, but the fact that those thoughts had been in my subconscious, or wherever in bliss the temple plugs had pulled them from, proves without a doubt that I have feelings for Clark, whether I want to have them or not.

I scan my wrist across the pane of black glass on the front of the door, which swiftly opens, and step gingerly into the room, where Clark is nowhere to be found. I turn, slightly relieved, before I see something on the bed I hadn't expected.

It's a dress that I've never seen before. It's beautiful, slim fit and covered from top to bottom in gold sequins that make it sparkle under the orange light of the sun, which is filtered by the now frosted glass of the balcony doors. I walk over to it, examining the material and cocking my head. That's when I notice that there's a note beside it on transparent paper. The blue holo-ink reads:

Valentine,
Put these on, then meet me on the balcony.
Your Husband.

I smile to myself.

Why so cryptic? I wonder, noticing shoes next to the dress. They're my size, and the same colour as the dress in gold. I pick up the clothes off the bed and decide to get dressed right here, not caring about Clark seeing me, even if he is already on the balcony and the glass doors have been made opaque.

Once I'm dressed, I take several steps toward the glass doors, which slide apart, revealing Clark behind them.

"What's all this?" I ask him, taking in the scene before me. He's wearing a casual slim cut suit with an open collar. Beside him, the table has been draped in a white cloth and atop it a single red rose is stood in a vase next to a silver cloche.

"You look..." He inhales and I twirl on the spot.

"Rather fancy for friends..." I cock my eyebrow and he smirks, his lips quirking up at the edges.

"Right you are, Valentine," he whispers, striding forward toward me in one fluid motion. He's so at ease with his body, and as I watch him I wish I were half as graceful.

"What's that supposed to mean?" I ask him and he lowers his gaze, taking my hands in his. I'm startled by this act, though what I spent two hours this afternoon imagining is far more extreme. The difference now though is that this is real, or at least I hope it is.

"Come." He commands me to step forward and so I do. I look out, seeing now that the sun is kissing the ocean with its fiery curves. The light it emits is reflected back at me, warped, by the silver gleam of the cloche.

"What's this?" I ask him as he removes it. I'm expecting what lies beneath to be food, but it isn't. "Clark!" I exhale as I place my hands, crossed, atop my collarbone in surprise. He's revealed a floating blue diamond necklace on the platter beneath.

"Do you like it?" he whispers in my ear as I feel his presence behind me.

"I love it. Where did you get it?" I ask him, confused. Upcyclers don't exactly spit out precious stones on cue.

"I've been carrying this around since our wedding. I bought it at the same time as your ring, but I wanted to wait to give this to you, until..." he begins, but I turn, cutting him off.

"Until?" I ask, my eyes widening as his shimmer, happy.

"Until I really knew you." He replies. I feel a flicker of disappointment. He got all dressed up to give me fancy jewellery just because we now know each other's coffee orders?

"Oh," I exhale, standing here, glistening golden.

"Do you want me to put it on you?" he asks me and I nod, turning back to the table and moving to pull my hair over my shoulder, before quickly realising that I've just had it chopped short. "I like your hair. It's sexy," he compliments me and reaches around my waist, picking up the necklace off the silver platter. The diamond tinkles against the silver as he undoes the clasp and raises it around my neck. Once he's re-closed it, he places a hand on the flesh of my back, which is exposed due to the steep drop line of the back of the dress. I shudder, pulling away and turning back to him.

"Clark, stop. This is scaring me. You don't want a romantic relationship, so why are you giving me diamonds and wearing that... and touching me..." I stutter. His mouth twists.

"You're right. I should explain myself, Valentine. But first, we have dinner reservations. The kind you won't want to miss."

"We do?" I ask him and he laughs.

"Of course, you think I'd waste you looking like this on the hotel room?" He asks me this question like I'm crazy and I smirk, unable to keep the smile off my face.

"Well, when you put it like that..." I reply and he looks excited all of a sudden, like he's gone back to a time in his youth before

211

the paranoia and the pain he carries had taken hold. He takes my hand again and we walk back through our hotel suite, my heart hopeful despite me knowing that it's the most foolish thing I can be.

Thirteen

The walk from the resort is brisk, and I smile, watching the enthusiasm Clark puts into each one of the steps he takes. We near the water, up the stretch of beach from where I'd taken my late night nude swim, and I look out over a dock from our higher inland vantage. It's where the water sports lessons available for couples take place, and we passed it when we had been out exploring the island earlier this week. My dress shimmers, the sequins that cover it rustling as a slight breeze chills my skin, despite the tropical heat. My stomach is in knots, nervous.

"Reservations on the beach?" I ask him, hoping he'll give me some sort of hint as to where we're going and he laughs.

"Not quite. Come on." He pulls me down a flight of faux wooden stairs, which descend haphazardly toward the sand. I try to take quick and careful steps, though my heels aren't exactly great for manoeuvring this terrain. As we turn a corner around a dune, following the wood of the path, my eyes fall on a dock I couldn't see from higher inland.

"What's this?" I ask him and he rolls his eyes.

"Patience, Valentine. Come, I'll show you." He pulls on my arm again, jerking me forward and into motion as I hoist up the sleek skirt of my gown. I wonder why on earth I'm dressed this way if we're on a dock, but soon, I see why. As we reach the end of the wooden planks, which form the jutting surface that leads out over the water, he turns me so I'm facing east, away from the setting sun.

Before me, a glass, transparent platform is stationary above the waves. It's not bobbing like the other vessels I've seen tied up at docks, but instead is so still not even the water in the clear vase on the elegant table atop it is moving.

"Dinner on the water?" I ask him and he nods, his lips spreading back over his teeth as his hair catches the orange and lilacs of the vivacious sun in its thick black strands. "Wow." I breathe, watching as he scans his tattoo on the transparent plastic gate, which connects with a half railing around the platform. He holds out a hand to me and I step forward, scanning my own tattoo, before placing my foot onto the translucent glass of the floor.

I look down, the blue waves frothing beneath. The platform is large, and is segmented into two. The closest segment to the dock holds our table, and the other one is empty.

"Take a seat, Mrs. Cavanaugh." Clark pulls out a chair and I sit, alarmed by his use of my married name. He's like a completely different person than the one I'd woken up to this morning.

"Why, thank you." I exhale, surprised as I lean back into the plush smart foam, which is covered in a soft scarlet fabric that I don't recognise. He quickly takes a seat on the opposite side of

214

the table and I watch as he looks out to the sunset across the dock. "This is amazing." I compliment him and he smirks.

"We've not started yet." He promises so much with his stare and I wonder what he's referring to. Suddenly, I hear a clunk as some kind of lock closes and we begin to pull away from the dock altogether.

"This thing goes out to sea?" I query him, surprised as not so much as a tremor reaches my feet.

"Yes, I thought we'd have a little dinner and dancing," he elaborates.

"Well, at least you can't storm off." I chuckle and he rolls his eyes.

"Well, there is also that." He nods with a reluctant smirk, gesturing to two plates with cloches atop them.

"The food is all prepared in advance, so we have complete privacy," he informs me, removing the cover from his plate. Underneath a steaming pile of meat, vegetables and potatoes is revealed. The smell of his food reaches me, making my mouth water, so I remove the cover from my own dish and pick up my cutlery as we begin to whir across the water at an even and steady pace. The platform rotates in calm momentum, giving the sense that the world is spinning ever so slowly.

"What is this?" I ask him as I place a piece of white meat into my mouth. I assumed it was chicken, but now I'm not so sure as it tastes different. Clark smiles to me, pulling a bottle of champagne out of the bucket laid between us and unscrewing the bottle cap.

"Turkey. I thought you'd like it. People used to have this for festive holidays and such, I think. It's only brought out on special occasions now. The turkey is quite a rare bird." He gives me this information.

"How do you know that?" I ask him and he shrugs.

"Jason. He knows loads about the olden days. He is fascinated with all that stuff," he elaborates and I nod, chewing gratefully and letting the succulent meat juices slick the back of my throat as I swallow.

"What's the special occasion?" I ask him and he looks suddenly surprised as he clears his throat quickly, pouring me some champagne before filling his own glass. I pick up the heavy stalk of the champagne flute; bringing it to my lips slowly and looking tentatively over the rim as the fizz of the bubbles tickle my tongue.

"Well, you said earlier today that romance and love are important to you," he replies and I almost spit out the sip of champagne I've just taken into my mouth.

"What?" I exclaim, unsure how to respond.

"Look, I... I've been unfair to you. I've been trying to keep things platonic, but I'm struggling, Valentine. I didn't realise that my wife would be..." he begins.

But I interrupt him, the desperation painfully obvious in my reply as I say, "What?", and he sighs out.

"A person. Like a real person. You're different. You're not like I thought," he admits, taking a broccoli stalk on his fork and placing it into his mouth. I sit back into the smart foam clutch of my chair once more, flabbergasted.

"What does that mean? I don't understand. I thought..." I begin, but this time it is he who interrupts.

"I know. I didn't think I'd actually like you. I thought this was all arranged and forced and you'd feel like a stranger. I'm scared, Valentine. I'm afraid of this. I've never felt like this before and I'm terrified. I'm afraid it's not real. What if it's the formula and not us?" he explains and I feel weak at his words, half afraid I'm still floating in the desersion tank.

"Why are you scared, Clark?" I ask him and he shakes his head.

"I'm afraid to tell you. It's awful and I don't want your pity," he admits and I blink a few times. He looks broken as we continue to drift out to sea. We've known each other so little time, and by some miracle it appears I've really had an impact on him.

"Well, why are you afraid it's the formula? Is it just because you hate Bliss Incorporated?" I ask him, hoping that if this is the case, it'll be easy to convince him to put his own happiness first.

"No. My parents, before they were killed. My father... he hit my mother, he hit me and Jason too. He was angry, because the formula made him so deeply in love with my mother. He said we had ruined her..." He admits this and I gasp slightly, bringing my hand up to my mouth.

"I've never seen love created by Bliss Inc. turn bad like that..." I admit, trying to think of a time I've heard of something like that happening. I come up empty.

"That's because it's not love, Valentine, or maybe it is... I don't know... I just know I'm scared to find out. I don't want to hurt you... I mean what if what Bliss Inc. isn't pairing us up for love at all? What if it's something else?" He doesn't meet my eyes this time, but continues to eat his food.

Silence falls between us for a few moments as I contemplate the situation, watching him as he slowly raises his eyes to mine. "What is it? Tell me what you're thinking, please," he begs and so I sigh, shifting in the seat.

"You think this is love?" I ask him and he bites his bottom lip, his brow furrowed and his features stunningly masculine as the last rays of the day disappear, catching in the bone structure of his face and casting deep shadows.

"I think it could be. I've known you so little time, I don't think I can say that I know anything for sure. I just know that you make me happier than I've ever been, and please believe me when I say that I've really tried to make things clean cut. I like taking care of you. I like watching you laugh. I even had a hard time finding myself repulsed when you threw up the other day, I just felt like I wanted to tuck you up in bed and hold you." He makes this confession in a whisper, like it's his darkest secret.

In this moment, I'm terrified and I don't want to get my hopes up. He's been so hot and cold ever since we met that I have whiplash from his behaviour, but I can't deny any longer that I like him. I find him attractive, funny and I want to keep him in my life for now, not that I have much choice. I realise with this thought that it could be only too easy for me to get carried away here, so ask my next question with caution.

"Okay. Well, what if things would be better if we stayed friends though? What if we try the relationship thing and it goes wrong? Like you said before, being stuck with someone you hate for life isn't exactly ideal." His face turns a myriad of expressions and I expect it to fall back into the one he wears most often, that of cool reserve, but instead he reaches out across the table for my hand. I oblige, allowing my fingers to weave through his as they drop to the fine table linen.

"I understand if you feel that way. I have fought myself on this for the last twenty-four hours. That's why I sent you out of the suite today. I needed some time to go over this decision myself. It's a risk. I never thought I'd be thinking about someone like this, Valentine. I didn't want to. I still don't know if I do, but keeping us apart for the sake of it is too hard. I didn't expect to have this kind of.... attraction." He swallows hard, looking into my eyes and imploring me with his gaze.

I feel irrationally angry all of a sudden. He has made it perfectly clear where he stands, and now, not even one week later, he is changing the rules on me. I wonder if he's not just playing with me.

"What attraction? You've been pushing me away since the day we met!" I snap, suddenly feeling ballsy despite the fact he's opening up to me.

"I know, and in spite of that you've still managed to infect my every thought. Can you imagine what would happen if we actually tried, Valentine?" he replies. It does nothing for my temper and I draw my hand from his, going back to eating before my food gets cold.

I take a few moments, chewing it over while enjoying my turkey. I want him, I know I do. Why else would I have been crawling red faced and flushed out of the desersion tank only this afternoon? But I don't think he knows what he wants right now. I mean, for someone who's been so icy in his reception of our marriage, how has he managed to flip his position on this so completely in such a small space of time?

219

"Are you serious?" I ask him, furrowing my brow. I don't want to believe him; I'm scared of getting my hopes up for nothing.

"Deadly. I'm not the kind of person who sits on the fence with important issues like this. I'm either in, or I'm out," he vows.

"Look, you'll have to forgive me, but this is a rather radical change from what you've said before. I'm just having a hard time believing that the man who put up walls between us on the first night now wants to try. I mean, what does that even mean?" I ask him and he exhales heavily.

"I'll take down the walls, Valentine. Share a bed with you when you're ready. Whatever you want," he breathes out and I want to believe him. My heart aches at his words, because it's what I've been dreaming of since our wedding vows when my fantasies had most spectacularly broken.

"Just..." He begins and I interrupt him.

"What, what condition do you have now?" I snap. I know I'm probably acting like a brat, but I'm desperate to avoid more disappointment.

"Don't think this is because of the formula. I don't like you because we're supposed to be together. I like you for a million little things. Things that no formula could possibly work out." I'm close to melting under his sapphire gaze.

"Could we go slowly? I mean, if your father was abusive like that, I don't want to push you beyond what you're comfortable with. Now I know about your parents, it seems like you have a pretty good reason to want to be cautious." I sigh, taking another sip of champagne as his lips quirk slightly.

"Of course, and if you think things are going badly, you can just say so. You're under no obligation to me, Valentine. We were married by the state, not by our own choice. You should know by now that I won't force you into anything you don't want." He goes back to eating his dinner, content that my mind has been made up.

I decide to remind him that I'm far from a closed case on this whole idea.

"Well, I think that going slowly would be best. I don't want this to go badly wrong. You were right when you said that if it does, then we're stuck with one another. I'm beginning to think you're right about more than just that as well..." I say as he watches me intently.

"What's do you mean?" he asks, curious, and I shrug.

"I don't know if I trust the formula anymore. I mean, I don't think we're exactly perfect for one another. Do you?" I ask him this, though I don't know why. I don't know whether it's because I'm trying to see how he reacts, or whether I'm longing for him to tell me that he disagrees.

"I think the formula has its flaws, yes," he admonishes and I consider his answer as I sit, allowing the world to spin around me, watching him as he eats. I know now that I must remember what I'm getting into with him isn't some magical fantasy, it isn't some transformative event that will have him emerge an entirely new person. I'm agreeing to try with him, for all his paranoia, his hatred of the system that I've grown up dreaming about. I have to make this work with Clark and his flaws, not without them.

I ponder this and realise that while he isn't perfect, perhaps people never are. I think about my mother, about how my father adores her despite the fact she thinks he's spineless. I think about my sister Eve and how she and her husband seem happy, despite

221

the fact he doesn't listen to a single word she says. Perhaps happiness and perfection aren't the same. Perhaps, real happiness is achieved in spite of flaws, not because there aren't any.

As I watch the sun's light disappear and the night above open up into a showering of glitz upon a black canvas, I realise that maybe this is what I've been waiting for. Maybe this is real.

Is Clark the right person for me? I wonder.

I don't have an answer, though I wish I did as I stare up at the cosmos, wishing for some great booming voice to come down and tell me that it is all going to be okay. Instead though, the silence makes me realise that this might be my only window to fall in love, so I should take it.

"Well, I'd like to try. Us… together." I swallow as I speak, nervous but excited as my cheeks glow a warm red. I feel flush at the thought of romance, of all the things I'd wanted since I said 'I do.'

"Really?" he asks me and I nod.

"Really."

The two of us grin at one another, stupidly happy amongst the cry of sea birds and the rush of waves.

Clark and I sit, silent, as though too anxious that whatever we say next will be the wrong thing.

I stare at him, pondering his face as his eyes bare into mine with an intensity I've only experienced once before, in the throws of my deepest desire. We don't do anything, lost in one another's eyes across the table as we continue to sip champagne, allowing the humidity of the night to settle, as the sea remains calm and the platform still. All too quickly, the moon is rising and Clark is getting to his feet.

"Time to head back already?" I ask him and his lips quirk.

"I promised dancing, did I not?" He bows his head and I find myself unable to control my expression as my eyes light up.

"Oh, yes!" I almost clap my hands like an excited child, but restrain myself, trying to play it cool far too late.

"You're so excitable, Valentine. It's adorable." He chuckles and I purse my lips, trying to control my face, before he adds, "and you appear even more so when you try to hide that fact." I let my face fall slack, irritated that he can read me like an open book when I long to be a mystery. I feel exposed with him, like I can't hide who I am, or how I'm feeling. Maybe it's because I suck at being subtle, or maybe it's just because when I'm with him I can't help but splay out my feelings like I'm only too available. I want to make things easy for him. I don't want excuses anymore, and yet I'm terrified of coming off as desperate.

"It's a bit cramped for dancing here…" I begin to speak, as Clark moves to the partition that separates us from the larger, empty part of the platform. I had assumed that was what had been driving us, but now I'm not so sure as the tiny gates slide open with a clunk. He gestures for me to walk through, so I get to my feet, feeling uneasy as the water around us moves, despite the steadiness of the platform beneath me.

Stepping onto the makeshift dance floor, I look around. The world is unblemished here; it is broad and wide from horizon to horizon around me as I spin. I wonder if I won't start to feel a little sick as I do, with the water swirling around on all sides.

Clark steps onto the platform with me and I scan my tattoo, closing the gate behind us. Once it's shut, I hear a chain begin to move through a metal loop, like it had on the rollercoaster a few days ago.

That's when I feel it; a gentle whirring beneath my feet, the only motion to penetrate the solidity of the floor. I glimpse down to where the ocean is, but now I'm seeing droplets start to form. What's going on?

I look up, and Clark is at my back, placing his hands on my hips.

"Don't panic. We're just getting a better view," he whispers in my ear as I watch us leave the water beneath. The platform, takes off, hovering soundlessly into the sky, while a chain tethers us seamlessly to the platform holding our table, which remains in the exact same place, below.

"Clark! This is crazy. This thing flies?" I exclaim, thoroughly surprised, and he smirks.

"You really didn't read any of the honeymoon brochures did you?" he asks me and I shake my head.

"No… I didn't. Is this normal?" I ask him and he laughs, gesturing out to my left. I look into the distance, where I see about five other platforms, with couples stood upon them, rising into the sky.

"How else are we going to get an uninterrupted view of the fireworks?" He smirks, stepping around my body to face me as we reach the height of our ascent and the platform shudders, coming to a sudden stop. I lurch forward, losing my balance, which is already compromised in the heels I'm wearing, and Clark catches me in his arms. I look up, getting caught once more in the sapphire allure of his stare, but shake it off, stepping back and trying my hardest to restrain myself.

"Did you say fireworks?" I change the subject, brushing my hair behind my ear as the wind catches a stray lock.

"Yes. Right over the horizon, according to the brochure. I've been reading them, they're great for sending me to sleep." he replies, his mouth quirking into a smile, which it seems he can't help.

"And also, dancing?" I ask him, realising that on such a small platform it's unlikely I'll keep my distance for long.

"Yes, let me just sort the band," he says, side stepping me and moving over to the transparent railing where we'd both scanned our tattoos to enter.

After a few moments, hard-light holograms appear, holding instruments, just like the ones I'd seen in the dance club we'd been to on our second night in the resort.

"I think I'll play some Van Morrison," Clark muses aloud. I'm surprised, I didn't realise he likes music.

"How do you know all these different songs? New music hasn't been recorded in years and the old stuff isn't easy to source?" I ask, really curious as he sighs.

"The orphanage where Jason and I grew up had a lot of music. I know it's not really that popular in Monopolis, but they play it in the work settlements, they say it keeps morale up." he explains and I swallow hard as the song starts to play.

"What's this one called?" I ask him, letting the sound of strings wash over me.

"Into the mystic," he reveals, striding over to me with long steps and anticipation on his face.

"That's beautiful."

"Music is. I love it. That's why Bliss Inc. keeps it for the labour settlements, or so I reckon. I think it's because when you hear a good song, it's a little like being in love. Not that I would know." He looks down at me as he takes my hand in his and places his other around my waist, pulling me close to him. I inhale the scent of his cologne, letting it fill my head and cloud my sensibilities.

"Why would that mean that they want to keep it away from the Jigsaw Project?" I ask him as we begin to sway. He leads me, precise in his motion, across the platform.

"Maybe because music makes us just... feel. Not always how we're supposed to. The reaction you have to a song can't be predicted or controlled. It just... *is.* Kind of like how I feel about you. There's no rhyme or reason to why I have feelings for you, there's no reason why staying away from you should be so difficult." He pushes me back, twirling me under the night sky as the floor illuminates at our motion, gold rays tracing our steps as we make intricate patterns in the sky.

"There isn't?" I ask him, cocking an eyebrow as I reach the farthest point in my spin away from him. He yanks me inwards, bringing both arms upward to cup the curve of my spine as goosebumps run rampant across my skin.

"Well, unless you count this..." His eyes linger on mine as he bends me back over, lifting and catching mine so completely in their trap that I inhale. He looks down, tracing the curve of my lips with his gaze, before bringing me up so I'm stood straight once more. "You feel that?" he demands and I exhale, feeling blood flood my face.

"Y... yes," I whisper as his lips quirk once more in that way I'm beginning to love.

"Uncontrollable, right?" he asks me and I shudder, his hands pulling me so close to him that his chin is almost resting atop my head.

"Absolutely." I agree, nodding and gazing down at my feet as we dance slowly, flushing in the dark.

"My point is, Bliss Inc. doesn't like that which it can't control. They control you, me, where we met, how we got married, where we've come on honeymoon. It's why I like surprising you so much. I like that I get to make you feel like this has even an ounce of spontaneity," he whispers and I smile to myself. It's true; he's continuously surprising me.

"Maybe the formula is their way of making us feel like they control how we feel... but maybe... maybe they don't really control that at all." I speak the words aloud, though they scare me. Clark's eyes twitch as they narrow ever so incrementally in surprise.

"So you're saying that falling in love on our terms is the ultimate rebellion?" he smiles at me, impressed, and I think on this a moment.

"Yes. Just, promise me one thing," I say, looking up and into his eyes. Their sapphire depths are full of adoration as his acute features soften into an expression so naturally forlorn that I cannot help but wonder if I was made to be looked at by him and him alone.

"What?" He asks me, raising my knuckles to his lips and kissing them softly. I sigh out, shivers running down my arm.

"Don't love me to hurt them, Clark. I'm not a weapon." I reply and he nods.

"You aren't a weapon." He replies, agreeing as we turn a half circle to the song, which is still playing out into the night.

A sudden firework explodes, taking over the night sky with brilliant white light as its shimmering trails of sparks fall like the branches of a weeping willow. My head turns to look at the night sky ablaze, but Clark's gaze doesn't follow. His eyes remain trained on my face, so I look back to see the fireworks reflected in the glassy sheen of his dilated pupils.

"Is this real?" I ask him, unable to stop the words spilling from me.

"I think this is the realest thing that's ever happened to me, Valentine," Clark replies and I blink a few times. Thinking on that statement. Perhaps what he's saying is true. He and I have been institutionalised since birth. Our interaction together isn't pristine or systematic, but perhaps that's what makes it genuine.

"Thank you for everything. I mean it; this dinner was amazing. The view, it's spectacular," I say, resting my head on his chest as another firework explodes, being born in a fiery explosion before fading into nothing, leaving behind only the memories of its beauty, engrained in my mind.

"Thank you for listening to what I had to say," he replies, continuing to dance with me as his hands stroke the flesh of my back.

"Well, it's not like I could run away," I joke and he chuckles.

"That is true."

"I'm scared," I whisper and he frowns.

"I know. I am too." He spins me away from him once more, as though the motion might distract me. "What can I do to make you unafraid?" he demands a solution from me and I think on this a moment, wondering what exactly would make me feel better. It's not like I can ask him for anything more in terms of commitment. We're married, whether he likes it or not.

"Show me you mean it. Show me you want to try." I almost feel like I'm bordering on pathetic. Why can't I just trust him? Why is it so damn hard for me to be happy? He's got me on a platform, floating under sweet moonlight with a jazz band and fireworks. What more do I honestly expect?

He tilts his head slightly and I watch as his lips quirk up at the edges again.

He takes one hand from my back, resting the other in the curve at the base of my spine. His free hand comes up to cup the side of my face and his lips come down on mine in a slow and gentle caress. It's not a forced kiss like it had been at our wedding. This one feels real. My stomach flutters and shivers run down my spine as I feel his honest care, and I kiss him back, placing both arms around his neck and letting him hold me as fireworks explode around us and the music reaches its climax.

As we kiss, hovering in the sky and surrounded by fiery glisten, I feel his heart race against mine through the crisp white cotton of his shirt, and I know that we're in this rebellion together.

Fourteen

I wake to immense heat, like I'm being pinned down by a furnace. As I open my eyes, I feel blood flush to my face and my lips ebb. Clark is draped across me.

We're both dressed, he's in his shirt and trousers from last night, and I'm in the silk shirt and shorts of my pyjamas. I still in the light of the early morning and watch specks of dust float a slow and silent ballet in the air. As I turn flat onto my spine beneath the crook of his arm, he stirs from sleep too.

"Good morning," I whisper, feeling the place where he'd kissed me over and over burn as I lick my bottom lip. It's tender, as is my heart and I feel suddenly the vulnerable nature of the situation I've fallen into with him.

"Hey..." His voice cracks, low and sexy in the morning, and his eyelids flutter open, revealing the sapphire blaze of his irises. I lean up on one elbow, looking down at him as he gazes up into my face. I cock my head and he puts a rough palm on my cheek. He pulls me down to his chest, pressing my lips against his and caressing my ebbing pink flesh with his lips and tongue. I let out a small sigh and he smiles, ending the kiss and staring at me for a moment, intense as the cogs in his mind whir and turn, processing my face.

"Your lips are red…" I whisper again, feeling bashful as he brushes a lock of hair behind my ear.

"Yours too, but they're still delicious." He looks to the rouge of my lips and I wonder if he's imagining kissing me again. My heart races slightly, picking up lazily in its early morning thrum.

"Well, today's Saturday, we don't exactly have anywhere to go…we could always…" I begin, but his face suddenly drops.

"Saturday?" he asks me and I think back, yesterday was Friday.

"Yeah. Saturday." I repeat and he sits up.

"We have counselling. What's the time?" he demands and I shrug. He turns around, moving to look at the flashing soft light clock on the wall beside the bed. "Shit. We're going to be late. Come on. Get dressed, I'll make you breakfast when we get back," he promises, getting to his feet and walking over to the bathroom to get dressed.

I sit up, realising that the time in which we had been so close, so intimate, is over and my heart deflates. Last night I felt things I have never dreamed could stem from Clark. I've let go and let him in. I have let his kiss capture me.

As I listen to him getting dressed, I begin to feel anxiety creep in. I've never been this happy in my life, but what if he doesn't feel the same? What if it all falls apart and I never feel this way again? Everything is changing so fast, and in the clear light of the morning sun, free from the glistening fireworks which had bloomed bright and dangerous just like our romance last night, I wonder if I've just made a huge, if not completely enjoyable, mistake.

We sit in the office of our sexology counsellor; a towering heart topiary in the corner of the white and sterile room. We have only just made it to our appointment on time by dashing down walkalators to the resort's own Bliss Inc. headquarters, and as I sit on the smart-foam couch next to my husband I'm both tired and nervous.

"My name is Jade," the counsellor informs us, crossing her hard-light and flawlessly smooth legs as she sits in an armchair in the centre of the room. She's wearing a calf length white coat, with a spotless white blouse and pencil skirt underneath and as she watches us her gaze alarms me. I have always hated the idea of official counselling and now I'm here, with a man who harbours intense paranoia for the person opposite me, I'm especially terrified.

"Hi." I wave at her with one hand, my palms sweaty. Clark is as far away from me as he can manage on the sofa, and I can't deny that this is horrifying. We haven't even had sex and we've got some stranger scrutinising us. I just pray we can get through this together without tipping off the counsellors that we're completely unsure of how we feel about one another.

"So, let's talk about sex. I know it can feel a little embarrassing at first, but let's start out slow. Have you two consummated your marriage?" she asks us and Clark answers, laughing and shaking his head. I almost hit him, it didn't seem like such an absurd idea to him when he was kissing the pants off me last night.

"No." His reply is almost too fast, and so the counsellor licks her hard-light lips and cocks an eyebrow.

"Okay, well, it's not uncommon. While many Jigsaw Project couples do consummate their marriages right away, it's not like that for everyone. However, we do look for there to be some sexual activity by the end of your one-hundred-day assessment period. Which is something you'll want to bear in mind. Many of our couples are concerned about pregnancy at this stage, but I'd just like to let you know that your food and ingredients are all infused with birth control, so your only concern should be enjoying one another." She says the words and I almost scowl. This seems odd to me, clinical and far too pushy.

"Well, we're both just taking things slow. I'll be honest, I don't think either of us has any desire to rush things." Clark replies, keeping his voice clipped as he crosses his arms with a defensive tone. He looks to me and gives a weak smile. The counsellor laughs and he turns back to her.

"What? Is that the wrong answer or something?" he asks, snide and yet tense at the same time. I know he's scared about failing the assessment, yet somehow, he still can't seem to curb his hatred for the system completely.

"No, Clark, not at all. I just think Valentine might have more of a desire than you realise. Let me just…" She walks toward the back of the room, drawing up a hard-light holo-dash, the first I've seen all week.

"What are you doing?" I ask her, nervous, and she smiles to me.

"Well, we monitor all our newlywed couples when they use our facilities. I believe you used the spa earlier this week?" she asks me, and my eyes suddenly widen.

Oh god no... that was in my head... she couldn't possibly have access to that.... Could she?

"Ah, yes, see here you used the desersion suite. I had a look through your activities this week before you got here; it's standard for us to review your progress before sessions. So, don't be surprised if your psychological counsellor asks about things you've been doing together, we have an all access pass to you while you're here. To ensure your happiness in your marriage, of course. So, anyway, Clark...let's take a look at what Valentine experienced in the desersion tank earlier this week, shall we?" She smiles to me, totally content with her intrusion of my psyche and I want to slap her. Clark *cannot* see what I was imagining earlier this week.

"Wait, no!" I squeal as she presses a file on the holo-dash and the soft-light projection flickers into life. I cover my eyes with my hands, leaning forward on the sofa and wishing that the entire thing would just swallow me up.

I exhale heavily as Clark leans forward and cocks his head, like a man possessed at the sight of himself, doing things to me that nobody should ever know about, let alone him. What had happened in my head had been far raunchier than what had happened last night, and I worry he's now going to expect me to want that right away. Apart from being utterly mortified, I realise that I don't know if I'm ready to give him that part of myself. He's sexy, smart and funny, but he's also damaged, paranoid and has a temper that never fails to surprise me.

After ten minutes of me squirming in my seat and peeking through my fingers as my cheeks flood scarlet, the counsellor turns off the desersion dream and I exhale, relieved. Clark looks back to me, his face surprised and flitting between two emotions like he's not sure whether to look angry or smirk.

"Was that really necessary?" Clark asks Jade and she smiles, hard-light eyes twinkling with something between malice and mischief.

"I think it's entirely necessary, Clark. I can tell that you two are struggling to communicate about the subject of sex, sometimes it's easier if we can just *show* you what the other person is thinking." She shuts down the holo-dash and walks back over to the armchair that is situated in the middle of the room.

"We met each other a week ago. It's barely been any time at all," Clark reminds her and she nods.

"Yes, that's true. So, I think we should see you both having an honest conversation about sex. Valentine, is there anything you'd like to say to Clark about the fantasy we just witnessed?" she asks, brushing the mahogany of her holographic locks back from her shoulder. She places her hands atop her knees, clasped together as I swallow and think on what I can possibly say.

"Uh... well, I want to say first and foremost that I hope Clark doesn't feel any pressure after seeing that. I mean, it's in my imagination; I don't expect that. I don't even know where it came from. I was expecting to have some dream about eating my weight in bacon," I express, trying to put some humour into the situation as, thankfully, Clark laughs at this.

"Pressure?" He quirks his mouth sideways and his eyes glisten.

"Yeah, you know, I don't want you to think that I expect you to be like that," I say, crossing my arms and worrying how he'll take this.

"Well, I'll be honest, Valentine. What I just saw was pretty tame. So please don't worry about my male pride, I'm sure I'll survive," Clark replies with a grin and this time it's Jade's turn to laugh, as my eyes widen and my mouth pops open.

"Tame?" I ask him, affronted, and he nods his head before looking back to Jade.

"I'm assuming porn is reserved for the Male District, then?" he demands an answer of her and she nods. I scowl as he exhales and runs his fingers through his hair, frustrated.

"What's porn?" I ask him and he chuckles again as his head hangs, leaving his body curved as it heaves with his outbursts of laughter. That's when I start to feel angry, he's making me look and feel like a complete moron.

"It's like a film, it helps men... relax," he explains, drying his watering eyes on his sleeve. I still don't get it.

"Whatever." I retort in an annoyed tone, shrugging my lack of knowledge off as Jade's eyes widen.

"Why don't you two watch a porn film together?" she suggests and Clark snorts as his head snaps up.

"Absolutely not." He leans back into the chair and crosses one leg over the other, resting his ankle atop his knee in a cocky pose.

"Where could I watch one... if I did in fact want to know what the hell everyone is talking about?" I ask her, sick of being none the wiser.

"When you get back to your hotel room you should be able to search for one on the soft-light channels. Okay?" Jade asks me and Clark rolls his eyes.

"Valentine, don't watch that stuff. Seriously, it'll rot your brain," he pleads, making me even more curious.

"Look, if it's that important to this whole sex thing then I want to know. Can you bring one up on that?" I gesture to the hard-light holo-dash and Jade turns, looking surprised.

"Of course. I'll set it up and then leave you two alone." She gets to her feet, a serious expression settling on her face.

"Valentine, I'm not sitting here and watching this with you." Clark whispers in a harsh and biting tone.

"Clark! You were fine watching something sexual when it was something I didn't want you to see. So, you freaking well *will* watch this. Besides, *you* brought this up!" I scold him and he sighs, shifting uncomfortably.

"Alright, but I'm not being held responsible for your innocence getting shattered into a million tiny pieces. Besides, this is just like another bit of Bliss Inc. propaganda. Only for men," he huffs, giving Jade a sideways glance, almost like he's silently begging her to interrupt.

"What do you mean, for men?" I ask him, feeling like the world is shifting around me as this conversation unfolds.

"Valentine, flowers and dresses... they aren't exactly what men spend their days thinking about. I mean, what did you think made men want to get married? Because I'll tell you right now it isn't the doilies." He rolls his eyes and I shake my head.

238

"Well, then I suppose I'll just have to risk my *innocence*, not that you were too worried about that last night." I snort at him and he laughs.

"Seriously, you think that was you risking your innocence? God, you're more sheltered than I thought." He runs a hand through his hair yet again, and I feel my heart deflate in my chest. I don't know what to say to that. I'm twenty-five goddamn years old and he's acting like I'm twelve.

Suddenly, the lights dim and the images begin to flicker across the screen. Jade walks from the room, her heels clicking against the floor, and Clark sits back in the hold of the sofa, a look of determined irritation plastered across his face.

I turn my attention to the movie, cocking my head at the screen and trying to work out what it is I'm looking at.

Then I realise.

Ohhhhhhhhh.

So, that's what a thingy looks like.

We sit in the waiting room, silent. Everything is awkward, even more so than it had been in the room with Jade, and I'm humiliated by how little I've experienced. Clark clears his throat as we wait with other couples that are whispering amongst themselves. The images I'd seen in the porn film flicker across the back of my mind, not disappearing despite my half desire to have them go and never return.

As I breathe in and out, painfully aware that my husband still harbours a half-amused expression, I recall him watching my reaction and becoming entirely amused by my shock. The thing he doesn't realise though is the fact that my shock hadn't stemmed completely from inexperience and the way in which I've had my mind opened, it is instead born of the fact that I've been imagining Clark and myself in place of the actors. I wanted it to be us.

"Mr and Mrs Cavanaugh?" a hard-light hologram calls as a door opens and reveals her. Our marriage counsellor is a woman again, a pretty one at that, with white hair cut into a short and trendy style and brown eyes which sparkle, as two long legs shimmer out from beneath her lab coat.

Clark and I rise to our feet, walking past the other couples that watch us go with envy, wishing that it were their turn so they could hurry up and return to their bliss filled honeymoon no doubt. If only they knew about who I've been matched with, they wouldn't be so jealous then.

"Hi," I greet the hard-light hologram as I brush past her, the light which makes up her form exuding cold, almost like she's a ghost or something.

"Hello, my name is Peaches," she says and Clark snorts. "Yes, I know. Terrible, isn't it?" She rolls her eyes and Clark smiles in agreement, chuckling as he forces his expression to become pity-filled. "Please take a seat." She closes the door and gestures for us to sit as Clark and I stand in the middle of the office, which is identical to the one we've just come from, red faced and embarrassed.

We sit in synchronised motion, and Clark remains distant, leaning over the armrest of the couch and maintaining his chilled body language as one ankle comes up to rest on his knee. I watch his face as the Counsellor sits before him and wonder if he's really as relaxed as he seems. Somehow, I doubt it.

"So, Clark and Valentine?" She looks at the file attached to her clipboard and we both nod. I sit bolt upright, this time not wanting to relax into the sofa. I'm feeling vulnerable and wondering whether or not Clark is still the person he had been when we'd woken this morning. I've opened myself up to his kiss, and then this morning he's been off, cold even. Especially when you compare his behaviour right now to last night.

I watch him as he licks his bottom lip and feel myself licking my own without being able to help it. It's like he's two totally different people. One way in private and another in front of others. Is he really ashamed of me because I'm the product of a system he detests?

"So, you two have been married a week! How have things been?" Peaches asks us. I look into her face and her brown eyes comfort me. She looks almost my age, and as the weight of everything that's changing so fast around me makes me panic, I decide to try and use this counselling for what it's intended function indicates, to better my marriage.

"It's been tough. Clark is... well, he's had a tough childhood, so he's not exactly very forthcoming," I blurt and Clark's head snaps sideways and his eyes flash a warning. I feel relief. Making him uncomfortable is exactly my intention. Perhaps if I can get him to talk about some of the things that make him so withdrawn then I can break down some of the obstacles that he keeps throwing up.

"Oh, you had a tough childhood, Clark? Why don't we talk about that? You are of course a Project prodigy, so what was it that was so hard? Surely, it'll be external, yes? I couldn't find your familial background, which I did think was a little strange." Peaches is babbling, her high-pitched voice breaking the tension of the room and causing it to crack. I watch Clark's rugged façade for any sign that he might be breaking too.

"My parents are dead," is Clark's only reply.

"Ah. I see. That would make sense, often records are lost or fail to be updated by the orphanages. They are so very busy." Peaches nods as she speaks as though acknowledging her reply as correct, looking down at her clipboard and writing upon it with a holo-pen. She gazes up once more and doesn't say she's sorry about Clark's loss, but merely watches us. I reach out a hand to lie atop his, which is resting, stone still on the couch, but he pulls it away.

"Yes, well I suppose it's not so much to do with my childhood, as it is to do with Valentine." Clark's words catch me off guard and I turn to look at him now, forehead crumpled in confusion.

"What is that supposed to mean?" I snap, panicking immediately. He has always said that his behaviour is no reflection of me at all. It is all him. Why the change now?

"Well, you're not exactly easy to please are you? You've got some pretty out of control expectations. I have been trying to make you happy, but it seems that after a week, I'm already failing. I guess that's what happens when you are raised to believe that you'll marry some prince charming." He flicks a hand out, waving his fingers as though brushing me and my silly fantasies away, like they and I don't matter to him.

I had known I was expectant at first, but I've been trying to protect myself since, not wanting to hope for anything from him.

"Okay, Valentine, would you like to respond to that?" Peaches asks me and I scowl, my heart pounding in my chest. I've let him in, and now he has the power to search and destroy. He knows me, so he knows just where to target to cause maximum damage. He's efficient at least.

"Well, I'm sorry. I didn't expect to marry some paranoid, cold, infuriating monster." I don't yell. Or scream. I just speak the words clearly and watch as his face turns impassive. He doesn't even care enough about me to get angry it would seem.

"I didn't realise you felt so strongly toward me," he retorts as Peaches looks between us. I stare at her, pleading with my gaze. I need help, backup, and it needs to come from a professional.

"I could feel incredibly strongly about you if you'd give me a damn chance, Clark. But you're hot and cold like no one I've ever met. One day you're saying you think we can be something, and the next you're telling me that *I'm* too expectant? If I'm expectant now it's only because you've led me on." I reply and he breathes out, his eyes still flashing a warning. Peaches coughs, wedging herself in-between our two raging hearts.

"It's actually more common than you might think for new couples to have arguments like this. It's a good sign. It means you care," Peaches states, smiling and trying to break the increasingly stifling atmosphere.

"Look, that's great, but I want Clark to open up and trust me. I can't keep having him shutting down when we come to a topic he doesn't like. He just… completely shuts down like no one-else I've ever met," I explain and Clark laughs beside me.

"Me? You shut down the second things don't go exactly as you imagine. You're so damn spoiled and entitled it's insane, but then with your mother that's to be expected I suppose." Clark's words cut me and I inhale too fast, feeling so hurt by his sentiment that I wonder if I might be sick. His eyes are hurt as they catch mine, only making me angrier. He's looking hurt? I'm just trying to be honest and get him to talk to me and he is taking cheap shots about my upbringing.

My eyes widen and I can't think of anything to say that will adequately express how I'm feeling without bringing me to tears, so instead I stay silent. Peaches looks between us and frowns.

"Well, I think that might be a little harsh, Clark, but it seems you can express your feelings in spite of what Valentine thinks. Maybe you should use that same honesty about your positive feelings toward her?" Clark snorts and she looks down at her hard-light watch. "Our time here today is almost up, so I'll give you an exercise to take home with you, okay? If you need me for extra time, you can always book additional appointments at reception." She scribbles down a few more notes on the clipboard she's holding, spinning slightly in her chair as I slump back into the smart foam of the couch. I'm aching, soul deep, from Clark's assessment of my character. How can he think those things of me? Hasn't he been the one pushing for us to try a relationship, after he had been the one warning me off? What the hell does he want from me? Is he after me wanting him without expectation so he can do whatever he likes without my objection, or does he just like the challenge of me making myself unavailable?

Peaches' gaze travels between us, fatigued as we all rise to our feet.

"Right, I want you two to try and spend one hour each night talking about how you feel about each other. No bailing. No hiding. Just talk honestly, even if what you have to say will be painful to say or hear. Okay?" Peaches is hurrying now, knowing she needs to move on to her next appointment and so I nod, on the verge of tears. Clark says nothing, but walks from the room without so much as a goodbye, opening the door for me like some kind of gentleman. I roll my eyes as he does so and walk through without thanking him, wondering why he doesn't just go for a run and not come back.

Back in our hotel suite I seethe, silently aching at his betrayal.

"Valentine?" Clark calls for me after an hour or so. He's on the balcony and I'm sitting on the bed, staring into space and using every ounce of my strength to not cry. I get to my feet, walking slowly out into the muggy heat of midday. My skin prickles, irritated by the clammy humidity.

"What?" I retort, unable to keep the disdain out of my tone as I raise one hand to shield my eyes from the sun.

"We need to talk about counselling," he growls. He's sitting in the chair where he always sits, looking out over the island and no doubt pondering how to next mystify me with his insane behaviour.

"Why? I think you made it pretty clear how you feel about me. Last night... it was a huge mistake," I announce, feeling my heart shatter at the thought of those touches, those kisses being reduced to the emotional equivalent of a champagne induced lobotomy.

"Look, I'm sorry about what I said, but you have to know I didn't mean it. You completely blindsided me!" he exclaims, outrage obvious as his lips, which had been used to make me feel so at home in his arms, spill hurt.

"Didn't mean it? What the hell are you talking about? You don't just attack like that and then say you didn't mean it," I snap, blinking quickly and brushing my hair back from my neck, which is beginning to become damp in the heat.

"Valentine, you can't just talk about my family with people like that! Especially people who work for... them." He explains his reasoning and I sigh. Of course. This. It always comes back to *them.*

"I didn't know I was doing anything wrong, talking about my husband's problems with a marriage counsellor!" I retort.

"I didn't think I had to tell you not to spill our private business to other people, Valentine. I thought privacy was a common practice between man and wife." His glare becomes scornful and the glimmering sapphires of his irises become hard, as though they could cut me to ribbons.

"How the hell do you know what common practice between man and wife is? We've been married a week and you don't even know enough about me to know that I hate my mother. I hate the way she brought me up," I snarl and he blanches. My heart is hammering, though everything around us is moving in lazy and slow time, as though the heat is draining the world of its energy and rhythm. My rage however, remains undeterred.

246

"Well, I'm sorry. I was just trying to stop you leaking my life story to some random stranger. You don't know who that woman reports back to!" He folds his arms across his chest, as though I'm the one in the wrong.

"Well if you'd have communicated with me that certain topics were off limits, maybe I wouldn't have said anything. As it is, you failed to inform me what was on the approved list, I'm not freaking psychic!" I feel my anger growing.

"I thought it was obvious, as someone who hates this whole fucking circus and everyone involved in it, that I wouldn't want my personal history broadcast like some fucking public service announcement!" He is yelling this time.

"Well, it wasn't. Though what isn't fucking obvious is why the hell I let you in last night. I must have been delusional, stupid even, thinking that this could actually work, Clark. You don't want to let me in and I'm done with attempting to give my heart to someone so two-faced." I get to my feet, ready to walk away.

"Do you really mean that? After everything last night... really, Valentine?" His face becomes suddenly unreadable as his anger fades, replaced by something I don't recognise. I look back to him, a shadow, as the sun causes him to silhouette before me. I sigh out, considering what to say as I watch him change before my eyes.

He's not good for me. I can't depend on him, and it's only been a week. He's been a million different shades of a man; one that I know now I can't trust to be what I need. Having made up my mind, I speak the declaration aloud, severing our most tenuous connection.

"Last night meant nothing."

Fifteen

It's been two weeks. Two weeks of awkward, strained and robotic motion.

Clark and I have adopted a kind of dance, whereby we exist in the same space, but never meet in said place. He gets up and goes to the bathroom to change, while I move to the living area and fetch something to eat. We pass in the doorway as he heads to make his coffee, before I take my food and eat it in bed. Then I move to the bathroom to shower and dress as I wonder where it all went so badly wrong and why I've not fixed it yet. During this time, we're also in a race to see who can leave the room first, because whoever does gets to go out for the day, leaving the other in the hotel room, watching movies or contemplating a way out of this numb and ambivalent state of affairs.

Today is our last day in the resort, we leave tonight and we've been sleeping in the same bed, no doubt Clark's antidote for his concern that our marriage counsellors are watching our every move. He spends a lot of his time in the evening on the balcony drinking, coming back into our room in a stupor and collapsing next to me, stinking of alcohol and telling me how he longs for me. I write this off as his drunken tongue and think nothing of it.

I think back on this as I hurry out of the hotel suite, savouring my victory. I've beaten him, and though it's our last day on this island paradise, I vow to enjoy it. Tonight, we'll be boarding our plane back to Monopolis before being shown to our new apartment where we will have only the Island in the middle of the lake with which to avoid one another.

I rush down the hotel corridor, bored by the repetitive décor and thinking about what I should do today, on the last day of my honeymoon. Now I think back on it, this honeymoon has sucked. The first week was okay, but ever since that argument, everything had become forced, an act, which is less than bearable.

Stepping into the elevator I contemplate the argument, on how I'd claimed the night we'd shared wrapped up in one another's arms, kissing, hadn't meant anything. I know I'm lying. It means more than I ever want to admit, so naturally I deny the effect it holds over me completely. I know I have hurt Clark, I know that this is partly my fault, and yet I can't quite bring myself to speak to him, to make amends.

Several times over the last two weeks I've thought about it. Tried, and yet found the words caught in my throat, unable to pass my lips. So, instead, we live in this purgatory, faking our way through counselling and avoiding one another. Connecting with him, sparking that fire which has already consumed us once, that night among the fireworks, is far too painful.

The elevator zooms downward, making my stomach plummet as I watch the resort floor move closer far too quickly. Opening swiftly, the doors part and I step through them, my heart heavy at the thought of leaving this place, but knowing that this day had to come. Soon, I'll be back in Monopolis, and that makes everything feel somewhat more vital, more terrifying. If Clark and I don't work this out, then what? What happens if we fail the one-hundred-day assessment? Are the counsellors buying the story we're spinning them? Or are my acting skills really as transparent as Clark claims?

I jog across the lobby of *The Oasis*, before setting out into the muggy heat of the day, and as the hot air clutches at me, I'm reminded of Clark's flesh on mine, making me all the more terrified.

———————————•●•———————————

When I get back to our suite, the sun is low in the sky. I've been walking around the island, aimlessly, all day. Stopping at every ledge, or outcrop of rock I can find and staring out to the horizon, wondering what on earth I should do. I've been avoiding these questions for the last fourteen days, but now we're close to being thrown back into the real world, I can't avoid my fears any longer.

"Clark?" I call out against my better judgement. There's no reply.

I look around the suite as the door closes behind me, but I can't see him anywhere. Then I remember that his favourite place to sit recently has been the balcony, so, swallowing my fears, I head outside as the glass door glides seamlessly to my left.

I step through it and out onto the wooden slats that make up the floor of the space.

"Clark?" I call again, this time there is a response, but instead of something cold, his voice is slurred but affectionate.

"Oh, look, it's my wifey," Clark replies as I turn to face him. He's sitting in his usual square wicker chair and on the table in front of him a half empty bottle of brown alcohol is sitting, the lid off. There's no glass on the table beside it.

So, he's drinking from the bottle now?

"Yes. I think we should have a chat before we leave. I didn't realise you were drinking... it's early," I reply, going to turn on my heel.

"So, what? You're judging me?" He slurs and I laugh.

"No, why would I do that?" I ask him and he shrugs, taking another swig from the bottle, which he lifts, slowly, as though it weighs a ton.

"I dunno... Isn't that what you wives do? Judge and shit?" he asks me and I chortle, unamused by his complete lack of tact.

"Whatever, Clark. I'm going to pack," I retort, knowing I have nothing really *to* pack but my wedding dress, which is still lying, crumpled, at the bottom of the wooden wardrobe, and the cuddly toy heart from Enamoury Park.

As I step back into the bedroom I hear his chair move, but continue to walk toward the wardrobe, regardless.

"Why do you hate me?" His voice travels over my shoulder, an unintelligible mess of emotions that make my heart falter.

"I don't hate you," I bite and turn to him, slowly.

"Yes you do," he replies, his voice becoming nasty.

"You're drunk. Go and have a shower, get sober and we'll talk," I retort, shrugging him off and averting my gaze. He's intimidating in this state, his gait and height becoming an unstable recipe for collapse if not something worse.

"Why should I?" he asks me and I roll my eyes. I'm not getting past him; he's too big, so instead I stand, aware that I'm most likely heading into a shouting match.

"Because you stink!" I yell, losing my temper. A burst of a giggle escapes his lips.

"See, you do hate me! You don't want me! You want Jason!" he exclaims and I scowl at him. When the hell did his brother come into our marriage?

"Clark, what the hell are you talking about?" I ask him and he blinks a few times, scratching through his overgrown stubble with his long fingers.

"You know exactly what I mean. I saw you two at *our* wedding!" he slurs. That's when something overtakes me that I've never experienced. Unbridled rage.

"How dare you!" I yell at him, taking two long and powerful strides across the carpet before slamming my palms into his chest. He teeters on the balls of his feet, reeling back and altering his stance, before falling forward toward me. I scrunch up my face, taking the brunt of his weight on my palms and shoving him toward the bathroom.

"What? Can't handle someone actually telling you the truth?" He mocks me, but I ignore him, shoving him again and grabbing his arm as he spins. I pull him around the bed, fury hot in my veins, before kicking open the bathroom door and shoving him inside.

"Shower on!" I call out, moving through the doorway and locking it behind me. He's not leaving this room without a good, long, detox.

"Relaxation mode?" the shower asks and I shake my head, knowing it can sense my tension but also aware that lavender and jasmine are the furthest thing from what I need.

"No! Wake me up setting!" I cry out, moving over to Clark and hauling open the glass shower door. He looks at me with a half amused, half angry expression and I roll my eyes, feeling a strength diffusing into my muscles that makes me capable of anything.

The water begins to plume out from the showerhead, intense in its pressure as the scent of oranges fills my nostrils. I don't even think about undressing Clark, I just grab the front of his t-shirt and pull him toward me, before redirecting him toward the torrent of hot and citrus-infused water with an abrupt shove. He gasps, the water hot as it drenches him from head to foot.

I stand, watching him become soaked as his t-shirt goes see-through and clings to his abdominals and pectorals.

"Valentine!" he growls, lurching forward in clumsy motion before he grabs me and pulls me into the shower. Before I know what's going on, I'm under the water as well. I'm soaked within seconds and, as he grips me at the elbows, I look up into his irises, within which the blaze extinguishes in a moment of complete confusion. Upon looking at my face his gaze becomes something I've never seen. From angry, to hopeless, to something new and unknown, something I've only seen in my fantasies; he is feral. "Dammit, Valentine! Why is this so fucked up?" he curses, shoving me against the back of the shower unit.

Within a second his sodden torso is pushing me against the tiles of the wall and his lips are on mine. They're angry and hot and I squeeze my eyes together, trying with every ounce of my being not to give in to him. It doesn't work as my lips emit a groan and Clark moans in retort. I put my fingers in his hair and tug, feeling him emit another snarl, though pained or not I can't tell. He kisses me, pushing his lips down on mine in besotted fury, and I let him.

"Adding soap," I hear the shower announce, before a flurry of bubbles explode from the wall behind me. I'm blocking the soap chute in the wall and so bubbles flow out around me and as I feel the heat seeping into my spine, I notice something else pushing up against my leg. I still, fear freezing the intense fire that is crawling across my skin, catching further with every contact of his flesh on mine.

"Clark, stop," I plead and he does, his eyes tracing my expression as he brings up a finger and moving it along my jawline.

"I'm sorry..." His bottom lip is red from its clutch on my own and he looks like he might cry. His eyes are wide and the acute scent of oranges is causing my nostrils to open and experience the scent of his sodden skin against me fully. It's intoxicating.

I slump against the wall, my body losing the strength that had been brought on by my anger. Clark still smells of alcohol.

"You're drunk," I sigh and he nods.

"I know. I'm sorry..." he apologises again, so I move to kiss him on the cheek.

"I know," I whisper, pushing him back so that the source of the water is directly above him. It drenches him and I move

255

forward a few paces, pulling his t-shirt over his head and throwing it on the floor.

"Get clean. Then we'll talk." I promise him and he nods, misery strewn across his expression like litter ruining a sublime nature scene.

"I'm sorry." He repeats the words again as I step out of the shower, dripping all over the floor, my shorts and t-shirt heavy with the weight of soap and water.

Stepping over to the upcycler, I shiver, quickly ordering a robe and waiting for it to appear, as I drip fast onto the tiled floor. I don't respond to the repetitive apologies of Clark as he continues to watch me, partially dressed, from inside the shower cubicle, I just grab my robe and exit the bathroom like it's on fire, not wanting to think about what's happening.

As I close the door behind me, I reach up and touch my lips with my fingertips. Both are sensitive and raw from Clark's desperate clutch on me and I feel like my heart will never stop racing.

───────●●●───────

After an hour, Clark emerges from the bathroom.

"That was a long shower," I comment, sitting with my legs curled beneath me on the satin sheets of our bed. He's in a robe too, with his dark, hair-spattered, legs poking out beneath. His hair is all over the place.

"I know. I didn't want to come out until I was sober." He shakes his head and I pass him a glass of water on the bedside table.

"Thanks," he replies, taking it in his palm before glugging some of it down. I wait for a few minutes before deciding to speak; I have things I need to clarify for him, because clearly I wasn't obvious enough two weeks ago.

"Before we start talking. I want to make one thing clear. I have no feelings for your brother, at all." I make the statement, breaking the silence between us, and Clark looks at me with a tired stare.

"He'd make the better husband," is Clark's response and so I look at him with a scowl.

"So? I'm married to you."

"Yes, but that doesn't mean you can't wish things were different," he retorts, taking another sip of water and sitting down on the side of the bed.

"I wish a lot of things were different. I wish you weren't so withholding, and so hot and cold. I wish I wasn't ignorant. I wish that you and I could be like every other couple. I wish that I'd never said that what we had two weeks ago, meant nothing to me. But I don't wish I wasn't married to you, and I certainly don't wish that I was married to your brother," I clarify and he looks at me, running his fingers through his thick black tresses and flattening them against his skull.

"You're not ignorant." Clark replies but I laugh.

"Oh, but I am. I don't know anything about how marriages really work. The only things I know are what I've been told by Bliss Inc., but I'm going to remain ignorant if you're not honest with me," I admit. I've had a lot of time to think these last two weeks and if I've realised anything it's that I don't know how to be an adult, I don't know how to think for myself, or to question

257

whatever I'm told. In a way, I'm envious of my husband, because he doesn't just believe with blind faith in the source.

"I can't be honest with you all the time, Valentine. I'm not putting you in danger in that way. I've been trying to protect you." His answer surprises me. I'd never thought that he might know things that could be dangerous. It scares me and I feel a wave of terror fall over the conversation like a black cloud.

"Oh," I reply and he looks guilty. His eyes drop.

"Saying that though, I'm sorry I got angry about you talking to that counsellor. I should have talked with you about it before we went... I just got so caught up, the night before," he apologises and I nod.

"I wasn't thinking. I just, I want to be like every other couple, Clark. I don't want all this extra anxiety." His lips quirk and his eyes soften as he gazes at me.

"You just want to live happily ever after," he paraphrases for me and smiles, as though he finds the notion sweet yet ridiculous. He places a hand over mine, the only tender contact we've had in weeks.

"I do. With you," I admit and he smiles again, like he's a teenager, before his face is overcome with worry once more.

"I wish I could give you that," he replies, before continuing on, "But I can't, it's selfish of me. I know that. This last two weeks have been awful, though. I can't fight like this again with you. Please, Valentine. Please don't cut me out again," he begs me, all of a sudden vulnerable as my eyebrows rise in surprise.

"Me? Clark you've been drinking yourself stupid these last two weeks. It's been hard for me too. I hate it when you drink," I admit and he shakes his head.

258

"I know, that was stupid of me. I just... I didn't know what to do. I'm scared anything I say will mess everything up. You're already giving up a lot being with me. I know that. I don't want you to be disappointed or angry at me any more than you already are. I hate it. I feel so guilty." He enlightens me and I scowl. Why is he acting like he's such a burden?

"I'm not angry or disappointed in you," I protest.

"You're not?" he asks, this time it's his turn to look surprised.

"Of course not. I like being with you. That's why these past two weeks have been terrible for me too." I remind him of the fact that he's not the only one to have suffered.

"Oh," is his only sentiment and it makes me sad. Does he really think he's that much of a failure as a husband?

"We've barely even started being in a relationship, Clark. You're getting too ahead of yourself. You're worrying about things we have no control over," I reason with him and he nods in agreement.

"You're right. I just... those counsellors, they make me feel like I'm failing at every hurdle," he admits and I laugh.

"Me too. I mean, I feel completely inadequate. You saw me watching that sex film. I had absolutely no idea what the hell was going on!" I laugh, remembering Clark's mortified expression.

"I don't know much about relationships either. Just about them going bad," he reminds me.

"Okay, well then let's just try to not screw it up. Take it a day at a time," I suggest and he smiles.

"Okay, but you have to trust me, Valentine," he warns, making my heart palpitate wildly.

"I don't know if I can do that. I mean, I need you to be honest with me first." I express my fear of trusting him after everything we've been through so far. I gave him my heart that night, and he threw it back at me only hours later. I suppose I can't help it if I'm a little bruised.

"I'll try, but you have to know, there are some things I can't tell you. Like I said, I'm trying to protect you," he admits and my lips pucker to the right. Is he really trying to protect me? Or is this just an excuse to be withholding.

"You can't just be fine with me one minute and then awful the next though, Clark. That's not fair," I express and he looks sheepish.

"Okay. I'll try to be more consistent," he promises, raising my hand to his lips and kissing the back of my knuckles.

"Just, don't think that things are going to be easy. I'm getting the impression that marriage is something you work on every day. It's not just something you pay attention to when things go wrong. Oh, and I want warnings on what I can and can't talk about in public. I need to know what you want, alright?" I almost scold him with the severity of my tone and he acknowledges me as he leans back onto one elbow with a slight nod of his head and his black locks fall forward across his eyes.

"Okay, I'll do my best. You need to tell me when I mess up though." I exhale at his words, feeling relief wash over me. My heart inflates seeing him like this. He's relaxed again, finally, and I'm grateful for the opportunity to fix things before we return to the city.

"I guess we kind of missed our 'honeymoon period'." I feel sad at the thought of leaving this place. While our stay has been far from easy, I love the constant sunshine and the facilities here. It really is everything that Bliss Inc. have promised. If only my husband and I had been able to fully enjoy it together.

"Yeah, I guess we did," he sighs, lying back on the sheets as we both fall into a relief filled silence.

Clark and I lay on the bed, looking up at the ceiling until it's time to depart, and as we leave the hotel suite for the very last time, I can't help but look back at the messy silk sheets and wonder what could have been. I suppose I can wonder all I like, but the truth is, the honeymoon is well and truly over.

Sixteen

The morning is dark and damp with a light fog as our flight touches down on the flawless tarmac of the airport from which we departed three weeks ago. I've barely slept during the flight, except for briefly for the last hour, which it turns out was a huge mistake.

I feel groggy and nauseous with lack of sleep as we walk from the aircraft back into the arrivals lounge with no luggage between us because my wedding dress and cuddly toy heart had been taken from me before we'd taken off and the hard-light hologram assured me that it would be in our new apartment before we made it there.

I'm nervous and excited at the prospect of seeing where we'll be starting our married lives together, and yet I can't quite bring myself to voice this excitement to Clark. Part of me believes that he'll look at it as me siding with Bliss Inc. over him, which is ridiculous, but seeing as how we only just got back on speaking terms yesterday, I'm thinking I'd better not push my luck.

After we walk through the long arrivals area of the airport, which is seemingly deserted, we quickly board a monorail to a brand-new destination for us both, the newlywed complex. This is where we'll be spending the rest of our one-hundred-day assessment period and as the monorail glides out of the station, I spot the city out of the window, surrounded by fog and the muted grey of the sky. My heart sinks.

I look at Clark quickly, who is sitting, groggy, beside me with one eye half closed. I turn back to the window and continue to examine the skyline. The separation of the male and female districts has never been starker than it is now in this early and ambivalent light.

The white matte towers of the female district rise high and contrast against the black sheen of the shard like sky-scrapers of the male portion of the city. I stare at the lake, watching its rippling waters and realise that the beauty I have always associated with it is entirely false. The waters are choppy, perilous and cold and it's there merely to divide the city, to keep us apart.

I wonder, as I lean against the pane of glass, gazing out, whether or not I like the fact that I'm not responsible for my own choices. I have no responsibility, I can claim anything that happens isn't my fault, but I have no control. I have always felt like I am in charge of my own destiny, and yet now, having been thrown in with a man who I'm not sure if I can ever have a stable connection with, I can't help but wish I had a choice. Would I choose Clark if I was given the opportunity?

I cross my legs, sitting back now into the plush seating of the carriage and realise that I don't know the answer and that this scares me more than anything.

The monorail races across a single track with only one destination, and I cannot help but feel like it's mirroring the way in which my life has been running. I'd been born from the Jigsaw Project, branded before I was old enough to know any different, and now thrust back into the same system with someone who is in the exact same situation as I am.

Clark is changing my perception and as the monorail arcs in its path, moving now across the lake instead of around it's perimeter, I wonder if I'll ever believe everything I'm told without question again. Is this the best way to be? Stuck within a system, knowing you are so and able to do nothing about it? Or would I be better off being left in the safe coddle of ignorance? Clark's hand brushes mine as he reaches for me and I let him, my mood melancholy as rain begins to fall around us and I continue to race toward my future, without escape or choice of deviation.

●●●

"New couples please report to the apartment registry office, thank you." The announcement is blunt and unfeeling as it rings throughout the carriage just before the doors slide open. Clark and I exit the monorail, both of us dressed in cotton t-shirts and shorts, not having thought about the change in climate upon landing. I shudder and Clark grips my hand hard as he feels the reaction to the chill run down my arm.

"Come on, let's get to that office. You're freezing." He looks me up and down and I nod, quickening my pace as we race across the platform, which spreads out from us in multi-coloured mosaic tiles. It's beautiful here; far different from the single district. This place is infused with colour and is a welcome reminder of the sunny climate from which we've returned.

We pick up our pace into a jog as other couples depart from the monorail and I recognise a few faces from the crowd I'd been a part of going up the stairs into Bliss Hall. The eyes around us narrow, as it suddenly becomes a race between the couples, each one grabbing onto their partner and starting on course for the same location.

The neon hard-light signs leading to the office glow bright purple as we rush down a flight of escalating stairs, ignoring their slow and steady momentum as the competitive air infects us with each heavy and hurried breath we inhale. We screech around the corner, following the next sign in our path and the rubber on the soles of my shoes squeaks loudly against the multi-coloured rubber of the floor. Clark watches as I skid slightly and pulls me behind him with a harsh yank on my wrist. Following him, I realise, eventually that we're in the lead. We run through the station, the cold air stinging our faces as we laugh, letting out the only sound we can manage as we reach the office first. It's fun. For no particular reason, for no planned motive, or materialistic merit, running alongside Clark makes me grin from ear to ear and I have no idea why.

The hard-light hologram inside the glass office booth looks between us, bored, as we reach the glass and almost slam into its spotless transparency. I'm breathless, and as we both erupt into a fit of giggles, the hard-light hologram rolls his eyes which sparkle lime in the ghastly fluorescent cyan of the booth.

"Names?" he asks me and I gasp for air, resting one arm on the outcrop of counter which slides beneath a glass windowpane.

"Valentine and Clark..." I pant as Clark cuts me off.

"Cavanaugh." He exhales, finishing my sentence. The man looks back into his head, his eyes rolling a torrent of ones and zeros before flickering back to lime.

"Right, this one is easy. You're in the penthouse apartment in tower number thirteen. Lucky you." He shakes his head, as though he's somewhere between losing the will to live and utterly jealous.

"Thank you." Clark nods in acknowledgement as the hologram shoos us away. The people behind us in the line, waiting to get their apartment assignments, scowl, as if having to wait an extra few moments to find out where they'll be living will most certainly kill them.

Geez. When did people get so entitled? I wonder, thinking on Jason, who is living in the labour settlements, alone and unable to lay a finger on the woman he's loved for so many years. My heart breaks at the thought of being apart from someone who I was certain of, as it also breaks at the thought of losing Clark, even though I can't be sure how I feel about him. We walk down more brightly coloured, semi-transparent, steps and out into the streets of the newlywed complex. The streets here are far more vibrant than those of the single districts. Everywhere, people are outside exploring the city, which boasts a spectrum of lush and vibrant hues. Couples are abundant and the noise is welcome, brightening my mood as Clark turns to me.

"Which way do you think tower thirteen is?" he asks me and I shrug, looking around the street, which has multiple towers rising in cut, coloured crystal on every side.

"I don't know. There are towers everywhere," I state. Clark grabs my hand again and we walk down the street a small way until, whilst I'm looking down at the coloured paving stones, I remember something.

"Hey, you remember in Enamoury Park how that map came out of the floor?" I ask my husband. At the word 'map', the tile beneath me activates, projecting a hard-light holographic diagram of the city upwards and before me like a orizontal desk has been laid out.

"Hey! Cool!" Clark states, peering down over my shoulder like he had that day when I'd been so terribly up and down, and not just physically either. We trace the way to our new apartment block quickly, finding the layout of the city much the same as the single districts in that every street on the right of Main Street is an even number, and every street on the left is an odd number.

We rush forward and past couples that seem lost to time, both tired and keen at the prospect of getting to our new place so we can stop for a second and take in everything. Taking a left, Clark and I come face to face with the tower in which our apartment is held and both stare up at the sapphire shard. Could it be calculated, the fact that the place we're living is the same colour as my engagement ring and Clark's eyes?

Probably, I muse, *almost everything around me is calculated.*

"Let's go in." I shudder; still cold despite the rush of heat I'd felt at our dash through the monorail station.

Clark doesn't reply verbally, instead pulling me after him as he moves toward the entrance of the building, and I realise that it's the first time we've been together in the city. This could be a problem, seeing as he was so hesitant to talk at Jungala despite the fact that so much of the island was lush, green and seemingly natural. I'm betting that in a city environment, his paranoia will only be worse.

We stride up to the entrance, rhythmically and methodically scanning our tattoos together across the turnstile barriers. This building is nothing like my apartment block in the female district as instead of white, the lobby spans out from us in a plush and deep azure blue, accented with dark woods. We tread across the space carefully, feeling all the way underdressed as silver handles gleam everywhere and a hard-light doorman presses the elevator button, calling it down to us. I stand for a moment as it descends, looking around and noticing a small palm tree sits in the corner, potted and out of place. It makes me smile as I remember the hotel from which I've just come, and I hope for the love of everything I thought I had known to be true, that this next part of the hundred-day assessment is easier than the first three weeks.

The elevator pings and as the hard-light hologram steps aside, the doors sweep open. The inside of the box isn't what I'm used to. It isn't white and clinical. Instead, it's clad of dark wood and silver with blue cushioned upholstery set into the walls.

"Whoa!" I exclaim my surprise, stepping inside as Clark gestures for me to move in first.

"Bit plush for an elevator," Clark grumbles, scanning his tattoo against the penthouse option on the holo-dash and leaning, with an exhausted sigh, against the padding of the wall.

"If our apartment is half as nice as this I'll be thrilled." I laugh and he smiles.

"You realise that this is excess." He says it, not as a question, but as a statement.

"I'm beginning to see it that way, yes," I admit and he laughs.

"Maybe I'm having more of an impact on you than I thought." He runs his fingers through his hair and I chuckle.

"Maybe, I've been thinking about everything a lot lately. About my mom too. I mean, when I saw all those other couples rushing toward the office, I just felt kind of bad for them. Like they're too good to wait a few moments? My mom is just like that. She thinks she deserves the best, and if she doesn't get it, it's never her fault. I just wonder how many things I take for granted. When I think about what my life would have been like if I'd not made it into the Jigsaw project... I..." I begin and he nods.

"I understand. We're lucky, but it's important that being lucky doesn't make us resigned to all this." He gestures to the elevator, looking between the corners of the space as we reach the height of our ascent within the blue shard.

"Exactly. I want to be grateful for everything. I mean, I'd never thought about it before I met you. What goes into making this kind of lifestyle possible," I reply, smiling. He looks at me as the elevator doors open and I could swear I catch him in the middle of an admiring gaze. "Come on." I hurry him, eager now to see the inside of our apartment. As we step out onto the top floor, I see that there's only one wooden door in the lobby like space.

"That must be us then," I hear Clark note, a slightly impressed expression curving his lips up into the beginning of a smile. As I watch him, I realise that he's excited too, even if he doesn't want to show it.

"Must be," I breathe, giddy. We walk forward and raise our tattoos to the black mirror of glass, which resides where a door handle would be. Scanning our tattoos together, a tiny light at the top of the door turns green, before it swings forward on hydraulic hinges.

We step inside to a full and uninterrupted view of the Bliss Inc. Headquarters across the water, and even beyond it to where the horizon fades into the wilderness. The entire back of the apartment is glass, with a balcony beyond it through two matching glass doors, providing an unfaltering stream of light, even from the dull sky of today, which falls upon the rich wooden floors and makes it feel like a real home.

"Whoa," I say, realising now what the hard-light hologram had meant when he'd said we were lucky. The apartment is cavernous, with dark woods and rooms that range from ice to midnight blue in hue.

"Holy crap," Clark announces, turning to his left as he walks into the main area. It's open plan and he immediately makes his way over to the kitchen.

"You'll be cooking me breakfast again now. You know that, right?" I tempt him, knowing that my breakfast diet for the last two weeks of our honeymoon, which has consisted of lukewarm ramen, has been less than satisfactory.

"Sure. I could cook for an army in here." His eyes sparkle and then turn sad as he revolves around in the space.

"Are you alright?" I ask him, hearing the door slide shut finally, cutting us off from the rest of the city.

"Yeah, I'm okay. It's just a little crazy. I thought our suite was big!" He sighs, placing both his hands on the back of his neck and reeling back on his heels as he spins in the space again, like he's unable to take it all in.

"I guess anywhere looks big once you've been resigned to an apartment unit the size of a shoe box," I remind him and he nods.

"What are we going to do with all this space?" He asks me and I shrug.

"I don't know. I didn't register for a lot really. I figured it would be fun for us to go pick out stuff together," I admit, knowing that the truth of the matter is that I'd opted to do it this way so my mother couldn't control my purchases.

"Okay, well we should go out shopping if that's the case. We need a bed and sofas and stuff," He reminds me and I nod. I'm tired, but I really need to stop by a store to pick up a hard-light watch too because I really do need to message Egypt like I promised.

"Yeah. Okay, let's look in the other rooms first," I suggest, walking over to one of the closed doors on the right-hand side of the apartment. It leads to a barren bedroom. There's no furniture in it, and the only actual object in the apartment apart from the holo-dashes and the kitchen and bathroom fittings is my wedding dress, which hangs in a new garment bag upon the curtain rail mounted on the midnight blue wall. "I guess I should have listened when they advised me to register for stuff." I huff, feeling a mammoth task before me now.

"Hey, don't look so blue. Shopping could be fun. Wait until we find out how completely we hate one another's taste in décor," Clark jokes, though his eyes are still sad, and I laugh to fill the silence as we stare around the empty apartment.

Knowing that we don't have anywhere to sit or rest except the floor, or possibly the bath, we both look to one another again as we swallow the somewhat sour anti-climax of our honeymoon, before journeying out into the city once more.

Leaving, I know I should be happy, but something about all this suddenly feels wrong. The scale, the grandeur, how everything is a little too perfect and yet I know elsewhere, people are alone, just like I have been for so long. As hard as I try, walking out into the city, I can't get the look of melancholy on Clark's face, at the sight of the kitchen, out of my head.

———————————●●●———————————

"Ma'am, can I help you with anything?" I hear the hard-light hologram ask politely as we stand in the middle of the furniture store. I turn to him, flustered and see that the moustache on his face is twitching, probably with impatience because I've been here far longer than I want to be. The problem is, it's insanely difficult to choose anything, mainly because there seems to be a million options for just about every single piece of furniture you can imagine.

"No thank you, just browsing," I explain as he turns on his heel without so much as a smile and stalks off.

"Clark! Help me decide!" I panic, looking down at my brand new hard-light watch with impatience as I flick past yet another option on the projector. The store space is completely empty, except for twenty blue-screens that allow shoppers to try out the furniture in a recreation of your new home. It startles me how many options there are, how am I ever supposed to narrow down this level of excess?

"Okay, that's it. You pick four numbers and I'll pick four numbers and that's what we're buying. It's not like we're even paying for this stuff," he exclaims, taking control of the unit as he looks up to me. The cyan light reflects back, cold in his sapphire stare.

"Numbers?" He asks me and I panic again.

"I.. I..." I start and he chuckles.

"You suck at being spontaneous! Come on, Valentine! Make a choice! Four numbers, go!" He pushes me and I can't help but feel utterly ridiculous, partly because of the amused gaze he's giving me, and partly because I realise that he's right, I don't know how to make choices on the spot.

"Four, Seven, two hundred and thirteen, and.... One." I spit out and he nods.

"Okay... so that takes care of the bed, living room set and vanity..." He says, biting down on his bottom lip as he swipes his fingers across the holo-dash which shines upward, lighting the hollows of his bone structure so he appears ghostly.

"Done!" he announces, making a final click on the dash and swiping his tattoo across the scanner, making sure that our information is stored so they know where to deliver.

"What else did you order?" I ask him and he looks to me, surprise in his gaze.

"The usual stuff, rugs, coffee maker, wardrobe, I also got a backpack for myself. One of those heavy duty ones," he explains and I scowl.

"Why would you need that?" I ask, suspicious and he shrugs.

"To carry stuff around of course." He reacts like it's the most absurd question I could have asked, but for some reason I feel a little thrown. Why does he need a heavy-duty bag, is he going somewhere?

"Oh. Right." I look down at my watch, checking the time for absolutely no reason, before striding over to the hard-light store manager. I sort of wonder why he's even here, I mean, this store which sells everything from backpacks to furniture is completely self-service.

"When will this be delivered?" I ask him, worrying now that I really have left it too late and that Clark and I will be left to sleep on the floor.

"It will be with you momentarily, worry not. As all stores in this Complex, we operate twenty-four hours," he explains and I frown, suddenly pitying him. Twenty-four hours? I've never heard of that before.

"You do?" I question him and he nods as Clark stops beside me before turning and looking down at the store manager's mere stature.

"You have someone to take over for you though, right?" I ask him and he frowns, looking me up and down with his beady hard-light eyes before staring up at me once more.

"No Ma'am. It is only myself. I am a hard-light hologram. We don't sleep." Clark stiffens beside me and frowns, a look of confusion on his face.

"Oh, well thank you," I reply, ending the conversation as he turns with an unimpressed glance and storms off. I turn to Clark.

"Ready to go?" I ask him and he nods, taking my hand in his. The look on his face continues to be troubled until we find ourselves back on the main street of the complex, where a mask of relaxed cold falls across his features.

"I hope the stuff you bought doesn't look insane," I snort, and he looks down at me before smirking also.

"Well, if it is we only have to live with it for the next eighty something days. You can't deny though, you do suck at making choices." He reminds me and I smile, embarrassed. Then it occurs to me: How many big choices in my life have been left down to me?

The answer haunts me.

None.

No choices that ever mattered have been in my hands, so I guess seeing as this one is, it can't matter too much. A seed of something unfelt buries deep within the recesses of my conscious, niggling away, as I let the sensation of stranglehold flitter away and we walk on through the cold, solitary isle.

<hr />

Back in our apartment, a mish-mash of furniture awaits us as the door slides back, revealing the now furnished innards of the main room. I walk through the living room set which, thankfully, matches in dark woods and lime green suede throughout.

"This is nice," I admit, turning on my heel as I see Clark's gaze has fallen to the kitchen island. In the centre of the dark wooden countertop, the backpack he ordered is sat, still wrapped in clear plastic and waiting for him. He walks over to it and I watch him as he does, sitting back into the plush, smart foam, hold of the new corner sofa.

"That's a big bag," I comment as he pulls off the plastic and examines it.

"Yeah. That's why I bought it," he expresses, quickly placing it on the floor, propped by the wooden stools, which are also new, before turning and examining the coffee maker.

"Want some coffee?" He asks me and I shake my head, yawning.

"No thanks. I'm actually really tired. I think I might go to sleep." I explain, looking over my shoulder and out the window. The sun has long since slunk behind the razor's edge of the horizon and dark indigo spattered with glitter has fallen atop the world.

"Oh. Okay. Sleep well." He smiles at me, closing the space between us and reaching down, stretching out a hand and pulling me into his arms. He kisses me, his lips tender on mine, not rushing but lulling me further into the drowsy mist which threatens to overwhelm my consciousness.

"Mmm," I mumble against his mouth as the warmth of his chest seeps into my own.

"Sweet dreams, Valentine." He turns me, directing me to the bedroom, before striding quickly across the floor without pause and opening the bedroom door. The bed is revealed in the midnight blue of our bedroom, an ornate black gothic frame with silver sheets. They're silk, just like the ones of our honeymoon bed.

I don't even bother to undress, but slip off my shoes where I stand, right in the middle of the floor, before using the last of my energy to take a few paces forward and collapse into the smart-foam of the new mattress. It smells of chemicals, of newness, but

I can't bring myself to care as Clark looks down upon me with an adoring gaze. He tucks me in, kisses me on the forehead and closes the door. As I ponder upon this suddenly tender act, the lights diminish automatically and I can't help but fall into an instant and dreamless sleep.

When I wake in the morning, it is to an empty apartment. Clark and the bag are gone.

Seventeen

Sitting on the lime suede sofa, I look into the wide dimensions of our brand new holo-dash, which is blank. No messages. No indication that another person even so much as lived here, let alone left.

I have a coffee mug in my hands, but am yet to take a sip of the contents as I contemplate what to do. It's still early, seven o'clock in the morning to be exact, but I'm wide awake; not that you'd know it from my lack of movement. I sit here, wondering where the hell my husband is. He's been gone all night and he's taken a heavy-duty backpack with him. Has he left me? Is he off to meet up with another woman? Is that even possible in the Jigsaw Project? I mean, we're on an island surrounded by other married couples, so how the hell would he even know someone here... he didn't even grow up in Pearl Falls. He grew up in an orphanage.

As I'm beginning to panic, I look down to my wrist. I'm still wearing my hard-light wristwatch.

Egypt. I should message Egypt. I realise, unable to believe that I've gone to sleep without even so much as letting her know I'm home. Leaning forward I place my coffee mug, still full, down on the glass coffee table in front of me and swipe open the interface on my watch. I'm no longer able to video call with Egypt, but I can still message her, provided she has enough cred that is. I look down at the blinking cursor, before deciding to start it simple. I don't want it to be obvious I'm completely freaking out.

Hey, I'm back! How have you been?

I type, hitting send as I lean back into the hold of the couch. Within seconds, I get a reply, causing me to smile.

Oh my bliss, you're back! How was it? Tell me everything! I've been saving my credit for this! How's Clark? Is he different than at the wedding? Do you love him yet? Where did you go on Honeymoon? What was the Honeymoon like? Where are you living? What's your apartment like?

I smirk at her reply, before laughing at the inflow of questions that I know she's been dying to ask since the day I left. I make sure to answer all of them as I type,

It was really fun. Clark and I are… well we're okay. I think I could really love him, but last night he went out, took a bag, and he hasn't come back yet. So, I'm scared. Our apartment is huge and we're on the top floor in tower 13, it's the blue one! We went to Jungala for our honeymoon! It was awesome and I spent lots of time in the spa and on the beach. Clark and I also had some nice dinners, you'd have loved the food! The service around here is insane too, they have these new hard-light holograms and everything's open twenty-four hours a day. So much better than the single district! I really missed you! But how have you been?

I click send with a single tap of my fingertip and wait for her reply in the silence. The smell of coffee fills my nose and though I'm alone, I feel a sense of comfort knowing Egypt is on the end of the messages I'm receiving. It might not be exactly the same, but she's still there for me when I need her most.

Her reply comes and I feel a rush of relief, as every time I hear from her, I grow increasingly worried that our conversation will be cut short by the limits of her cred balance.

He's gone? Where did he go? Didn't he tell you? Maybe he went out to surprise you with a gift or something? I mean you said everything is open twenty-four hours, right? Have you two slept together yet? If so, what was it like? Was it good? You also say you think you can love him? Don't you know? Can you see why the formula matched you two up?

More questions come flooding through the watch face as I scroll down the conversation.

As I'm about to reply, I hear the door open and Clark walks in. He looks totally fine, bag slung across his shoulder and his face sporting an expression of contentedness, as though everything is totally normal. In fact, he looks the most relieved I've ever seen him except when he was drunk.

"Where were you?" I ask him, knowing that I'm probably going to get a non-response but also knowing that if I don't ask, then it'll nag at me forever.

"I went out for a run, sometimes I do that at night. The cold air helps me think, keeps me level," he explains. I look him up and down. He *is* in running gear. But why the hell would he need a backpack for a run?

"Why did you take that bag?" I ask him, still suspicious. I wonder if this is how he feels about Bliss Inc. and momentarily pity him, because being suspicious is tough when you have someone to question, so I can't imagine how frustrating it must be when you're suspicious of a company you can't get answers from.

"Weight. I put weight in, it makes the run tougher. It's called weight training, look it up," he replies, dumping the bag on the floor. He strips his shirt and shoes off as he walks across the living space, enters the bedroom and then the adjoining bathroom before closing the door shut promptly behind him. Ignoring the sound of my watch alerting me to the fact that Egypt has replied, I move over to the bag he's just discarded. I pull open the magnetic clasp, surprised at the weight of it, only to discover that there's nothing inside at all. No weights, no clothes, not even a bottle of water. Nothing.

I clip the bag closed again before placing it back exactly where I found it and making my way back over to Clark's running shoes. I don't know what exactly it is that possesses me to pick up a man's sweaty footwear, but I turn them over, only to be greeted by a hideous smell. The soles of the shoes are dirty, covered in water and some sort of sludge which I have no way to describe, other than by saying it quickly makes me want to throw up.

Placing the shoes back down again, I wonder where exactly Clark could have picked up that kind of debris on the soles of his shoes. I mean, everywhere in Monopolis is paved with plastic, rubber and silicone. How is it possible that his shoes smell absolutely rancid?

281

I move back around to the couch, taking up the position I had been in before Clark's return. I take my cup in hand and take a sip of now lukewarm coffee. It tastes a million times better than the stuff from my old coffee maker, but for some reason I know that right now, when my husband is obviously lying, I'd rather have crappy coffee and good company. Looking down at my watch, I realise I've got two more unanswered messages from Egypt. Clicking on the conversation, I read quickly, hoping she hasn't gone back to sleep.

You're okay though right? The first message says, before I scan downward and see the next line of text, which reads, **Valentine?**

Looking back to her previous messages I begin to type my reply, knowing I need to be as concise as possible.

Sorry, he just came back. Apparently he went for a run? All night? No, we haven't slept together, just made out once, which was nice, but now I'm not so sure I can trust my own judgement. I really like him, but he's lying to me and this is one of the reasons I can't be sure whether or not it's love! I have no idea why we were matched to be honest, I mean, we don't have anything in common. He's the most confusing person ever and he's totally different from one second to the next. What should I do?

I click send, wondering if my unmarried friend really can be of any help. I could message my sisters, but I don't know if I can bear the thought of getting them involved in all this, especially when I think about the torrent of smug and self-satisfied responses I'd probably be getting. Egypt replies once again in seconds.

That doesn't sound like the truth if I'm honest, but maybe he has a reason for keeping you in the dark? What if it's some weird man thing? I guess it's good you haven't had sex, especially considering you're still not sure why you've been matched. I'm glad making out was fun, I'm sort of jealous! I have been real lonely since you left. Do you think the formula got it wrong for you two? How's counselling and stuff, does that help?

Her reply makes me realise that my fears are right on point. She doesn't understand, because she's not married. I think about her last question, about counselling. I'd totally forgotten about our appointment yet again, and as I swipe left on my watch face, I can see that my calendar reflects that this afternoon is our first post-honeymoon session and I'm nervous.

I get to my feet, walking into the bedroom and sitting down on the bed, unable to keep still as my pulse begins to heighten.

I know I'm not supposed to speak about certain things, but how can I keep this kind of anxiety inside? I'm scared he's in love with someone else. I'm wondering where he's been all night. I'm scared that I'm falling for him against my better judgement and that he's off longing after someone, someone he should have been matched with. What if he knew someone from when he was a kid? What if he fell for someone before he got selected for the Jigsaw Project? It's not common, but I've heard rumours of it happening before.

I exhale heavily, waiting on Egypt's worried message from my lack of reply as I let the fear gnaw at me. I twist the silver silk sheets in my palm, taking out some of my frustration on the material as I scrunch it up beneath my fingertips. I should just be able to ask Clark about it, confront him, but the last time I'd accused him of talking to someone else on our wedding night, he had explained it all away seamlessly, believably even. I mean, I also asked him today about it, and he had obviously lied, so what makes me think that he'll be honest with me if I just come out with it?

I realise that talking with Egypt, as helpful as it had once been, isn't going to make me feel any better about this. The only person who has the power to do that is Clark. I type out my reply to Egypt in a flurry of tapping fingers as I hear Clark get out of the shower.

Not really. Clark doesn't like it when I talk to the counsellors about our problems. He thinks it might risk our place in the Project. I don't know, he's a hard person to figure out. I'm sorry you're lonely, I miss you too! Please don't be envious of me, I'm sort of wishing I was back in the Single District with you if I'm honest. Anyway, I have to go, Clark is just getting out of the shower and I don't want him to think I'm talking to you about our relationship. He can get super cranky! Speak to you tomorrow, I promise.

I click send and turn the screen back to the time, which blinks, notifying me as to how early it really is. My stomach grumbles as the door opens Clark steps out into the bedroom with a towel around his waist, steam billowing out behind him. I scowl to myself as I quickly look away.

"Good shower?" I ask him and he nods without saying a word, stepping around the bedframe and over to the upcycler in the wall where he requests some fresh clothes from the catalogue with a bored expression. "Did you forget we have counselling this afternoon?" I ask him and his head snaps around as his eyes widen.

"Oh, shit. Yeah. I did," he mumbles and I nod. There's a moment as I look into his eyes and he gazes back, where I almost confront him. I almost say the words, and ask him who she is and why he just won't admit it, but instead the silence hangs between us and it's awkward. I don't have a way to force him to be honest, the only way I can do that is to make him uncomfortable, or threatened, so he doesn't have another alternative.

I think back on what Egypt had asked. Is there a reason good enough that he would be lying to me? He keeps saying he's protecting me, but I don't even have any evidence that I need protecting. The only thing I have is his word, and even worse, I've just caught him lying straight to my face.

An idea strikes me as I break eye contact with him before saying, "Well, it's important we keep on top of it. We have a long way to go if this marriage is going to work, right?"

"Right you are," he responds with a gentle smile. "Breakfast?" he suggests, but this time I notice the distraction tactic. He did it last night too, when he'd tucked me into bed just so he could sneak out unnoticed.

"That would be lovely," I reply, my smile not reaching my eyes. I'm tired of his lies. I'm tired of the games, of the ice and fire between us. Counselling hasn't helped us so far, but maybe that's because Clark's put a filter on what I'm allowed to discuss.

I feel suddenly unhinged as he walks over to the bathroom to get dressed in private, putting the door between us, knowing that, more than his approval, I need him to come clean.

285

I sit back in the hold of the smart-foam sofa. Once more I'm sat in a counsellor's office, and for the life of me, I can't tell the difference between this office and the one in Jungala, because they're completely identical. The hard-light hologram, Peaches, is sitting in a chair opposite us, legs crossed and with an impartial expression plastered onto her hard-light face. I admit I find it beyond strange she's still our counsellor despite the fact we're hundreds of miles from where our last session occurred, but I guess that's the wonder of these new hard-light holograms.

"So how have you two found your re-integration into city life?" Peaches asks us and Clark snorts.

"That's sort of a stupid question. We only got back yesterday," he reminds her and she frowns before nodding, ignoring his irritable nature. I sigh silently under my breath, finding his lack of trying annoying to say the least.

"How about you, Valentine?" she asks me and I take a deep breath, wringing my fingers and looking at the glow of my tattoo before allowing my eyes to rest on my wedding band. It's beautiful, no doubt, but I'm beginning to see it as a beautiful shackle and the jigsaw pattern on my wrist as a kind of branding. It makes me angry, perhaps irrationally so, that I have so little control already, and Clark is choosing to take away even more by keeping the truth from me. So, I decide to push him.

"Well, I thought things were going better. But then Clark went out all night running. I woke up and he was gone," I explain and Peaches scowls. Clark turns to me, a warning flashing in his irises once more, but I ignore him.

"And how did that make you feel?" Peaches asks me. I blink a few times, contemplating what to say next as I watch Clark's fist tighten on the upholstery.

"Well, abandoned. Say, I do have a question. What were to happen if, just theoretically, one partner in a married couple was caught being unfaithful? Just for example," I ask, throwing all caution to the wind and watching as Clark's mouth pops open. My heart is racing in my chest as Peaches makes a note on her clipboard.

"Is there something you want to say, Valentine?" she asks me and I shake my head.

"No, I mean I'm just curious. Nobody ever talks about it, but it must happen, right?" I ask her and she looks startled. Her eyes widen slightly and her hard-light cheeks flush, which is an odd thing to see.

"Well, it's a serious violation of the project rules, I'll tell you that. But it's unheard of. The formula makes it almost impossible for you to fall for someone else once you've clamped eyes on your matchmate, so I wouldn't worry." She smiles, though is clearly uncomfortable as she quickly rotates to face Clark, who I could swear has turned to stone.

"Clark, do you want to respond?" she asks him and he turns to me.

"I'm sorry that you felt abandoned, Valentine. I was just glad of the time to myself and that I was finally able to go running without collapsing from dehydration. You know how hot it was in Jungala." He gives me an explanation for why he was gone so long, but I don't believe it.

"Well, you could have told me where you were going," I counter and he sighs.

"You were asleep," he reminds me, looking deeply into my eyes.

"So? You could have mentioned it before..." I know I'm beginning to sound ridiculous, like a small child, but instead of doing what I expect and getting angry, his eyes soften and his lips quirk up at the edges.

"The fact that you could think I have feelings for anyone else is absurd, Valentine. You know how I feel about you. You're beautiful, smart, funny, sweet. I love spending time with you. I just wanted some time alone, which I think I have every right to. Everything has been so intense and crazy, that last night I needed a second to... re-integrate." He takes my hand in his and raises it to his lips, laying a kiss on the back of my knuckles in that way which causes a shudder to run up my arm.

I narrow my eyes at him, but he keeps his charming expression on with a ferocious determination in his eyes. I could mistake it for passion toward me and how he feels, but now I also wonder if this is an act for the counsellor.

"See Valentine, Clark is being honest with you. His body language is relaxed, he's looking you in the eye, and he's speaking his mind. I know it can be difficult to believe that someone can love us so completely, especially when we are still learning about who we are and how to love ourselves, but you have to let Clark adore you. You're very lucky. He's being open about his emotions, which is something a lot of men have trouble with early on," Peaches interjects and I turn to her, feeling entirely awkward and defeated as I realise that my plan to get Clark to come clean has completely backfired.

"I guess you're right," I admonish, frowning as I brush a lock of my dirty blonde hair behind one ear. Clark exhales beside me, noticeable only by his shift in position, which I can feel, however subtly, through the sofa cushions. I turn back to Peaches, exhaling and relinquishing to the fact that whatever game it is Clark and I are playing, I am losing.

***

Back in the apartment, I expect an argument to erupt over the fact I'd spoken honestly to Peaches, but instead Clark becomes more attentive than I'm used to.

"You know, if you're anxious about something you should just talk to me about it," he reminds me as he sits down on the sofa, looking up at me with a kind expression. I stare at him, taken back as the crisp sunlight streams in through the window and is captured within the thick black locks of his hair. His eyes are wide and seemingly frank as I fidget on my feet, uncomfortable at his sudden candour.

"What's the point when you just lie to me?" I ask him, feeling my rage come on all of a sudden and escape from my lips with only a few wicked strokes of my tongue. I take a quick and direct step forward, sidling across the dark, hardwood floors and closing the space between us.

"I haven't lied to you." He says, plain faced, taking my hands in his.

"You say... while lying to me," I snap and he blinks a few times before letting a sigh loose from his lips.

"Alright. That's a lie. I have lied to you. I didn't go out for a run last night. But I wasn't with another woman either, so don't even go there," he warns me and I frown.

"Why won't you tell me where you went?" I ask him, reluctant to let the topic drop.

"Because it's not important right now. You just need to know I wasn't out longing after some other woman. Have you forgotten how I feel about you?" he asks me and I flush slightly. It's been two weeks since that night when we lost hours to one another's kisses, and since the shower incident, everything has been polite and purposeful.

"Well, it's been two weeks since we had that little talk," I remind him and he suddenly looks concerned.

"Come here." He pulls me down onto his lap as I twist under his arm, spinning on the ball of one foot. He gazes up into my eyes as his hand comes up to caress my cheek. "Have I been slacking on my husbandly duties, Valentine? You can tell me if I have." I feel a sudden nervousness come over me and I wonder why. Have I been going crazy because I'm worried about Clark's lies, or is it just because I don't believe that he really has feelings for me? I'd known that night, on the revolving platform above the ocean, but it's been so long since then, it's hard to believe, after all the discontent that's been between us, that anything survived.

"I just... we had that night and then everything went to hell," I remind him and he bites his bottom lip.

"It did. I'm sorry it did. You shouldn't be left wondering if things have changed. So, let me be clear." He pulls me close, resting my forehead against his before his lips push against mine. I feel the fire within my chest reignite at this nostalgic motion and my breath catch in my throat as he kisses me deeply. "There is nobody else, I promise you. Only you," he whispers, breaking the kiss.

"Okay," I whisper back, realising as I stare into his gaze that I don't think he can be lying. If he is lying, then I can't tell and I'm at the mercy of his seemingly besotted hold on me.

"Let me take you out tonight," he pleads at me with his stare and I nod, not knowing what to say. Should I just let last night go? Or is his sudden amorous behaviour just another distraction from what's really going on? I'm afraid of what that might be; especially now he seems so certain of his feelings for me. If he's not sneaking out to run off with some other woman, then where is he going?

The questions continue to whir around my brain as I put my arms around Clark's neck and pull him close to me, hanging on for dear life in a world where everything is out of my control.

"Don't worry, Valentine," he states, trying to lull me into a sense of entirely false security, "I'll take care of everything."

Eighteen

The clinking of fine cut crystal and the clattering of heavy knives and forks against flatware fills the restaurant as Clark and I finally get inside and out of the cold. He's looking refreshed after taking a long afternoon nap while I flicked through the soft-light channels, bored but none-the-less grateful for a break from all his intensity. The smell of food fills my nostrils and my stomach grumbles as I begin to wonder why I thought it was a good idea to skip lunch.

Hard-light holograms flit around the room in a sort of slow, yet precise choreographed ballet as the warm light of the room washes over us and we bask in the heat. I watch them, unable to shake the unnatural feeling I get whenever I observe them, the technological ghosts which have only most recently come to haunt the city, where everything is clean, and each night the moon rises, erasing the memories of the day past and readying the sky for a new, clean and sterile day, when the sun breaks over the horizon, stark and unyielding.

It seems unnatural to have these holograms, which are so close to people and yet not so, walking among us as though it's totally normal, and I wonder as we approach the host, who is standing at a tall aluminium podium, who came up with the idea of making people hard-light in the first place.

"Table for two?" she asks us and we nod, not even bothering to reply vocally, as she turns promptly on her heel and her holographic locks of hair flip back over one shoulder. We follow her into the hot clutch of the space, where the architecture and decor is unlike anything I've ever seen. The entire inner space is carved out in black, slick marble from ceiling to floor, and geometric patterns spirograph across every surface in liquid gold. The lighting is warm and bright, making the space intimate and private as it bounds between the walls which sheen dark.

We approach a table in the far corner, the surface of which is glass placed upon a stand shaped like some kind of gold bird. Its long, curvaceous neck just tall enough to the hold the table to the correct height, and we are seated quickly around it by the woman who quickly stalks off.

"This place is ornate," I comment as I pull my seat in under the table. "What's with all the birds?" I ask Clark as he sits, taking his faux leather jacket off his shoulders and slinging it around the back of his chair.

"Well it's called the Golden Swan, right?" he reminds me and I cock my head.

"Yeah, so?"

"Well, swans are birds, aren't they? Well, they were, before they went extinct. An interesting fact about swans, is that before they went extinct they used to mate for life." He makes this comment like it should have some kind of profound significance to me, but instead I merely feel stupid as I scan my tattoo across the glass of the table and bring up the menu.

"Huh?" I say, acknowledging his comment as he laughs.

"Don't you see the irony?" he demands and I cock my head.

"What irony?" I ask and he chuckles again, looking at me as though I'm cute or something equally as irritating before shaking his head and letting his thick black locks capture the golden gleam of the lights.

"Never mind. What looks good?" He brushes my question away, changing the subject as I stare down at the menu and flatten the bulge of my lilac skirt's under-netting. I'd chosen something simple and sweet for tonight's dinner, wanting to appear as innocent as possible.

"Urm... ooh look they have lobster!" I inform him, surprised. I'd never seen lobster on an actual menu before, only in magazines. It's supposed to be quite decadent, and totally not the kind of thing you waste on someone who is unmarried apparently.

"Ooh, I've never tried lobster. Should we go for it?" he goads me, drawing up his own menu with a wicked grin, transforming his face into that of an adolescent once more. I melt slightly at his enthusiasm, having forgotten how attractive I find his appetite.

"Sure, it says it's a sharing dish. Come to think of it, all the dishes on here are sharing dishes." I scowl a little at that, not liking the idea of having my dining choices resting on someone else's tastes.

"Figures." Clark replies, hitting the order button on his menu. As he does so, two very odd things happen at once. The first is that a new server pops out of the floor. Actually appearing atop the black glistening floor tile beside us, from where before there was nothing, in an instant. I've never seen a hard-light hologram just appear before, so it takes me by surprise entirely and I jump in my seat, knocking the underside of the table and causing a slight clatter of cutlery.

The second thing that happens is perhaps the most bizarre, as Clark goes white as a sheet at the face of the hologram server before us. He's a bald man, with rough stubble around his jawline, brown eyes and dark hair. He looks at us with an unamused stare and Clark's jaw falls so his mouth is hanging open as his eyes blink rapidly.

"You rang?" He sighs, flipping open a holographic notepad and looking between us with a bored stare. I open my mouth to order, watching Clark suddenly jump to his feet.

"Clark..." I begin to ask him where he's going, but before I can even process the words to articulate this, he's grabbed his jacket and dashed for the door, barging past tables and running into the hard-light waiters with a hurried desperation I've never seen from him.

I get to my feet, observing the trail of chaos he's left behind which consists of several smashed glasses, disgruntled couples, and dishevelled staff sprawled on the floor and utterly confused in his wake. I don't scowl; I just stand there as all the eyes in the restaurant turn to me, locating my person as the source of the disruption.

I cringe, wondering what to do next as the waiter turns to me, un-phased and simply demands, "What was his problem?"

I walk back through the streets of the Newlywed complex, shivering and hungry. I hadn't stayed to eat after Clark bolted, I merely turned scarlet in my seat, ordered a glass of wine, and stayed stationary, sipping it for the mandatory amount of time before the total population of the restaurant had ceased staring and returned to their meals. I feel my stomach turn at the thought of those eyes on me, judging me, and my rage curdles in my gut like sour milk, wondering what the hell Clark's problem is this time.

Where before I'd have assumed it is something I've done, this time I'm pretty sure he freaked out over the waiter, not me. I think back to the face made up of hard-light, trying to place it, trying to recall anything I know about Clark that would explain why on earth he had taken off so suddenly, but I come up with nothing.

My rage doesn't quell at this, but heightens, as I'm left wondering why he would just take off without me or so much as an explanation. I turn the corner, realising that I'm actually striding with purpose down the street of honeycomb multi-hues as the hexagonal paving slabs illuminate at my tread, like one of those old-fashioned puzzle cubes my mother had taken me to see in the museum in Pearl Falls as a child. That place was supposed to teach us an appreciation for technology, by showing us some of the old toys children had to play with, but I'd always found the puzzle cube nifty looking and neat. My steps have quickened as my anger has flared, not extinguished by the harsh chill of the wind as it whips around me. I didn't think to bring a coat, which is probably stupid of me, but I've gotten far too used to not needing one on honeymoon.

I continue through the city, watching the paving stones slowly morph to blue as they lock together, leading toward the sapphire shard I now call home. I look up to the top floor, where a single light shines out into the dark. Clark must be in, so hopefully I can get some answers.

I step under the awning as I feel a large spit of rain fall down the back of my neck, making me shudder, before I step through the glass revolving doors and then swipe my tattoo, allowing me access to the lobby. I step across the floor, my gold stiletto heels clicking against the unforgiving marble as the hard-light hologram beside the elevator calls it down to me. I stand, waiting awkwardly in my lilac cocktail dress, wondering whether or not I should try to talk to him or not. I decide on not as the elevator pings, signalling its arrival, and the double doors slide open. Inside, Clark is revealed, rucksack slung over his shoulder, and expression still fraught with an emotion I can't recognise.

"Oh, hey. Why yes, Clark, I got home just fine. Thanks for asking." I place both hands on my hips and he rolls his eyes.

"I can't talk now. I have to go out," he blurts, taking two large steps across the threshold of the elevator's cushioned space and into the lobby, manoeuvring around me as though I'm toxic.

"Where are you going?" I demand of him, seriously pissed about him abandoning me. Isn't he supposed to be proving he can handle husbandly duties? Well, if this is him handling it he gets an F for effort.

"I can't talk right now. I just said that. I'll be back in the morning," he growls and I narrow my eyes.

"Clark Cavanaugh, I'm your god damn wife! Tell me where you're going... or I'll... I'll..." I stutter, faltering in my resolve as I realise that I don't have anyone to tell on him. Besides, even if I were up for going to someone with more autority than me on the subject, then I'd be shooting myself in the foot too.

"You'll what?" He queries me with a semi-serious smirk, turning on the balls of his feet as he spins around so he's stepping leisurely backward toward the turnstile. I take a few steps forward, grabbing him by the wrist and trying to get him to come clean with me.

"Just tell me where you're going! For Bliss' sake, Clark! I thought I mattered to you?" I look him deeply in the eyes and for a moment I think I'm breaking through to him. As quickly as this thought occurs to me, his eyes flit to the left, his gaze gliding over my shoulder and landing firmly on the hologram who is watching us, expression passive and uninterested in our conversation. I roll my eyes as he sighs out, snatching his wrist back from me.

"Go to sleep, Valentine. I'll be back in the morning." He drops his gaze, sighing as he turns from me and hurries through the turnstile with a practiced swipe of his wrist. I'm left standing in the lobby when I hear a roll of thunder break outside and a flash of lightning illuminates Clark's form as it disappears into the night. I spin on one foot, not sure whether to cry or scream as I storm back into the elevator and smash my wrist against the black mirror panel of the top floor. The doors slide shut, calm and even in their motion as always, and I sit down on the backbench of the padded box as it ascends against the side of the building. The steady sureness of the motion makes me want to scream more, as I put my head in my hands and groan. I'm so angry, but

I know I can't cry. I am so done crying over this man. I'm done putting in all the effort while he remains unchangeable, elusive and secretive in his nightly happenings. I'm done feeling powerless.

The doors of the elevator open as a ping sounds, but I don't move. I don't rise to my feet. I just stare out into the lobby, at my front door. I could walk out of this elevator and into my apartment, close the door behind me and crawl into bed, fuming. I could message Egypt and vent and cry. Or... I could go down to the lobby and follow Clark. If I wait any longer it will be too late, but if I go now I might just be able to catch him.

Making my choice, I slam my wrist against the lowermost black dash, scanning my tattoo and causing the elevator to plunge downward again. I feel a calm settle over me. Either way, after tonight, I'll know the truth. Even if it's awful, even if it breaks my heart, at least this is my choice, and nobody can take it away from me.

I storm across the lobby, my feet pinching in my heels as they click against the floor in time with my hurried steps. Scanning my wrist quickly, I jog through the turnstile before I push my way through the glass revolving doors and out into the rain. I gasp, surprised by the sudden onslaught of cold water against my bare arms and legs while lightning illuminates the street around me. That's when I catch Clark's backpack at the end of the street, turning the corner right as the honeycomb paving tiles illuminate him against the shadows of the encroaching storm. I turn, quick on my feet, as I grit my teeth against the wind, which is somewhat feral, nipping at my ankles and making me shiver.

Hurrying down the street in the direction of my fleeing husband, I exhale heavily as the paving stones continue to light up underfoot, worried now about the possibility of getting caught. If Clark catches me following him before he reaches wherever it is he's going, I'll never know the truth, because he'll always be looking over his shoulder on future jaunts like this one. The rain continues to fall, heavy against my skin as my hot blood courses, veins dilating, close to the surface, trying to keep me warm but failing with the onslaught of cool water chilling right through.

As I make my way through the city, shrouded by the pelting water and intermittently exposed by the lightning which forks across the sky, I wonder if what I'm doing is completely mad. I mean, when I'd taken those steps down that very long aisle a few weeks back, I didn't exactly think I'd be spending my first nights as a married woman, following my husband in order to expose his lies, his secrets, and yet here I am, sodden and cold, stalking him like some desperate woman in love.

I know I'm desperate, but I wonder now if it's because I'm so deeply in love with him that it scares me to think of him getting into trouble, or whether I just want to know where I stand so if it's the latter and we fail the evaluation at the one hundred day mark, which now seems increasingly likely, at least I can say I did my very best.

Couples walking down the street toward me stare, probably wondering what I'm doing out alone, or why I am hardly dressed for such terrible weather. I use the flocks of them, hurrying and with hard-light umbrellas above their heads, to shield myself just in case the speck of shadow in the distance, that Clark has become, turns and catches sight of me.

Main Street of the complex feels as though it will never end, but soon I realise that Clark has no intention of turning off anywhere. He's making a straight shot for the edge of the island, where the complex meets the water.

I quicken my steps, feet sloshing through puddles and trying not to slip as I scurry, nearing him as we get close to the guardrail that separates the land from the surrounding lake. I stand near the edge of the final building on the enormous high street running central to the complex. It's a coffee shop, and the light it exudes from its window and hard-light hovering sign produces just enough light for me to watch Clark put his hood over his head and look left, then right, before bending down and loosening a man-hole cover. I wouldn't have known it was there if I wasn't seeing it with my own eyes, but he strains, lifting it and setting it down on the street as quietly as possible before he lowers himself half way into the space it's left open. He descends into the hole until he's waist deep, before hauling the man-hole cover back toward the opening and placing it back where it came from. It seamlessly disappears into the pavement as does he, leaving no one any the wiser that anyone had ever been there, let alone that they've disappeared into the floor.

Where on earth could such a thing lead? The sewers? I mean, it's never advertised but our waste has to go somewhere I suppose. Then the question is, why on earth would my husband need to go down there? My mind wanders across all the terrible possibilities, maybe he's a smuggler, or worse, maybe he's committing a crime.

I sigh out, no longer feeling the rain pounding on my back as my skin goes numb. I have a choice now. I could follow him, but realistically I'm not really dressed for the sewer, and I have to ask myself whether or not I want to get involved in whatever it is Clark is doing. I'm cold, wet and beginning to feel terror creeping into the edges of my consciousness, wondering whether or not I really am better off not knowing. Clark had said he is trying to protect me by keeping me in the dark, but I thought he has just been being overdramatic, or trying to push me away. Now however, I know he was speaking some semblance of truth and despite this, I still get the feeling that I have a right to know what it is he's up to. Especially if he's married to me. I mean, if Bliss Inc. ever did want to find him, they'd come to me first, I'd be the one who would have to lie for him, to protect him.

I lean back against the wall of the coffee shop, which is slick with rain, panicking slightly as my breath quickens and indecision makes me feel lost. I decide what to do quickly, taking a few steps before turning back on myself and entering the door of the coffee shop. I feel the warmth of the space envelop me and the smell of coffee hit me hard in the face as I inhale, knowing that I need to warm up and think a while on what to do next.

I order myself a cup of coffee and sit as the rain falls outside and people return to their apartments for yet another night of newlywed bliss. I watch them as lights in the surrounding apartment buildings dim and the early hours of a new day break over a city of sleeping and contented couples begin. If only my life with Clark could be so simple.

The sun is just breaking over the horizon as I see Clark's familiar form pass by the coffee shop window. I'm on my third cup of coffee and my second banana and blueberry muffin and I'm shaking slightly, the thoughts from the last few hours rattling around in my head like angry bees, buzzing and stinging me the more attention I give them. Getting to my feet, I throw my half empty plastic coffee cup in the upcycler next to my table and walk from the coffee shop into the early drizzle of the morning. It's been raining all night and I'm still damp from my journey here. I'm also stiff, having been sat stone still in the same booth, contemplating all the terrible things that Clark could possibly be involved in down in the sewers, or wherever that manhole cover leads. I'm not brave enough to have followed him, and a part of me wishes I'd been reckless enough to go into the man-hole.

Instead though, I've decided to confront him, let him know I've followed him and force him to tell me. I rub my hands against my skin which is rampant with goosebumps as a light spray of rain coats my flesh and causes the chill of last night's downpour to return.

I follow Clark all the way home, making sure to stay a certain number of hexagonal paving steps behind him at all times and ignoring the looks of those people who are out this early. I know I must look horrendous with a rain-stained face and damp clothes, not to mention the fact that my hair is now the consistency of rat's tails, hanging limp and wet down the back of my neck.

Clark reaches the sapphire shard, pushing through the revolving glass doors where he'd left last night and through the turnstile the other side. I wait a good few minutes before I too enter the building, getting odd looks from the hard-light hologram who still stands, stationary, in the lobby as he calls the elevator down to me. Inside I relish the warm air as the doors slide shut and my stomach fills with anxiety, twisting and knotting itself like a vice as I think about Clark's secret. I know that if I don't find out, then I'll never be able to trust him, never be able to move forward, but a part of me wishes it didn't have to be this way, wishes that there was no secret.

The elevator moves up quickly, too quickly, and before I know it I'm walking through my apartment door and dripping onto the floor as I see Clark in the stark morning light of the front room, looking into the bedroom for me.

"Clark." I say his name as he spins on one heel, his face mad with worry before it relaxes the instant he lays eyes on me. Then it becomes confused as he sees that I'm soaking wet and shivering visibly.

"Valentine... what on earth?" he demands an explanation, raising an eyebrow with an alarmed expression.

"I followed you." I speak the words into the air, my voice cracking as a shudder wracks my body and a droplet of rain runs down the back of my left leg.

"You did what?" Clark begins to look angry, but I scowl at him, crossing my arms and trying to send the message that I'm done being lied to.

"I followed you, Clark. I saw where you went," I announce and he takes a few paces forward.

"Did you now..." He growls, fists balling at his sides for a moment before he strips off his coat and tosses it across the back of the sofa cushions.

"Yes. I think we need to have a little talk," I say, raising my chin and puckering my lips before brushing my fingers back through my wet hair. He narrows his eyes at me, taking yet more steps forward and my breathing quickens at his proximity. Invading my personal space, he looks down upon me, his jawline strong and assertive as he whispers,

"I think you're right."

Nineteen

Clark stares down into my eyes, somewhere between fury and fear in his expression as he turns and walks, purposefully and with harsh steps, across the living area and over to his backpack. He opens it, before pulling out a small black device. He walks over to the wall and suctions the black box onto the rich blue of the paint, waiting a few seconds before the device beeps once and then turns to me.

"Right. We can talk now." He crosses his arms and leans back onto his heels, propping himself against the arm of the sofa while I stare at him with a confused expression.

"What's that?" I ask him, looking over to the box, which blinks every few seconds with a tiny green glow.

"It's a device that blocks any and all surveillance technology in operation within fifty feet," he elaborates and my eyes widen.

"Surveillance?" I ask, unsure if he means what I think he means.

"Yeah, like cameras, microphones, that sort of thing," he replies and I nod, speechless.

"What's going on, Clark?" I sigh, as he shifts.

"We may be about to have our very first completely honest conversation, Valentine. Are you ready to hear it? If not, say now, I can't protect you once you know everything." He looks at me, somewhat forlorn as his sapphire gaze becomes riddled with concern. This one look says more than I expect, it says that he really does care.

"Yes. I need to know. I can't be married to you and not know. Whether you like it or not, in marrying you I've been made a part of this," I remind him. He grimaces, guilt wracking his face.

"Okay, well, I was seeing my mother." He drops this bombshell and I inhale a deep breath quickly.

"But your mother, she's dead," I exclaim, as though I'm reminding him of a fact he's forgotten. He laughs.

"Not exactly. When my father was exposed as violent to us, she went to Bliss Inc. They didn't take too kindly to her claiming that the formula had failed, so she was exiled. That's where I've been going, Valentine. It's why this programme is so important to me. I've been taking her food, supplies, things she can trade down there." He looks down to the floor and my mind races. Bliss Inc. exiled her? Why would they do that? Why wouldn't they just relocate her to the labour settlements? Did she threaten to tell people the formula was a fake?

"You've been taking your mom food and supplies? That's it?" I ask him, cautious in my words and he frowns.

"What, did you think I was some kind of criminal?" he asks and I pause before replying, feeling my stomach flood with relief.

"I didn't know what to think. That's the thing about secrets, Clark. People tend to imagine the worst." He frowns at my reply

307

as I speak the words aloud, feeling the truth of them ring in my ears.

"What I'm doing is dangerous, there's no mistake about that. But it's not morally bankrupt. I just want to help my family," he confesses and I melt. His eyes are full of emotion and for the first time I feel like his façade has completely dissolved. This is who he really is.

"I don't understand how it can be dangerous, I mean Bliss Inc. must be aware that the people they exile have to survive, right?" I ask him and he frowns again, rubbing his stubble with his fingers as he shifts from his left foot to his right.

"They drop them off at the city limits. Or at least they used to. There haven't been any exiles found for a long time," he informs me and I feel my forehead crease. How do they survive without an upcycler, or a holo-dash? What about their tattoos? Does Bliss Inc. know they're still hanging around?

"So how has your mom survived until now? I mean, we've only been married a few weeks, and we've been away for all of them," I ask him and he smiles.

"Monopolis is built on top of the remnants of an old city, I mean, even the lake is manmade. It looks deep, but it really isn't; it's just there to deter people from moving between the districts. When the company picked the land to create this settlement they just levelled the buildings and built over the top of it. The sewer structures remain though. That's where they live. The ones who spoke out, the ones who fail the hundred-day assessment and threaten to protest or go public with their story, the few infertile couples, there's more than you'd think. I mean, my mom has been taken care of by her partner for a long time. Now it's time for me to help her give back to him and the rest of them for what they've given," He implores my understanding and I wonder if he really thinks I'd be opposed to helping those in need.

Nodding, I feel the weight of the responsibility, that has pinned him down, encroaching on my own shoulders as well.

"So, Bliss Incorporated... they just abandoned them?" I ask him and he nods.

"Yes. Then yesterday, something amazing happened. You know the hard-light hologram?" he asks me and I nod, rolling my eyes.

"You mean the one you ditched me over. Yeah, I don't think I'd forget that," I remind him and he cringes.

"You'll understand why I bolted when I tell you this..." He exhales, "That was my dad," he announces and I scowl. What on earth?

"Wait, what? How is that possible, you said he was dead too?" I express, feeling my heart rate begin to heighten, the thought of the man who had abused my husband making me angry. How is it he's allowed to just walk around?

"I thought he was dead. I mean, I know I lied about my mom, but I thought that after she came forward about the abuse, Bliss Inc. had 'disposed' of him. Then he pops up yesterday, quite literally, right in the middle of our dinner," he states, his eyes wild with discomfort at the memory. I feel my heart falter in my chest, confused to say the least.

"But Clark, that hologram, whoever he is... he didn't recognise you at all." I remember the look of utter confusion on the hard-light face as he watched my entire face flush with embarrassment. "Are you absolutely sure it was him and not just that they've used his form as like a template for the holograms or something?" I ask him and he shakes his head.

"That's the thing, Valentine, I'm not sure. But Jason said that people have been going missing in the labour settlements. Ever since these hard-light holograms got approved for the trial phase of development. It's weird." His explanation causes me to frown. I can't deny the hard-light holograms make me feel a little on edge, they just don't seem natural.

"So, what are you saying?" I ask him and he shrugs.

"I don't know. I don't know what to think. I just know that my father's face popped up in the middle of a crowded restaurant yesterday where it didn't belong. I had to go and see my mom, because I wanted to ask her whether or not she had any sort of confirmation of my dad's death. It was heartbreaking though, the look on her face as I told her I'd seen him. It wasn't good," he admits, his eyes dropping to the floor, and I nod. I know it must have been hard for him too.

The air around us stills and I feel my heartbeat slow as I think on the huge amount of information that's been unleashed in the last few minutes alone.

"She's why you decided to accept the Jigsaw Project place, isn't she?" I ask him, thoughtful. His eyes rise to mine and he looks like he might combust with angst.

"Not that I had much choice, but yes. She's the reason why I knew I had to go through with this, make it work. I do have feelings for you, ever since I laid eyes on you, and in spite of my prior judgements about the idea of an arranged marriage. But she has always been at the top of my priorities. After all, she gave up her place in Pearl Falls to give me and Jason a better life, away from all that abuse, it's the least I can do." Hearing him talk about his mother in this way makes me feel like taking him into my arms and holding him, just as I had done when I'd heard the lie about his parents' death.

"Clark, you are telling me the truth, right?" I ask him and he suddenly looks surprised.

"Of course. Why would you even ask that?" His face turns from shock to agitated quickly and I feel my anger spike too.

"Gee, I wonder why I'm asking if I can trust you after all the lying, Clark? I mean this whole time I've been walking around thinking you're an orphan. Now, I find out that your mom has actually been alive this whole time and your dad might very well still be kicking around too. Don't you think I have a right to be suspicious? You're not exactly Mr. Forthcoming!" I exclaim, out of breath as I blink a few times, realising that I need to control my temper. It's a sensitive situation and I don't want him to recoil into himself again. If that happens, I may never coax any truth out of him again, if that is in fact what I'm hearing right now.

"I've been trying to protect you from this, Valentine. I don't want you to get drawn into all this. I mean, if I get caught fraternising with these people, I could just disappear one day," he explains and I sigh out.

"Yeah, great. But don't you think it's a little selfish to leave me in the dark? Say you did disappear, don't you think I have the right to have some inclination of what's happened? I mean if I knew, then maybe I could... I could..." I stutter, trying to think of what exactly it would be that I did in that situation.

"Do what? You can't do a damn thing if they get hold of me. You're one person, Valentine. One person can't stand up to a

311

company that size and win. Why do you think so many people are trapped in marriages that make them miserable and producing children that they don't want? Because I'll tell you one thing, it isn't freaking love." He's standing straight now, both feet planted on the floor and spread wide, his stance aggressive as his chest rises and falls heavy with his breathing.

"You really think that everyone in the Jigsaw Project are staying in their marriages and having kids because they're scared?" I scrutinise him, wondering if he's not in fact right. My mom and dad have had their bumps in the road, and with her schedule she made sure she was never in the house for long. If I hadn't been out at my various classes with her, I was always at home with dad. I think back on my childhood, the truth of those late nights at ballet with my mom now exposed in a stark and unfaltering light. Are my parents really happy?

I think about my sisters, about how Portia sounds so tired now she's married with two kids, and how Eve's husband Desmond is always looking at other women. I think back to those couples on the honeymoon, about how rose tinted glasses from the experience of meeting your true love might in fact be why they had seemed so utterly caught up in one another. Could it be that this fantasy I've been presented isn't just a by-product of presenting the future as an ideal, but also a way in which instant infatuation is produced? Could it be that the honeymoon period for most couples is just fuelled by them wanting to be so deeply what the other desires?

"Children are a weapon," I whisper, suddenly realising what he's been trying to tell me all along.

"What?" Clark asks me and I feel like I've just had a veil lifted from over my eyes.

"You're right, Clark. Bliss Incorporated, they are just controlling us, keeping us distracted. I mean, once we're married off, we have children, the ultimate bargaining chip. Your mother, she tried to protect you, but they punished her for it, she risked everything to keep you safe. They punished you for it by taking you away from her. I bet, given the same choice, knowing what would happen to you, she would have stayed with your father, taken the abuse to stop herself from being separated from you. They don't care about well-adjusted children at all, do they? They just use children as a way to keep people inside unhappy marriages that they claim are 'perfect.' Because what parent wouldn't bear the unthinkable to protect their family? You can fall out of love with your husband, but I've never heard of someone falling out of love with their child."

"I thought you believed in the formula?" he asks me, cocking an eyebrow as a smile plays on the edges of his lips.

"I just... the further I get into this relationship, the more I realise that you can't quantify emotion. How can they possibly know whether or not we're right for each other, when we don't even know?" I counter and this time he does smile.

"I don't know whether the formula exists or not. But you realise that we're proving that it does. Every time I look at you, a part of me wants to be disgusted, wants to hate you, to prove to myself that they don't own my happiness, nor can they patent it, but I can't. I just can't. You're too... I don't know... something. Especially now." He takes a few steps forward and I look up into his face as his hands come up to rest on my shoulders.

"Now?" I ask him, fluttering my lashes as he smirks.

"You're saying all the things and clarifying everything I've always believed, but never been able to voice. It's... attractive to say the least. I feel like you understand me, at last," he admits, leaning down and placing a kiss on my forehead. I want to lean into his chest and relax, letting all the tension drain from my body, but I'm still bruised from his lies and the way in which he's treated me. I know he has his reasons, but it still hasn't made my time being married to him any less turbulent.

"Clark, I want to believe you. I do. I mean, I can see exactly what you mean about the Jigsaw Project now. But I want to see it for myself. I want to go into the tunnels with you, next time you go." I make the leap, wondering how I ended up in so deep with a man who is fighting the very system I've been brought up to crave.

Why do I want to push the limits? Why do I want to wake up from the fantasy life I've always wanted to live? Maybe it's because now I know what I know, I can never go back, or maybe it's because I wish things could be different.

"No. You can't. Don't you believe me?" He demands a response of me, gripping the tops of my arms hard with his long fingers and lowering his eyes so they meet with mine.

"I need to see all this for myself, Clark. Besides, I want to help. I want to meet your mother. Don't I at least deserve that, since you're risking getting us exiled trying to help her?" I ask him this, plain and simple, scared he'll deny me again before adding, "Besides, I followed you to that manhole, or entrance, or whatever it was. So, if you don't take me, then I'll just have to go by myself." I threaten him and his body visibly relaxes, as though the thought of no alternative has put the decision at rest.

"Well, then I suppose I don't have any choice," he mutters, leaning in and kissing me on the cheek.

He walks over to the wall to disconnect the device from the wallpaper, before turning and informing me, "We can't use this thing that often. If we do, the people monitoring this place will think something is up. If we only use it occasionally, then it could just be a brief power failure, or a glitch in their system and they won't know the difference. If you want to talk to me freely, otherwise, the best bet is the balcony." He gestures to the enormous transparent back wall of glass, which leads out to the unfurnished jutting platform.

As he says these words and I nod in response, he detaches the black device from the wall. The holo-dash lights back up again, and everything in the kitchen begins to hum as the sound of electric power returns.

"What do you want to do now?" I ask him, feeling the questions whir around in my brain. There are so many things I want to ask, so much I want to know now about the inner workings of the company that rules my life. Clark looks to me with a cocked eyebrow, as he walks back toward me.

"Well, I suppose it wouldn't be so terrible if we assumed our cover of man and wife again," he whispers to me, stroking my cheek with a finger as he curls the other arm around my waist.

"Clark, I have so many things running through my mind right now, so many questions. How can I possibly quiet all that down after what we just talked about?" I ask him and he smirks.

"I can think of a way. After all, what else are we going to do to pass the time?" With that sentiment, he kisses me and doesn't stop until my mind is empty of questions, empty of uncertainty.

With each kiss chosen, carefully planted and painstakingly felt, we revolt.

Twenty

I lay in Clark's arms, fully clothed in my pyjamas and silent as the day passes. We've kissed until my lips are raw and plump once more, and now I'm lying here, unsure what to say or do and with a million questions running through my mind. Clark's asleep beside me, having been up all night again, and even though I've been up for just as long, perhaps longer, I can't bring myself to shut my eyes. I'm just too busy questioning everything I had once known was true.

My heartbeat thuds, heavy in my chest, as I sit up, slipping from beneath the crook of Clark's arm, which has been cradling my waist, and getting to my feet in the melancholy light of late afternoon.

I shut the bedroom door, walking over to the sofa before scanning my tattoo over the holo-dash causing it to wake, and sitting down with a sigh. I know I haven't messaged Egypt like I promised, but now I'm also scared of putting another person at risk. With this thought I realise that Clark was right in how he has acted. I also wonder if Egypt would believe me, if she'll be able to see through the cleverly woven persona of Bliss Incorporated or whether or not she'll just be like I have been; blind to it, because the lies are still her reality.

I sit back on the sofa, crossing my legs in front of me as I call out some random soft-light channel into the air of the room, breaking the silence, in an attempt to make my mind idle. The holo-dash flickers for a moment, before projecting the Newlywed Channel, which is of course littered with relationship advice straight from the source; Bliss Inc.

As a commercial break comes on, Pippa Hart's smiling face is projected in soft-light, high-definition glory. I watch the advert, observing her as she journeys through the Bliss Inc. headquarters, and I wonder: How can someone so seemingly transparent be a part of such a huge system which endeavours to control every single thing in an individual's life? I watch the commercial for a few moments more as Pippa Hart greets a new hard-light hologram and begins talking about how they will be a part of revolutionising our world, of making things easier for everyone, of making it so the labour settlements will one day become redundant. My eyebrows rise in surprise. I've never seen this advert in particular before, which is surprising, seeing as my entire single life had been saturated by adverts from the company.

I wonder, is it possible Clark has it all wrong? Is it possible that his mother is in fact a criminal? Did she threaten the company more than she's let on? I mean... he is her son after all, so wouldn't he be bias toward her?

Feeling suddenly uncomfortable, I stand, stepping behind the couch and over to the glass doors. The sky outside is an ambivalent pewter, and the wind whips around my form as I

318

stride out into the city air, looking out over the people below, who scurry along the streets which run like veins, spidering through a much bigger organism.

I sigh out, feeling the heat of my anxious flush lift from my face and slump over the railing, before I straighten almost immediately as the sound of the doors opening behind me reaches my ears. His arms fold around my waist, pulling my spine to his chest and flooding my back with warmth whilst his lips come up to tickle my ear.

"I can't stand waking up without you. Are you okay?" he whispers as I spin in his arms, turning away from the underwhelming view and choosing instead to look into the intense dark blue of his eyes.

"I'm... I'm struggling with all this," I explain and he cocks his head to one side as a tiny furrow of concern forms between his eyebrows.

"What's wrong? If you have questions you know you can ask me," he promises. I think for a moment, wondering why the advert I've just seen is making me flushed and panic ridden.

"I just... Bliss Incorporated... In their commercials they seem so... well, honest. I mean, I'm struggling to trust my mind over what I can physically see. I can't just write off the fact that they openly broadcast adverts showing their facility and the people within it. How do I know I'm not just being crazy? I'm having a hard time trusting my own judgement," I explain and he nods.

"Exactly, Valentine. Why would any company, who is trying to hide secrets, operate so openly? Why would anyone show the inside of their facility when they have something to hide?" He asks me the question and I think on this for a few minutes, the

319

sound of the high-speed monorail bringing me back to myself as the answer dawns on me.

"Well, I guess if Bliss Inc. is making the adverts and broadcasting them, then they can show us what they want us to see? If they're seen to be hiding things, people might go snooping around, but if they appear to have public transparency, then nobody has any reason to ask questions... right?" I ask him and he nods as a coy smile overtakes his lips.

"Clever girl." He kisses my forehead and I sigh out as the knowledge makes me feel safe. This feeling is merely momentary, as a few seconds later I realise that it is possible that everything I know of the world is a complete lie. They say there's nothing else out there in the world, that everything is barren and wild, but how do I know that? What if it's just a way of making people feel like they have no other choice but to stay here?

My mind reels as the information I've taken on in only hours muddles together, becoming a flurry of facts, lies and half-truths that I've been drip fed since early childhood. My stomach grumbles as the light around us continues to dim.

"Can we eat?" I ask Clark and he nods.

"Would you like me to make you breakfast?" he asks me and I look at him, mischief spreading across his face like wildfire as he watches my reluctant pleasure and I'm unable to stop myself smiling.

"Breakfast? At this late hour?" I put on a fake posh accent and he chuckles.

"Well, if we're breaking all the rules anyway, why not have breakfast in the evening? I didn't think you'd object to bacon past five o'clock." He smirks and I slap him across the arm.

"God, it's like you actually know me or something." I roll my eyes, laughing, as we head back inside, eager to eat. After all, for what the night will bring, I'm going to need all my strength.

———————●●●———————

As we leave our apartment in the middle of the night, I look down at myself, keeping my head low and wishing to be utterly unremarkable. I'm quite a different person now than I had been just a few short weeks ago when preparing for my wedding. I've always wanted to stand out, be different, be memorable, but now, now I want the ground to swallow me whole for fear of being discovered.

We walk down Main Street, careful not to make eye contact with any of the passers-by as the paving stones illuminate beneath our silent, heavy tread and I feel fear grip at me, trying to take me over. Hurrying through the cold, hand in hand and dressed in dark, unremarkable clothes which cause us to illuminate as nothing more than absent shadow above the lit street, we near the place where, last night, I'd watched Clark disappear as a tight knot of fear lodges permanently in my stomach. I'm scared. What if his mother is crazy? What if everything he knows is a lie, or something that she's made up to get back at the system she hates? What if she doesn't think I'm right for her son?

"Get a grip on yourself, Valentine!" I whisper to myself, angry that I'm being so ridiculous. I mean, I know that most women are nervous before meeting their mother in law, but this isn't exactly a normal situation. Could it be that Cynthia Morland had ingrained her ideals about making the perfect first impression more deeply than I thought?

We approach the man-hole cover, which Clark promptly removes with a grunt as he bends down to the ground. He gestures for me to enter first and I feel my stomach drop as I look down into the darkness that lies below. I suppose this is it. The moment where I have to decide how much I really trust my new husband.

I swallow my fear, knowing that standing around for too long could garner attention from those walking not too far away, and lower myself slowly into the hole, gripping the slick top metal bar of the almost invisible ladder so hard my knuckles practically glow a fierce white. I take one step down the ladder, which is nothing more than a few metal rungs that have been sunk deep into the mortar between bricks. I've never seen bricks before, not like this, but I knew they had been used in our past, before they were deemed too damaging to mother earth to make. I take another step, then another, carefully positioning the balls of my feet on the rung below before loosening the grip of my hands. I descend the vertical tunnel, reaching the bottom just as Clark begins his own descent, pulling the manhole cover down over himself and eclipsing all the light.

I hear something snap before a bright neon orange glow illuminates the tunnel. The light source falls to the floor, landing in a puddle at my feet. I look down, picking it up without thinking about the fact I'm standing in a sewer. My hand disturbs the water as it plunges for the glow-stick and a vile smell plumes upward, making me wrinkle my nose.

"Ugh!" I exclaim, feeling my hand recoil coated in faecal smelling slime.

"You okay?" Clark calls down, his voice bouncing off the walls in a worry-tainted echo.

"Yes I'm fine, you just dropped that glow stick in a puddle full of...." I begin as I hear him groan.

"Oh, don't worry I'll retrieve it when I get down there," he says and I sigh.

"No need, I've already...." I begin to explain, but see that Clark is on the same level as me at last. He takes a few steps forward, his blue eyes turning an eerily odd half shade as the light in my hand illuminates his face tangerine.

"Oh, I'm sorry." He apologises but I laugh, shrugging it off.

"It's the sewer, I don't know what I expected," I reply and he smirks, pulling out a towel from his backpack's front pocket and wiping my hands clean before taking the glow stick from me and wrapping it in the cloth.

"Come on, this way," he calls out to me, not lowering his voice.

"You're not worried that Bliss Inc. has cameras down here?" I ask him and he shrugs.

"Why would they? As far as they're aware, they think this place is empty except for a few upcycler tubes that take stuff to and from a few labour settlements. It's how my brother manages to get away a few times a month. Besides, Jason would know if they had cameras watching this place. He's got a friend in surveillance remember?" He explains his logic and I nod, suddenly catching the glow of my jigsaw puzzle piece tattoo.

"But what about us, Clark? What about these tattoos? Can't they see we're here?" I ask him and he turns back to me.

"Oh crap, I forgot." He stops in his tracks in the middle of the rancid smelling, circular, brick sewer, bending down as he slings the backpack off one arm and then the other, before opening it and pulling out a small black device, just like the one I've seen him use in the apartment. He scans it over the tattoo on my arm, sighing out as he watches the neon blue glow diminish beneath my skin.

"What did you do?" I ask, looking at the tattoo's now dim outline in surprise.

"Our tattoos are made from a kind of liquid ink with a slight electrical pulse, powered by your biological system. It's how they unlock things. This device temporarily blocks the signal it emits and takes us off the grid. Never for too long though, or the people upstairs start getting suspicious. Though, it is almost impossible to permanently disable them, which sucks," he explains and my eyebrows rise.

"Who the hell designs this stuff, Clark? Like how did you get hold of this kind of technology?" I ask him, realising now that this should have been one of the first kinds of questions I asked when he had taken our apartment off the grid yesterday morning.

"Jason. There's a whole group of people in the labour settlements, people who hate Bliss Inc. as much as us, if not more. They've been salvaging parts of old technology, the stuff that Bliss Inc. abandoned and designing new, useful items for years. It's only been a recent thing that we've been able to block signals from entire rooms, but the technology for the temporary blocking of tattoos has been around for a while." He explains this like it's totally common knowledge, like what he's talking about isn't entirely illegal.

"How is it that Bliss Inc. doesn't have some kind of police force to stop this happening? I mean I know they tell us that they don't need prisons and stuff, but surely..." I begin but he cuts me off, reclipping the front of his bag before beginning to walk forward again through the dark tunnels.

"We don't know. I think they have a small task force for dealing with trouble, but I'll be honest, they don't need that many people," Clark explains and I feel myself frown.

"How is that possible? The city is enormous!" I ask him, unsure of what it is he's actually saying.

"Well, we watch ourselves. It's called the panopti... something... I can't remember. Like they put cameras up everywhere, and knowing that we're monitored, by tattoos and the like, we become too afraid to rebel, even in private, because we don't know if people are watching or not. It's clever," he explains and I nod, getting his point. My first inkling once I'd discovered that Bliss Inc. surveillance was more extensive than I'd thought was to check myself, to run through a list of my private behaviours to make sure that none of them violated Bliss Inc. ethos. I shudder at the thought of this invisible power being exerted over me without my knowledge.

We take a few more turns around the winding cylindrical corridor maze, until we reach a metal grate. Clark knocks his glow stick against the metal bars of the construct, the sound ringing out in the tunnel and echoing around me, causing me to startle. I'm on edge I know, but I can't help but feel like I'm doing something highly unorthodox only by being here.

"Clark? Is that you?" I hear a gruff voice call out as Clark raps the neon glow stick against the bars twice more in quick succession.

After a few moments, a man shrouded in the shadow of our dank surroundings comes forward and silently removes three of the middlemost bars from the grate, with some kind of magnetic device he's holding firmly in one hand.

Once the bars have clattered to the floor, one by one, Clark steps aside so I can move through the gap. I hear the man, still covered in the shadows of the tunnel, cough before saying, "Who's this and what is she doing here?"

"This is my wife, Valentine." Clark introduces me as he steps into the next tunnel, joining me as the man replaces the bars.

"You sure that's wise, boy?" he asks and Clark sighs.

"You can trust her." he retorts, his stare settling on the man, who steps forward, squaring up to Clark as the neon orange of our light illuminates his face. His skin is patchy with dirt and his dark hair is cropped so short he's almost bald. His facial structure is intimidating, as his chin and cheekbones jut out from his skull and his dark eyes sink deep within it, creating shadows in all the most terrifying places.

"You gonna lead the way then, Jeremy?" Clark straightens, showing that he's far taller than his opponent. Jeremy looks to me and then back to Clark.

"I sure as hell hope she is as you say, Clark. We've got a lot at stake to just be bringing princesses down here for some kind of guided tour," he snarls and Clark cocks his head.

"You think I'd risk her safety?" He asks Jeremy, though I get the inclination he is no longer talking about me. At that, Jeremy backs off slightly, turning to me and holding out a dirty hand.

"I'm Jeremy," he says as I take his palm in mine right away, not wanting to show him how nervous I am.

"I'm Valentine." I retort, feeling no inclination to make nice with this man at all. He turns on his heel, promptly dropping my hand and stalking off into the shadows ahead, Clark and I follow him, until suddenly, as we turn a corner, stark and acute light floods the passage ahead.

"Argh," I blurt, shielding my eyes as Clark grumbles.

"I should have warned you about that. Sorry. This is where the exiled begin to draw power off the grid of the city," he explains and I nod, fascinated by this half way of life.

We tread lightly down the length of the tunnel and suddenly I feel eyes on me from all angles. I turn my head, coming face to face with a sheet, that is drawn back, and a pair of eyes are staring out from a dark side passage with a dead-end. I stare back into the dim light, able to make out a hammock hung between the two sides of the passages circular arc.

People live like this? I think to myself, slightly disgusted.

How do they shower? How do they cook down here?

I feel phantasmal bacteria crawling all over my skin, despite the fact I'm fully clothed in a black turtleneck sweater and tight slacks.

"You okay?" Clark asks me as the ragged curtain, which looks to be no more than an old sheet, is pulled across the opening, eclipsing the inhabitant from view.

327

"Yes, I..." I begin but his eyes soften and I realise that I've been stood still, gawping this entire time.

"It's okay, it shocked me too at first. Come on, we don't have long before our tattoos become active again. I want you to talk with my mom." He grabs my hand as I hold it out, letting him drag me behind him, keeping me moving so I'm not tempted to stop and stare in shock at the abhorrent uncleanliness and unacceptable living conditions belonging to more people than I would have thought possible.

After navigating an impressively intricate system of tunnels and tunnel junctions, Clark finally stops in front of a curtain of silver silk.

"Our bed sheets?" I ask him and he looks sheepish.

"The upcycler must have remembered what the delivery people ordered from the catalogue. That's why these came out when I ordered sheets our first night in the apartment," he explains and I nod, smiling a melancholy smile at the way in which the garment from our apartment is completely out of place.

Looking around here, I'd gladly give them every single piece of furniture I own. After all, I can always get more, or sit on the floor in my beautiful apartment. They need it more than I do living down here.

"Mom?" I hear Clark call out as he sweeps the curtain sideways and moves inside the dead-end passage, which seems identical to the one I'd peeked in before, if not a little larger.

"Clark, is that you? Back so soon?" I hear a woman's voice call; it's not old. I had pictured Clark's mom to be elderly, but instead she sounds vibrant at the inkling her son has come to visit. I step inside the makeshift doorway, ducking my head as Clark holds the curtain open for me.

Inside the dead-end passageway, I instantly spot things I recognise in the half-light, that look utterly out of place. Instead of a hammock though, this make-shift home has an inflatable mattress, covered in the same silver silk sheets as the flimsy partition I've just walked beneath.

"Hello." I say, dumbfounded as I meet the same blue eyes that I've looked into for hours. These don't belong to Clark though, they belong to his mother.

"Why, you must be Valentine!" I hear her voice squeak with excitement as her long black hair, which is pulled up into a high bun, bobs atop her head and she gets to her feet.

"I am. You must be Clark's mother. You look so much like him!" I exclaim, looking around at Clark whose face is alight with an unexpected happiness.

"She's gorgeous, Clark! You didn't say she was gorgeous!?" She accuses him, reaching out and slapping him across the arm with a cheeky grin. I'd put her at the same age as my mother, but she looks a lot older, even if her voice doesn't match. Her face is lined with worry, the crevices of her skin exaggerated by a collection of grime and dirt.

"Mom!" He complains, setting his backpack down on the surface of the makeshift wooden desk she'd been sitting at when we'd arrived. I take a second to look at what sits on its surface which is a jumble of dehydrated food, a portable cooker as well as some new looking plates and mugs.

"Well, look at her! She's a stunner." His mother grips at my hands with hers, examining me with intrigue as the sleeve of her ragged jumper pulls back and I inhale, horrified.

"Oh dear, don't you worry about that. It healed a long time ago," she whispers.

"What happened to you?" I ask her, bending down to look in her eyes. She's shorter than me and tiny in stature, though I can't tell if this is through hunger or if she's always been this way.

"Oh, this old thing? Bliss Inc. left me with a little parting gift." She sits down on the wooden chair and gestures for me to sit on the crumpled mess of her bed. I do as she asks, making more floor space in the cramped living quarters. As I get settled on the air mattress, she pulls back her sleeve once more, before shuffling her chair a few paces forward and grabbing my hand in hers. She pulls it against her wrist, aligning the faded tattoo on mine with the marbled scar that lies on hers. "You see?" She asks me as my eyes widen.

"They did this to you? They... burned you?" I ask her, my eyes threatening to fill with tears of disgust. How can any human being do this to another and still be able to live with themselves?

"Yes. Couldn't risk me accessing monorails, or anything else for that matter," she explains and I blink a few times, shocked, as I watch Clark unpacking his bag on the table behind her. He's brought her a lot more dehydrated food, toiletries, clothing. I watch him in wonder, suddenly questioning why it is I've been leading a life of privilege while others are struggling to survive. Clark is an honest to god hero.

"As happy as I am to meet my daughter in law, why did you bring her down here, Clark? You know that the less people who know about us the better. You're supposed to be keeping her safe." Clark grunts, a half exasperated, half amused sound.

"I'll let her explain that." He nods for me to answer for myself with an amused expression.

"It's my fault. After he ran out the other night with the hard-light hologram, I followed him. I told him if he didn't bring me to see all this for myself, then I'd come down here alone." I admit and she chuckles.

"That's brave. I'm surprised you believed him. Most women your age would have written him off as a raving loon," she laughs as Clark comes to sit next to me on the bed.

"Well, he's my husband," I state, proud and unable to express why exactly it is that I'd believed him.

"You're lucky. If my first husband had been half the man Clark is, I wouldn't be here." His mother snorts, leaning back into the chair and turning to see the haul Clark has brought with him. "Would you like some tea, either of you?" She offers this to us, kind and generous in intent, but I shake my head, worried about the kind of hygiene standards.

"Speaking of down here, do you mind if I ask... how did you end up down here? Why didn't you just leave?" I ask her and she blinks a few times.

"We don't know what's out there. We don't know if the world is in a suitable condition to be explored. I mean, Bliss Inc. had all the resources and money you can imagine when they built this city, we don't have that luxury. It's safer here, at least this way we're close enough to civilisation that we can steal that which we need. Or, if you have a wonderful son like mine, they bring you what you need to survive." She smiles at Clark who sits upright, attentive to her.

"Have you heard anything more about the missing workers from Jason?" he inquires, his face turning curious, and she shakes her head.

"No, I haven't." she admits, her eyes saddening. I think back to Jason's face and my heart falls at the thought of him being in danger.

"Is it people he knows who are going missing?" I ask her and she shakes her head again.

"No, I mean as far as we know it's rumour at this point. The people who've been going missing aren't from the telecommunications sector, the rumours are coming out of the public services sector apparently." His mother imparts this information as she crosses her legs and looks between us. "You really are a perfect couple," she whispers, though I think it's more for her benefit than being directed at either one of us. Clark looks to me, grasping my hand in his as I feel my heart pound. This situation is so unique; I'm not quite sure how I'm meant to be feeling.

"Well, we hope. If not, then after seeing all this, I'm really rather worried what might become of us, and of you." Clark voices my concern and his mother scowls, as though she can't bear the thought of being a burden to her son.

"You think it ends at the one-hundred-day assessment? Oh no. I mean, you know me and your father passed that assessment, and beyond that there are other reasons Bliss Inc. can want to make one disappear." She sounds ominous as she speaks and her face becomes hard, a mask of reserve sliding in unlike anything I've ever seen except on the man to whom I'm married.

"What do you mean?" I ask her and she laughs.

"Well, birth defects, genetic diseases, infertility, and as you'll know from Clark, domestic violence. Anyone who encounters these things is at risk of becoming exiled. Anyone that puts the vision of 'happily ever after' at risk is a threat." She says this into the dim, cold light and a shudder of fear runs through me as a breeze races through the tunnel behind the curtain. I'm scared, I'll admit it. Just being here and talking about feeling the wrath of Bliss Inc. terrifies me.

"I'm afraid." I turn to Clark this time, looking into his eyes and ignoring the fact that his mother is watching us closely.

"I think that's the wisest thing to be when it comes to Bliss." The voice isn't Clark's. Instead it belongs to another man, a man who stands in the doorway of Clark's mother's home.

"David!" She exclaims, getting to her feet and moving across the space to kiss him on the cheek. I'm taken back by the candidness of her affection for this man.

"Who's this?" I whisper to Clark and he smiles.

"My mom's partner. Her romantic partner." He adds the second part of the sentence on for clarification as my expression moves toward becoming confused. His mother has a.... what do you even call someone who isn't a fiancé or a husband?

"This is David, my manfriend," she giggles slightly, pulling him into the middle of the room as she takes her seat once more. He leans against the brick of the circular wall, a brave move seeing as I have no idea what they're slick with.

"Manfriend?" I ask her and she nods.

333

"I love him, well most of the time when he's not driving me mad," she explains, giving him a sideways glance with a chuckle. He grins back at her unabashedly, the affection clear in his deep brown eyes. His hair is brown too and falls in short waves against his head. He's shorter than Clark, with a crooked smile and kind face.

"Nice to meet you," I breathe as Clark turns to me.

"David's sister was exiled after Bliss Inc. discovered that her baby was going to born with a genetic disease. David works in the Bliss Inc. headquarters, as one of the male readiness test technicians. He's known my mom for a long time, and is the reason we found out what happened to mom right before our Jigsaw Project readiness test. He spotted our names on his test schedule and knew who we were immediately; the rest is history," he reminisces and I nod, realising suddenly that this man must be quite dear to Clark as well as his mother. He'd risked it all to reunite a mother with her sons.

I feel a sudden and encroaching sense of inadequacy surrounded by those who would risk it all for one another without a second thought. I sit here, wondering if there's anything I can do to help.

Suddenly, I have an idea.

Reaching down into the high folded collar of my turtleneck jumper, I find the clasp of my necklace and unhook it, before catching the blue diamond pendant in my hand as it falls free from my neck. I take a second to examine it, before realising the true value of what I'm holding.

"Here," I say, passing it to Clark's mother. Her face turns surprised as I drop the necklace into her palms and she examines the stone.

"Valentine... you don't have to do that." She gasps, eyes widening.

"I do actually. Clark gave this necklace to me because I began to mean something to him. But it's now I realise meaning something to him is worth more than any diamond. I've done a lot of whining since I got married, and now, seeing you, I realise utterly ridiculous I must sound to Clark. Please, take it. It'll do far more for you than merely looking pretty around my neck." I make this small speech, unable to stop myself from looking into Clark's face.

His mother means more than anything to him, and it's time I start supporting him and thinking about his needs, rather than my own selfish motives. There's a bigger picture here than my story, and it affects so many more lives than I've ever realised, in a negative way. My happiness, it would seem, is no longer worth the suffering of others.

Twenty-One

The door to our apartment slides open, revealing a panoramic view of the now rising sun. My tattoo is restored in its glow, and Clark places a hand on my shoulder as I walk forward into our home. Examining my surroundings, they look wrong now. Too bright, too shiny, too clean. Too much. I look down at my engagement ring as I stand in the middle of the room like a spare part.

"You alright?" he asks me and I frown, knowing I can't speak freely about what I've seen, what I know. He watches me as he throws his backpack onto the couch, his eyes gentle as they glide over my form in an observant caress.

"Yes, I'm just a little on edge. Everything is... different now," I admit and he nods, walking over to the holo-dash and scanning his tattoo without saying a word. He frowns at the hard-light interface as it opens out against the back wall, taking a few moments to look around the projection before sliding his fingers across several hard-light tabs. A song comes crooning from nowhere, as there's no source for the music I can see. It's familiar, the song Clark and I had danced to on the hovering platform that night above the sea as fireworks had broken overhead.

"Into the mystic?" I ask him and he nods, a smug smile coming to his lips as he remembers that night.

"Care to dance and talk, Mrs. Cavanaugh?" He bows to me, acting silly, and so I do a fake curtsey in return before bounding forward, light on my feet, and into his arms without so much as a second thought as he begins to spin me slowly. His lips come in close to my ear.

"Speak to me. You must be reeling." The music blares and I realise what this is. It's his way of checking I'm okay without the need for any covert meeting on the balcony. The music covers our voices and the motion of the dancing makes sure that we're in a constantly changing trajectory so any cameras can't read how our lips are speaking. A few weeks ago, I'd have thought he was being romantic, but now I know better. My eyes are irrefutably open.

"Just… everything is so intense. You're amazing. You're a hero…" I say, unable to stop myself and he laughs.

"No. I'm just doing what's expected of me. My mother, she's the amazing one," he replies in a breathless sigh beside my ear and his breath tickles my flesh.

"Honestly, Clark, I don't feel… I don't know… worthy of any of this. When we first met, I thought you were so… so… hot and cold, and now I see you're a survivor. You change to be what society needs of you and what you need to be to undermine it. You're amazing." I stutter in my reply, my heart racing inside my chest. I'd taken on a lot of information in the last few hours, it's true. But I'm also getting the desperate inclination that I'd been underappreciating everything that Clark is at his core. I couldn't have married a better man. A more loving one.

"You think that's what I am? A survivor? I don't feel like one, I just feel like a guy who can't win. I am afraid of loving you, because of what my father became, and yet the idea of never loving you terrifies me in a way I never expected. You keep surprising me. I mean, what you did for my mom by giving her your necklace, I never expected that of you." I feel his voice breaking beneath the weight of his words, which are dripping with emotion it seems he's been keeping inside forever. We continue to sway to the music and I put my head on Clark's chest, unable to look fully into his gaze.

"I didn't do it because it was expected. I did it because I wanted to," I explain and he sighs out.

"You're sweeter than you know," he expresses and I feel my stomach flutter at his words as his hand comes up to caress my cheek.

"Well, I trust you," I say the words and his breathing stills, heavy with emotion.

"You do?" he asks me and I feel my voice shake as I respond, realising his uncertainty of this declaration is evidence of how tumultuous our romantic past has been. I continue to rest my gaze firmly on my feet below, careful not to step on Clark's toes.

"I do. If I didn't... well I wouldn't have gone down into the sewers with you," I explain and he exhales a sigh, tentative.

"I don't think that's trust, Valentine, as much as you may want it to be. I think that's your stubborn curiosity getting the better of your sense of self preservation." I look up at him, my eyes wide and unassuming as I take in his face.

"You don't believe me?" I ask him and he shrugs.

"It's just a little soon for that. I lied to you, snuck around, I don't expect that to just disappear only because you've now seen there was a just cause." He expresses the most logical breakdown of my behaviour I've ever heard and I frown. This heaviness in my chest, the fluttering of my heart and the churning of my stomach isn't because I don't trust him. It's because I do despite my reservations. It's because I think I love him and it terrifies me because I'm afraid he doesn't feel the same.

"Clark, why don't you believe me?" I whisper to him, my heart breaking as I hold his gaze with an unwavering intensity. It takes him by surprise and his expression becomes worried, as though the last thing he'd ever want to do is hurt me.

"It's not that I don't believe you, Valentine. I just, I couldn't blame you for not trusting me. You've just learned that everything you've ever known is a giant manipulative lie, you've just discovered that the dream you've been fed is a device to keep you placated. I'm a big part of that. I'm your husband and I don't want to mistake fear of the real, of the unknown, for trusting me." He looks down at me and I laugh quietly to myself, letting a small smile spread across my face.

"That's the thing though, Clark. You've never been a fantasy, or a dream come true. You're infuriating, stubborn and at times cold. You're not a manipulation. Or a lie. You're just you; you don't know how to be any other way. And in spite of everything I could find to hate about you, about the fact that you've taken me out of the idealist bubble I was living in, I can't hate you. You told me once that I'm the most real thing that's ever happened to you, and now I know what you meant." I feel myself getting out of breath as I ramble on, worried he's not taking me seriously, but when I look up again into his face, I see that he's enraptured.

"We're not a dream or a fantasy. We're just real." He repeats back at me.

"Exactly. I can't help but want you, despite your broken edges, the parts of you and me that don't fit together like puzzle pieces, but we're still perfect. They just don't want us to know we can be this way without them." I look at my tattoo, which rests by my face as my palm touches Clark's arm. I hate it more with each parting second.

Without falter, he bends down and kisses me deeply, cupping my chin with two fingers and groaning into my mouth. We've kissed before, but the intention of this kiss is different. He picks me up in his arms, turning on his heel and kissing me as we walk through the apartment. My heart hammers against the inside of my ribcage, and my mouth becomes hungry and insatiable as he continues to move his lips in rhythmic time against my own. His flesh is scorching and I feel his cheeks heat as they brush against my fingers whilst I'm reaching up to bury my hands in his hair.

He places me down on the bed, looking me deeply in the eyes as he towers above me.

"You trust me?" he asks, crawling over me and pressing his taught torso against my chest.

"I do," I say, unable to stop the words spilling from me, just like that day I'd spoken them at the altar. Clark smiles against my skin, as his lips begin to run down the inside of my neck. I pant, feeling myself getting tingles at the apex of my thighs, before he growls as though he's restraining himself and his lips come up to kiss me once more.

He breaks the embrace with another growl, yanking back from me and pulling his shirt over his head. I have never been like this with him when he's been bare chested before and I reach up, running my fingers down his pectorals, which shake with his heavy breath as his eyes burn a feral sapphire.

"Clark..." I look up to him and he leans down over me again as I shuffle up the bed, trying to buy myself some time before he gets too carried away.

"Yes?" he demands, the urgency in his tone arousing as he crawls after me and leans down over my body, caging me in with his arms so I can't escape.

"Do you want me?" I ask him, suddenly timid, as my cheeks flush and he presses his hard crotch against my lower stomach.

"What gave it away?" he asks me and I giggle at the feel of him, moving in to kiss him and feeling the fear I had always garnered about losing my virginity dissolve. It isn't just anybody, it isn't some random stranger like it has been when I've pictured giving it up on my wedding night. It's Clark. Clark Cavanaugh. The man who had woken me up to the fact that love isn't perfect and had made himself perfect in my eyes in one fell swoop. My husband.

"I don't really know what I'm doing here..." I explain, my anxiety rearing its head again fast and getting the better of me as he kisses me on the cheek, a sweet notion, sweet enough to even melt my fears of inadequacy.

"Me neither, but it's okay... I think we're doing pretty great so far," he whispers into my ear making me shudder.

"Me too," I reply, slightly out of breath as I decide to just go with it as I place my hands around his muscular torso and dig my nails, ever so slightly, into his back. I run them down the length of his spine and he shivers, groaning and bending to kiss me again, this time slipping his tongue in between my lips and causing me to moan too as he begins to undress me.

I'm not as nervous as I thought I'd be, not even when he and I become so lost in one another we form a single entity with jarring, broken edges which create an excruciating friction.

The sun rises over the Monopolis skyline as our fingers trace patterns across one another, each one different, but each one screaming the same answer to all the important vows we could promise, but have never spoken, as synapses fire and we implode like the fireworks under which we had danced. We make love together, all the while, whispering 'I do' with our fingertips and re-branding our hearts as our own to give.

Clark's skin presses heavily against the base of my spine as he runs his fingertips down the curve of my naked back.

"You are so beautiful," he breathes, laying on his left side and looking me deeply in the eyes. My head is turned toward him and as I examine his face, I sigh out, as though I exist in a dream.

"Thank you," I murmur, closing my eyes a moment and enjoying the feel of synapses waking once more as his hands run across my skin.

"Did you enjoy that? I mean... I hope it was okay," he asks me and I smile, a small chuckle escaping me at the idea that he thinks what has happened between us was anything but okay.

"You see this face, Clark? This is a contented Valentine face," I explain and he leans in, kissing my forehead and continuing to examine me. I thought I'd be embarrassed about being naked, I've always been afraid that losing my virginity would be awkward and that I'd feel under scrutiny, but now, I can't bear the thought of putting clothes on ever again. I like everything about being bare with Clark. I like how his eyes linger on me like I'm a three course meal, I like the way he touches me in places I've never been touched before, but most of all I like the fact that he's the only person who's ever loved me in this way. Or at least, I think it's love.

"Clark?" I mumble and he pulls me into his chest, resting his chin on the top of my head and inhaling deeply.

"Yes, beautiful?" he answers, relaxed as he leans back into his pillow once more and takes a deep look into my face.

"Is this love?" I ask him, my eyes widening and my skin flushing with colour. I watch him, expecting him to become uncomfortable, or to draw away, but he doesn't. Instead he just thinks for a moment as the warmth of his naked body seeps into mine and I find myself unable to tense.

"What do you think? I mean, are you okay after everything that's just happened?" I feel like he's chickening out a little, deferring the answer to me, but the genuine concern in his eyes makes me inclined to answer regardless.

"I'm wonderful. A little sore, but I've never felt this... relaxed or contented with anyone," I express, knowing that the words cannot possibly encapsulate how I'm feeling. I've just had sex with my husband for the first time. Clark Cavanaugh, the man who has infuriated me. I have just loved him in a way I've never loved anyone, and it feels so unbelievably right I can't quite believe that I'll ever be able to feel this way with another.

"You didn't answer my question." He smirks, running a finger along the length of my shoulder and down my arm as I shudder.

"Neither did you," I retort, getting close to him once more beneath the sheets and moving up to kiss him. The kiss deepens fast and his eyes blaze again with unrestrained desire as the plump flesh of his lips takes that of my own and causes it to tremble. "I think if you're not sure of the answer, Valentine, then I'm doing this wrong," he whispers to me, his hands coming around my naked torso and running down my spine before he grabs my buttocks with his hands and squeezes with a small moan. He leans into my neck and kisses me, in that way he had done before, as his hands run rampant over my skin and I feel his pleasure as he presses his body flush against mine. Suddenly, I'm not tired, only ready to be made sure.

Clark rolls off me, his body slick with sweat and his heart hammering as his breathing finally begins to slow. I'm feeling undone as his weight lifts from my body and my limbs seem to disconnect from me in a jellied mess. My heart is hammering as he rolls onto his back beneath the silver satin and his arm comes out, wrapping around me and pulling me closer onto his heaving chest as we both catch our breath.

"Are you sure yet?" he asks me with a smirk and I smile like a contented lioness.

"What if I say no?" I ask him and he laughs, coughing slightly as his too fast breath gets caught in his throat.

"Jesus, Valentine, I'm only one man, give me a second!" He exhales as I laugh.

"Sorry, am I being too demanding Mr Cavanaugh?" I quip, nuzzling into his chest and I practically feel him looking down on me with an adoring stare. I look up to him, not wanting to miss a single moment of this experience and he begins to rhythmically stroke his fingers down my spine once again, as though the sensation not only calms me, but soothes him as well.

"I believe greedy is the word." He rolls his eyes and kisses me on the forehead again, like he can't bear to stop kissing me for too long.

"It's not my fault you're good with your... thingy." I blush up at him, feeling a wave of guilt as I worry he's not enjoying things as much as I am.

"Good enough to make you sure?" He presses the issue and I flush a deeper red, my heart picking up pace to an excited thrum.

"Yes. I'm sure," I whisper, dropping my gaze as a sense of embarrassment and vulnerability make my chest tighten.

"Me too," he whispers back, brushing my hair from my face with his fingers and cupping my cheek with his dextrous thumb and palm.

"Say it," I beg of him, wanting nothing more in this moment than to hear him declare his feelings aloud. I worry that as soon as the words leave me, he's not ready. That it's too soon, but he smiles, bringing his hand around the back of my head and lifting my lips so they're but centimetres from his own.

"Valentine Cavanaugh…. I…." His eyes drop to my lips, before rising again and threatening to consume me with their deep unbridled blue as I wait, hanging on the edge of his every syllable.

Suddenly, as I'm on the cusp of hearing the three words I've been desperate for since the day I said 'I do,' a sound interrupts us.

Clark's eyes dart to the closed bedroom door in alarm and the moment is lost, our post-coital haze dissipating within only seconds. Just as we both freeze, unsure of whether or not the sound could have been something imagined, it comes again.

Rap, Rap, Rap.

Someone is knocking at the door.

Twenty-Two

Clark gets out of bed, walking over to the upcycler and requesting some clean pyjamas before quickly throwing them on and opening the door a fraction so he can slip through. I hold the sheets to myself, bereft at the fact that he's no longer holding me. It'd been hours since we'd fallen into bed together, but I'm not done being alone with him like this. It feels like only moments since he'd first started kissing me in the living area, even though I know better, and I feel an ache where his fingers had been that I know can only be soothed by his return. After a few minutes, Clark re-enters the bedroom with a puzzled look on his face.

"Who is it?" I ask him, wondering who on earth would be calling at this hour. Then I realise I actually have no idea what time it is and so turn, seeking my hard-light watch which lies on the bedside table. It's 10:30 at night... already?

My loss of time aside, I wrap the sheets tighter around me and get to my feet, moving in close to him and taking his hand in mine.

"What is it?" I ask him again and he sighs.

347

"It's David. He came here to talk to me about something urgent. I know it must be bad, because the technology he used to get into the building isn't the kind of thing you waste on a house call if you can help it. I'm hoping it won't take too long. Why don't you take a long shower and I'll join you in a couple of minutes. He won't be able to stay too long anyway." He looks me straight in the face and seemingly can't stop himself from smiling down at me. I've finally got him communicating, or so it would seem, and I can't deny that I'm enjoying the fact that he's finally being open and honest with me without any games.

"Okay. A shower does sound nice. I'll uh… wait for you." I breathe and turn on one heel, looking back over my shoulder at him with hooded eyes. He shakes his head and chuckles at my obvious flirtation before running his fingers through his ruffled hair and slipping out of the room silently.

Dragging the sheets from the bed, I walk the remaining distance between the bed and the bathroom door. I press down on the silver handle and step inside the cool tiled room, the deep azure of the ceramic floor seeping all the remaining heat from the soles of my bare feet. The shower is enormous, just like the one in our honeymoon suite had been, and as I scan my tattoo on the dash to turn it on, I remember shoving Clark into the shower only a few days ago. He'd been drunk and unhappy, and I was clueless about everything. How is it everything can change so quickly? I've never felt this close to anyone, and yet for the majority of our relationship I've been battling with Clark, while he was pushing me away and I was tiptoeing around his mood swings.

As I step into the shower, I reflect back on the time we've been together. I know it hasn't been very long, but as the hot water begins to flow down my spine, reminding me of Clark's fiery clutch, I honestly can't imagine being without him now. I can't fathom never having known him. I know that he hasn't said it yet, but I know that I love him. If this isn't love, then what is? I don't think I can imagine caring more about another person. I've always wondered what love would be like, whether it'll be a slightly amplified version of my closest friendships. But this isn't really like that at all. This goes deeper. Much deeper.

It's not until I've finished washing my hair and my mind begins to wander to what being with Clark would be like in the shower, that I realise he's been a while in the main room.

My heart drops in a single moment and worry begins to infect every facet of my thought process. He had said that David wouldn't just risk coming here for no reason, so whatever he has to say must be important. Has Clark been discovered defying Bliss Inc.? Have I done something that's exposed us? I tried to be as careful as I could as we left the sewers last night, even insisting we stop in the coffee shop I sat in the night before to give us a reason to be out so late if someone really was watching our every move.

The thought of losing Clark becomes too much, and I find myself suddenly crying under the hot water. I've only just discovered what Clark really means to me. I've only just begun to trust him fully and share myself with him in the way I've always imagined, and the thought of that being taken away so soon fills me with gnawing, inescapable, terror. After all, my virginity is gone now. I have given him that and I can never get it back.

There's certainly no chance that anyone else would ever want me now, even if it were a possibility. Everyone knows that once you've given away your virginity you're damaged goods to another man.

Clark is the person I've chosen, and instead of joy at this revelation, I'm suddenly nervous and shaking.

I exhale, taking a deep breath in the moments that follow and finding myself desperate to know why it is David is here. I ponder this for a few moments, wishing that everything could be simple, but realising I need to know, or I'll always be worrying that I'll come home and Clark will just be gone.

I don't turn off the shower, anticipating returning shortly with Clark in tow; instead I step out of the fragrant air, which is clouded by steam as the water continues to shower the floor.

Treading lightly, I exit the bathroom and move briskly across to the upcycler on the far wall. I order a robe made of towel, which arrives slightly warm, and wrap it around myself. Placing the hood of the robe over my head, I hope that the material will soak up some of the water running from my hair and down my spine in a cold stream, making me shudder. I take another deep, scared, breath and walk over to the wood of the closed doorway. I take another deep, scared, breath walking past the bed and over to the wood of the closed doorway.

I reach out, placing my hand on the handle, but something stops me and I freeze, pulling back my outstretched fingers and instead moving to press my ear against the wood of the door. It's thinner than it looks, and I can hear the conversation taking part in the living room with an alarming amount of clarity. I hear David's strained voice speak and I can tell he's distressed.

"Look Clark, we need her help. You have to tell her the truth. It's not fair to anyone. You know the importance of this." My eyes widen as these words reach me and I wonder who the 'she' is to whom he's referring. My heart continues to hammer as I press my ear harder to the door, afraid of what I might hear, but unable to keep myself in the dark any longer just because I'm scared.

"I'm not dragging her into this, David. No." He says the words firmly and my heart flutters. Is he talking about me, or his mother? Or is there another 'she?'

"Clark, we've been working towards this moment for as long as I can remember. I know that what I've done isn't exactly ethical, but you have to see this from my side. This could change everything. It could end Bliss Incorporated! Think about your mother, about all the exiles down in the tunnels. Do you really want to stop us from potentially freeing them? Your mother deserves better than that."

So it's his mother they're talking about? I listen in further, the dripping of my hair no longer bothering me as my palms begin to sweat with nerves.

"I've hurt her enough, David. I can't tell her this now. You don't know her, she believes in true love. She says that she doesn't, but I can see it in her eyes. She's falling in love with me and I with her…. How can I just destroy that?" Clark's voice is desperate too now, and I realise that it is me he's talking about.

"I did this for everyone. Now we need her to help your mother, and everyone else. That's the whole reason you agreed to this charade to begin with! You have to tell her the truth, Clark. You know that you can't pretend you're her matchmate if this is going to work. You know she deserves to know the truth. She deserves to know that I switched you and Jason at test stage. She deserves to know that he's her matchmate, not you. I know you love her, but you're being selfish. Besides, it's not like she can leave you." I no longer need to have my ear pressed to the door, because David's voice is raised in a yell. My heart pounds.

Clark isn't my matchmate?

I feel sick.

"Look, David, you don't think I know she'd be happier with Jason? I do. They're perfect for one another, and it kills me to see that every fucking day. Don't you think it makes me want to scream when I realise how right the formula got it with them? I mean, you're the one who suspects it's all bullshit, right? So why should it matter whether she lives her life with me or not? What difference does it make!? If she doesn't know, it won't hurt her. It's hard enough for me to see her with him every time I close my eyes, I can't handle seeing her longing after him when I'm awake!" Clark's yelling too and my heart shatters.

He's been lying to me? He knew all along? Was that why he'd been so awkward with me at the wedding when his brother had kissed my hand? Why he'd yelled that I wanted to be with Jason during his drunken stupor? My eyes fill with tears again and I cover my mouth with my hand in shock to stop myself from giving away that I'm only metres from the heated argument.

He's been keeping me for himself because he's selfish and wants to use me as a weapon to hurt Bliss Incorporated and prove that they can't control his emotions. The one thing he said he'd never do. He would rather take the risk that I'd never fall in love with him and be miserable for my entire life, than tell me the truth, than give me the option to go to the authorities about the fact that there's been a mistake.

My breath comes in shallow wisps as I glance back to the bed and realise what I've done. I've given a man who isn't my matchmate my virginity. Even if I went to the authorities about this and they understood the mix up, they'd never let me be with Jason, not after the fact that I've been soiled by someone else. If that's not bad enough, Jason certainly wouldn't want me now either, because I've had sex with his brother. I'm spoiled goods. I'm damaged. I've given my worth to the wrong man, a man who has been manipulating me and my emotions, trying to trick me into falling in love with him for his own selfish reasons.

I think back to our honeymoon, about how he'd tried to keep his distance. I should have let him get on with it. I should have known that someone so manipulative and dishonest was just playing with me to achieve ulterior motives.

I've never felt so used in my life.

He's saying he loves me, but how do I know that's not just more lies?

I'm betrayed as I stand here, utterly broken up inside, not about the fact that he's not my matchmate, I think I could overlook that, but because he's kept me in the dark this entire time without a single thought for my happiness or what I want. In this moment, where he's taken my choice away from me, he's just as bad as Bliss Incorporated, having manipulated my life and my emotions for the sake of keeping control of me for selfish motives.

Taking a deep breath, I straighten, pulling my hood from my head and wiping my eyes on my sleeve. I'm flushed beetroot red with embarrassment at how I've acted. At how wrapped up I've allowed myself to get with the wrong person. I should have trusted my gut; I should have known right after the wedding that he wasn't the right man for me. Have I just been deluding myself this whole time? Or has he been sweet-talking me and leading me down the path which he has seemingly carved out for this relationship long ago?

Squaring my shoulders. I open the door.

"Valentine." Clark says, his voice laced with shock and dread as he inhales slightly, like a child with his hand caught in the cookie jar.

"I'm not your matchmate?" I whisper, my gusto suddenly gone as I feel the fight leave me at the sight of his face. David stares at me, his expression going slack before returning to its usual casual cocky smile.

"It's better that you know, Valentine. We need your help," he expresses and Clark's head snaps to one side.

"Get out," he says the two words and David opens his mouth to speak. I watch Clark's muscles tense up as he inhales, his chest expanding as he begins to look like he might yell. Instead, he balls his fists at his sides, as I stand here on shaking legs with wet hair and a tear-stained face, before saying, "Get. Out," with a ferocious wrath contorting his face into something feral. David's expression goes stern, before he walks over to one side of the room and detaches a black device from the wall, leaving in even and unhurried steps.

I stand, unable to move or breathe as the door closes and Clark and I are left alone.

"Valentine... I...." he begins, just as he had begun to say that he loved me not twenty minutes ago.

"No. No more lies. I don't believe anything you say to me. You're just manipulating me for your own selfish gain. You swore to me, you promised you wouldn't make me into a weapon to hurt them, but you did." I speak, my voice trembling. He takes a step forward toward me, sensing my distress, but I step away from him, flinching slightly as I do at his enormous height. He's forced himself on me in the shower before in an argument and placated my rage. I can't let that happen again. "Don't touch me," I snarl, feeling my devastation begin to curdle into rage.

"Valentine please..." he begins again, but I hold a hand up.

"No. Whatever it is that I thought you felt for me is a lie. You don't care about me. If you did, you would have told me that Jason is my matchmate. You would have given me the chance to choose him... to set this right," I blurt, not thinking about what I'm saying, but knowing I want to hurt Clark as much as possible. I don't even know if Bliss Inc. would allow me to be with Jason, or whether they would just exile me.

"You think being with Jason is right? You think that what we have isn't real?" he asks me and I nod, eyes brimming with angry, broken tears.

"You lied to me. You've been lying to me ever since we met and I can't trust anything you say. Jason wouldn't have done that to me. Jason wouldn't have lied, because he would have really loved me. He would have put my needs first."

"You don't even know Jason," Clark bites out, his face turning glacial.

"Says you. But you're forgetting that nothing that comes out of your mouth means anything to me anymore, Clark Cavanaugh. So, talk all you want. I'm not listening anymore." Realising I'm now standing in the doorframe, I take a final step back from him and grab the bedroom door, slamming it in his face.

Twenty-Three

I sit on the edge of the bed for at least an hour, sobbing. After my tears have dried, I realise that my stomach is cavernously empty, making me feel sick, so I reluctantly get to my feet, face tear stained and my eyes raw from crying. My hair is in a tangled damp mess against my spine and I feel a tiredness that extends beyond what is physical.

I open the door to the living room, having heard no activity coming from outside for the past hour. Clark hadn't tried to come in after me, which makes me irrationally angry even though the sting of his betrayal is still fresh. I shouldn't want him to chase me, I shouldn't want him to come after me just so I can shoot him down again and watch him crumple. Yet, I can't help it. I want to hurt him; I want to show him what it's like to have your choices taken away, because in defying the ruling power he hates, he's become exactly like them.

I pad over to the kitchen, being greeted by an empty room and don't need to see that Clark's backpack is gone to know that he is too. The air in this place is cold, chilled by the way we've parted as the night continues to roll on outside the giant panoramic window. The kitchen reminds me of Clark, which is ridiculous because we've barely even started to make it a home, and yet the hob looks wrong without him propped up against it, cooking and relaxed. I shake my head, willing the memories of his stupid face to dissipate as I order a single, lonely cup of instant ramen from the kitchen upcycler. I turn on the sink's third faucet and allow the boiling water to run for a moment as I yank the lid of the ramen cup and shove it under the hot torrent. Within a few seconds, the cup is filled to the water line, and so I turn off the tap, moving to sit at the island and looking down into the swirling fake broth of chemicals and plastic-ish noodles. I'm hit with a kind of sick nostalgia as I let my anger fall from the boiling point which it's been simmering at and exhale deeply, my nerves steadying and a kind of clarity settling over me.

I can't be with Clark. That's the reality of this. I can't trust him. So, either I'm stuck in a marriage with someone who I wonder now if I'll ever be able to look at with affection again, or I'm going to be exiled by Bliss Incorporated.

Maybe it won't be so bad. I think to myself, recalling the meeting I'd had with Clark's mother only yesterday. She seems happy. David makes her happy, doesn't he?

I ponder this for a moment before releasing I haven't brought anything to eat with and so fiddle around in one of the draws set into the island countertop for a fork. Twirling it in my hand as I quickly grab one, I continue to wonder about what my life could be like if I was exiled.

What about Jason? I find myself wondering this, despite the fact I don't know Jason at all. Clark was right about that, and wasn't Jason also in love with someone else?

358

I plunge my fork into the now inflated ramen and twizzle it between my forefinger and thumb, raising it to my lips and blowing hard to get rid of some of the heat. I put it in my mouth and cringe slightly at the taste. I've been spoiled on good food and cooking by Clark.

Damn him. I might as well be eating Styrofoam.

I look around at the apartment I'm sitting in, wondering why it is that when I'm surrounded by the very hardwood floors I'd always thought would make me a home, I'm sat eating the same old processed crap that I'd been subject to in the single district and feeling worse than I ever had when I'd lived alone. I'd always been lonely, but I'd never felt this low about myself or my life in general. There had always been hope about the future, and someone to share it with; there had always been friends...

I straighten on my stool and look to the window. Is it possible Egypt is still awake? I mull this over momentarily, knowing that reaching out to her could be dangerous for us both if I say too much, but wondering if just knowing she would be on the end of the line would be enough.

I get to my feet, abandoning my ramen and hurrying into the bedroom before grabbing my hard-light watch off the bedside table. I take it in my palm, swiping the interface open and finding myself alarmed at the amount of messages I have from her. My stomach floods with guilt and I feel a sense of panic coming over me.

Val? You okay, thought I'd hear from you today?

I scroll down to the next message.

Val? I'm getting kind of worried. I know you're busy being married and all but you sounded so upset yesterday. Message me when you get this.

And the next.

Guess you're busy with Clark or something... drop me a line?

There's more below it but I can't bring myself to read through the worried one-liners so instead I open a new message window and begin typing with my fingers.

So sorry I haven't gotten back to you. Been really caught up in decorating. Clark and I finally slept together, it was amazing, but it turns out he's been lying to me this whole time. I don't know what to do. I don't think I can be in love with someone who lies.

I press send and wait a few minutes for a reply but nothing comes, it is pretty late though and Egypt is still on the single district schedule, so I guess I'll just have to wait until morning. Depressed, I walk back through the empty apartment and resume staring into the cup of ramen, thinking.

●●●

Just as I'm draining the powder dregs at the bottom of the cup dry, I hear the door open and my heart fills with dread. I've said my piece, and I don't know if I can take more excuses.

"Valentine?" His voice seeks me as he calls out into the apartment and I freeze in place, sucking in breath and wanting to stop myself from locking eyes on his face. As he comes out of the narrow hallway and into the open space of the kitchen and living area, I exhale. I don't speak, I just sit, numb to everything.

"Valentine, we need to talk," Clark demands, his eyes blazing passionately. His jaw is firmly set and his stance is determined as he crosses the space between us and places his backpack on the floor before leaning in on the opposite side of the island.

"I don't want to hear anything you have to say. I've already told you that," I reply, stubborn as I move to get to my feet. I turn to place the cup of ramen in the upcycler to be taken away, but as I do, his voice makes my head snap sideways.

"I didn't know," he announces and I can't help but finish my rotation to turn back to face him. Does he think I'm totally stupid?

"What did you just say to me?" I breathe, feeling fury beginning to rear its ugly head again.

"I didn't know that Jason was your matchmate until tonight. I swear to you." He pleads at me with his blue gaze, but we've been here before and I'm not falling for it again.

"How stupid do you think I am? I heard your conversation with David, Clark. I heard all of it." I cross my arms after placing the plastic cup down on the counter so hard it almost breaks.

"Well, if that's true then you know I'm telling the truth. That's what he came here to tell me. He came here to tell me that we're only together because he switched the test results." He blinks, still imploring me to believe him. I cock my head.

"So why is it that you didn't just say this before? What, need a little midnight walk to give you time to concoct your story?" I ask him, raising one eyebrow in suspicion and he frowns.

"You yelled at me and slammed the door in my face, Valentine. There wasn't any reasoning with you. You didn't want

361

to hear it." He acts like I've forgotten my own rage, my own disappointment, making me even more bitter.

"What, more of your lies? I still don't," I snap and wonder momentarily why I'm even entertaining him. Why haven't I just made a break for the bedroom? As I watch his fists clench, I wonder if it's because I know this time he'll follow me.

"I'm not lying!" he exclaims, standing upright and inhaling sharply.

"Fine, if you're not lying, why did you tell David that you see me and Jason together whenever you close your eyes? Why would you be thinking that if you didn't know we were matchmates?" I ask him and his expression drops instantly. For a moment, I think I've finally caught him in a lie, before he looks embarrassed.

"Because... Because... I just do alright! I mean look at you, you're so innocent and optimistic and kind. I'm angry, stubborn and jealous. I'm not like you. Jason and you would be perfect for one another. I can't help but think it, Valentine, because I'm guilty as hell I can't give you what you've always wanted. I'm just not good enough." He looks at me and I'm stunned.

"That's ridiculous. You're the one who is choosing to lie and deceive me. You're doing all this, but you didn't have to. You're a good person. I know you are. Someone who has given as much as you, to your family, couldn't be bad," I express to him, feeling irritated by his self-pity.

"Jason does exactly the same." He looks miserable as he says the words and I want to shake him. Why has he suddenly become this kicked puppy, he's never been this way before?

"Clark, I don't care about Jason, I did care about you. I thought I loved you. But I can't be in love with someone I don't trust. You say you love me, but either you have been lying to me since the beginning or you were going to hide the information about Jason from me. Either way, you were right, I can't trust you." I find him confusing, to say the least, as I stand here, my heart breaking. I've been angry, but now that's falling away at the thought that he actually believes what I have yelled in anger. I thought I'd been clear about how I feel. I gave myself to him physically without any regard for the consequences because in that moment, I trusted him implicitly. I mean, he might not be the right person for me, but he's still a hero to those who depend on him down in the sewers, why can't he see that? "Why wouldn't you just tell me about it? If you only just found out? Why do you insist on lying to me? What's the point?" I ask him, wondering why exactly it is he feels the need to control me.

"Because I am afraid that now you know, you won't have feelings for me anymore!" he admits, balling his fists once more in frustration. His eyes drop to the floor.

"Clark, that's not how this works. That's not how any of this works! You're the one who keeps saying how we should be together on our own terms, not because some company tells us to. So why the hell do you think I'd leave just because that exact same company says we're not supposed to be together? Where the hell is the logic?" I exclaim, getting frustrated again. I don't want a heart to heart, I don't want him to distract me with sweet words or compliments. I want the truth.

"Valentine... I... I'm just scared. I've never felt like this before about anyone. I don't want to lose you." The words leave him and instead of the effect I expect them to have on me, I feel oddly numb. I can't get past his lies. I can't get past the fact that while his face is extremely pretty, I'm afraid his motives aren't as pleasing. I've gone all in with my heart, and now it's time I pull it back off the table. The hand that's being played just isn't in my favour anymore.

"You already have, Clark. I don't trust you. I can't give you my heart, or anything more than I already have, without trust. I'm just... I have to do what's best for me. Nobody else is. Not you. Or Bliss Inc. The only person in this world who has to get up every day and live my life is me. So, it's time I took my choices back," I express, feeling my heart pound painfully with every word that falls from me.

"How exactly do you plan on doing that? We're stuck in the system now. We're married," he asks me and I frown slightly, feeling the stranglehold of the world around me growing tighter by the second.

"David said you need my help in some kind of scheme? Something to help turn the tables on Bliss Incorporated. Is that true? Would it get me out?" I ask him, wondering if he'll just lie again as I give him a stern stare.

"Yes, but I can't guarantee your safety, or your ability to stay in the Jigsaw Project once this goes down, Valentine. We've been waiting on something like this for years. Decades even. So many cogs have had to stay in motion without being noticed to even get us this far, so if you're not willing to go all in, I think you're best left out of it," he says this and I ponder his response.

"You're not just saying this because you want me to stay stuck married to you?" I interrogate him and he scowls at me.

364

"Valentine, I'm surprised at you. I thought you knew me better than that. I told you the very first day we met that I don't relish the idea of staying in a marriage with someone who detests me." He looks miserable, heartbroken, and yet I think my words have finally reached him as the edge in the way he talks is starting to return.

"You were happy to keep me in a marriage by lying to me though," I remind him and he shakes his head.

"I thought you were happy." He sighs, it's not a question. It's a statement and one full of melancholia. I feel wistful in spite of myself as he turns away.

"What about if I don't help with this scheme? What about if I just go to Bliss Headquarters tomorrow and tell them about all this? About the mistake. Do you think they'd place me with Jason? Do you think they'd fix all this?" I ask him and he turns back, a surprised look on his face.

"And what makes you think that going to Bliss Inc. and telling them about this mix-up isn't exactly the scheme we have in mind, Valentine? After all, David switched Jason and me for a reason." He whispers this last sentiment, looking around the room with a suspicious glance and I inhale.

"So, you're saying that you want me to go and tell them about the mix up? That you want me to go and expose David and what he did?" I ask him and he smirks.

"Yes, Valentine. That is exactly what we want you to do. Now, take some time and think about it. After all, life as an exile is no picnic. I might have made my choice. But this is yours and yours alone. You have to ask yourself, now that you have the choice, is getting out of this marriage, trying to expose this system for what it really is, worth being exiled, or worse, killed?" His words shock me as he turns and moves into the bathroom, no doubt to wash away the scent of sewer and despair.

I sit on the edge of the bed again, with my knees hauled up under my chin, rocking slightly as I think on everything that I now have to decide. I've wanted the right to choose, but I didn't realise that this would come with such utter fear. I don't know what I'm doing. I'm the product of a system that has determined the direction of my every waking hour for my entire life, and now at the thought of making a choice for myself I'm frozen. I know what I want to do. I want to try and fix all this, not just for me, but for everyone living in the dark, dank filth of the sewers. But what if I choose wrong?

I want to get out. But I'm afraid. Afraid that I'll end up exiled, or dead in a ditch somewhere with no gravestone, no memory that I was ever alive. Just my absence and a lot of unanswered questions from those who have been a part of my life.

I sit, looking down now at the tattoo on my wrist. At the wedding band and engagement ring on my finger. They are supposed to be signs that I've found true love, that my soul in fact has another half, and yet the man with the other half of this tattoo isn't my matchmate, the man who's given me this ring doesn't love me, or at least not in a way I want. He isn't what I've been promised, or what I've imagined or been hoping for. He's complicated, messy, a liar.

I sigh out, thinking of all the girls in Monopolis who trust Bliss Inc. with their future happiness. I think about Egypt, about my sisters, about my mother. Are they really happy? Or are they just being placated by a system designed to take away their autonomy?

I know the answer. I know the truth of it all.

This isn't real. It's a façade. Just like the haunted house, just like the rollercoaster in Enamoury Park, the illusion is perfect, except for the fact it's an illusion. It's not real life.

I ball my hands into fists, watching the hard, blue glow of my engagement ring demand my attention. It's very beautiful, but the promise it represents is one that has been broken over and over again by Clark's lies, to the point now where the pieces of our relationship are jagged and hostile, broken beyond repair.

I get to my feet, knowing that I need to do this. I need to stop anyone else from being stuck in this situation.

If I can help put an end to Bliss Incorporated, then I can give people the option to love who they want. It might be at the cost of my life, or my place in this society, but at least when it's all over, I can say that I fought for true love. Even if that true love isn't mine.

Twenty-Four

Light bounces off the slick walls of the cyclical sewer tunnel as our damp, heavy tread echoes around us. My tattoo no longer glows, having been deactivated by the device just outside of the sewer entrance by Clark, who had caused me to shudder as his fingers brushed my wrist.

My heart has been racing since the second I decided to tell Clark I wanted to help David, regardless of what that means for my safety. I think he finally gets that I want out of this relationship, because our interaction has been minimal at best and as we walk through the dark, approaching the living quarters of the exiles, we're silent, awkward even, reminding me of the day we met.

Clark raps a neon green glow stick against the bars where we met Jeremy before, but instead of the short haired man with an intimidating face, this time someone I'm familiar with comes to let us in, making my heart leap.

"Jason?" I whisper, as Clark exhales heavily beside me. I turn to him, watching his face glaze glacially and his eyes deaden at the sight of his brother, whose face lights up at the sight of me.

"Oh hey, Valentine! So, David convinced you, huh? I'm not surprised, that guy can be persuasive." He chuckles to himself as he brings out the same magnetic device that Jeremy had used to let us into the exile's living quarters before.

After a few moments of watching his large brown eyes focusing on the bars he's lifting, I wonder how he and his brother have ended up so different, and I feel a little guilty.

Does the fact that he should have been my husband make me wonder if I could love him in a way I could never love Clark?

Absolutely.

Does it make me wish that it'd been him at the end of the aisle?

I ponder this as I step across the grate and into the connecting tunnel, coming face to face with him as he holds out a hand to Clark, who takes it and pulls him into his chest in a manly embrace. Clapping one another on the back, they part, and I realise that I wouldn't want either of them to be standing at the end of that aisle, because either way they'd both be strangers to me. Shouldn't the person you vow yourself to, forever, know you first? Shouldn't they love you first?

"What?" Jason asks me, and I realise that I'm standing here staring at both of them.

"Uh, nothing," I reply, blushing as Clark rolls his eyes and makes a snorting sound. I turn on the ball of my foot and walk away from them, no longer wanting to look at the pair of brothers. Everything just feels so ridiculously complicated with them right now.

I turn a corner and move into the stark light of the tunnel, which had blinded me last time, striding through the patchy puddles that plume dark as my boots disturb the residue suspended within. I hear whispers as I pass various homes, speaking the word 'Valentine' like it's holy.

What do they know? Is what they're going to ask me to do that dangerous?

I swallow hard as I turn a few more corners, avoiding the eyes which peak out behind sheets hung from rusty poles and running my fingers through my hair, which hangs loose down my back. There's a chill to this place, a dank depression that causes me to shudder as I reach the vibrant silver curtain of Clark's mother's home. I halt, not wanting to intrude without the presence of her sons.

"You can just go in, Valentine." Jason ushers me forward, his voice soothing to my ears like liquid chocolate. His gaze falls upon me with a gentility that Clark does not possess and I watch him before my eyes dart to my husband's face. Clark is wearing a mask of cold disapproval and, for a moment, I flash back to his fingers tangling in the strands of my hair and his lips on my neck.

I turn from Jason at this image, the thought of hurting Clark suddenly too much.

Drawing the curtain aside, I step into the shadow of the cramped space. The air mattress has been collapsed and several chairs have been procured from seemingly nowhere. David is astride one, which is positioned backwards so his arms rest across its back.

"Valentine. You're here." His mouth forms a smile and I kind of want to slap him.

"Yes, but don't think this means I forgive what you did. You screwed with my future for your personal gain. I can't forgive you for that," I snap and his eyes lose their fire.

"I know. That's okay. What I did wasn't ethical, but it was for a greater good, I promise you." He licks his bottom lip nervously as I take a seat beside him.

"If I didn't already believe that, I wouldn't be here," I respond, sassy and determined as Jason and Clark enter the room. Clark's mother is stood, leaning over the portable campfire that is heating a pot of water, no doubt for tea. Her black hair gleams in the dim light, being loose today as it falls to her shoulders. She pivots to face me, a smile gracing her lips as her blue eyes well, full of emotion.

"Are you sure this is what you want?" she asks me, her face intense in the directness of her inquiry.

"Yes." I nod to her, not elaborating. I don't think I can make a justification for this, maybe because the reason I'm doing it is because I can't bear the thought of anyone else having control over my life anymore.

"Right. Let's begin," Jason says, leaning back against the table and folding his arms against his chest. He's wearing a ragged looking tan coloured shirt and khakis with holes in the knees. I've never seen a labour settlement worker in uniform before and it alarms me.

They really dress them in that? I want to cry, thinking about perfectly good people being forced into poor living conditions because of the results of some test. I sigh out, calming myself as best I can and focusing on the task ahead.

"So, Clark said you want me to go and tell Bliss Inc. about the mix up with…" I begin but my voice trails off because Jason is staring at me as I speak, he's really listening to what I'm saying and I don't want to mention the fact we're matchmates. I'm worried I might flush, or worse smile at the thought of the mix up. Clark watches us both intently.

"That you and Clark aren't matchmates?" Jason finishes my sentence and I nod before he continues, having lost my voice. "That's right. We have been waiting for the technology to be developed that would allow us to gain access to their holo-dash systems, and this has become recently available to us. All we need now is for someone to have an issue important enough for

Pippa Hart herself to step in. We need access to her dash in particular, because we want to see what's going on inside. Once we know, we can leak that information to the city. The labour settlements are ready to riot with the recent disappearances, we've been preparing for war for a while, but we know we need a reason for the Nuclear families and the singles in the Jigsaw Project to want to join us. We need to show them how corrupt this company really is." Jason speaks and the information detonates a million questions inside my head.

"How are you going to leak the information?" I ask him and he smiles.

"That's easy enough. I work for the soft-light broadcasting network. So as soon as we have the footage we need, it'll be on every channel in every settlement," he explains and I nod, realising I should have known that.

"Footage? What do you mean we're going to put a camera in there?" I ask him and Jason nods again.

"Come with me. I'll show you the technology we'll be kitting you out in and explain the rest of the plan." He holds out a hand to me and I rise to my feet but don't take it.

Shrugging his shoulders, he holds the curtain open as I follow him, hearing Clark's mother offering her son and lover a cup of tea as Clark moves too quickly out of my way.

Jason leads me down the tunnel, passing a few more curtains where more eyes track my movement and more whispers greet my ears. I sigh out, realising that these people are relying on me, they're trusting me, a stranger, with a rare opportunity to secure their freedom, or at least attempt to overthrow the people that put them here. Suddenly, we come to a door in the wall of the sewer. I frown.

"If there are rooms here, why don't you use them for housing?" I ask him and he turns to me.

"This is the only room down here with a lock, you'll see why we keep it locked when I open it." He slips a hand into his trouser pocket and produces something metal. I've never seen anything like it before, and watch, fascinated as he slips it into a hole in the door in front of him. He turns it and the door gives a click.

"What's that?" I ask him, staring as he moves to place the object into his pocket.

"A key. Why, haven't you ever seen a key before?" he asks me with a cocked eyebrow and I shake my head.

"No. Never," I admit, blushing.

"I suppose that's to be expected. They're like tattoos, but they don't need to be on your skin to let you into places," he explains, pulling the door open with a yank. The hinges groan and a thin layer of rust flakes down from the frame, fluttering to the floor like bloody snow.

"What if you lose it?" I ask him and he chuckles.

"You don't."

"Oh," is all I can think to reply, stepping onto a flat concrete floor.

The room is packed full of wooden pallets which are stacked high with something I've only ever seen once, in history class with my mother when I was small. My heart stops in my chest for a moment.

"Jason…. Are these…" I begin and he nods his head, his face looking solemn.

"Yes, Valentine. They are," he whispers, turning to me without blinking.

"Where did you find them?" I reply in a hushed tone, immediately terrified, worried that the ground beneath my feet will explode with one careless motion.

"These bombs were in the museum in the labour settlements. The one to remind us why we need to be where we are. Why we're marginalised. Why we don't deserve happily ever after. We don't even know if they still work. Didn't make transporting them here any less scary though I'm sure you can imagine." He laughs slightly to himself and I wonder how he can be joking as I imagine the domed metal casings being transported. My heart races at the image, worrying that with every tiny imaginary motion, Jason could die in a blazing inferno.

"Are we okay to be in here?" I ask him and he nods, pursing his lips.

"Yes, it's fine. They've been moved here from one of the outermost labour settlements. If they made it that far without detonating, then I'm sure we're fine. This is just where we keep the valuable stuff, the stuff we don't want anyone to have access to if the exiles are ever discovered. Come, sit down." He directs me to a small wooden table with a single wooden chair in the corner, illuminated by a bald lightbulb that hangs upon a single string from the grubby ceiling. I take a seat on the chair as it creaks and Jason pulls a black duffle bag from a metal locker in the far corner of the room, before walking back over to me and dumping it onto the table. He yanks the zipper open and rummages around inside.

After a few seconds, he pulls out a tiny silver box.

"Right, so this is why we need you mainly. Other than the fact that you're going to be turning David in as the wife who's had her matchmate switched, we need your eyes," he explains, popping the lid on the case and turning it to me. "These are a new version of an old technology that was used before the war, surveillance contact lenses. These are the only ones we have right now and they're brown. Clark couldn't wear them, or we'd be putting the risk on him." He explains this to me and I nod.

"So, what, do I just wear these and turn David in?" I ask him and he hands me the box. Inside the case is slick black plastic with two darkly tinted, brown glass discs.

376

"Well, not just that, we need you to plant this too, anywhere close to a holo-dash interface within the headquarters. Just be discreet." He hands me a tiny black plastic card smaller than a cracker, it's thin and doesn't look like anything special so I examine it curiously for anything visibly complex or technological. "You could put that on the bottom of a desk, or on any vertical surface, it sticks using static electricity," he expresses and I nod, placing the card on the table beside me.

"So, David is coming with us? He's okay with all this?" Jason nods at this.

"Yes, we've given him a pair of these too, so even if you don't make it back with them, we should be able to see them on this monitor. He's given his life for this cause, he's risked so much already, he'd rather go out fighting than anything else." He pulls out a thick black box with a screen. This screen though isn't hard-light, instead it appears to be made of plastic. He smacks the side of the box with the flat of his palm.

"Oh, I guess that makes sense. That's a screen?" I ask him, getting to my feet and turning to look at it. It flickers to life as he pulls an enormous metal stick out of the top and I can see my chest on screen. I look down to the lenses, realising I'm focusing them right on my cleavage and snap the case shut with alarm. Jason smiles, laughing as he turns the boxy screen off again.

"So, if I record this from my point of view, won't they know it was me once the recording is out there?" I ask him and he looks suddenly sad.

"Yes, they will, but we can do things to protect you. The first of which is giving you this." He reaches into the depths of the duffle bag once more and procures a laminated plastic card.

"What's this?" I ask him and he looks at me very seriously, the soft chocolate brown of his eyes affecting me more than I'd like to admit.

"This, Valentine, has been the hardest thing to procure. This is a master key. It will allow you past any door, or onto any transport in the entire of Monopolis." His expression is completely lacking in humour.

"What about if I lose it?" I joke, actually realising that this could be a serious concern.

"Don't," he replies, his expression becoming hardened. In this moment, he looks a little like Clark, before the toughness fades and his face turns concerned as he runs his hands through his blonde hair.

"Are you okay?" He asks me and I shake my head as I sit back down.

"This is just a lot you know. I just... I found out about you and me and Clark and then about the fact that I can potentially help all these people. I'm afraid I'll mess it up. All of it," I express, wondering which I'm more afraid of, potentially getting exiled or ending up without a direction in my life, without anyone to love me.

"You should know that Clark loves you very much. I knew it from the moment he saw you. I watched his face on that monitor in Bliss Hall," he expresses and his deduction takes me by surprise.

"What? He looked terrified!" I laugh, remembering back to when I'd thought that Clark's reserve was my biggest problem.

"You don't know him like I do. Clark was prepared for feeling nothing; he was prepared for not loving you at all. The morning of that wedding he was relaxed as anything. In fact, I've never seen him so calm. It wasn't until he actually saw you that he became Mr Frosty," he expresses and I grimace.

"Is that because he knew I wasn't his matchmate?" I ask him and he shakes his head.

"No. He didn't know about what David did. Neither did I until this evening. But that's the thing, Clark doesn't believe in that stuff because he's seen our mother fall in love on her own. He watched what real love can do, how it can heal." He expresses this and licks his bottom lip as I look into his face, feeling guilty that I haven't believed Clark's innocence.

"I thought I loved him. But he keeps lying to me. Trusting him is impossible." I sigh, remembering quickly why it is I don't trust his word, and Jason cocks his head with a frown.

"Yes, well it's become second nature to him. Every single day we operate in this damn hellhole is a lie. The only time Clark can be himself is when he's down here. It becomes automatic. I catch myself now, and sometimes I can't remember what's really the past and what's a lie I've concocted to get away with helping them survive down here. It's a burden to live a double life, and that's very much what this is. Except..." He stops himself mid-sentence and I raise my eyebrow, leaning back into the wooden grain of the chair.

"What?" I ask him and he looks at me reluctantly once more as he props himself against the table in a too familiar pose.

"You accept that I know Clark better than you, right?" he asks me and I nod. "Well, then I'll tell you that before, when he came down here, he didn't ever talk about his life up in the city. I don't know what his single life was like, even if he had any friends. But I do know that since he's been married to you, he's started talking to me and mom about the other part of his world. About you," he explains, taking me by surprise yet again.

"He has?" I ask him and he nods.

"I think he's conflicted." He sighs out and runs his fingers through his hair.

"He is?" I ask again, knowing I sound desperate for information, but that's because I am.

380

"Yes. I think he doesn't hate the idea of living in Fantasia Pastures with you as much as he thought," he says and I feel my heart break slightly, coming apart at the seams.

"Oh," I whisper, realising that what he's saying might be right. Could it be that he's afraid to want what Bliss Incorporated is offering us, because they're so cruel to everyone else that he loves? I exhale and Jason stands up straight once more.

"Anyway, enough of that. We've got to get you briefed on what's happening with your tattoo."

"My tattoo?" I ask him, and he tilts his head with a slight cringe, his eyelids fluttering slightly.

So I guess this is really it. I'm really going to become an exile; I'm really going to risk everything to change everything.

"Yes. This is the part that I need to really talk you about. It's about keeping you safe afterwards. We can't have Bliss Incorporated finding you. We need you to get rid of this tattoo after you've had the meeting." He breathes out, as though he's suddenly nervous.

"But my tattoo stays active because of my pulse, right?" I express what I feel is an embarrassingly minimal understanding of the mark I've possessed since I was sixteen.

"Yes." He rummages around in the bag again before procuring a bottle of something. He hands it to me. The bottle is made of brown glass and the cap is unlike anything I've ever seen.

"Jason, what is this?" I ask him, my heart pounding hard in my chest as I get a feeling of terrible anticipation.

"There's a label on the other side," he says with a jerk of his head. I roll the bottle around in my hand, finally reaching a paper label with a single word scrawled upon it in old-fashioned ink. I read the word aloud, not knowing what it is I'm looking at, let alone what I'm getting myself into.

"Vitriol."

Twenty-Five

I awaken, cradled in the smart foam hold of the double bed, alone. I take a moment to relax into the clutch of the material, knowing it may well be the last night where I can claim to be so comfortable, as a sudden and unmistakable feeling of dread floods the empty cavities of my body. I squeeze my eyes tight, not wanting it to be the day. Not wanting it to be here so abruptly and without apology.

Eventually, I leave my longing for delaying the inevitable behind and accept my fate, opening my lids and blinking one, two, three times, reaching out for Clark's warmth even though I know he's not there.

For a moment I'm angry with myself for needing him, before I swallow hard, acknowledge that I'm only seeking someone familiar because of my fear, and get out of bed.

I take my time in the shower, savouring the scents and high water pressure before reluctantly emerging from the bathroom with a clear head. What I'm doing is what's best for everyone, not just what's best for me. It's the first time in my life I've had a choice like this, and I know I need to make the one which is right, not that which is easy.

I get dressed cautiously, scrolling through the catalogue and checking out which options are best for those objects I have to conceal. I could take a handbag with me, but I don't know what security is like inside the building and worry that I'll be searched. It's much less likely that they'll search my person, especially if I turn up empty handed, and so I go for black jeans and a warm, black V-neck sweater with a vest beneath and a bra that's slightly too big. I pair this with a large black overcoat with three or four pockets and a hood for warmth. This might be the last night I have a flat with heating, not to mention a roof over my head, so I need to make sure I'm prepared.

Placing a pair of sturdy, flat, black boots on my feet and zipping them up, I grab the items which I'll need from the nightstand. I don't take my watch, knowing it's just one more way I can be tracked, so stare at it as I shove the vitriol bottle into the cup of my bra and feel the cold glass press against my racing heart. I put the master key in the innermost pocket of my coat, as well as the tiny black card that I'll need to allow the exiles access to the Bliss Incorporated holo-dash system. Placing the contact lenses on the bed for me to use in just a few moments, I look down at my wedding and engagement rings as I debate taking them off. I haven't mentioned it to Clark, but after everything is said and done, I know I need to leave after it's over. I'm not going to be in any state to be in a relationship while I'm learning to live as an exile, or while I'm on the run, especially with someone I can't trust. I also can't bear the fact that in living where his mother is, I'll be close to Jason, close to what could have been.

No. I think.

I'm better off trying to make it alone.

"Valentine?" There's a knock on the door, which startles me as I turn and it opens. Clark is standing in the doorframe after spending the night on the sofa.

"Yes?" I ask him, keeping my face passive as I walk over to the upcycler and order a hairbrush. It arrives in a few seconds and so I take to running it through my hair as I wait for him to answer me.

"I just wanted to say I made breakfast. After all, it might be the last time we have a solid meal for a while." He gazes sheepishly at me. He's trying to be sweet, kind, but all I see is the fact that he lied to me. That he didn't want to tell me he and I should never have been he and I.

"I'll be with you in a moment," I state, turning from him and rubbing my hands down the front of my body, feeling the bulge of the vitriol vial close to my heart and wondering what it'll feel like to eviscerate the perfectly good skin on my arm. I shudder, knowing I need to do this. I need to get out, out of this apartment, this relationship and off this conveyor belt Bliss Incorporated is running. This doesn't mean I'm not scared though, because I am. I'm terrified.

I stand in front of the mirror in the bathroom as I watch my expression turn pale, pulling my eyelids apart and placing the glassy cold contact lenses onto the surface of my irises. I blink a few times, hating the feel of these foreign objects in my eyes before they settle and it's like I'm not wearing them at all.

385

As I leave the bathroom and then the bedroom, I wonder what my mother and father will think. What my sisters will conclude happened to me. Will I put my family in danger? Maybe, but what am I supposed to do? Let people continue to go missing from the Labour Settlements? Let Bliss Inc. continue to marry young men and women without giving them any other choice? Let the exiles die in the sewers?

I can't do that. Not to Clark, or to Jason, or to Egypt.

Maybe my sacrifice won't make a difference, maybe everything around me will crumble and I'll disappear like a wisp of smoke, silenced by the voices of the powerful, but maybe, just maybe, my voice, my sacrifice, will inspire others to act. To revolt. To change the world.

Maybe just one voice, my voice, is enough.

Breakfast and the journey to the station pass with little interaction between Clark and I. Everything is tense, and to be honest, I'm grateful for the silence, because it means I can focus on the task ahead. As I sit back into the plush bench of the glistening monorail coach, I ponder how everything has come to this so quickly.

The jostling of the chandelier above our heads alerts me to the fact that the monorail is beginning its journey to the Bliss Incorporated headquarters. It seems fitting really, the fact that I'm returning to the place where all of this started. I remember how desperate I'd been to get here, to get to this life, and now I'm running from a relationship with the wrong man.

I find my heart palpitating as I think this and I turn to Clark, who is sitting beside me. He looks pale and stressed, and as I lay eyes on his face I momentarily want to hold him, to tell him everything will be okay, to give him some comfort. I don't though; instead I sit here, unable to speak, unable to move, speeding toward my uncertain future like a bullet to a glass pane, which will undoubtedly shatter.

As we depart the monorail, which terminates at the main headquarters building and lies just behind the male and female test centres, I keep my eyes peeled for any sign of David. He is going to be meeting us outside the building so we can turn him in, and as I descend the glass steps of the station, I wonder if I'm going to be sick. My heart rate heightens at the sight of the enormous building, at the sight of the huge hard-light letters announcing Bliss Incorporated. I look behind me a moment, seeing the barriers between the male and female parts of the district, before picking up my pace as Clark starts to pull in front of me with determined strides. I catch up to him and he places my hand in his, though I think this is more for his comfort than mine, as he looks practically green with nerves. Exhaling, I wonder if it's too late to turn around and head for the horizon without ever looking back.

As we approach the colossal steps of the Bliss Incorporated headquarters though, this seems increasingly likely.

I hear my name called and Clark and I swizzle a full half circle immediately as David appears from nowhere.

"Valentine!"

"David, hey," I mumble, nervous and unsure of how to act around a man who has seemingly turned my entire world upside down on a whim.

"David." Clark's single word makes me realise that he might still be mad at him too. After all, whatever David has done to me he's also done to Clark.

"Are you ready?" he asks and I nod, not wanting to wait any longer. As the sun shines high above over the genetically modified grass, which sways uniformly in the light breeze, I feel the heat of the morning pouring down over me, making me claustrophobic and panic-stricken. I move over to David, grabbing him sternly by the elbow and leading him with me up the stairs of the headquarters building. The steps are vast, and I feel but a speck upon them as we move through a set of silent, double glass doors and into the lobby.

I've never been in here before, mainly because the counselling Clark and I attended was in an entirely different building. I look around at the slick alabaster floors, the sterile and cavernous high ceilings which are unending in a bland and boring white, and find this kind of dichotomy with everything natural unnerving. The place is practically empty, a sign of exactly how many people feel that Bliss Incorporated is a place they can run to with their problems. There are no sofas, no seating, no coffee tables, yet another sign that the public is not welcome.

I look around as we take determined and purposeful steps, a sign to all that we're here and we mean business, and observe men in white suits, the same men I'd seen the day of my wedding, stood at the entrance of Bliss Hall. There's more of them near a metal detector and, as we walk forward, I feel my heart start to race.

"Good morning Sir, what brings you to Bliss Inc. headquarters today?" The man in white asks in a robotic voice. Clark grabs David's other elbow and yanks him away from me.

"This... *piece of garbage...* expects me to believe he switched my Jigsaw Project test results with someone else's to screw you guys over. I want to know if it's true and you've married me to the wrong damn person," he growls, his tone dripping with the sum total disdain I know he's harboured for this company practically his entire life. The man in the white suit is wearing sunglasses, so I can't tell whether or not his eyes widen, but his eyebrows certainly rise on his forehead.

"Well... that's startling news. Wait one moment please." The man turns smartly on the ball of one foot and the heel of the other before marching off past the semi-circular desk behind him. It looks like a reception area, where yet another man in a white suit, this time with blonde hair, is sitting. Nothing rings, beeps or signals any kind of interaction with the public though, so I wonder what exactly it is he's even there for. We stand in the silence, glancing to one another with racing hearts and sweating palms as I exhale, wiping my hands on my black overcoat and trying to stay calm.

Minutes later, the man returns, his shoulders squared and his face a mask of stern calm. He approaches us and I feel my stomach flutter with anticipation and fear.

"We'd suggest you head over to the newlywed counselling building and ask for a match test," he expresses and I feel my heart drop. Suddenly, I have an idea.

"You look here. We've already had this screwed up once! I'm not trusting anyone else with this who isn't Pippa Hart herself!" complain, drawing breath and mustering my most intimidating stare courtesy of Cynthia Morland, because if there's anything my mother taught me, it's that being pushy as hell usually gets you what you want. "You're the ones who have to prove your competency here, not me. So, I want to see Miss Hart. Or else I'm not leaving and I'll scream myself hoarse if you try and make me!" I scowl, stomping my foot as a sign that I won't be trifled with.

As he opens his mouth to speak, I see a woman in a stark white and cyan blue suit appear from the long corridor on the left side hand of the desk. As she grows nearer, I look around, wondering exactly how many cameras caught my little tantrum on tape for her to see.

"Pierce. Let them through." I hear her voice echo out into the lobby as her heels click against the floor in monochromatic time. I recognise her immediately as the woman I've been demanding to see. This really is Pippa Hart the Eighth.

"You're Pippa Hart," I gush, wide eyed and utterly stunned. She's exactly like she looks on television, and as far as this woman is concerned I want her to believe I think she's a goddess.

"I am, Valentine." She says my name in a serene and even tone and I get a slight twinge of panic at the thought she knows exactly who I am as well as why I'm here. "Let them through!" She barks again as she finally reaches the metal detector. I hold my breath as we walk through, having been warned about this particular measure by Jason. He'd told us that everything they'd given us to take into the headquarters was metal-free, but part

390

of me wonders if the metal detector will go off just so they have a reason to search my person.

The alarm doesn't go off though, in fact nothing happens and so I breathe easier once we're through the front door and security, knowing that my next challenge is walking back through them alive.

"Scan your tattoos please." Pippa directs us, her poker straight caramel brown hair falling to just above her shoulders in a calculated bob. Her eyes are brown too, and she examines both myself, Clark, and David as we press our wrists to the black mirror of the panel.

"Right, come this way. Leave him here." She's stern now, her face utterly serious as she gestures to David. Clark drops his arm, giving him one final look of fake disgust as Pippa Hart takes off quickly down the hall from which she's just come. Clark and I walk side by side but we don't hold hands, we just glance at one another nervously every few seconds, following as quickly as we can in the wake of the woman who is responsible for everything that's ever happened to either of us.

The hallways continue on, endless, turning and twisting with labyrinth like precision on a cavernous scale. Finally, as we reach a glass door at the end of a long hallway that holds no other doors, Pippa scans her wrist on a black glass panel, and we're ushered inside her office.

The room isn't like I expect, in fact, it's the total opposite. Her office isn't barren, or bare, or sterile, in fact it's warm and filled with photographs of her family. Everyone knows that the Hart family live at an undisclosed private location outside of the city, and so it startles me to see so many images of her children, of her parents, scattered across the walls and various surfaces. The floor is made from hard, dark wood with an apparent grain and her desk of the same dark material which sheens. Behind the desk is a panoramic view of the wilderness beyond city limits, which I take a few moments to consider before lowering myself into a smart foam armchair, facing her as she sits down. She crosses her hands in front of her on the desk, her expression unwaveringly stern as Clark reaches across the space between our chairs and takes my hand in his. It's a small gesture, but Pippa Hart watches us with interest, this becoming apparent only because she tilts her head slightly.

"So, why is it you felt the need to come in and disturb the day to day operation of this facility, Valentine? Surely you should know by now that stamping your feet and complaining isn't effective." She smiles at me, though it doesn't reach her eyes.

"I don't know. I'm sitting in your office, so I'd say it's effective enough." I smirk and she's taken back.

"You should be careful. This company is more powerful than you can possibly imagine. If we say so, then you're nothing more than history, and even the reliability of history is debatable these days." Clark shifts in his seat and I blink a few times, unsure of what it is she's trying to say. Regardless, I hold my tongue, knowing that if I'm going to take this woman down then I'm going to need to at least be civil.

"You have a very beautiful family." I compliment her, gesturing around to the photos that garner the warm aubergine walls.

"Thank you. They are my pride and joy. The reason why all this is necessary." She gestures to the office and I smile at her, knowing full well she's talking a load of crap but trying to act as convinced as possible of her legitimacy.

"That's why we're here. I care about my future, about the future of my children and who they'll have as parents. I need to know if Clark is the man I was supposed to be paired with or if there's been a mistake. I need to know because I don't want my children growing up as a result of a marriage that isn't scientifically guaranteed to give them everything they need to contribute to society. They don't deserve to suffer because of the scheming of one man." I make the spiel and Pippa smiles at me once again.

"I understand. Here at Bliss incorporated, you know that your happiness and that of your future children is paramount to us. So, let's pull up some of your records." She swipes her tattoo across a black panel in front of her as a holo-dash interface materialises from nothing, parallel to the flat horizontal wood of her desk. I watch her motions carefully, as her long and dextrous fingers play with various options on the dash. After a few moments, she sighs.

"You have a brother Mr. Cavanaugh?" She asks and Clark nods.

"Yes, he works in the labour settlements," he replies, shifting once more in his seat. Pippa stares at his face for a moment, her brow becoming more and more furrowed the longer she examines his features.

"I see," she mumbles, no longer looking directly at either of us. I watch as her expression becomes masked with an unfeeling deadness once more and my nervousness begins to heighten. I fiddle with my engagement ring on my finger as time passes too slowly and we continue to watch as she looks over everything Bliss Inc. knows about us. Finally, Pippa Hart gets to her feet and closes the holo-dash.

"Mr Cavanaugh, you're going to have to come with me for a blood test." She rounds the desk and Clark gets to his feet as I continue to rub my finger around the band, an idea suddenly striking me as I loosen it, tucking my hand inside my coat. I get to my feet, and Pippa looks at me expectantly before walking past me and leading the way out of her office. I feel the band fall and watch it roll a few seconds out of the corner of my eye as Clark walks back through the glass door of the office and into the hall.

"Oh, my god! My engagement ring! I must have dropped it!" I run my hands down my body, looking frantically around as Pippa's eyes widen from the other side of the doorframe.

"Are you sure you were wearing it this morning?" she asks me and I nod.

"Oh yes, quite sure, Dr Hart. I've not taken it off since the day I got married. I take my role as a wife and mother in this project very seriously you know. If not I wouldn't be here!" I exclaim, scowling as she momentarily gets a slight look of pity across her face. Have I appealed to her sense as a mother, or as a wife?

Either way, I get onto my hands and knees and start scouring the floor for my ring, even though I know exactly where it landed, because I've aimed it that way. Crawling around the back of her desk, I rummage around for a few moments around the legs of the plush office chair, before making my way under her the wooden inlet. I reach back into my coat's inside pocket as I sweep my hair back around my ear, grabbing the black card in my palm and slamming it into the bottom of her desk. It sticks as I yell out,

"Ow!" as though I've hit my head. A few seconds of totally fake searching later, I yell, "Got it!" with a relieved tone and return to standing. Pippa has watched the entire ordeal and not even noticed that I've planted the device under her desk. I feel smug as I walk back over to her. "See, I can't lose this, it's a blue diamond, just the colour of Clark's eyes." I smile, showing her my ring as I slip it back on and she nods to me without smiling.

"It's beautiful. You should take better care of it, maybe look at getting it sized tighter?" She suggests and I nod, smiling enthusiastically.

"That's a great idea. I can't bear the thought of losing it, it's so beautiful you see, and so sentimental," I gush, hoping she buys that I'm just as stupid, naïve and infatuated with the idea of a perfect love as all the other women who she matches with total strangers. I hope the act is believable; after all, I had been exactly like this until only a few weeks ago.

"Dr Hart?" I ask her, my voice dripping with ignorance.

"Yes?" She asks, her face becoming irritated quickly at my persistence.

"What happens if Clark and I aren't... well, Clark and I." I ask her and she turns to me.

"I doubt that's the case here. We'll have to see what the blood tests say. It's probably nothing, after all, you two seem pretty smitten to me. I wouldn't have taken the word of someone like David Abernathy seriously, he's probably still disgruntled because we haven't promoted him above technician yet, and now we never will." She condemns us, like it's we who are being stupid. I almost want to laugh in her face. This is her system, her rules, so it's hardly our fault if her employees hate her.

"Oh," I reply, realising that it's unlikely I'm going to get a straight answer.

"Don't worry, Valentine. Clark and I are going to take a left here. You should go and wait for him in the lobby. It might take a while," She explains. I'm surprised that she's trusting me to walk back to the lobby alone, but then again, I suppose with the amount of security in this place, I shouldn't be able to enter a single room without her knowing about it.

"Alright." I turn to Clark, slipping both my rings off in my pocket and grasping them in my fist, I take his hand in mine, passing them to him with a subtle and single motion and hoping he realises that this means everything is over between us.

I kiss him on the cheek, smile and say, "Good luck," in a sweet tone before turning on my heel and walking away, pausing just around the corner.

I wait until he and Pippa have turned a corner and begin my journey back to the lobby, walking slowly and looking at each door and the label beside them. I pass a long corridor and take a step back, checking to see whether or not any of the men in white suits are lurking. They aren't, so I step quickly into the ominous looking hallway. It's long and narrow and the lights above are flickering on and off, almost like something is draining them of power. The door at the end has no label, no name, no identity. It's just a grey metal door with a single black panel to the left-hand side. I look at it, reaching into my jacket as I stare behind me, checking that no one is coming. I can hardly believe my luck, believe that I've been left to walk unattended and lose no time scanning the master key and slipping inside.

I don't intend to stay long. I just want to get a look at whatever it is inside and satiate my curiosity, after all, what if it's something important? Like weapons or something equally as devastating? Jason would need to know about anything like that before unleashing bombs on this place.

As I step inside the room, I'm hit by an alien blue glow. I gasp, my heart suddenly racing and my blood pounding in my ears as my eyes widen and I feel suddenly sick.

What the hell have they done?

Twenty-Six

I stare out across the gargantuan pit beneath the ledge where I'm stood. Hundreds, if not thousands, of pods stand filled with a cyan fluid, which glows not unlike the ink I'd had injected into my skin the day Bliss Incorporated had branded me.

I take a step forward, my mouth a tiny 'o' as I realise what it is I'm looking at. I don't want to be right, I don't want this to really be happening, but I need a closer look, I need to record all this. I need to stop it.

I take a few measured paces forward, dulling the echo of my boots against the ghastly dim cement of the floor before reaching the edge of the platform, which leads out of the room. I turn around to face the door, which is surrounded by blinking lights, and vow that I will return through it as soon as I'm able. This place, what it stands for, what it holds, is disturbing to say the least and, as I begin my decent down the ladder which gives access into the pit of pods below, I feel the hairs on the back of my neck simultaneously rise and my hands become chill with sweat.

Once I'm at the bottom of the ladder, I turn, hoping I'm wrong, hoping this is all perfectly justifiable, but soon my eyes are resting upon their faces. Upon their open, glazed eyes, I know I can't be wrong. This is happening. This is real.

I walk along the rows of pods, each one holding a human being inside. Tubes course in and out of their bodies without apology or restraint, making me think back to the tentacled man atop the horror house at Enamoury Park. Clark had said it was ridiculous, that it wasn't even slightly scary, but seeing these silicone and plastic tentacular tubes penetrating the mouths and nostrils of each of the poor souls who have been left here to pickle, I find myself terrified beyond what I've ever thought possible.

I look into the pods, upon the faces of the zombified citizens, and wonder what could possibly justify something like this. What is it that they're even doing in these tanks?

That's when I see it. A face. A familiar face, which beckons over to me. My eyes widen as I approach, my fingers extending out to touch the chill glass holding her captive.

The woman from the salon, the girl who had consistently filed her nails and rolled her eyes at me, is suspended in this blue viscous fluid, her body violated by science. That's when I realise it. The Hard-light Holograms. They're not just people from the labour settlements. Real people. They're people who can't move, or think, or breathe on their own, without the say so of Bliss Incorporated.

I want to break the glass, to smash it to a million jagged pieces and watch the fluid leak onto the floor, but I don't. There is too much at stake. I have seen the inside of the beast. This is it. This is what they've been doing with the labour workers, with people like Clark's father. They've been bringing them here and turning them into static vegetables to work for them in hard-light bodies. A potentially immortal, utterly controllable army.

I stare out across the rows of people, suddenly feeling overwhelmed. The burden of what I'm witnessing weighing heavy on my chest as I simultaneously feel relief. I have the chance to save all these people. To free them, return them to their families. I could break the glass on one pod, but I'd probably be caught and suffer the same fate.

Instead, I know that I need to get back into the sewers; I need to get this information to the Exiles as fast as possible. I need to find out exactly *why* it is they felt the need to capture humans, strip them of their rights and use them as hard-light puppets. What's the reasoning? I wonder this and realise that I'm standing motionless, still staring upon the face of the spa receptionist. I need to move. I need to get as far away from here as possible with the footage of what I've seen before it's too late.

I turn on my heel with unbridled urgency, my feet suddenly carrying me faster than I anticipate back up the row of pods from which I've come. My boots pound on the concrete, but I don't hear it, all I hear is the sound of blood pounding in my ears from my heartbeat's frantic rhythm. Everything seems so normal on the surface, so perfect, and it's not until now that I've seen the cost of that. The cost of absolutes and flawlessness.

I reach the ladder after what feels like an eternity of running through the muggy air, which smells of fluids and slow decay. Grabbing onto the bottom rung and beginning to climb, I try to calm myself enough so that I can walk back through the door and into the Bliss Inc. lobby like nothing ever happened.

Hauling myself to my feet atop the platform, I turn for a second to look back over the fields of people, the people who are being used for someone else's agenda against their will. Horror floods my system and I realise that the society I've been living in is built on treachery and morals so black I scarcely want to believe it's true. Yet, here they are, right in front of me, undeniable in every respect and so I vow to free them all, even if it takes my life from me in return.

I turn from the frozen, the damned, stepping towards the grey door and take a deep, steadying breath of stale air before I scan my master key on the black mirrored panel and step back out into the ominous hallway with flickering light. On the other side of the doorway, everything seems normal. A man in a white suit passes the hall and backs up a few paces as I shove the master key back into my pocket with haste.

"Hey! What are you doing down there?" he calls. I turn my face innocent as I allow my mouth to fall slack and my eyes to widen.

"I'm looking for the bathroom. I think I'm lost. I just tried this door but it wouldn't open. I was on my way back to the lobby but... you know, women's time..." I pull out this excuse, hoping to make him uncomfortable as I shift on the balls of my feet and take a few steps toward him. He coughs, immediately becoming twitchy and uncomfortable.

"Oh, well the bathrooms are down here. Come on, I'll show you." He grabs me by the elbow, forcefully, but I don't mind because I've already found the most damning secret in the place, or at least what I hope is the most damning. I mean... what about if they're hiding even worse secrets somewhere else?

The thought alarms me and as the man in the white suit, with slick hair and sunglasses scans his wrist tattoo, that of a green triangle, across the black mirrored panel outside the ladies room. I step inside, unable to stop my mind racing.

Inside the bathroom is sterile, just as I expected. I pace up and down across the white tiles a few times, unable to bear the thought of stopping moving. I turn to look into the mirror under the stark fluorescent buzz of the lights and my face is pale. wonder if it had given me away, or made the lie that I was getting my monthly visit from Mother Nature more believable. I place my hands under the faucet, letting the sensors detect their presence and sprinkle them with water. I bring my palms up to my face, splashing liquid across my hot, ghostly skin and bracing myself against the basin as I let water droplets fall from my nose. I look up into the mirror once more, into the face of the person who no longer recognise. My eyes are ringed with dark circles, my lips creased in an expression of alarm and I realise that the light behind my irises has extinguished. My hope for my future is gone. The hope I've held dear, that everything will be alright for me, that Clark would be the one, is gone too. All that's left is me. Me and a secret which needs to be exposed.

Gritting my teeth, I ball my splayed fingers into fists and hold my nerve. I need to remain steady, to stay calm in spite of the fact everything I know has completely imploded all over again. A knock at the door startles me and I realise my moment of reprieve is up as I grab a paper towel and use it to wipe my hands clean before balling it up and throwing it down the upcycler next to the door. Pulling open the bathroom door, the man in the white suit is raising his hand to knock again, making me irritated.

Geez, can't this guy give me two seconds? I think, biting my tongue to stop myself from snapping at his impatience. He nods at me curtly and grabs my elbow again, hurrying me down the corridor and back towards the lobby. I sigh, sick of being manhandled, but let him whisk me closer to my goal of the exit willingly.

As we reach the cavernous white space of the lobby, I realise that the only thing left for me to do is wait for Clark.

"I have to wait here," I say to the man in the white suit, who continues to walk me across the lobby. His hand tightens on the crook of my elbow and I suddenly start to realise that he has no intention of letting me wait around for my husband. He's taking me somewhere else. Urgency grips at me and I start to panic, realising that I need to get out of this building, with or without Clark. It's stupid of me to think they are or were ever actually going to return him to me unharmed.

We've questioned their authority, and the 'blood test' Pippa Hart was taking him for was probably code for torture or worse, sedating him for one of those pods. Bile floods my gullet as I realise that the thing I might lose may not be my life, it might be Clark, and the possibility of ever seeing him again. I don't love him, I know I don't, but for some reason, call it attachment or affection, I'm suddenly furious.

Panicking, I bring my fist sideways and smash it into the side of the man's head. His grip falters and I take my chance, bolting for the doors. I don't look behind me, but soon I hear a deafening siren and the doors are beginning to close as I approach them. I speed up, barging through the metal detector ahead, scared I'm going to fall and smash a bottle of Vitriol into my own chest, causing burns if not death. I take the risk, pulling away from men in white suits beyond security who are converging on my position appearing from nowhere on all sides, reaching out to try and grab me, to subdue my motion, but they narrowly miss as I twist out of their desperate grasps, realising that my size is definitely an advantage. I reach the glass doors of Bliss Incorporated headquarters with only seconds to spare. Twisting sideways, I slip through the narrowly closing gap between the two glass panels and fresh air hits my face. I breathe a sigh of relief as I glance back over one shoulder only to see men in white suits blocked in by their own security measures, and take no time in making a break for it down the broad steps and into the courtyard of the headquarters.

David had told me where the entrance to sewer is around here; I just need to find it before the men in white suits find me. I take a deep breath, halting momentarily and throwing my hood over my head, not only to disguise myself, but also because large spots of rain are beginning to fall from puffy, angry clouds overhead. I feel my heart continue to race and wonder if it'll ever stop, before realising I need to get moving. I can't stand for even a moment, because all too soon this place will be swarming with people and synths out for my head. I turn on my heel and begin a swift jog, tracing the sidewalk which runs parallel to the left and right wings of the enormous headquarters building towering high overhead, casting me in its shadow.

I take a left as the building ends, remembering what David said about the entrance to the sewers. It wasn't far from the building's edge, so I scurry along the pavement as the rain begins to fall heavy around me with the density of what feels like lead pellets. The sky rumbles and a roll of thunder breaks the silence, which is interrupted only by the sound of my boots splashing through puddles and my breathing coming fast and heavy in my chest. I turn another corner, finally laying eyes on it, on the manhole cover.

Yes! I think, savouring victory as I hear footfall coming closer behind me. I panic, beginning to speed up in my tread and not caring for the sound any longer. Skidding to a halt, I know the men in white aren't far behind me, and so haul the metal disk out of the hole as fast as I'm able before slipping inside. I hear a voice call, "Hey, I think she went this way!" as I lower myself into the vertical tunnel and hear the splash of boots turning the corner onto the street I'm descending into as I finally manage to place the metal manhole cover back over myself, hiding my entire body from view.

I lower myself into the sewers, heart pounding as the heavy tread bangs overhead, echoing out as the bottom of boots strike the ground in a repetitive onslaught. Once I reach the bottom, I stand in the flickering light of the tunnel for a full five minutes, catching my breath. Every time the lights flicker on and off, I see my tattoo flash neon blue and I realise that unless I act quickly, I won't be staying hidden for very long. I feel a pang of terror at the thought of massacring my own flesh, and yet I know there is no other way to ensure I stay hidden and safe. There is no other way to be sure that they won't track me down and kill me before I can expose them all.

"Okay, Valentine. Be brave. It won't hurt that much," I whisper to myself, reaching down into my cleavage and pulling out the vitriol vial.

I know I need to be quick, to get it done while I can still fade from existence without them watching me, but I can't help but feel hesitant as I slowly screw off the lid of the glass bottle and take a deep breath, hanging in the moment. Pulling off my coat and throwing it to the floor in terrified abandon, I take one last look at the unmarred and flawless skin of my arm as I pull up my sleeve, trying to comfort myself by thinking, *oh well, it's just a bit of skin.* Then, with shaking hands, I upend the cold vitriol onto myself, burning away any claim that anyone but me has over my heart.

"Valentine?" I hear the voice come from the distance and I startle awake. I don't exactly remember when I passed out from the pain, but I know it wasn't soon enough as my mind still reels from the memory of my own screams, magnified and thrown back at me by the surrounding tunnel walls. I feel my arm before I receive any other notion of conscience, and I can smell the chemical burning of flesh and feel the need to be suddenly and horrendously sick. I sit up, before vomiting spectacularly all over the floor beside me, tears streaming from both my eyes as the endless throbbing and burning of my exposed nerves continues to taunt me. I feel a hand on my back and wince away amid a sob, that escapes my throat in a strangled and mutant cry. "It's okay, I got you."

I feel two arms sweep me up and a warm chest press against my damp side. My head is pounding too, and I guess that must be because I'd hit my head when the pain had become too much to bear and my legs had buckled from underneath me. My rescuer lowers me slightly, urging me to pick up my coat, which had narrowly escaped me spewing my guts. I throw the black material over myself, emitting a shudder as I realise that the damp puddle I've been lying in has left me chill and exposed.

"Clark?" I whimper, the sound coming from me is pitiful and scared, like that of an animal that's been shot or something equally as uncalled for.

"No. It's Jason." I feel my heart fall as Jason announces himself, but I'm then distracted by the coat lain across me touching my arm. I scream, the agony crawling across my skin like unstoppable tree roots, splitting me apart from the inside and gaining new ground where it doesn't belong. I bite my lip, trying to distract from the terrible pain, but I can't. It takes over everything, and soon, I find comfort only in the sensory absence of sleep.

───────●●●───────

When I wake once more, Jason is still walking and I'm still in his arms. I realise that there are two bag straps on his shoulders as I look at him through speckled vision.

"Where are you taking me?" I slur, feeling my eyelids still heavy against the glassy sheen of my eyes.

"To the Single district. We need you to be looked after. You can't stay down here for a while, not until that burn has healed up, there's too much risk of infection. The vitriol, it went deeper

407

into your skin than I thought it would. I'm sorry, Valentine." He apologises, looking down at me with pity as he continues to carry me through the dim light of the sewers, taking lefts and then rights in a combination I know I'll never remember.

"Clark... they took him... for a blood test." I sigh, remembering how I'd said *good luck* and given him my rings back. What have I done? What if he dies? Oh no. No, no, no.

"We'll get him out, Valentine. Don't worry. I saw everything, the pods, everything. We won't leave him there I swear to you." He sounds certain of this, which makes me feel better. I still can't get the feeling that he won't come out of that place the same way he went in. What if they ruin his mind, his sense of humour? What if he's not Clark anymore?

Then I wonder why I care so much. It shouldn't matter to me because I shouldn't want to be with him. He's not my matchmate. I don't trust him. I can't love him.

"What if they put him in one of those awful machines? It'll be all my fault. I should've grabbed him and run." I voice my terror aloud and Jason looks to me with a scared expression.

"Valentine, I won't let them do that to him. He knew the risks going in. You both did. You were a hero today. What you saw in that room... Bliss Incorporated needs to be stopped," he expresses and I nod.

"They're turning people into hard-light holograms. They're using their minds or something... I saw this girl, she was on my honeymoon, in the spa... if I'd had known..." I whisper, tears coming to my eyes now. The only image I can see in my head is Clark suspended in the cyan fluid, his hair hanging like dead seaweed and his eyes glazed. I scrunch up my face, slamming my eyelids shut and bearing the brunt of the shock from everything 've seen today.

"How could you have known, Valentine? I didn't even know and I work in the labour settlements where people have been vanishing for months. I knew the numbers of workers were becoming outweighed by the number of nuclear families, it's been that way for years, but I never imagined this would be their solution..." he muses and I open my eyes again.

"That's why?" I ask him and he nods.

"From the files we're currently receiving, it would seem so. I came to find you when you didn't turn up. Luckily for you, your senses showed us where you lost consciousness, but in the last few hours, we've uncovered more than we ever thought possible." He jostles me against his body, reaffirming his grip on my back and I wince, pain shooting up my arm.

"Sorry," he apologises and I grimace.

"It's okay. I'm lucky I'm not dead I suppose. I just... I still don't understand why Bliss Incorporated decided to imprison those people and use them like that? Why wouldn't they just assign more kids to the labour settlements?" I ask him and he shakes his head.

"I can only imagine, but I think it's easier to keep people in tanks. It's certainly cheaper. You don't have to provide them with housing, food, clothes, not that you'd think anything the labour settlements are provided with is anywhere near expensive. They've been trying to crack artificial intelligence for years, to create something that would eradicate the 'impure' workforce all together, but I guess they couldn't do it. So instead they made the intelligent into something artificial. Something they could control." He explains this and I feel a wave of exhaustion hit. My heart is slowing, finally, in my chest, but my mind isn't showing any signs of letting go of the rapid rhythm in which questions are flooding my consciousness. "We're nearly there," he assures me, his footfalls continuing to be something reliable, something I can focus on as we move through the unending labyrinth of those discarded and forgotten.

"Will they be searching for me now? I don't want to put anyone in danger. I don't have anywhere to go," I express and Jason looks thoughtful.

"Maybe, either way I've got you everything you'll need to stay off the radar, but remain in the city, in this backpack. You need to heal somewhere safe. Do you have anyone you can stay with? What about Egypt?" He asks and I suddenly feel fear clutch at me.

"What if I put her in danger? I don't want her to get hurt." I feel a little more alert at the mention of my friend, but then I wish I didn't because my nose is filled with the smell of my own desecrated skin and I wonder if I'll be able to stop myself being sick.

"Everyone is in danger now, Valentine. This isn't the end, it's the beginning. The rebellion is ready. We're moving ahead with this. You just need to heal up and stay inside, let us worry about the rest. Let us carry the rest of the burden. You've done enough." He smiles at these words, and I think he's proud of me.

As we reach a final turn in the sewer tunnels he halts. "I'm going to set you down. Can you stand?" he asks me and I nod, unsure of whether I'm portraying a reality or a hope.

He tilts my body and my legs slide out under me. I take a second to catch my balance, feeling my head swirling in a cocktail of pain, exhaustion and resignation to everything that is happening. Eventually, I manage to stand on my own, but I can't bring myself to look at my arm. Jason hands me my coat, which I hold under the arm that I haven't willingly destroyed, and then the backpack which he slips off his shoulders before helping me get into the harness of straps.

"There's a device in there to stop the camera feed and microphones in any room. You know what to do with that I assume? Also, a cell phone. My number is in there, you call me if you need anything. I'll always find the time to help you if I can. The line is secure." I nod, remembering the cell phone I saw Clark use on our honeymoon, and the device he attached to our apartment wall. Jason looks down at me as I remove the contact lenses from my eyes, wincing as my fingers shake against my eyelids. I hand them to him and he slips them into his jacket pocket.

"What about David? What about me? Where do I go after I'm healed?" I ask him, urgently seeking any kind of information that will aid me and he frowns.

"We're trying to sort out something for you. A way out. I'll know more soon. As soon as I do I'll call you. Okay? But Valentine, you need to stay off the streets. Don't worry about David, or Clark, we'll find them. Stay inside. You promise me that?" He asks me and I exhale, knowing that staying put will be hard.

"Yes. But you promise me something?" I look into his face, seeing not Jason, but Clark in the familiar architecture of his jawline, of the way his forehead spreads wide and his brow hangs, casting moody shadow at will.

"What?" he asks me.

"You get Clark out alive. You hear me? He can't die." I shake my head, unable to believe the thought is even one of plausibility.

"You know, for someone who says she doesn't care about my brother, can't trust him enough to love him, you're awfully concerned about him. Are you absolutely sure he's not the right man for you, Valentine? He's a good man. He might have lied, but I think you'll find it was out of fear of losing you and putting you at risk, not purposefully deceiving you." He brushes his fingers back through his hair in a way I once again recognise and I sigh out.

"That's the problem though isn't it? Everyone has lied to me, no matter what their reasons are. Since they day I've been born, my whole life has been a lie. I just want something real." I express, feeling the truth of my words sting, perhaps more intensely than the chemicals still present on my raw and bloody skin.

"I see. Well, I'll call you when I know something." He smiles and I nod, feeling grateful for his level head and quick thinking. God knows how long I'd have been stuck down here without him.

"Take care of yourself," I express and he nods back, turning away from me and vanishing into the darkness without another word. I pivot full circle, finally feeling myself steady after so much physical exertion. Behind me I find a ladder, which I promptly climb after taking a moment to remove my backpack, gingerly place my coat back onto my shoulders and pull my hood over my head before picking back up the bag once more and slinging it over one shoulder.

I pull myself up out onto the street, alarmed to see that it's dark. How long have I been unconscious down in the sewer?

412

What has passed in that time I've been dead to the world? I take a second after placing the metal manhole cover back over the sewer entrance to take in my surroundings. I spin, realising I'm not far from Egypt's apartment, and look out over the water to the Bliss Incorporated headquarters from where I've come, wondering whether Clark is even still alive. If he's in pain.

The thought depresses me and so I turn my back on the churning waters of the lake and the newlywed complex and head to Egypt's place. I don't want to drag her into this it's true, but Jason said that the things in the backpack on my shoulder will keep me out of sight, so maybe it'll protect her too.

Either way, I have nowhere else to go, my arm is throbbing and raw with pain, plus my eyelids are drooping from exhaustion. The wind bites into me as the rain continues to pound down. It must have been raining for hours since the streets are flooded and full of puddles. The hood atop my head soon becomes heavy as I watch the familiar sight of a high-speed monorail glide overhead, illuminating the white, sterile streets below with a glamorous, lush light. I had been so envious of the people in those carriages, but now the thought of them makes me angry. They're fools. Not seeing the world as I do, not seeing what's right in front of them and it makes me scornful thinking about their chewing mouths, loud lips and thirsty gullets being satiated while others suffer.

Turning a corner, I keep my breathing level, trying to ignore the pain in my arm as I approach the front of Egypt's apartment building. I scan my master key on the black glass dash by the front doors and walk into the familiar lobby as a wave of nostalgia hits me so hard I want to cry. I can't wait to see Egypt, I can't wait to

413

be safe in her apartment unit with pizza and coffee again. I can't wait to hug her and tell her everything I've been through.

I scan my master key again on the turnstile, careful to keep my face eclipsed by my hood as I step across the white floor and into the elevator. I select her floor, and feel anticipation pool in my stomach as I rise. The elevator seems to take forever to shoot upward, but eventually the tone sounds and the doors slide open.

I stride across the hall, almost tripping over my own feet and with tears in my eyes just as I had been the day I'd taken my last readiness test. I raise my hand, knock on the door and wait.

As I hear a scuffling behind the door and a sudden whooshing sound of the door drawing back to reveal her, hair messy pyjama-clad and wide eyed, I stand in her doorway, looking into her face and unable to be strong any longer. Her arms open without question and I take a single step across the threshold before bursting into tears.

Twenty-Seven

Egypt holds me for a good hour before we speak. Sitting on her sofa, just as things had always been, I clutch my arm to me, unable to bear the thought of exposing the wound so I have to stare upon it properly for the first time. After a while, my sobs exhaust me and my tears run dry, she looks at me, at my snotty face and what is probably a complete hair malfunction beneath my hood and her eyes are so full of worry. It's a look I've only seen once before, and it came from the face of the man I'm married to.

"So, are you going to tell me what's going on?" Egypt's face betrays no sense of humour, no happiness; she's merely serious and concerned. I lean back into the hold of the chair and sigh out.

"I did something..." I express and she nods.

"I gathered that. What happened?" she asks me. After a second, I realise that I'm being careless and so get to my feet, cradling my arm and walk over to my backpack, which is propped against the kitchen island. I open it and pull out the tiny black device I'd seen Clark use in our apartment before, right before he'd revealed everything to me, and place it onto the wall behind

the sofa where we've been sat. The suction cups grip onto th
white paint of the boxy apartment and after a few moments, th
light on the front of the box flashes green. Sitting back down ont
the sofa, Egypt gives me a surprised stare.

"What's that?" she asks, and I look to the box.

"It's blocking the signals to the cameras and microphones i
this room. It gives us privacy," I explain and Egypt nods as I lowe
my hood from over my head.

"Is it Clark? Did he hurt you?" she asks me and I shake m
head.

"No. Not at all. It's Bliss Incorporated, Egypt. I went into th
headquarters, to prove they're corrupt. To show them for wha
they really are..." I begin and her eyes glance down to my arm.

"They did this to you?" She gestures to me and I shake m
head again.

"No... I did it to me. To get rid of the tattoo." Her eyes wider
even further.

"Valentine, what's under the coat?" she asks me and I pucke
my lips.

"I don't know. I haven't seen how bad the damage is yet. Bu
Jason said it's too dangerous for me to stay in the sewers unti
it's healed. That's why he brought me here." I continue to explair
and she reaches out to grab my hand.

"Valentine, let me have a look. You need to get it looked at."
I pull away from her and her dark eyes shine with tears. "Please
Val. Come on, I'm scared. At least let me clean it? While you
explain? I need something to do. I feel totally useless right now."
Her face is completely pure in its intent so I nod slowly, my heart

racing again at the thought of having to look at the damage I've caused myself.

"Okay," I mumble as she immediately moves to her feet. I lean forward while she walks across the room to the upcycler. "That won't work," I call out, moving to take my coat off and wincing as the lining brushes against my injured arm.

"Why not?" she asks me and I gesture to the black box behind me.

"It cuts all the electrical power off in the room I think. I don't know, I don't know anything about any of this really." I express my feelings of inadequacy, fearful now more than ever that I'm not cut out for this life, and she continues to move over to the upcycler anyway.

"It looks like it'll work to me," she says, ordering some bandages and cleaning solution.

"Huh. Must work off a different power source," I muse, wondering if it's a safety measure.

After a few moments of silence, the upcycler sounds, indicating that the items Egypt had ordered have arrived. Reaching into the device she takes them out and I finally have the courage to look down at my arm.

I gasp, not recognising what it is I'm looking at.

Luckily for me, my hand had escaped completely unscathed, but that's where the good news ends because my arm looks like a complete mess from wrist to elbow. The skin is red raw, bloody and marbled. It looks like someone melted hot wax onto my arm and left it to dry and I want to cry, looking at it. As Egypt returns to the sofa with the medical supplies in her hands, she looks down at me and inhales sharply.

"Holy shit, Val! What did this?" she asks me and I cringe.

"Vitriol. It's another name for Sulphuric acid," I murmur unable to take my eyes off my wound for more than a few seconds, transfixed. She shakes her head as her mouth opens and closes several times in fish-like succession.

"Why? I mean why did you do this?" She looks crazed, scared so I take a deep breath.

"You clean my wound, and I'll explain. It'll distract us both," express. With this, she promptly moves over to the sink and begins filling it with cold water.

"Come on over here. If it's acid that's done this damage, we need to soak it for a little while to take out the sting," she expresses and I cringe at the thought. She looks sort of pissed sort of terrified, as I walk over to her. As the sink fills with cold water she looks me straight in the eyes, there's a kind of determined maturity there that I haven't seen before.

"You better start talking, Valentine. This is going to hurt like a bitch." She grabs my arm and plunges it into the water, ripping off whatever pain tolerance I've managed to achieve since the vitriol had first touched my skin with it's cold and brutal clutch.

As I screw up my face and debate over whether or not it would be easier just to cut off my arm and be done with it, I try to regain some kind of focus. I look into Egypt's face, I muster the energy I have left, and I begin to explain to her everything that has happened to me since the day we last parted.

———————●●●———————

418

A few hours later, my arm is finally clean and bandaged. It's throbbing and raw, but at least I know now it won't get infected. Egypt is watching me from across the room as she begins ordering cup after cup of ramen noodles.

"What are you doing?" I ask her, half sleepy, from the bed.

"I'm stocking up. If what you say is true, if the labour districts are planning a revolution or attacks, we're going to need food and lots of it." I laugh at this expression, a piece of the old Egypt finally making an appearance. She's been so quiet and serious since I arrived, which is understandable, but as she stands next to the upcycler ordering more bottled water and noodles, I watch her with interested worry.

"Are you okay?" I inquire, my eyelids heavy as I tilt my head.

"No. Are you?" she asks me and I shake my head, unable to speak.

"My father always told me this would happen. He always said that one day the people would rise up and take down Bliss Incorporated. But I didn't know it would be so soon. I didn't know it would be like this. I thought... I don't know. I thought there'd be a sign. Something to let me know this was going to happen, so I could prepare." She's breathless by the end of the sentence and I sit up, propped against two fluffy pillows, staring across the space between us. I'm looking at her in a whole new way.

"Your father? He's a rebel?" I'm intrigued and she shoots a look at me.

"I thought you knew that. I told you about the books," she replies, her eyes saddening at my total and complete lack of acuteness.

419

"I didn't know. I guess I should have worked it out," I express, feeling like everything in my world has tilted on its axis so fast I have head rush.

"It's okay. I wasn't obvious about it. I never am. It's too dangerous," she replies, stacking cups of ramen atop the island in the middle of the kitchen.

"I understand. I was afraid to come here. I didn't want to put you at risk, but I didn't have another choice." I feel an instant pang of guilt at the fact I'm lying in her bed, taking her credit and her food, her supplies. She doesn't owe me anything.

"You don't have to apologise. You know you're always welcome. I've missed you so much... and I think... I think what you did was brave. Braver than you know, Val. I mean, I never wanted to get married to a man I'd never met... not really. I don't like men." She says this aloud and my eyes widen.

"What do you mean? I thought you wanted a red dress and a guy with a great personality?" I question her, raising one eyebrow.

"Well, if I had to marry a man, then yes. I'd want him to not be awful. But I don't want to marry a man. In fact, the only person I've ever felt attracted to is..." She stops and I look at her.

"Who?" I ask, intrigued, and she flushes scarlet.

"You," she says the word and I'm not surprised. I know I don't feel the same way, but I've always known that I mean more to her than just a friend. The day she'd gotten me ready to walk down the aisle, the tears she'd shed at the thought of having to say goodbye, I've known they were more than just tears from a friend. I've never wanted to ask, or put her in the situation where she has to tell, so instead I'd just tried to be there for her as much as I can. I look at her face and her gaze drops to the floor. "I know you don't feel the same way, Val. I mean, I'm not a complete idiot, but I just needed to tell you. Now that you know about Bliss Incorporated, about their real motives, I feel like you understand what it's like to not be free to love who you want," she explains and I nod.

"I do. I hope that at some time in the future, you can find someone who loves you the way you deserve. I hope that you get to choose." The sentence resonates with me. Who would I choose to be with now? The memories of my time with Clark are seared into my memory, a permanent scar like that which is forming on my arm where the tattoo, matching the two of us, had once been visible. I think back to the times he's made me breakfast, how he's held me, how we've danced and my heart begins to pound as fear floods over me. He's gone. He's out of my life forever.

I thought I'd feel relief, like I'd feel like I could start over. But instead, I feel like my life's been left with a gaping and irreparable wound. Like he's been ripped from me before I'm ready, or before I've had a chance to realise that which I know.

I do love him.

I know it in my gut. I know it because every single time I think about him being in pain, or dead, it makes me want to go to sleep and never wake back up again.

"Valentine?" Egypt says into the air, I know she probably thinks I'm being silent because now things are awkward between us, but instead I'm struggling to find the words to talk about anything that isn't the fact Clark is in danger. It seems like anything else compared to that just isn't so important.

421

"Sorry... I was just thinking about, well, Clark actually," express and she looks at me.

"I see. You love him." She states what I'm afraid to and pucker my lips.

"How do you know that?" I ask her and she shakes her head

"Well, while you were telling me that story, the entire time you just kept saying about how Clark is a hero, but how you can' trust him, about how he isn't right for you. You repeated yoursel a lot, and I know you only do that when you're trying to convinc yourself to believe a lie you're telling yourself to make everythin easier." She pins me to the post so completely, I wis momentarily I could be attracted to her. She understands me o a level I've not easily found with Clark, so naturally it's alarmin and refreshing all at once.

"You think I should be with someone who lies?" I ask her an she shakes her head.

"No. I think you should be with him. He's not just anyon Valentine, he's Clark. Yes, he lied. But if I was in his position, I' have lied too. He didn't want to put you in danger, and then h didn't want to cause you pain by telling you that you and h aren't matchmates. But you've already said that you don't thin the formula even exists. *You* said that. And I think you're right Because if I love women, how could a system that only matche me with men, find my perfect love? How is that possible? You sa you don't believe the formula exists, so why does it matte whether you got matched by some stupid system or not? You were together, and that's what matters. You found something ir him to love, or you wouldn't have slept with him. I know you. You don't trust people so easily." She begins ordering more ramen as

422

I begin to feel my fatigue take over. She's right. Everything she's said has been correct. But I've blown it, and now it's too late because Clark is gone. He's either being tortured, turned into hard-light, or dead by now. I love him, but I've thrown it away because I've been too caught up in my own stupid ideas about what the perfect marriage should be to look at the situation and realise that nothing about marriage can be completely normal or perfect. Clark and I operate by our own set of rules, and somewhere between marrying him and sleeping with him I've forgotten that.

"I'm tired," I murmur, yawning and stretching out my arms. I cringe, forgetting that I've got a fresh burn as the last of my strength is sapped away by the pain.

"You sleep, Val. I'll wake you right away if anything changes," Egypt assures me.

With my final thoughts being those of regret, and terrible torment as images of Clark floating with tubes coming in and out of every orifice pass in and out of my mind, I fall into a place of dark unconsciousness.

I'm woken not by the sound of Egypt's voice, but by the blaring of the holo-dash. I momentarily wonder if everything had been a dream, if I'd imagined it all, but then I realise that I'm still in Egypt's apartment. I sit up to see her stirring on the sofa. The light is blinding, and I'm wondering how the holo-dash is even working. I glance to where the black device is still attached to the wall and operational before shielding my eyes as the soft light broadcasting channels begins to blurt out increasingly intelligibl sound.

"Breaking news bulletin from the labour districts!" th speakers blurt. I realise now that this must be what Jason mear when he said he could intercept the soft-light broadcastin channel. I've always known there was an override which give Bliss Incorporated the option to power up and broadcast to a holo-dashes simultaneously, like in case of flooding, natura disasters or that kind of thing, but I didn't realise Jason would b using it too. I sit up in bed, groggy and uncomfortable as the ligh hurts my eyes.

Egypt moves from the couch to sit next to me on top the be so I shuffle over, watching as the broadcast begins to show th footage and files that had been discovered from inside the hear of Bliss Incorporated. The footage from my eyes is shown i terrifying and glorious definition, and I feel myself haunted as watch mine and Clark's last moments together. I feel even sicke as I watch back the footage of my discovery of the hard-ligh holograms and where they have come from.

After a few more minutes of explanation about why Blis Incorporated had done this, about the fact they want a cheap and efficient workforce they can control to do away with the labou settlements altogether, an interesting fact comes to light which have suspected, but never known.

They've discovered that the formula for true love isn't real. I doesn't exist.

I have known this deep down, but seeing the flashing image on screen, the documents which show how Pippa Hart had beer trying to create a 'pure' and 'perfect' race of people who do not question or resist one overarching power, I begin to feel furious.

"How can she do this? How can she sleep at night, knowing she's just using us for selective breeding?" I coin the term I'd heard Clark use when talking to David down in the sewers, my heart pounding in my chest as we watch on, neither of us able to look away.

The exposé concludes after a few more moments. Warning the public to stay inside until further notice, because action is being taken to remove Bliss Incorporated and their executive power over our lives, before they display the slogan of the rebellion:

Ignorance is Bliss.

Egypt and I look to one another as the room goes dark again and the moonlight from outside casts dark shadows across our faces.

"I think you've changed the world, Valentine," Egypt whispers, and I sigh.

"I think you're right," I reply, knowing in this moment that there is an inescapability to the truth of her words. In one day, my own acts have changed the future of this city. I have rebelled, and I am still alive.

The only thing I need to work out now is whether I've changed it for better or for worse.

Twenty-Eight

I wake the next morning with a sense of dread in the pit of my stomach. I sit upright and realise that what's woken me is the familiar smell of my old coffee maker. Egypt is standing by the counter, watching as I look around in confusion.

"Don't worry. Everything is quiet. It's like... dead outside. Like the city has just gone silent. I guess everyone took the warning in that broadcast pretty seriously," She explains, her eyes red.

"Have you been crying?" I ask her, blunt and insensitive in my groggy state and she smiles weakly.

"Yes. I'm afraid about what's going to happen next. The future is now looking uncertain, at best, for everyone." She takes a sip of her coffee and sighs outwardly, shifting from foot to foot in her pyjamas.

"I'm sorry," I whisper, the guilt at what I've done and how I've changed the course of Egypt's fate weighing heavy on my shoulders.

"You did the right thing, Valentine. You have nothing to be sorry for. But I don't think these next few days, months or maybe even years, are going to be easy or certain for anyone. It's going to be a lot of wait and see. I've been up on the roof since dawn doing exactly that, waiting to see something, anything, that would indicate that Bliss Incorporated has lost power." She looks at me and my eyes widen.

"I want to go up with you next time," I express and she frowns.

"Are you sure that's wise? Aren't people going to be out searching for you? Looking for the girl who destroyed Bliss Incorporated's veil of lies?" She cocks an eyebrow, brushing her raven locks behind one ear and I shake my head.

"I'll wear my hood. No-one will know it's me." Egypt continues to look unsure at my response, but nods anyway.

"Okay. I trust you know what you're doing." She smiles at me and I swing my legs over the side of her bed.

"Thanks for letting me sleep in the bed." I blush slightly, feeling bad that I've taken over her entire apartment. She laughs.

"With your arm like that, I wasn't exactly going to make you sleep on the sofa." Turning back to face the kitchen island, she grabs a mug full of steaming coffee and hands it to me as I pad across the room toward her. I reach out to take the cup with my injured arm, but realise quickly that tensing the muscles in my forearm is likely to be agony, so quickly switch, inhaling the familiar fumes as they plume upward into the cold morning air of the apartment unit.

"Thanks. I guess I expected to wake up and everything would be immediately different. It seems like everything is changing so fast," I say, taking a sip of the coffee and feeling myself relax slightly as a sense of familiar routine begins to creep in.

427

"I think it might be a few days before we know anything" Egypt replies, walking over to the sofa and sinking back into the hold of the chair.

"So what do we do now?" I ask, wondering exactly where all this leaves me. Am I fugitive? An exile? Is Bliss Incorporated too busy with the revolution to worry about the single person who started it all?

"Now," Egypt states thoughtfully, "We wait."

We wait in a citywide silence for two days, before suddenly the peace is broken. On the third day, I wake to the smell of smoke and the sound of thunder, until I sit up, with Egypt standing over me, to discover that what I'm hearing isn't thunder at all.

"Val! Wake up! Bombs, they're detonating bombs!" She squeaks, her voice fraught with terror.

"Oh my bliss, where? Do we need to leave?" I am instantly looking around for my clothes, for my bag, for all the things I could possibly take with me that would aid in keeping both me and Egypt alive.

"Not here, at least not yet. It's all happening over at the headquarters. There's smoke and everything. Come and see!" She grabs my coat from the back of the sofa and throws it at me, as I scramble out of bed and put it on over the top of my pyjamas. I throw the hood over my head and place my boots on my bare feet, so they ride up under my cotton pyjama bottoms. Egypt scans her tattoo across the holo-dash in front of her door and I feel a pang of emptiness. My own tattoo is gone, and as I follow her up the fire escape stairs and onto the roof, my tread

428

pounding in my ears against the harsh concrete of the steps, I wonder if I'll ever be able to be part of society again. I've removed any trace of what Bliss Incorporated had made me, and right now they seem to be under threat, but what if they fight back and win? What if I'm hunted down and killed like a dog for my inability to sit down and shut up when told? I ponder this, feeling increasingly anxious and claustrophobic, until I reach the top of the building and Egypt opens the fire escape door. A rush of cold air, rank with the smell of burning, bowls into me and rips any warmth from my form. Egypt and I step out onto the rooftop together, looking out over the city to see what has become of our world.

"Whoa..." I say, my mouth dropping open. My heart drops along with my jaw as I realise that what I'm looking at might very well mean that Clark is gone, dead, burned to a cinder. That is if Jason hasn't managed to get him out first.

The remains, of what had once been the Bliss Incorporated headquarters, are smouldering, with plumes of black smoke rising into the sky in an unending turret. The testing centres for the male and female districts have been obliterated too, and it looks like it's been done from beneath as from this distance, I can just make out that the pavement has been scarred, blown to pieces and left gashed wide open.

"Does this mean it's over?" I ask Egypt and she shakes her head.

"No. I think this means it's just beginning."

The bombings continue for two days, and yet they cease to reac either of the civilian districts. The places worst affected are th marriage complex and the headquarter district.

For three days Egypt and I huddle in her apartment, cringin and having our hearts set racing by the impact of mor explosives. The bombs are coming from beneath the streets, s everywhere outside is deserted and everyone is huddled awa\ just like we are, terrified for their lives.

On the morning of the fifth day, post arrival at Egypt' apartment, she looks at me with a disheartened smile.

"What do you want for breakfast? We have ramen... o ramen?"

"Ramen it is," I sigh, glad for her quick thinking. Upcycler haven't worked since the first day of the bombings, and withou her initiative on stockpiling the basics, we'd probably be trying t smother each other for the last cookie right about now.

"At least we have food. I mean, I don't know how everyon else is managing." She tries to lighten the mood, tries to sta positive, and I can't help but admire her for that. As she's fillin one of the ramen cups with boiling water, a sound interrupts us

"Breaking News from the rebellion!" The sound is so sudde that Egypt jumps, almost spilling water all over herself as I turn my head snapping toward the holo-dash, which has been dea for days.

"Citizens of Monopolis. You will have seen our bombings, ou first and hardest strike against the corporate minds that have imprisoned us for the half a millenium, but now it is time for yo to join us. As of noon today, the walls between the districts wi be destroyed. You will be free to intermingle with the opposite

430

sex, and free to voice your opinions about what is happening within the city. All you have to do is make your way to the headquarter district at noon. Faces of the rebellion will be there to hear you." I look at Egypt who has become so dumbstruck by the announcement that she's dropped the ramen cup she was holding in the sink and is staring at the soft-light broadcast in utter shock.

"In additional news, we are sad to say that both Clark Cavanaugh and his wife Valentine, who risked their lives in the exposure of Bliss Incorporated and their crimes, have been killed. A merciless and tyrannical act by Pippa Hart herself. Please, don't let their sacrifice be in vain. We need to come together now, not as marrieds, singles or labourers, but as humans. We need to hear your voice to know how to govern our future, so please, come and join us at noon to honour the sacrifices of Clark and Valentine, by having your say in the days to come." The announcement has pictures of both Clark and myself, no doubt those stored in the Bliss Incorporated database because I can't remember ever having had my photograph taken by anyone else. There are ones of me and Clark on our wedding day. There are pictures of us separately when we were single. It's a beautiful montage, but then I start to wonder.

I might not be dead, but what if Clark really is dead? What if they're using the fact of his death to make mine seem more believable to those who are possibly still seeking me out? My heart shatters. I've known it isn't likely Clark will have survived the bombings, if he'd still been in Bliss Incorporated, but I've held onto the hope that Clark had been rescued by his brother, before.

431

"Egypt, you need to go to this thing. I can't... but you can st
go and have a say," I express and she looks at me like I might b
mad.

"I don't know, Valentine. What if it's a trap to lure us all ou
and then bomb us all? What if it's not really the rebellion, bu
Bliss Incorporated pulling something?" she asks me, her parano
resonant of Clark as she purses her lips and her brow furrows i
irritation.

"How about if I call Jason, he'll know." I quickly stand at th
thought and walk over to my backpack, which is on the floo
propped against the wall. Pulling it open I sit back onto the sof
and rummage through the contents. I quickly find the thing I'r
seeking, pulling out the thing Clark had called a cell phone.

"A cell phone? That's pretty old tech!" Egypt notes wit
excitement in her voice. She's intrigued by the old technology
and so she watches me with intensity as I press the 'on' butto
and pull out a large silver stick from the top of it, just like Jaso
had showed me the day before Clark and I had lost one another

"Yeah, Clark used this the first night we were together and
thought he was talking to other women." I laugh, rememberin
how naïve I'd been back then.

"That's funny?" she asks me and I nod, pressing buttons an
learning to navigate the screen in an annoying slowness, whicl
makes me wonder how anyone had the patience to use this kin
of technology every day.

"Yeah. It is. When I think about that night, I really had no ide
what I was doing," I express, brushing my hair back from my fac
as I find only one number in the phone book and press the cal

432

button. After a few rings, the phone is answered, and through an intermittent clicking and popping I can hear Jason's voice.

"Hello?" He says and I instantly begin to babble.

"Yes, it's me, Valentine. Um, I saw the broadcast. I wanted to know, is it true? Did you really invite people to voice their opinions? Are you really taking the divide down between the districts?" I'm speaking ridiculously fast, desperate for answers.

"Yes, that was us. It's true. It didn't take a lot, but Pippa Hart fled early yesterday morning. We're planning on taking over the headquarters, or what's left of it, at some point over the next few days. We need to find out what the best course is to take first though, and to do that, we need to hear the masses speak." He sounds like a leader now, like he's found his true place in the world.

"What about Clark?" I ask, unable to help myself. I hear him cough at the end of the line, clearing his throat.

"Valentine, I can't talk about this over the phone. I need to see you in person. I'm at your old apartment right now, but I'll have more information for you in a few days and then we can meet here. I'll be in touch." He hangs up the phone in an abrupt manner and I feel my heart shatter. If Clark was okay, Jason would have just said so, wouldn't he? That must mean that he's dead, or worse...

"Is it for real?" Egypt asks me and I nod at her as her eyes widen.

"Yes. Jason didn't answer me when I asked about Clark though... what about... what if he's dead?" I ask her and she moves to sit beside me. "He said he was in my old apartment." I

433

speak the words in a wistful lull of sound, like it's an afterthought, as Egypt's frown deepens.

"So, what he just didn't want to tell you? That's not okay! You're his wife!" she exclaims, outraged for me as I look down at my hand.

"Actually, I'm not. I'm not even wearing my wedding ring," I admit, feeling tears spring to my eyes. I should've tried harder. I should've remembered what I vowed to him and tried to get past the lies. I should've tried to see why he was lying, and realise that it was because he had really loved me.

As I sit here, I think back on that last day we'd spent together before everything had fallen apart, I'd been so sure of him then. I'd known that with every single touch he wanted me. So how had I allowed my own insecurities to get bigger than what I knew he felt for me? Could it be that because everything around me had been shifting so quickly I'd lost my footing and become overly paranoid and defensive, become scared to love him because it wasn't certain, it wasn't safe? Had I been looking for an island in a sea of confusion and missed the point that nothing in this life was certain? There are no islands. There is only me and the current, taking me where it wills.

"Egypt, I have to go to that apartment," I say, determined as I realise that there's no way in hell I'm possibly going to sit and wait around for two days, not knowing whether Clark is dead. That's torture.

"What if you get there and it's empty?" Egypt asks me and shrug.

"I don't know. I guess I'll just wait it out. Besides, David talked about meeting me there soon so he must be visiting it

434

sometimes. At least this way, I don't have to wait around for him to call. I think I'll go crazy," I admit and Egypt still doesn't look convinced.

"Is it safe for you to leave?" she asks me and I shrug.

"I don't care about that. I care about him. I screwed this up Egypt and I pushed him away. I have to know if he's dead, because what if he's not? What if he's alive and suffering, and I have the chance to get Jason to take me to him so I can make things right. If there's a chance I can see him again, just once, I need to take it." I make the decision in these words, and I watch as Egypt realises there's nothing she can possibly say that will change my mind.

"Okay, I'll walk with you to the station." She grabs my hand and squeezes it as I look up at her, wondering how on earth it's come to this.

We walk from the apartment unit while I pull my hood down so it half covers my face and adjust the straps on my backpack. The wind is chill and I immediately realise that Egypt doesn't have to worry about me being noticed.

Everywhere, women are walking, some are holding signs, some are holding one another's hands possessively and others are running through the crowd, barging people out of the way and yelling 'Ignorance is Bliss!' in high-pitched screams. I'm afraid for a moment, wondering if so many people have been wanting change all this time and I've never realised it.

435

"Seems like lots of people want their say," Egypt whispers to me and I nod, worrying that speaking will cause someone to recognise my voice from the tape.

We walk down the street, picking up the pace, but soon realise there's a bigger problem than we'd anticipated as people begin to halt in front of us. "What's this?" Egypt asks a woman who has her arms crossed across the rumpled double breast of her standard issue single shell suit.

"This is the queue for the monorail. There's only one running and now they've disabled the need for tattoos everywhere. It complete madness!" She throws her arms up in fury and Egypt looks to me.

"You can't wait in this line, it'll take too long." Egypt turns to me and I pull my hood lower over my eyes. The woman in the line huffs loudly as she announces her displeasure at what she thinks is Egypt's entitlement.

"Well, if you're too good to wait, you could always swim there!" She's joking, but it gives me an idea.

"Hey, Clark once told me the lake isn't as deep as it looks. Do you think I could just walk or paddle across to the newlywed complex?" I ask Egypt this in an urgent whisper and her eyes widen.

"Do you trust his word?" she asks me and I think on this a second.

"Yes. I do." I realise that while he's lied to me about certain things, concerning our relationship, I do trust what he's said about the world I live in. I mean, I've seen how right he was about Bliss Incorporated for myself, so I turn on my heel, making my way back through the crowds and pulling Egypt behind me.

436

"Wait!" Egypt pulls back on my arm so I turn, not wanting to stop in the middle of the street but not sure she's giving me much any other option.

"What?" I snap, feeling immediately bad as she points to the left and a gust of wind blows my coat out behind me.

"We can just take that exit. It's quicker." My face relaxes as she speaks, making me realise how much I'm completely stressing out over getting back to my apartment. I don't even know if anyone will be there, and yet, the thought that I might miss Clark's final moments, or anything else important that has to do with his life, is making me crazy.

"Oh, right. Sorry," I mumble and she laughs.

"You really do love Clark." She says it as a statement and I nod my head.

"Yeah, I feel pretty stupid right about now. I've pushed him away over what feels like something completely ridiculous in the scale of current events." We turn and begin to walk down the street to our left, parting from the crowds as Egypt turns to me with an expression that's kind and endearing all in one. Her brown eyes sparkle despite the fact the light of the day is dim, and I wonder if she'll be able to find happiness now, or ever be married.

"You didn't know. As far as you were aware, he was lying to you for no good reason..." she expresses and I shrug.

"Yeah, I guess. I just, I regret not listening to what he had to say. Not giving him a chance to explain. He was just so withholding, so scared of everything happening, that it made it impossible to gauge how he was feeling. He was too good at living across two totally contrasting worlds, and I didn't know how to

437

separate perception from reality," I say as we reach the end of the street too quickly and meet with the guardrail at the edge of the water.

"This is it," Egypt states ominously, looking down into the sloshing of the water below.

"I guess so." I look into her eyes and I find myself wondering if I'll ever see her again.

"Egypt… what if I never see you again?" I vocalise the thought and she looks immediately sad.

"I… I don't know. I guess, maybe that's just life. If life was fair, you'd be in my apartment everyday drinking coffee and eating pizza with me… but…" she begins, her eyes filling with tears.

"Life isn't fair." I finish for her and she nods.

"Just, look after yourself, and call me whenever. You come back to me if you can, okay?" She pulls me into her body and holds me close. It doesn't feel strange, even now that I know she has feelings for me, because the embrace isn't romantic. It feels sort of like she's letting me go and moving on to something new. Something in the future with someone who she can really love and who will love her back. That doesn't make it any less painful though.

"I hope you find the woman of your dreams," I whisper in her ear and she laughs.

"I hope that you make it to the man of yours." She lets me go and I take a few steps back, hesitant, but knowing if I don't make the leap now I never will. I climb onto the metal of the guardrail, standing tall upon the second highest steel bar, and letting my knees rest on the top of the construct, helping me balance. I look down into the water and Egypt calls.

"Mind over matter, Valentine!" At her words, I grit my teeth, realising that it's time to let go. It's time to trust in *my* beliefs, not those I've been fed.

"It's just perception versus reality, right?" I call back with a laugh, and with that, I take the plunge.

Twenty-Nine

My heels hit the water and a second later the soles of my feet h
something hard. Icy liquid fills my shoes and my knees buck
under the strain of hitting something so solid unexpectedly. I fa
forward, my hands plunging beneath the frothy lake's surfac
and hitting the floor lying only inches beneath.

"Well that was an anti-climax!" I hear Egypt call and I laug
again, my knees, hands, and feet, sodden but the rest of m
happily dry as I get to my feet and test the ground beneath m
feet. It's sturdy, and to be honest I feel a little short-changed. Thi
journey should have been epic or something, like in those ol
movies where the couples really struggle before finding eac
other for a final happy reunion, but in this case it just looks lik
I've got a bit of a damp walk ahead.

"Ya think?" I call back, chuckling as I turn to begin my walk.
look back for as long as I can, and Egypt and I wave to on
another. Eventually I've walked about half the distance, acros
the water in around ten minutes, which is far preferable t
swimming, and I lose sight of her as she becomes a speck in th
distance, before she turns and walks away. I focus ahead afte

440

...at, not looking back, not wanting to acknowledge her absence ...om my life as permanent. I hope one day, I'll see her again, ...ore than anything, but I've waited nine years to find the love of ...y life, and I'm not letting him go so easily If I can help it.

Clark Cavanaugh, who would've thought that he would be ...*ght for me?* I think back to the first time I'd laid eyes on him. If ...ou'd have told me then what I know now, I'd have slapped you, ...r called the authorities, whatever good that would have done. ...ow however, I can't imagine not seeing the world how I do, and ...ll of that is because he'd opened my eyes.

I walk across the fake lake, realising that what had once ...eemed like such a giant obstacle is no longer much of one at all. ...My feet splash and slosh through the water, making easy tread ...n the surface beneath, and I pull my hood down further over my ...ead, hoping for the love of all things that nobody sees me or ...hinks of me as a threat, because the last thing I need is to be ...rrested or something before I even make it to my apartment; ...hen I'd truly never know Clark's fate. It's probably an entirely ...tupid move for me to have come out here, but I suppose if I'm ...ot ballsy enough to try a move like this, then I have no place ...nfiltrating a tyrant corporation, let alone outing all their secrets.

"I can't believe I really did that," I mutter under my breath as ... shake my head. If I hadn't everything would be different. It ...night be safer for me, yes, but it wouldn't be for the exiles, or ...he labourers, or the people who had been made into hard-light ...olograms.

As I reach the three-quarter point across the vast distance of ...he lake, between the single district and the newlywed complex, ... hear a multitude of screams. I look back over my shoulder.

441

People are beginning to notice me, to see me walking across th
surface of the water. They dangle, specks now, over the met
railings watching me in alarm. I stand, stone still, petrified as the
gawp, before realising I'm probably too far away from them to k
able to recognise me.

I exhale, relieved, and watch as the people begin to follow n
example. They leap from the guardrails into the water, settir
their fears aside and plunging into the unknown of what is real
watch the crowds descend atop the water, a spectacle unlik
anything I've ever seen as they all appear to be floating, an a
most divine. They don't follow me though, instead turning an
making a right, moving toward the headquarters district. I smil
They're free, free from illusion at last.

Finally, as I tread onward, I reach the opposite side of the lak
My thighs ache from sloshing through the water, but other tha
that I'm pretty much dry from the ankles up, so it could hav
been a lot worse.

Once I approach the waterside platform, marking the start c
the newlywed complex, I make a small jump before grabbin
onto the brutally sharp brick edge and beginning to pull myse
up onto the pavement behind the guardrail where the islan
stops and the lake begins. My arm stings when the bandages ar
pushed against the harsh material of the brickwork, and I grun
as I strain to lift my own weight despite the burn. Eventuall
though, I manage to get some hold with my boots and pus
myself up and over the ninety-degree edge, onto dry land onc
more.

After I've rolled onto my back in the middle of the sidewalk,
get to my feet and see that the streets here are pretty much

442

empty, realising that the people from this part of the city must have all gone to the headquarter district too. It would have been a lot faster for them than those from the single districts because they had access to a more frequent monorail service. I walk the familiar sidewalks, watching my feet illuminate the paving stones beneath me, and a terrible anticipation forms in my gut. What if I walk into the apartment and find Clark's things, or his body, or something else? I toughen my resolve, knowing that I need to do this. I can't be afraid of knowledge, of knowing, anymore. I need to face the fact that bad things are going to happen. If you love someone, you run the risk of losing them; after all, I suppose everyone dies eventually.

I wonder now if I'd take back those days with Clark, altogether, if I'd known it would prevent me this pain.

No. Not for the world. I conclude, thinking back over the many breakfasts, the many kisses and the many smiles we've shared together.

I turn a corner, after about ten minutes walking, and realise I'm here. Without knowing it, my legs have carried me to where I wanted to go faster than I thought possible. My heart beats faster as I approach the door of the sapphire shard, and my hands become moist with sweat as I grab the master key and swipe it across the dash to gain entry. Once I'm inside the lobby, I look to the elevator as I swipe my master key once more to gain entry through the turnstiles, and smile. The hard-light hologram who had once stood guard next to the elevator is gone, and I relax, knowing this tiny piece of evidence that Bliss Incorporated no longer holds power here allows me to exhale a deep breath.

I did the right thing. I remind myself. It hasn't been the ea: thing, and it hasn't been the choice that most benefits me, b one that has been the choice that has changed the world f many and will free many more. I guess now, no matter what I fir in the apartment, I can't regret what I did.

I step into the elevator, leaning back against the rear wall the box and feeling my backpack dig in between my should blades. The last time I'd been in this elevator, everything ha been about to change. And as I step out once more when I reac the top floor, I wish, in a way, everything behind my apartmer front door could be frozen, kept where Clark and I could b together without the real-world interrupting.

I scan my master key card one final time and the door glide left. At this sound, a voice calls through from the apartment an my heart stops.

"Jason?" The voice belongs to Clark. I take a few hurried ste forward across the hard wood floors, revealing myself as I tur the corner into the main room and my eyes fall upon him. He' stood in the middle of the room, staring at the entryway fror where I've just come, and his face is in stilled awe. He's bruisec with a black eye and a purple jaw bone. He barely looks lik himself, thinner in baggy pyjamas, and yet the sapphire burn c his gaze is unmistakable.

We hang for a few moments in the silence, neither on wanting to move, before suddenly I cannot stay still any longer Letting my backpack drop to the floor where I'm stood, my fee carry me the distance between us and he strides forward to mee me too. I crash into him, my arms coming around his torso an

444

y head slamming into the place where his heart lies beneath, ounding audibly beneath my ear.

"Clark!" I exclaim, my voice a breathless whisper as his arms ome to encircle me too. He's shaking in my grasp, and so I pull ack, looking up into his pained and multi-coloured expression. e stand, staring at one another for a moment before I reach up, y fingers gingerly stroking the places where his skin is black and ue. "What did they do to you?" My eyes fill with tears and his ain becomes unbearable to me. "I thought you were dead," I hisper and Clark's expression melts.

"I thought you were too. Pippa Hart, she told me they killed ou. She told me they tortured and killed you," He whispers, his oice crackling and gruff as his eyes water, though from pain or motion I cannot tell.

"Jason... he wouldn't tell me whether you were alive... I anicked, so I came here," I express and Clark nods.

"I told him not to, I didn't want you to see me like this. I mean, m vulnerable and I didn't want..." he begins and I feel my xpression fall as he trails off mid-sentence.

"Didn't want what?" I ask, and he sighs.

"I didn't want you to answer the question I have to ask you ntil I was well again. Until they could find out what else they did o me during the surgery," He explains and my eyes widen.

"Surgery?" I ask and he nods.

"Yes... they sterilised me." His eyes become so emotional, motional in a way I've never seen, and my heart fractures as my ands come up to my mouth and my eyes fill with tears.

"Oh... Clark." I pull his head down to my shoulder so it's esting there and let the weight of him bear down on me. I

445

withstand it, letting him relax, and sigh and drink me in as th apartment falls into silence around us, tears trickling down m cheeks.

"It's okay. I just... I need to ask you..." He reaches into h pocket with a wince and I notice that the back of his hand burned just like mine. Once again, we match.

After a few seconds, he draws his hand back and opens palm up to me, exposing where my wedding band an engagement ring lie. "Did you mean it when you gave these ba to me?" he asks and I stare at him, and then at the rings, my ey still overflowing with tears.

"I thought I did. I thought all the lies, all the deceit was to much. I thought it meant you didn't love me," I express and h shakes his head.

"Valentine, my words might have been lies at times, but m actions never were. Every time I kissed you, or held you... thos things were real. I thought I made that clear. I didn't want you t get hurt, I didn't want to lose you. That's why I lied. I'm sorry, bu I'd do it again if I had the chance. If it meant that both of us ge to stand here, right now, together after everything, I'd lie million times," He expresses, still holding out the rings to me, th blue diamond glittering unique and beautiful in the light.

"I thought you had died... and when I heard that, I realise that... life is too short not to try and be with the person you love. His eyes widen and I realise it's the first time I've actuall admitted that I love him.

"Can you love someone who can never give you children?" H asks me, his expression pained, and I realise that he's deadl serious.

446

"Wait... why did they do this? Why sterilise you? Why not just kill you and be done with it?" I ask him, suddenly wondering what the logic is behind this most inhumane of acts.

"It's to punish you. Pippa Hart knew what children meant to you. She knew you got away... I guess it was her way of making sure that you'd never know true happiness even if I got out, or a way to blackmail you into turning yourself in. I guess she also didn't want my recessive allele getting passed on by accident."

"Your eyes... That's how she knew we weren't matched without even testing us." I whisper, my hand coming up to cover my mouth as he continues and shock settles over me.

"And that's why I need to know. I need to know if you can be okay with a man who can't give you a baby. I don't want to cause you anymore pain than I already have," Clark admits, his eyes glistening with melancholia.

"You can't tell me that you think making a baby biologically is the only way to have a family? After everything we've just fought for. There will be children who need good homes. If we want a child, we will adopt one." I think back to the fact that Clark was an orphan, that his childhood was hard, and I realise that I really do believe what I'm saying. Bliss Incorporated had been wrong about many things, but I do see the sense in that one of the key things a child needs, to be a successful member of society, is a stable, loving home. Perhaps we can help children achieve that, children who would otherwise be lost in the system.

"You're sure. I don't want you to want..." He trails off as I lift one finger to his lips, silencing him.

"I want you." I stare deeply into his eyes, sure of myself, finally. I have been drifting for so long, watching everything I

447

know crumble to dust, only to be terraformed moments later in something new. Perhaps now, after everything, I'm fina starting to see beyond what appears to be to what is. Clark lea down, putting his hands in my hair, and kisses me gently and wi an unwavering passion and adoration I have never felt from hi before.

"I love you, Valentine," He whispers in my ear as he ceas the kiss and pulls me close to him. "I want to start over. From th beginning. No counselling, no rules, just you and me, giving th marriage a real shot. Is that something you want? " I nod at hi and smile, feeling finally contented in his arms

"I do." As these words spill from me, a brand new and ve real vow, he grabs my hand and places the rings upon my finge both of them this time, before kissing my knuckles.

"Come here and look at this. We're about to see history bein made." He walks me over to the panoramic view of the skylin from which I can see out over the still lightly smoulderin headquarters district.

"What am I looking at?" I ask him, seeing only two crowds o people coming together, one from the left, and one from th right side of the district. Then, I gasp. "The male and femal districts... they're coming together!" I feel so excited, like I'v made the fantasy I've held onto for nine years, about being abl to simply walk over to the male district and find my matchmat a reality for so many others. If only really getting to knov someone, and falling in love with them in spite of their flaws, wa as easy as taking down a barrier.

"What happens now?" I ask a few minutes later, havin simply watched as the men and women of Monopolis reunite fo e first time. It is awe inspiring, but makes our situation, netheless, complicated.

"Jason is arranging for us to be taken far away from here. He ys that right now there are a lot of people who are all for the olition of Bliss Incorporated and their power, but as things gin to change, some people will start to lash out against the iles and the labourers too. We instigated all this, so we aren't fe in the city," he explains, his eyes full of sadness as I think on hat this means.

"My family..." I say and he shakes his head.

"I'm sorry, Valentine. It'd put them at risk, and your nieces d nephews need to be protected. It's better off for everyone if e make a clean break. It won't be forever. Just until order is stored and things are stable again." He takes me hand in his d holds it tightly, comforting me.

"What about your family, Jason, your mom and David?" I ask, alising that I hadn't really thought about David's fate. I feel mediately guilty.

"David is dead. They killed him moments after we arrived at e headquarters. Mom is devastated, but Jason says he'll take re of her. He said we've done enough," He expresses, imploring e with his gaze. In his mind, things are clearly settled, and I can't eny that staying here would be risky. Even though I'm reluctant, can see that it's probably best if we go.

"Where are they sending us?" I ask him and he frowns.

"An island off the coast of Jungala. Pippa Hart has a holiday ome there and it's extremely secluded. They're securing the cility right now, which was empty, according to Jason's pilots hen they last flew over." He explains this and I feel like

449

everything is once again changing quicker than I c...
comprehend.

"So we're going on a second honeymoon?" I ask him and I...
shakes his head.

"No, we're going on a first honeymoon. A real one where n...
one will be watching us, where we can just... be." He smiles
this thought and I can't help but relax beside him as I relish th
idea of real privacy.

"We really are starting over again," I admit and he laughs
little, bending down and kissing me on the cheek tentatively.

"Yes. This is a new beginning for everyone, but I'm not
politician, or a fighter. I've always just been a guy who could se
what everyone else was blind to. Now that I've cured th
blindness or begun to do so, I'm ready for a nice long vacatio
I'm ready to be married to you." His eyes bore into mine and
feel my heart flutter.

Above the city where we have freed so many, and broug
change to everyone, I begin to think about my own peace, m
own happily ever after. The thing that makes it so happy thoug
is that it's my choice who I spend it with, and I choose Clark.

Thirty

Well, it's official. Mom and Dad are divorced," I call out as I walk om the double glass patio doors and out onto the powdery hite sand of the beach. Clark is laying, body stretched out in the in, near the water's edge as I call to him. He rolls over onto his tomach lazily and looks up over the top of his sunglasses.

"Well, if they're not happy, then I guess it's for the best," He xpresses and I nod, frowning. My mother is now Cynthia Spinnet nce more, and it's only now that I realise that perhaps she isn't uch a bad parent after all. Since leaving Monopolis, we've had ome of the most honest conversations, the type I'd never nagined would be possible between us. She has explained why he pushed me and my sisters so hard as children. Her fear that ve would become the downtrodden, the labourers, driving her o make us into the best candidates for wives we could be. She as been unhappy a long time, but she is quick to remind me that he'll take unhappy in a beautiful house with her babies over nhappy in a sweatshop any day. It turns out, that has been the ase with a lot of Bliss Incorporated marriages. We've been gone two months now, and the divorce rate is up to almost six percent. Both my sisters are moving to divorce their husbands, which surprised me because of how happy they'd always claimed to be. Clark and I, however, are still blissfully happy, and as I fall down to my knees with my long flowing skirt blowing around me, I bend down to kiss him.

"I love you so much, Clark Cavanaugh." I chuckle as he pulls me down onto his warm, sunbathed chest.

"Yes, who would have thought that an arranged marriage could flourish so spontaneously?" he quips and I laugh as he moves into lightly tickle my sides with his fingertips.

"I just can't help but wonder what we'll be like in twenty, or thirty years. What if you're sick of me by then? My parents have been married a long time. Maybe humans just aren't meant to be with only one person," I muse, looking into his eyes as he props himself up in the sand on his elbows and gives me a bemused expression.

"You wound me. And if I ever find you with someone else, not that there's anyone else on this island except the odd monkey, then I'll chop his hands off. Whether he's human or not." He laughs and I cock my eyebrow as I brush my hair back behind one ear.

"I'm serious, Clark!" I giggle, imagining him chasing a monkey with a machete.

"Maybe most people just don't have something worth hanging onto. It's hard to find. I mean, it's not like there's an instruction manual or a scientific formula to tell you what's right for you," he reminds me and I nod, remembering the calls I've gotten from Egypt crying over multiple girls who had used her to

452

periment with their sexuality, drunk on their new sexual
eedom, and then discarded her.

"That's true, on paper we look like we'd kill each other, but
tually you're not so bad," I joke and he rolls his eyes.

"Oh, I'm still plotting your death. Didn't I mention that? That's
hy I insist on cooking you all your meals." He winks and I laugh.

"Yeah, because it couldn't possibly be because I can't cook
d you don't want to live off ramen for the next hundred years."
e sun bathes my back and I feel happiness swell inside me as
grins.

"Yeah, it's lucky one of us can cook or we'd be dead by now,
r sure. You're cranky as hell when you're hungry. Jason would
d me beaten to death in the sand. He'd be pissed though,
ainly because he'd have to find another best man at such short
otice." He runs his hands across my back at a leisurely pace as I
arrow my eyes, trying to placate me. I let him.

"Yeah, for someone who hated Bliss Incorporated and all the
eremony and stuff, he's sure getting carried away with this
edding. I'm amazed he has the time with everything he's
urrently working on." I roll my eyes, thinking about the fact that
ter two months, Jason still hasn't managed to revive the human
odies of the hard-light holograms. They've woken a handful,
aybe more, but they're all brain damaged beyond repair. I
onder sometimes if Clark finds relief in this, because despite the
ct that there are hundreds of innocents in the pods, his father
among them. I think on his father walking free, after what he
d to Clark and his family, and a shudder runs through me. I
on't, however, brush this bad thought away. Instead, now I
cknowledge that bad things happen, but that I can always make

453

Clark's days brighter, can always make up for the love he misse
in his childhood. I focus on what I can change, on the positive ar
my husband.

"Yeah, but he has waited a long time for this. I can't wa
personally, this time I'll get to embarrass him in front of his ne
wife." He chuckles and I laugh, remembering the memory
walking down the aisle toward him, terrified. I had thought n
world was ending that day, but little had I known my world wa
growing, and my life was just beginning.

"I guess I got lucky with you," I express and he frowns.

"If you count being stuck with me forever, lucky." He laugh
kissing me gently and I laugh against the flesh of his lips.

"Funnily enough, I do."

We spend the rest of the day lying in the sand, talkin
laughing and flitting away the day as we do most every other.
thought I had known what I wanted. What happiness was. Ho
to be free. I thought I knew how to love and what love felt like
But I'd been wrong.

This is love. This is freedom and happiness. This, is bliss.

Acknowledgements

Four hundred and something pages later and I've finished my 'short story', my 'palate cleanser' novel... so yeah, that went as expected (not). A big thank you to my wonderful partner Mark who as always has listened to my fears and pushed me to keep writing this story to the last word. Though I've never based a character on you before, I'll admit that a big ass part of Clark came from you, so thanks for the inspiration and being imperfectly perfect for me. Thanks to my family, who as always, continue to support my ambition, my dreams, and who respect the fact that when I'm typing, you stay the heck away. I also can't begin to express how grateful I am to my one of a kind, absolutely awesome, editor Jaimie Cordall, who never fails to make me realise when I'm being an idiot, like when I refer to acetate as PHP and boggle both you and the internet. I loved working on this project with you, so thanks for taking the time to help make this book everything I imagined. To my betas, Dawn Yacovetta, Emma Harrison, Winters Rage, thanks for reassuring me that though this novel isn't my usual brand of imagineering, that It was worth writing all the same! To all my telltails, I just want to say that you have no idea how much you mean to me, but in particular I want to shout out to Brenda Lee Moreno and Kaela Cueppers who helped me pick Valentine's wedding dress! What you guys came up with is stunning! So, that's all my gushing for today, onto more Infiniverse musings. This book is done, so I guess I better start on the next!

Want more from Kristy Nicolle?

Website: www.kristynicolle.com

Facebook: https://www.facebook.com/AuthorKristyNicolle

Twitter: Nicolle_Kristy

Instagram: authorkristynicolle

Goodreads: Search Something Blue

Photographs by the fabulously talented Trish Thompson.

Current Available titles from Kristy Nicolle

THE TIDAL KISS TRILOGY:

The Kiss That Killed Me
The Kiss That Saved Me
The Kiss That Changed Me

Coming Soon to the
Kristy Nicolle Infiniverse...

TIDAL KISS NOVELLAS
Vexed

TIDAL KISS SHORTS
Waiting For Gideon
The Tank

OTHER QUEENS OF FANTASY TRILOGIES:

THE ASHEN TOUCH TRILOGY
The Opal Blade
The Onyx Hourglass
The Obsidian Shard

THE AETHERIAL EMBRACE TRILOGY
Indigo Dusk
Violet Dawn
Lavender Storm

FOR PREDICTED RELEASE DATES VISIT
WWW.KRISTYNICOLLE.COM

68586557R00283

Manufactured by Amazon.com
Columbia, SC
02 April 2017